"...This first novel in Joseph's This Generation series is a suavely futuristic story about a major shift in the paradigms of Western civilization and religion. It effectively combines humanistic sympathy and ambitious speculation about the cosmos' trajectory. The narrative is steeped in the author's knowledge of the prophetic traditions of Abrahamic, Eastern and esoteric religions, and engagingly mixes science fiction with psychological drama.

"An unusual, enjoyable novel for readers interested in religious history and speculative fiction."

—*Kirkus Reviews*

"This book deserves a high mark for presenting an unusual combination of intimidating possibilities—doomsday hysteria, New Age philosophy, extraterrestrial abduction, and even alien impregnation. In a realm where dreams and visions could be reality, where a place of worship could trigger cataclysmic events, nothing is definitive, and everything is subject to interpretation."

—*Foreword Clarion*

"The first installment of TC Joseph's This Generation saga—a science-fiction-nuanced and presumably apocalyptic storyline following three Christian women and their families—is, in broad strokes, comparable to Tim LaHaye's bestselling Left Behind series, which examines the end of the world from an eschatological perspective... the story is an undeniable page-turner right up to the end, so those who don't mind committing to the whole series may very well find a rewarding reading experience."

—*Blue Ink Review*

PRECIPICE

THIS GENERATION SERIES: BOOK 1

PRECIPICE

THIS GENERATION SERIES: BOOK 1

TC JOSEPH

ARCHWAY
PUBLISHING

Scripture references are taken from the New King James Version. Copyright
1982 by Thomas Nelson, Inc. All rights reserved. Scripture references
in this book fall within Thomas Nelson's Fair Use Guidelines.

Archway Publishing books may be ordered through booksellers or by contacting:

Archway Publishing
1663 Liberty Drive
Bloomington, IN 47403
www.archwaypublishing.com
1-(888)-242-5904

ISBN: 978-1-4808-0783-9 (sc)
ISBN: 978-1-4808-0785-3 (hc)
ISBN: 978-1-4808-0784-6 (e)

Library of Congress Control Number: 2014940876

Printed in the United States of America

Archway Publishing rev. date: 11/4/2014

To my parents, my sisters, my brother-in-law, and
the best nephew and niece in the world

ACKNOWLEDGMENTS

I value my privacy and have joyously written under a pseudonym to preserve it! All in all I think it is a marvelous decision, but it is troubling when it comes to an acknowledgments page, because it precludes me from thanking, by name, so many who have been instrumental in the production of this book. The failure to mention individuals is no reflection of the gratitude that I feel. So I would like to offer a special thanks to the cadre of family and friends who read this novel in draft. Each of your changes made this book better. Each word of encouragement was met with a grateful heart.

I also would like to thank the staff at Archway Publishing for taking a chance on me, for taking care of me, and for taking time to make this the best book series that it could be.

AUTHOR'S NOTE

Like many others, I watched with fascination as the world approached December 21, 2012, the supposed date for the end of the age, according to the Mayan calendar. This intrigued me. Given my passion for Christian end-time prophecies, I have been transfixed by the movement of history following the birth, against all odds, of Israel as a sovereign nation after thousands of years. For certain Bible scholars, this is the single event that triggers the inexorable fulfillment of end-time prophecies.

As I researched the Mayan calendar and other prophecies outside of the Judeo-Christian tradition, I was fascinated to learn that cultures all over the Earth have end-time prophecies and pinpoint *this generation* as the one to witness their fulfillment. For example,

- Judaism awaits its Messiah;
- Islam awaits its Mahdi;
- Christians see Armageddon on the horizon;
- New Agers believe that humanity is on the brink of enhanced awareness and contact with alien species;
- many suspect a plot to subjugate mankind in an emerging world order; and
- others have a sinking feeling that the world is spinning out of control.

You may say, "What a coincidence!" But the questions screamed at me: What if they are all right? What if they are all speaking of the same events but from different perspectives? What would that look like in the lives of three families?

And a book was born ... a series of books, in fact. Going to my Bible prophecy roots, I tagged the generation in question to be those people who were alive when Israel became a nation. Israel declared its independence in 1948, but the United Nations formally recognized it in 1949. So my plan was to view the lives of these families since 1949. I decided to look at them in ten-year increments, starting in 1969, and examining the prehistory (1949–1969) at the end of the series. The characters are intriguing, knowable, and great fun, and their lives illustrate the changes to society that have been orchestrated since the end of World War II.

Throughout the writing of these books, I have spent well over a thousand hours studying differing viewpoints about events that have occurred since World War II and the events that are prophesied by other cultures and belief systems. Added to a lifetime of Bible prophecy study, I am convinced that we are poised to see incredible events unfold. To assist readers who are curious about my research, I have included a partial reading list at the end of this book.

One thing is for sure: this generation is on the precipice of incredible, life-altering changes! Whether you see them as positive or negative depends upon your worldview. So why not pull up a chair, grab a cup of coffee, and join really intriguing characters on a roller-coaster ride through recent history with a view toward determining where we all are headed?

Enjoy the read!

TC
March 2014

1969

ONE

Kimberly Martin's BMW raced down the highway. What she was doing was madness, but to do nothing would be madder still. She could think of no other way to save herself from the nightmares, if that's what they really were. The hot Georgia air blew through the open car windows, tousling the long, dark hair of the nineteen-year-old heiress. Maybe if her parents were alive, they could have helped her. But Kim was an orphan. She needed to tend to this matter on her own. The radio blared one of 1969's biggest hits by Credence Clearwater Revival. The words seemed personal as she sang with the radio. "Don't come out tonight. It's bound to take your life. There's a bad moon on the rise."

As her car passed the county line, Kim crossed the line from Kimberly, the young heiress, to Kimbo, the bimbo of Franklin County. The landscape changed as well. Gone were the large homes with manicured lawns and shade trees. Peach orchards and the neat rows of well-tended gardens gave way to ramshackle homes and burgeoning trailer parks as Kim sped to the Tic Toc Tavern. She had heard about this place at the prep school from which she had just graduated. Imagine what the girls would say if they knew she was cruising off to the Tic Toc in the muddy town of Alphona, Georgia.

How had her life become so complicated? Until very recently, she was just the slightly spoiled daughter of Stanford Martin, one of the wealthiest businessmen in the country. Stan, as he was known to his friends, made a handsome profit on anything he put his hand to, and government contracts during the Cold War moved his accumulated wealth to the stratosphere of American society.

Stan was a hard man who did not suffer fools graciously. While Kimberly was the light of his life, her older half brother, Benny, met with Stan's constant disdain. He could not endure the otherworldliness and slightly effeminate mannerisms of his stepson. They had shared an uneasy peace predicated on their mutual love of Kimberly and their dedication to giving her a happy life after the death of her mother. And for the most part, they, along with a host of nannies and servants, had succeeded. Her life was quite stable by the time Benny became a Catholic priest. She had always adored him and took comfort that he was able to perform Stan's funeral service after his tragic car accident.

Since then, she and Benny had become very close. He was her only family, and she spoke to him several times each week. She also invested heavily in his career once she came to realize that the right word in the right ear, coupled with a generous donation, could open wondrous doors for Benny. Plumb assignments and the constant recognition of the bishop could also come from years of dedicated service. But her well-placed donations put Benny on the fast track and assuaged her feelings of guilt that she alone had inherited Stan's fortune.

Aside from the pain of losing her parents, life had given her everything she could ever have wanted. So why this panicked race to a tacky bar to find a suitably tacky man to take advantage of her? It was the night visitors ... aliens. Sometimes she believed they had to be nightmares, but what if they weren't? She couldn't take that chance. Whatever they were, they took a perverse interest in her reproductive organs. Night after night, they probed her, preparing her for something. Instinctually she felt that they wanted to use her as a sort of incubator for a hybrid. She was sure tonight's defilement of her womb would send them packing. She was at the peak of fertility in her cycle, and she didn't think she had a month to spare. To her mind, there was only one way to end this ordeal—and it had to be now.

She pulled off the road to a secluded, wooded spot about half a mile from the bar. She would go the rest of the way on foot. Checking herself in the rearview mirror, she choked back a sob. Mama would be heartbroken if she could see what her precious little girl had become. Her makeup was heavy, to the point of being garish, with trendy white eye shadow and hot-pink lipstick. The auburn highlights in her long brown hair shimmered in the light of the setting sun. Her miniskirt was more mini than it was skirt, and her underwear was, well, non-existent. It would only get in the way of her stated objective, namely Rory Blanchett and/or his brothers, Terry and Georgie. They were trouble, but they sure were handsome trouble. If she was to go through with this plan and not chicken out, then the guys she chose had to be handsome. Rory had blazing blue eyes, dark reddish-brown hair, and a gorgeous smile. His brothers were paler versions of him. Terry had the same smile but dull eyes, and Georgie had the eyes but a taciturn look on his face that seemed to never smile. Rory was her choice, but then again it wasn't like she was giving her virginity to a man she loved. She was tossing it to the wind in a desperate act to protect herself.

An involuntary, sharp, gasping cry escaped her lips as she realized what she was about to do. She thought about how this would hurt poor Benny. He'd never understand.

She wiped her eyes, locked her car, and began the walk to the Tic Toc Tavern, her go-go boots clicking down the side of the little road that led into town. Arriving at the door, she took a deep breath to calm her nerves. She could smell the Tic Toc even in the street. The air was filled with the strange mixture of booze, aged grease in a deep fryer, and stale cigarette smoke. She exhaled, pulled hard on the door, and entered the tavern. Dirty aquamarine paint graced its walls. Kimberly would have to walk the breadth of the aged, red-and-black-tiled floor to get to the bar. She made it a slow, deliberate walk, her tight, well-formed tail traveling twice the distance as the rest of her body. To her left was the pool table under a dimly lit fluorescent light. The Blanchett brothers were there. No turning back now. She found a barstool and gazed intently at the brothers, who were engaged in their own bit of local drama.

Kim could tell the brothers were already half-drunk. Cigarette smoke hung like a dirty cloud over the pool table, where Georgie and Terry watched Rory sink the eight ball. Another twenty dollars from another youngster who thought he was good enough to challenge the Blanchett boys. A little too drunk, a little too loud, and a little too angry about losing to Rory, the boy called him a name under his breath.

"What was it you just said, boy?" Rory asked indignantly.

"Nothin'."

"The hell it was," Rory growled. "You should know better than to be bustin' on the Blanchetts in their own bar, now shouldn't you, boy?"

"I know it's your bar. Everyone knows it," the boy said as passion ignited his voice, "but you three's always together. Nobody challenges you 'cause it's always three on one."

"That's right, boy, it is. Now why don't you pick your sorry self up and get out of here before we show you how we deal with sore losers." He smacked the boy along the back of the head and pushed him toward his brothers.

One of the brothers gave the boy a good shove, and he landed at Kimberly's white go-go boots. He scampered away and made for the door, leaving the brothers to take notice of Kimberly. She could feel their eyes on her but didn't want to jinx the effect by looking their way. *Stay calm, Kimberly. It's a different kind of charm than you learned in finishing school, but it is charm nonetheless.*

She sat on a barstool and crossed her legs. Her miniskirt stretched to look as if it had been painted on. She pulled a Virginia Slims cigarette out of her purse and played with the feel of it in her fingers. She waited a few seconds to see if any of the Blanchett "gentlemen" would offer her a light. She looked their way invitingly. They stared at her like dogs looking into a butcher shop window, but it didn't dawn on one of them to light her cigarette. At this slight, the competitive nature of her father came to the surface. She had come to seal a deal, and, darn it, she was going to get these hillbillies to give her what she came for.

She lit her cigarette, smiled at the boys, and turned to the bartender. He smiled at her request and soon returned with a bottle of whiskey and four shot glasses. *Just enough to make them pliable and to give me the nerve to go through with it,* she thought. She laid fifty dollars on the bar and slowly slid off the barstool. With the bottle in one hand, glasses in the other, she sashayed over to the pool table and asked seductively, "Can I play?"

Kimberly was unaccustomed to this type of behavior, but she played it to the hilt. It was as if assuming a different personality would somehow shield her, exonerate her, from the events of the evening. Regardless of the consequences, she knew it had to be done to stop a torment far worse than the Blanchetts could deliver.

At least Rory was attractive and well built. Between that and the alcohol, she was able to convince herself the time spent in the back of his pickup wasn't all that bad. As the eldest, he had called "dibs" on Kim. Only he had full intercourse with her, but Terry and Georgie found other avenues of pleasure at her expense. As the evening wore on and she let herself be passed from one brother to the next, the numbing effect of the alcohol started to wear off. The boys were laughing and cheering at whichever one was busy with her at the moment. In the midst of that laughter, something horrible grew in Kimberly. Even though she had sought exactly this situation, she hated them for their cavalier treatment of her.

The night seemed to go on forever. Finally, Rory yelled to his brothers that they had work tomorrow. He also grumbled something about needing to get a shower before his wife could smell alcohol and slut all over him. In one gesture, they pushed her out of the pickup, threw her clothes to her, and laughed as they pulled out of the alley. *Not so much as a "Thank you, ma'am,"* she thought bitterly as she slid her miniskirt over her thighs.

As she walked to her car, she could feel the bruises forming on her body. The boys had not been gentle, but a few bruises here and there might help her spin a tale that would satisfy Benny. She needed to fake being traumatized. That shouldn't be too hard actually. The experience certainly had not been pleasant, but she was sure she had accomplished her goal.

The timing was just right, and it was as if she could feel the new life growing inside of her. She had no desire to be a mother at this tender age, but pregnancy … well, that was a different story. It would end the night visits, and she could always hire nannies to take care of the child. All in all, it was well played—anonymous sex with a man who would never remember her, never be tempted by her fortune, and never be able to tell of the night's desperate events to any of her acquaintances. Most importantly, the night visits would stop. She knew it.

Back at her car, she changed out of the miniskirt and tight top into a granny skirt and a tunic. She used mud from the side of the road to soil the clothes, and then ripped both the skirt and tunic. Looking in her rearview mirror, she removed the garish makeup. *I look tattered and torn, but I'll need to look more battered if I'm going to be convincing.* With that thought, she slammed her forehead against the steering wheel and raked her nails across her face. As blood coursed down her cheek, she put the car in gear and headed home.

Although convinced she had done the right thing given the unusual circumstances, Kim's resolve dissolved into hot tears as she saw her home at the end of its rambling driveway. The Georgian manor she had inherited from her parents was huge, but every inch of its twenty-five rooms was fully used when her parents were alive. Weekends filled the guestrooms with attendees to Stan's constant parties and barbecues. Tonight, every light was on. Joseph had waited up for her. She might have known it. Joseph had been the loyal butler and friend of her father. Her father's death resulted in the transference of Joseph's loyalty and protectiveness to Kimberly. As she pulled up to the manor, the front door flew open and Joseph appeared in his suit, pressed and clean, as if he had just put it on.

"Miss Kimberly!" Joseph exclaimed.

"Oh, Joseph," she cried. "A terrible thing has happened." Tears poured from her as she remembered the night she had just been through. The emotion was real, even if the story was a fabrication.

"My car overheated, Joseph. I pulled over to let it cool down. Some men in a pickup truck stopped to offer help, and then ..." She cried harder remembering Rory's hot breath, laden with the sickening smell of tobacco, weed, and cheap whiskey.

"Miss Kimberly, we have to call the police."

"No, Joseph. I can't do that!" Kimberly protested, her entire body trembling at the thought of making public an event she intended to forget altogether. "I'll *never* tell anyone, not even the police, what those creeps did to me! I plan to forget it, Joseph. To just ... put it out of my mind." She stared at him intently, trying to conjure the demanding look her father used when he would broach no further discussion of a matter.

"But, miss. These men have to be brought to justice."

"No, Joseph, they don't. I have been through too much lately. I need a bath, some ice for my face, a couple aspirin, and my bed."

Later, Kimberly lay exhausted in her bed. The room was dark, and the sheets felt cool against her skin. She wanted to meet them head-on and fully coherent, not in some somnolent haze, but she was losing her battle with sleep. As she dozed, she became aware of a bright light. It was them. "Come on, Kimberly, wake up!" she screamed in her head.

As with all the other times, she felt drowsy and lighter than air. She felt the bed lose contact with her back as her body began to float into the light. She tried to open her mouth to scream, but she was paralyzed. Her bravery was quickly abandoning her in the glare of the pulsating bright light just outside her bedroom window. She was definitely more awake than she had ever been during these encounters. This was *not* a dream.

She levitated slowly, almost gently, toward the wall of windows on the south side of her bedroom suite. Seeing her room pass by, she felt a growing homesickness. She didn't want to leave. She wanted to remain in the security of her bed. She longed even for the simple security of the dreamlike state that had protected her in the past. Perhaps it was too much to be fully conscious for these events.

She heard a lilting, powerful voice in her mind. "Relax, we won't hurt you. It's just a visit. Try to sleep. Relax ..." The voice didn't sound totally human. It had a buzzing, insect-like quality about it. Nonetheless, the words were soothing, lulling her. She felt herself giving in to the temptation to fall asleep. Her eyes closed as her body floated unharmed through the closed windows.

There was a flash of light; then the room was dark and silent.

———

While Kim was driving toward her evening of desecration, her brother, Benny, was hearing confessions at St. Patrick's Cathedral in New York City.

New York City in July—they didn't call them the dog days for nothing. The humidity and the ninety-five-degree temperature made the atmosphere so thick you could cut it with a knife. Downtown construction was booming on the biggest tower to hit the New York skyline—two, in fact. They would be twins, each with more than a hundred floors. Benny loved Manhattan.

"And I got angry, Father, about four hundred times."

This guy really needs to get a life, Benny thought to himself. The confession droned on and on.

"In fact, it may have been more than four hundred times. I try to keep track of these things, but it's tough, you know, Father?"

Benny had to cut this short for his own sanity. "Four hundred will do. You've made a very good confession. I don't need to hear any more. For your penance, say three Hail Mary's, one Our Father, and a Glory Be."

"But Father ..." Then Benny slammed shut the veiled window that led to the confessional. This guy was clearly a whiner. Benny knew he would have to hide out in the confessional until the guy was done with his penance, lest he follow Benny to the rectory, lofting ever more sins to be forgiven.

He thought about how he had come to this place. He loved New York, and the priesthood was better than he thought it would be. He had to admit the idea of an angry God killing one man for the sins of us all was ludicrous, clearly an archaic idea in light of the dawning Age of Aquarius. But the priesthood was much better than the draft, and it was a hell of a lot more socially acceptable than becoming a drag queen. He loved the robes, the chasubles, the finery, and the control it gave him over others. Imagine the psychological power when people think you can set them free from the ravages of sin they didn't know existed until you pointed it out to them. Stan would have killed to have this kind of control over the fates of men.

Good old Stan. *God, I hated that man! Why mother married him is beyond me.* Stan never appreciated Benny's finer points. Benny's mother had often suggested that Stan adopt him, especially after Kimberly came along. She thought it would be nice if they all had the last name of Martin. Alas, Stan could not bring himself to call Benny his son or to let him share in his fortune. Benny was stuck with the last name Cross, a gift from a Jewish father who anglicized the family name of Croszynski, and it would be a daily burden to him as he grew up in the Martin household. What is that line from the gospels? "Pick up your cross and follow me." That's how Stan had acted toward Benny, as if he were the Cross that the Martins had to endure.

Maybe the cruelest thing Stan did was to allow Benny access to the high life, the exquisite wines, the fine dining, and the lavish vacations. Stan had shown him how to live the life, but he had never intended to leave him the wealth or position to continue in such a life. All of the money and power went to Kimberly.

Yet he couldn't help but have special feelings for Kimberly. She had loved him from the time she was a tiny baby. When she was an infant, she cried if not held constantly by her mother or Benny. As Kimberly grew, she continued to favor Benny, who was twelve years her senior. Kim was one of the few bright spots in Benny's young life. She didn't see his heavy physique with womanish breasts. She didn't notice his premature balding or interminably bad skin. To her he was the big brother she adored with no conditions, no prerequisites, and no demands of reciprocation.

When Benny left to pursue a degree in philosophy at the University of Georgia, Stan gave him the talk about it being time for him to go out into the world, to find himself, be a man—all of that crap. Benny was sure Stan really just wanted to get him off the dole. By this time even his mother had turned against him, insisting Stan was only trying to do the best thing for him.

How sad Mother betrayed me prior to her death, he thought. He had taken the summer off between college and seminary, convincing his mother he needed the time to contemplate this next big step in his life. Things hadn't gone well. Mother was constantly minding his business, insisting his lifestyle didn't seem to be that of someone entering a lifelong commitment to the Church. Her disappointment with him was visible in every look and every word. It was as if her disappointment had manifested in a physical deterioration. Unable to find anything physically wrong, her doctor tried lithium to lighten her mood, but the illness got worse as the summer wore on. Finally, she caught a summer cold that her poor body couldn't seem to shake. It grew into pneumonia, and she died. Benny, to his own surprise, felt no remorse. In fact, it was rather liberating when her constant criticisms were finally silenced. *Bye, Mom.*

Mother's death had really shaken Stan, and Benny had taken great pleasure in seeing his torment. Then an odd thing happened. Stan began to rely on Benny to help in the rearing of Kimberly. She adored him, and the seminary was a short drive away. Stan had even written Benny a lovely letter thanking him for the hand he had taken in Kimberly's formative years.

In those years, Benny was the hit of the seminary. Friars and faculty alike joined him in frequent outings to the Martin mansion. Joseph served mean poolside martinis and was always available to look after the more mundane aspects of Kimberly's upbringing. Benny's role was more that of a friend and confidant. For the longest while, it looked like he had found a way to have it all.

But then ordination hit like a summer storm. One day, he was lying on his face, pledging loyalty to the bishop, and the next he was installed as a pastor in a Georgia stink hole of a town. "Few people in America do poverty like backwater Georgians," he would snipe at his congregation. The entire thing was tasteless to him. Worse still, Kimberly was nearly grown. She didn't need him as she had … and that meant Stan didn't have much time for him either.

Shortly thereafter, Benny learned a few things about the hierarchy of the organization he had just joined. There were definitely those on whom philanthropy was not lost. Luckily, Benny still had credit cards Stan had given him to use for Kimberly's care. They appeared limitless. Soon Benny had much of the Georgian hierarchy eating out of his hands.

Once, while he was spending a few days with Kimberly, Stan took him aside. Two hundred eighty-three thousand dollars of credit card charges in the past year had come to Stan's attention. When he looked into them and found that none of the funds had been spent on Kimberly, he went ballistic. He threatened to take away the cards and Benny's visits to Kimberly unless he exercised more financial restraint.

There it was again. Benny Cross could look at the Martin wealth. He could touch it and even play with it. But he would *never* be allowed to own it or control it unless he took matters into his own hands. He reasoned he wouldn't need to control the wealth to benefit from it. All he needed to do was control his adoring little sister. How fortunate for her that he was there to comfort her the weekend her father died. Brake failure was uncommon, but when it's your time, it's your time. The Lord calls you home at a time of His choosing. At least that's what Father Benjamin Cross had said at Stan's funeral. *Rest in peace, Stan.*

In recognition of his exceedingly generous sister, Benny had secured an associate pastorate at St. Patrick's Cathedral in New York. *Saint freakin' Patrick's!* He could barely believe it himself.

He entered the rectory, grabbed a glass of red wine, and turned on the television to watch the news. Like everyone else in the world, he was awestruck at the pictures coming from Tranquility Base on the moon. Man had come so far; the imagination couldn't even conceive of how far he could go.

The moon is by far our closest celestial neighbor, but Armstrong's giant leap for mankind was merely the opening volley. It was now perfectly logical to think of a future when man ventured far into the cosmos. What would become of Benny and his kind once that happened? Could they really expect the sophisticated world to take seriously the accounts of a messy death in Palestine more than two thousand years before?

Benny, like many of the younger priests with whom he associated, thought the Church needed to change fundamentally. It needed to embrace a larger ideology, one that had room for Jesus, Mohammed, Buddha, and all the great men of faith. It needed to establish its relevance not only to a world that got smaller every day, but also to the solar system, the galaxy.

In short, if the Church was to avoid being "Lost in Space," then it had to beam on board the starship *Enterprise* and boldly go where it had never gone before. It was clear to Benny there was an overriding cosmic consciousness that man could access. Many called that consciousness God. It seemed to him all of the differing religions on Earth were really methods of tapping into this greater self. Benny was convinced Jesus' life and death weren't the end of cosmic revelation. They were a beginning.

Thankfully, Vatican II had come about to allow more freedom in the Church. While not espousing any of the ideas Benny was forming, it provided a cover under which he could move people along to this new view of religion. His sermons, which resonated strongly with youth, were about each person finding his own path. In this regard, Benny was beginning to make a name for himself. Other young priests began to follow his lead, reaching out to the liberated youth with what had become known as the Aquarian Gospel.

And others noted Benny's philosophies and preaching style as well. Benny smiled faintly as he remembered the time Cardinal Cesare Bilbo visited from Rome. An old, frail-looking man with only a few reckless remaining hairs, Bilbo had spoken to him at great length about a powerful lodge within the Vatican—one recognizing that the suffering savior model was now passé. This group of devotees believed in a cosmic consciousness that permeated all religion. In particular, they were investigating the role of Lucifer in the next generation of Christian thought.

"You must understand," Cardinal Bilbo intoned with a thick Italian accent as he sat across from Benny at Delmonico's famous triangle-shaped restaurant. "This Lucifer we talk about is not the same as the devil. We need to put away this archaic notion of a devil. He does not exist.

"We need to look beyond medieval myths. Lucifer is a symbol for the light bringer. We have to embrace enlightenment. We need to take responsibility for the world, and we need to liberate it from the vestiges of colonialism, imperialism, and capitalism."

Benny was enthralled. This man was able to crystallize his own thoughts about the state of the Church. "Teach me, Eminence. I have often longed to belong to something bigger than the day-to-day existence. I have long suspected there is more for me than fasting and rosaries."

The cardinal smiled knowingly and began to shepherd Benny in the new spirituality that was infiltrating the Vatican.

Benny's reverie faded as the news coverage moved to a live broadcast from Tranquility Base. As he watched Armstrong and Aldrin bounce along the surface of the moon, Benny knew there was more.

After finishing the bottle of wine and eating an outrageously good Italian dinner, Benny slipped into bed without changing his clothes. Sometime in the middle of the night, he had the dream again. It always started the same way. A bright light awakened him. When he opened his eyes, he would be in a very brightly lit, circular white room. In his dreams he was never afraid. He had more knowledge here than he did in his real life.

"Time to open your eyes now." It was his spirit guide. In the dreams, he knew her so much better than in his waking existence. "Come on," she teased. Her voice had a soft, lilting quality to it. Every time she spoke, it was like the soft pounding of waves upon the sand, drawing him in.

"Hello, my lady," he said as he opened his eyes. She was like no lady he had ever met. She described herself as being Pleiadian, from a planet far away and a dimension that circumscribed the four we call home.

The Pleiadian look had startled him at first. She was large, perhaps six feet tall, with long, thin legs and arms. Her hands had four thin fingers. Her face could be most easily described as a humanoid insect. Her large, moist eyes were like round, totally blue orbs. Her cheekbones were very high, and her nose was thin and angular. She had a pointed chin, which gave her face the distinct shape of a narrow heart. Her skin was very pale, as if it never had been exposed to sunlight. Her hairless head rested precariously on a long, thin neck. Her insect-like movements were quick and reflexive.

"I have summoned you tonight," she said in a conspiratorial whisper, "for a marvelous event. We have tested the subject you provided to us, and we think she would be a good candidate for insemination."

"It won't hurt her in any way, will it?"

"No. In fact, she may never even know she is pregnant. Our plan is to extract the fetus after thirteen weeks of development. Past that point, our methods are vastly superior to human incubation."

"We've discussed this before," Benny said with disgust. "Spare me the gynecology. What will the baby be like?"

"A blend of our two species. If humanity is to survive its self-imposed nuclear threat, it will need avatars to guide its evolution to global consciousness."

"Will he look alien?"

"He will look human but will have the attributes of Pleiadian intellect and spiritual insight. Your subject has retained her virginity, I presume."

"As her brother, priest, and confessor, I have been very strong in my dialogue with her about premarital sex. She has committed to waiting for marriage."

"Then this should be a simple procedure."

"My lady," Benny intoned almost reverently. "Please tell me, do I have a role in the coming shift in global consciousness?" He knew the answer but needed to hear it again.

A reassuring smile in her voice, she said, "You will shepherd the people of Earth into a new dawn, a life of peace and tranquility."

He smiled and took a second to imagine the unimaginable. It seemed so wonderful, so real, but it wasn't. This was, after all, just a dream.

TWO

C alvary Bible College was a small school hidden in the parched hills south of Ozona, Texas, the seat of Crockett County. The county, as well as almost every public building, park, and highway, bore the name of the famous US representative from the state of Tennessee. David Crockett had once told his fellow legislators, "You can all go to hell. I'm going to Texas." While the distinction between the two had been lost on many a visitor to Crocket County over the years, the small student body at Calvary was by and large a happy crew.

Two of its seniors sped down the road in a bright-green Studebaker convertible that had been quite the car in 1959, when it was manufactured. Even though the Studebaker belonged to her roommate's fiancé, Fran Sharpe drove it to town. Her roommate, Sarah Matheson, was scheduled to marry Mack Jolean, the car's owner, the following day. Sarah manned the radio. The arrangement spoke to their friendship. Fran was the grounded one, while Sarah was a slave to her emotions.

Fran had been the school's reigning beauty for the past four years. Her toned body was shapely and tall. Her long blonde hair accentuated the high cheekbones of the Native American part of her heritage, as well as the violet-gray eyes of her Northern European background. A fiercely independent and fun-loving spirit matched her beauty. And yet when it came to the Lord, she was serious and respectful. For Fran, the world was her oyster, but her faith was the pearl.

As they drove, listening to the blaring radio, Fran pondered how she and Sarah had become so close. Their viewpoints were as different as their looks. Shorter than Fran, with a more rounded torso, Sarah was the Judy Carne to Fran's Goldie Hawn, not that either Bible school

14

woman would admit to ever having watched *Laugh-In*. Where Fran held a very traditional view of her faith, Sarah was progressive, always looking for the next new thing. But each was an only child who desperately wanted a sister, and a close bond formed.

Mack Jolean, Sarah's fiancé, had graduated the previous year and taken over the pastorate in the small town of Riverside, Texas, home to five hundred Walker County residents. Mack was a go-getter. He fully believed in a vision to transform Texas and beyond with power evangelism.

Their wedding would be a small affair, held in Calvary's white Georgian chapel, with a reception at the student union. As maid of honor and the roommate with organization skills, Fran had become the de facto wedding planner. She had gotten use of the school cafeteria, where she and Sarah made ham, potato salad, cookies, and punch for the guests. She and Sarah had already used Mack's car to get the necessary supplies. Today's trip was about fashion. As a wedding gift, Fran agreed to do Sarah's makeup, not the Bible-school brand of bland, but full model makeup with large patches of white eye shadow and cherry-red lipstick. Fran was planning a much more traditional look for her own wedding to Tom Ellis in six months, but this was Sarah's wedding. Fran's job was to make it happen according to her best friend's wishes.

As the car sped down the roadway, Sarah raised the radio's volume even louder as the Fifth Dimension sang their hit, "Aquarius."

"What is it with this song?" Fran asked. "It's like there is a twenty-four-hour 'Aquarius' channel or something. You can't get away from it."

"I think it is very spiritual," Sarah answered. "It resonates with people our age."

"Spiritual? To me it sounds like an astrological guide to a love fest."

"Maybe it's not," countered Sarah. "I've been thinking a lot about this. Maybe God is doing a new thing."

"Why would God need a 'new' thing? How's He supposed to top Calvary?"

"I don't think it has anything to do with 'topping Calvary,' Frannie. I think it is all about drawing the world closer, pulling them into the Calvary experience without grossing them out over all the blood and gore. Maybe it's time to look beyond Calvary to the Kingdom."

Fran's spirit balked at the idea, but she didn't want to challenge Sarah. She wanted merely to enjoy riding in the old convertible on a sunny Texas day. Her mind wandered to her own future.

She would graduate at the end of the fall semester. Then she would marry her fiancé, Tom Ellis. From there it was off to Africa and the mission field. Tom was a delightful man, full of passion for the Lord and the love of life. Fran loved every moment in his presence. They seemed to click on so many levels, as if they were one person living in two bodies. And then there was the physical attraction. Tom had light blond hair that fell in loose curls around his face. That face! It was, in a word, beautiful, like a Michelangelo sculpture. In fact, if it wasn't for his muscular body and physical prowess, Tom's refined, facial beauty would seem nearly feminine.

Fran couldn't wait to graduate and be with him. She ached to know him physically. She was nearly jealous of Sarah, who would know Mack fully in another day. Unlike Fran, Sarah didn't seem to be nearly as excited about the upcoming intimacy. She and Mack seemed to share a dream of taking the world for Christ, as if conquest was their shared aphrodisiac.

The song ended, and Fran started the conversation where her thoughts had ended. "So, Sarah, have you picked a lovely negligee for the big night?"

"No. I assumed there wouldn't be much need for clothing, if you get my drift." Sarah smiled as she screamed over the radio.

Fran laughed, lowering the volume. "And all along I thought you enjoyed a more cerebral passion. You go, girl!"

"I'm different than you, Fran. I'm not the type that can look hot. So why try, right?" Fran noticed Sarah was wringing her hands, a nervous habit from childhood.

"Sarah, you're wrong. I bet you get Mack plenty hot and bothered. Still, for the wedding night, you could help the process a little bit."

"Do you really think so, Frannie? I would love to feel really sexy at least once in my life."

"Now you're talking! While we're in town, I'm going to treat you to a really sexy negligee and some perfume that will bring out the animal in Mack."

Sarah cackled at the idea. "I think I'll take you up on the offer."

"I also read an article about milk baths. We could get your whole body so soft and silky that he'll never want to leave your side."

Sarah looked over her granny glasses toward Fran. "Well, if you're sure Gloria Steinem wouldn't mind ..."

Both girls laughed.

"Gloria only attracts trouble," Fran said. "It really is okay to be your own woman and *still* attract men, you know."

"Preach it, girl," Sarah joked.

"It's not 'girl'; it's 'woman.' Don't call me 'Miss'; you can call me 'Ms.' 'Ms. Sex,' to be precise."

"But I don't want to Ms. Sex," Sarah chortled. "I want to *find* sex!"

"Now you're talking, sister!" Fran continued, "You're going to have good old preacher-girl sex. You're going to be a loving sex kitten to your preacher husband, and he's going to want to ring your chimes and have a tent meeting every day!"

The day with Frannie had been great fun, but the warm evening enticed Sarah to drive into the Texas countryside for some alone time. She wanted to catch the sunset in an isolated place, to feel as if she alone was being treated to the glorious red hues painted on the canvas of the sky just for her by a loving God.

No radio this time. She wanted to be alone with her thoughts. She may never have a time like this again. Soon there would be various parish meetings and children that would occupy her time. At a minimum, she would have to share some of these times with Mack. She knew that may seem romantic to some girls, but Sarah would miss her alone time. There were wondrous times ahead in the life she would share with Mack, but she hoped to be able to carve out time for herself. She was ready to be an equal partner in life and in ministry, as long as she did not have to lose herself in the process.

The sun had slowly dipped below the horizon as the old Studebaker grunted up the dirt road to the top of the bluff. Something deep inside had led her to this location. She marveled at the beauty before her. The setting sun was casting a red-orange glow on the horizon to the west. In the east, the first bright stars were bursting through the indigo sky.

No moon tonight—just the backdrop painted by the setting sun and God's very own diamonds peering through the darkness.

Taking in the incredible sight, she noticed movement on the eastern horizon. One of the stars appeared to be moving. Very slowly it was growing brighter, as if approaching her. Thinking of the Betty and Barney Hill story told a few years back by *Look* magazine, she laughed at the prospect of little gray men from outer space, although she had to admit it would be fun to live in a world that knew its galactic neighbors.

The light moved insanely fast and just as quickly stopped and hovered above her. Startled, she looked up to see a beam of light descending to a spot next to her. In fractions of a second, the light in the sky dissipated, and standing next to her was an incredible being of light.

The being was beautiful in an androgynous way, glowing in varying shades of light. Its long hair was a yellowish white, while its flowing robe was a striking blue-white light, and its eyes were large, slightly slanted, and a most beautiful shade of blue.

Reaching out to her, the being said, "Do not be afraid." Her mind instantly raced back to the many angelic appearances in the Bible that started with the angel's admonition not to give in to fear. The words had a calming effect on her, as if their mere utterance had spoken the reality into existence.

It strode effortlessly, as if gliding, to the car. She was caught up in how incredibly real this all was. She saw its reflection clearly in the polished hood of the car as it made its way to the driver's door.

"Are you an angel?" she asked softly.

"Yes," the being replied, more by thought than by mouth. "You can call me an angel. Others have."

"Has the Lord sent you?"

"We all serve the Lord. I am merely a servant sent to help you accomplish His will."

She was confused as to what could demand such a dramatic burst of eternity into reality. "What is it you want from me?"

"Our Lord would have you give birth to an exceptional son. Unfortunately, you bear an affliction that renders you incapable of becoming pregnant." These thoughts were communicated to her without words, but with an attendant conviction that buried into her subconscious mind. Hearing the words made her believe fully that they were the truth. It was as if she had always known she would be unable to bear children.

"What do you want me to do?" she asked.

"Come with me. We are permitted to perform a procedure on you that will enable you to bear this child."

"Wh–where do you want me to go?" Sarah stammered.

"To the beam of light I just came from," the angel said with a smile that exuded great love.

She felt herself longing to go with this beautiful stranger and readily agreed to do so. The bright light in the sky began to shine above them. Everything turned white.

Next she found herself on a metal table in an extremely bright room. The angel was nowhere to be found. Into the room strode an insect-like being. Through mental prompting, Sarah knew to refer to her as the Lady.

The Lady referred mentally to something called DNA. Sarah had never heard of it. The Lady explained in thought patterns that mankind's DNA was deteriorating. She was going to implant some healthy DNA into Sarah's womb. To Sarah's untrained mind, this healthy DNA was the fix to allow her body to bear children.

The Lady held up a long needle and plunged it into Sarah's abdomen. Sarah screamed in pain until she passed out.

When Sarah returned to consciousness, she was in the front seat of the Studebaker. Looking at the dashboard clock, she saw it was midnight. She was cold and got out of the car to raise the convertible roof. It was so late. Could she possibly have fallen asleep while watching the sunset?

After raising the top on the car, she got behind the wheel, turned the ignition, and turned on the car's heater. Sitting there for a moment, she tried to recapture memories of the evening. She remembered the beauty of the sunset and the evening's first stars on the eastern horizon. Then she remembered a great flash of light above her.

With that memory came a flood of others, although not necessarily true memories of real events. She rushed to tell Frannie what had happened.

Fran had spent the evening praying ... and pacing. It had been hours since Sarah left. What if the old Studebaker had broken down somewhere? If Sarah was looking for a quiet place, then she would have headed toward the bluff. It was very lonely out there. There would be nobody to help her. When she finally heard Sarah's key in the lock, she ran to the door.

"Where have you been, Sarah? I've been crazy worried something horrible happened to you!"

"Oh, Frannie." Sarah's eyes started to tear as she recounted her memories of the evening's events. "I saw an angel tonight." She hugged the unsuspecting Fran and squealed with delight, "An honest-to-goodness angel!"

"What are you talking about?" Fran asked cautiously.

"I was out on the bluff outside of town. I just wanted some me time, you know? The sunset was gorgeous, and I was marveling at it, when a bright light shone above me. I looked up, but then the light was beside the car. When the beam of light went away, there was this incredibly handsome man. He glowed, Fran. He actually glowed all over. His face shone like liquid gold, and his robe was brilliant white. And the eyes! Oh, Fran, his eyes were blue as the ocean and just about as deep."

Fran was concerned. Sarah had always been prone to high drama, but this was starting to sound like a full-fledged break with reality. With labored, deliberate calm, she said, "So you're out on the bluff looking at the sunset and some golden Adonis shows up at your car?"

"Not an Adonis, Fran. I mean he was handsome and all, but he really did glow. It was really freaky. I could feel power emanating from him. It was spooky, and I was scared spitless. But then he smiled at me and said, 'Don't be afraid. I'm here from the Lord.'" She told the rest of the tale in minute detail as Fran held her hand. Fran willed herself to take long, deep breaths to appear calm, but inside she was afraid her friend had lost it.

"So you came away from this feeling okay?" Fran asked tentatively.

"Better than okay, Frannie. I'm healed of a problem I didn't even know I had! The Lord saved me years of trying unsuccessfully to become pregnant. The angel told me that I'm going to have a son. Oh, Fran, a son! I've always wanted a son. And he'll do great things for the world." A cloud of consternation furrowed her brow. "But I've got a strong feeling I shouldn't tell Mack about this."

Fran hoped she could put a cork in this bottle before Sarah tried to make Mack into a modern-day Joseph destined to care for her 'child of promise.' "Sarah, I believe in complete honesty between husband and wife. But this ... incident ... was so personal. Maybe it should stay between you and God."

She handed Sarah a cup of chamomile tea. "I'll tell you what," she patronized. "I agree to forget this talk. I'll put it out of my mind, Sarah. We'll pretend you never told me. That way, it can be just between you and the Lord. Let's just get some rest and start tomorrow off fresh."

Sarah agreed, the chamomile having its desired effect. Fran went to her bed, pretending to be tired, but she knew she wouldn't sleep. She intended to stay awake to make sure her best friend was indeed all right.

THREE

The sun had not yet risen on Springfield Lake, but Chris Altenbrook had. The twenty-two-year-old athlete started his day on the deck of his parents' house with a cup of coffee and his Bible, as was his custom. The home was rustic with exposed beams on its ceilings, four fireplaces, exposed brick interior walls, and rough-hewn pine floors. It fit perfectly into its lot along the lake in Springfield, Illinois. Chris had been fortunate to grow up on the lake. His youth had been idyllic. He was the only son of devoted parents, his father a pretty well-known journalist and his mother a homemaker in the June Cleaver fashion. Summers were spent swimming, paddling, and fishing in the lake with beachside fires in the evenings. Fire-roasted hot dogs, mountain pies, and toasted marshmallows were the order of the day in summer. In the winter, the fireplaces were often dotted with clothes drying from Chris's adventures in the woods, ice-skating and ice fishing. And of course, there was football. Chris was a gifted athlete. As quarterback, he led his high school team to the state championships. They lost there, but Chris was heavily recruited to join a number of large football programs across the country. He turned them all down in favor of hometown college Southern Illinois University.

The decision to go to SIU wasn't based on their football program. It was based on unfinished business. Chris drew a deep breath of the morning air as he contemplated the fateful day that changed his life forever: March 15, 1964. *Beware the ides of March.* Chris was a junior in high school then. It was like any other day. He got off the bus at the intersection and walked the quarter mile to his home. Normally his mother would be waiting for him to ask about his day. On this day, the police were waiting. Both parents had been killed in a freak car accident. Or maybe it wasn't an accident. The evidence was inconclusive because of the horrible fire that consumed the car after it crashed, but the police had suspicions that the brake lines had been cut. They took Chris to police headquarters for an interview. Chris was never really a suspect. Springfield was small enough that the police department had a pretty good read on what a good kid he was. They spoke with him for hours, trying to determine if Chris knew of anyone who would want his parents dead. Chris told them that he could think of nobody who had a grudge against his parents. He lied. His father had been sitting on a story of government corruption of the highest order. He had been threatened. Chris reasoned that there was no use telling the local law enforcement that he suspected national government involvement in his parents' death. Some things were never meant to see the light of day. That same night, he burned his father's notes in the family room fireplace.

Chris lived the next couple years in a state of numbness. Between the insurance payout and some money that his parents had stashed away, Chris was able to keep the house and have some money for college. The remainder of his junior year and the following summer were a blur to him. He joined the school's baseball team, entered a summer soccer league, and took jobs as a lifeguard during the day and a waiter at night. His trauma turned him into a dynamo of nervous energy. To sit too long created an opportunity for the memories to come flooding back. The emptiness of his parents' home was an assault to his senses. And if his parents had actually been murdered, Chris figured his continued safety depended on a public display of his desire to move on rather than ponder the details of their death. The only way to survive it was to stay busy.

During that time, Chris grew into a man. He filled out significantly, building a muscular upper body, six-pack abs, and heavily muscled legs. He had his father's hair, straight with just a bit of wave to bring it gracefully off his face as it grew longer. His hair was dark brown in the winter but turned nearly blond from his summer activities. Crystal-blue eyes set atop high cheekbones glowed from his tanned face and balanced his perfect white smile. His smile came easily, and his manner appeared effortless. A casual observer would think he was the most popular kid in school, with girls drooling around every corner. The truth was different from the expectation, however. Chris had been forced into a sudden maturity that the girls his age found daunting. Sure, he was handsome and athletic and smart, but he was also driven by pain to be always busy, always unavailable.

It wasn't until Christmas 1964 that Chris finally broke. He had put up all of the Christmas decorations his mom loved. He used her recipes to make the family's favorite Christmas cookies and bought his parents the gifts he wished he could give to them. But when Christmas Eve hit, it was like a ton of bricks. Returning home from midnight Mass, he turned on the Christmas tree lights and fell to the floor in tears that were months old. Hysteria gripped him, and heavy sobs moved him into a fetal position. Although he could barely breathe to speak, he called out the name of the only one he knew who could breach this kind of pain: Jesus.

Instantly, the sobbing slowed and Chris opened his eyes to see that the Christmas tree wasn't the only source of light in the room. Everything had a golden glow that comes from the strong presence of God. He tried to speak to the Presence in the room. His words became jumbled into a new language as he felt the golden glow move from the room into his heart. Where he had been lonely and in despair only moments before, he was now bubbling over with joy that welled up from the deepest part of his being. He never left the floor that night. He fell asleep in that Presence and let it work inside him to heal him and change him.

From that day forward, daily Bible reading, daily prayer, and daily Mass were added to Chris's routine. The addition of Jesus into his life made it happy again but added new complications. His local parish priests were at a loss to explain what had happened to him that night. They were impressed with Chris's devotion, but they found the Pentecostal experience of speaking in tongues to be an affront.

They counseled him not to speak about it, to concentrate on a life of service to the Lord. Chris complied. His was becoming a life of secrets anyway.

Attending SIU was the only option if Chris wanted to keep his home on the lake. He flatly turned down other options in favor of the chance to live in his parents' home, but that decision created a distinction between him and the other students. Again he felt like the only adult in a classroom of children. While they were worried about going to the spring formal, he was worried about the cash flow crunch that came when real estate taxes were due in the spring. Those responsibilities, coupled with a growing puritanical set of values, made him the odd man out in the "turn-on, tune-in, drop out" mentality sweeping college campuses.

Things had changed a bit in his senior year when he met Sophia, an exchange student from Argentina. She had also come from harsh circumstances and felt the loneliness of being separated from her family. She had light hair and a gorgeous olive complexion. More than that, she had a kind, gentle, and graceful manner that Chris found irresistible. Before he knew it, he was spending more and more time with her. She was committed to waiting until marriage, and his relationship with Jesus caused him to agree. She was behind him one year in college, but he could squeak out another year of eligibility to play football. It was all settled. He would stay in school an extra year and try to bang out a great football season that would enable him to apply for the NFL draft of January 1970. He and Sophia would marry, and life would be great.

The plan made sense on an intellectual level, but somewhere deep inside it brought about uneasiness. He rationalized that it was cold feet or a fear of finally leaving his parents' home and their memories, but he knew it was more than that. At daily Mass he found himself daydreaming that he was the one administering the sacraments. *Administering was such a sterile word.* Ministering the sacraments was what he wanted to do. Priesthood! Who would have thought? He couldn't even speak about the feelings rising within him. Instead, he followed the plan, a shot at professional sports and marriage to a beautiful girl. And he had waited for the Lord to make clear which path he should follow, until a few months ago.

He had been in a rowboat, fishing on the lake. Nothing was biting. He remembered the biblical account where Jesus told the fishermen to fish from the other side of their boat and their nets were filled. As he was wondering how the fishermen must have felt, he sensed a nudging in his spirit. *Cast your line to the other side of the boat.* "No way," he said to himself, laughing. "Lord, is this You, or is it my imagination?" *Cast your line on the other side of the boat!*

This time he followed the instruction. He dropped his line on the other side of the boat. It barely hit the water when it hooked the largest catfish Chris had ever seen. "Come on!" He laughed as he reeled in the fish. *Again!* He followed the instruction again with the same result. This time he was giggling. It was all too weird and too much fun! Again and again he dropped his line for fish to throw themselves on to. He had to wipe his eyes from the tears of joy and laughter as God revealed Himself out on that lake. Finally, he baited the hook and held it over the edge of the boat, waiting to hear, "Again," one more time. He didn't hear it. Instead, he heard a soft breeze in the trees along the lake's edge. Then the breeze left the trees. Chris watched the water ripple underneath its pass as it skimmed over the lake. When it reached him, he fell backward, as if dropped by a solid punch. He dropped his line as he heard, *Chris. I want to make you a fisher of men.*

Chris cried out loud with joy. Something in him had snapped. Now he wanted to be a priest more than anything else on Earth. Months of indecision gave way to feelings of exultation and joy. He screamed and laughed as he righted himself in the boat. On shore he saw Sophia waving to him. Sophia.

She didn't take it well. Hell hath no fury ...

"Coño carajo!" Sophia spit into the smoke-filled air of the Theta house. *Abe Farley is one hot piece of meat.* And more importantly, he was on the football team with Chris. He would do nicely. She couldn't believe that she had been saving herself for the day she and Chris would be married. Married! How stupid she was! All the time they were talking about marriage, he was planning a life without her.

Breaking up was hard enough, but being lied to for all those months! How could he not have told her that he was even considering the priesthood? She would have put up walls. She would have stopped herself from falling hopelessly in love with him. But he forgot one very important fact—she was Latina. And she knew how to get a man back—at least any normal man. If she was at home, a few public appearances with one of his friends would be enough to make him come crawling back. If there was another woman to confront, she could do it. And she would win. But how do you fight when the man you love has thrown you over for some mental delusion that he considers to be from God? She had some ideas, but they were desperate ones.

She moved close to Abe. Abraham Lincoln Farley. Corn-fed 220 pounds of muscle in a tank top and flip-flops, Abe was already three sheets to the wind. He took another hit from the bong, grinning happily. She sat down next to him, rubbing her hand on his thigh. He was the perfect choice to incite jealousy in Chris. He was by all accounts a great athlete but was forced to play second-string quarterback behind Chris. There had never been an outward rivalry, but Sophia had seen the discontent in his eyes when Chris received all the postgame adulation. She had seen the lust in his eyes when she walked hand in hand with Chris.

"Where's your boyfriend?" he asked warily.

"We're not going out anymore," she said with a pout. "I don't think I'm his type."

He grinned at his potential conquest and handed her the bong. She put down her drink, the fifth one of the evening, and stared at the alien contraption. He moved closer to her to show her how to take a hit.

"What's his type?" he asked as the smoke from her first bong hit exploded out of her mouth.

"You," she said with a naughty look.

He took her that night. Her first full-blown sexual experience was filled with passion. Her emotions ran wild with the joy of knowing that soon it would be Chris who would be her lover. She just had to shame him into it.

The next morning, Abe was more than happy to drive her to Chris's house to collect some albums and a swimsuit she had left there. The startled look on Chris's face when he opened the door was worth a million dollars to her. She could tell by that look that he loved her and that she had hurt him.

"I didn't expect to see you," he stammered as she led Abe through his front door.

"I just want to pick up a few things I left here," she said nonchalantly as she went into the house, leaving him with Abe.

"Hey, Abe," he said, eyes downcast. Abe grunted a response.

She returned with the few things she had left and kissed Abe hard, turning to see Chris's reaction. He colored.

"Well, we better be going," she said, handing her belongings to Abe. "We're tired. We didn't get much sleep last night."

Abe left first. Sophia followed. As she reached the door, Chris grabbed her arm. "Sophia, can I talk to you a minute?" Here it was. He was ready to throw over his stupid delusion and declare his love. She turned to him with a hard gaze. When he came back, it would have to be on his knees after the pain he had put her through.

"Sophia, you don't have to do this," he said.

"Do what?" she demanded.

"Throw yourself at Abe." He laid his hand on her shoulder. She relished the touch.

"Maybe I'm not throwing myself at him," she teased. "Maybe he just knows how to treat the woman he loves."

"He doesn't love you, Sophia. We both know what's going on here," he said tersely.

"Are you saying that you're the one who loves me?" she asked.

"Sophia. You know I love you, but it's just not meant to be for us."

Rage filled her. How could he stand there and say he loved her, all the while refusing to take the relationship further?

"Chris," she pleaded, "I will drop him for you in a minute." She reached between his legs to show him that their new relationship could be much more intense. He pulled away.

"I told you. I'm going to the priesthood, Sophia. Don't throw your life away in bad choices meant to get even. You deserve more than that. Treat yourself with some respect."

A torrent of Spanish curses streamed from her mouth as she pounded his chest with her fists. He grabbed her hands to stop the hitting.

"I hate you, Chris Altenbrook! I curse the day I met you!" She spit to the floor and ran from the house in tears.

It had been years since SIU had placed well in the NFL draft. Coach wasn't getting any younger, and his legacy was going stale. Young Chris had been the brightest thing on his horizon for years. There was a strong chance he would do well in the draft picks of January 1970. Of course, he wasn't about to do better than Terry Bradshaw or Phil Robertson from Louisiana Tech, but he would do well enough to bring attention to the SIU football program.

Looking ahead to the football season of 1969, Coach should have been ecstatic. He had convinced Chris to play for another year. Everything was looking up, except this news: his girlfriend was telling everyone that he preferred pole dancing! Chris had always been a bit of an enigma. He wasn't driven by the typical lusts of kids his age. Coach passed it off as a result of the tragic deaths of his parents. Something like that can make a person grow up pretty quickly.

And yet, there was something more. He had always wondered if Chris had the passion and the drive to move on in football. He was a wonderful player—fast and smart, with a wicked arm and the ability to scramble in the pocket—but he didn't *live* football. It just wasn't his passion. Coach should have taken a closer look at the kid before pinning so many hopes on him.

There was a knock on his office door. He looked at his watch. Chris was exactly on time for their meeting. He called out, "Come in."

Chris entered with his typical smile. It disarmed people, putting them at ease, but it was also a barrier. It was hard to get past this kid's smile to figure out what he was thinking. "You wanted to see me, Coach?"

"Yeah, Chris. I wanted to talk to you a bit about things to work on over the summer. When we file the NFL draft forms, I want to be able to highlight—"

"Coach," Chris cut him off, "about that. I won't be able to play this coming year, and I won't be filing for the draft." The smile was replaced by a somber seriousness.

Coach didn't want to hear it. The rumors were true. He needed to take control of the situation now. "Chris, there are more people like you than you realize in the NFL. It's not a matter of what you feel, it's a matter of controlling the information that people get. Understand?"

"No, Coach. I don't get what you're saying. Listen, something has happened to me ... something that you're going to find hard to understand—"

"Chris, I understand," Coach said sternly. "Now you listen to me. It

29

doesn't matter if you like some occasional male bonding. What matters is keeping your girlfriend happy enough that she doesn't tell people about it. Do you understand? Nobody cares what you are. They only care about what you appear to be."

"I think I'm beginning to understand," Chris said gravely. "I broke up with Sophia, and she's trying to get even."

"Well, she's doing a hell of a job at it!" Coach slammed both hands against his desk. "She's slept with half of the team, and she's telling everyone that you never touched her ... that you prefer boys! If this gets out, you can kiss your career good-bye!"

Chris's face reddened. "First of all, it's not true," he said sternly. His tone wasn't the least bit conciliatory as Coach had expected—no explanations, no protests, no pleas for understanding. "As for a career in sports, I don't want it. I've decided to become a priest. I'll be leaving for the seminary soon."

Coach nearly fell out of his chair. *The priesthood!* How the hell was he supposed to talk the kid out of this! "Chris, these types of decisions aren't to be made lightly. I'm sure Sophia embarrassed you, but becoming a priest? Kind of dramatic, don't you think?"

"Coach, I told you those rumors aren't true. I'm becoming a priest because I love the Lord and I've heard Him call me to it."

Chris's demeanor suggested that he was sincere. *Damn!* Coach knew he should wish the kid well, but at this moment he wished he had never met him. He pleaded, "Chris, can't you wait just a bit longer? Think of the time and energy that I've put into this! Play one more season, enter the draft. I'm guessing that God can wait another year, don't you think?"

"I can't wait another year, Coach." Chris smiled, putting up the barrier and closing the discussion.

"Are you sure about this, Chris?"

"As sure as I've ever been about anything, Coach."

"Well, good luck to you then," Coach said stiffly, turning his chair to indicate that the conversation was over as far as he was concerned. He heard Chris leave his office and then turned his chair back around.

There was only one thing left to do. He had to turn up the heat in recruiting that kid from Biloxi, Lionel Antoine. Chris Altenbrook was dead to him.

FOUR

s Sarah related her experience to Fran, a small white dot shone on the horizon in Georgia.

Even through her closed eyes, Kimberly was aware of the bright light that surrounded her. She knew where she was; she had been there before. Still it strained the bounds of sanity to admit it. Naked and shivering, she opened her eyes to see the now-familiar rounded room of light. She was lying on a metal table that seemed to have grown out of the floor, wider at the bottom and sloping to the single bed–sized rectangle to which she felt glued. Even though there were no visible restraints, she was unable to move her arms or legs. Turning her head from side to side, she examined the two small beings that had brought her to this room and removed her clothes.

They were each about four feet tall, with huge heads and childlike bodies. Four long fingers fit at the end of skinny arms. The length of the arms compared to the body size made them look oddly simian. Their movements were quick and jerky, almost as if they were having a hard time getting used to the gravity in the room. The predominant feature on their faces was a set of huge eyes that slanted toward the backs of their heads. Each eye was totally black, devoid of any distinguishing iris or pupil. In the areas of the eyes and forehead, their craniums were bulbous and quickly tapered to a point where a chin would normally be. Their noses were flat, like a piece of skin hanging over two breathing holes. They had no lips, just a slit where a human mouth would be. Their complexion was a light gray. Kimberly couldn't tell if they were wearing very tight-fitting jumpsuits or if they were naked. There were neither discernible genitalia nor body hair.

The attitude displayed by these little guys was nonthreatening. In fact, Kimberly could honestly say they did not scare her. If she hadn't been abducted from her bedroom and glued naked to this table, she might have even thought they were kind of cute. A lot of their actions looked like those of a toddler.

One of them was now staring at her. The darkness of its eyes was broken by glistening pools of tears that glided over their surfaces. As it stared, Kimberly stared back. She could feel its mind reaching out to her, touching her.

"Good. You are not nearly so afraid this time," it thought at her.

"No," she admitted, "but I am a little angry at being abducted and held against my will. Can you understand that?"

"Humans have a preoccupation with the illusion of freedom. For only a brief period of time we interrupt the illusion. In the end, you will pick it up again and feel as if this were only a dream."

"You've taken my clothing," she complained, "and I'm cold." The small figure drew near to her with a rod or wand of some type. He tapped it to her forehead and instantly she felt comfortable.

"Rest for a while. Our leader is not yet ready for you." He tapped her forehead again, and she drifted into a semiconscious state. While vaguely aware of her surroundings, she was very relaxed. She felt as if she were drifting, much like being on an air mattress in a pool. After a short while, she felt a change in the atmosphere of the little room. There was a slight odor of sulfur and burned wood, very much like the smell after a match has been lit. The smaller gray beings scampered away from the table on which she was imprisoned, and the shadow of the larger female entity loomed largely overhead.

Kimberly looked into the Lady's large blue eyes as she heard these words in her mind. "I will not hurt you, little one. I just need to perform a few quick tests."

"But you have no right to pluck me from my bed and perform 'tests' on me!" Kimberly replied sharply.

Benevolence left the Lady's face as she hissed, "I have every right!"

She then touched Kimberly's forehead with a rod, inducing a feeling of serenity. Once Kimberly had calmed, the Lady inserted a very long needle into her navel. Kimberly felt no pain but nonetheless had the sensation of the needle in her abdomen. Drawing a bit of fluid through the needle, the Lady moved to another part of the room to analyze it.

A humming growl grew from the creature as she examined Kimberly's specimen. In a burst of speed, her insect-like body jumped to the examining table. A kind of tongue extruded from the thin opening that served as her mouth. She stood quietly, as if tasting the air around Kimberly.

"You're pregnant," she hissed at Kimberly and then left the room.

Take that, you smelly old bug, Kimberly thought as the Lady exited the room. It felt good to frustrate the plans of this alien witch who thought she had the right to invade Kimberly's life. Better still, Kimberly had the feeling this would signal an end to their visits. It was more than a feeling; actually, it was an inner knowledge. She didn't know how she knew it, but she was certain there would be no more abductions, no more bad dreams, and no more terrors in the night.

Soon she found herself surrounded by three of the little gray beings and the Lady, who looked down at her with a malicious grin on her slit of a mouth. She picked up an instrument like a forceps and said with undeniable malice, "The situation is salvageable, with a slight change to the child's DNA. This will probably hurt." At that she invaded Kimberly's body, sending searing pain through her. She wanted to scream, but she couldn't make her lips move.

"*Stop!*" her mind screamed. *Please! Stop!* She never knew she could endure such pain. It felt as if her insides were being ripped apart. "*Oh, Jesus, make it stop!*" her mind screamed to a Savior she had barely known. At that moment, the pain stopped and she fell into a deep sleep.

Benny awoke to the sound of the telephone, which was dutifully answered by the housekeeper. He checked the time: six o'clock. He thought of going back to sleep until he heard her heavy orthopedic shoes clomping up the stairs. *What a night!* He was sure he had some wild dreams, but he couldn't quite remember them. It was as if they were just beyond his ability to perceive. And yet there was an odd feeling, a sort of sixth sense that something had happened to Kimberly. *Pregnant?* Had he dreamed that the Lady told him Kim was pregnant?

"Fah-ther, the phone is for you," the housekeeper called through the door with the last vestiges of an accent she had brought from Ireland nearly half a century before. "I told them you hadn't come to breakfast yet, but they say it's important."

Putting on his robe, Benny called back, "Tell them I'll be right down, Mrs. O'Reilly." Throwing open the door, he saw her still standing there, looking distressed.

"It's yer fahmly," she said before bustling to get in front of him as he descended the stairs. Reaching the phone seconds before he did, she dutifully grabbed the receiver to fulfill his earlier command. "He'll be right down," she said as he plucked the phone from her.

"Father Cross speaking," Benny said as he shooed Mrs. O'Reilly from the room.

"Master Benny," Joseph began desperately.

"Joseph, what's the matter?"

"A horrible thing has happened. Miss Kimberly was attacked last night." A lump rose in Benny's throat. He was at once stunned by the fact that he had sensed something was wrong with Kimberly and by the realization that he loved her beyond her utility as an avenue to Stan's fortune.

"Is she all right, Joseph?"

"A few ugly bruises and scars, sir, but I fear the more profound damages may be emotional. She wouldn't tell me the details, but I believe the attack was sexual in nature."

Benny gasped at the torrent of emotion engulfing him. Immediately he was sick for the pain and humiliation she must have suffered, and he was confronting an inner conviction that she was pregnant—not only pregnant, but with a special son, one that was ordained by the universe.

"Did you take her to the hospital? Notify the police?" he barked.

"She refused to go to the hospital and would not even entertain the notion of going to the police, sir." Benny knew of her stubbornness; it came from her father. He softened his tone with Joseph.

"Joseph, I'll notify my superior and catch the first flight. I should be there by midday. Do you think it would be a good idea if I spoke with her now?"

34

"She's still sleeping, sir. I'm sure she would be unhappy with me calling you. She acts as if she can make it go away by ignoring it."

"I'll be there this afternoon," Benny said as he hung up.

The sun shone brightly through the sitting room windows of Kimberly's master suite. Her head ached. Putting her hand to her head, she felt the scabs from her self-imposed injuries. She heard a quick knock at her door, followed immediately by Benny's sweeping entrance into the room.

"Benny?" she asked groggily.

"Yes, honey. I'm here."

"Did Joseph call you?" she asked, forcing her eyes open.

"Yes. Don't be angry. He is only looking out for you."

"I know." She smiled and then winced at the pain it caused her swollen cheek.

An unexpected tear came to Benny's eye.

"Don't cry, Benny," she pleaded. "You'll get me crying too. And I'm pretty sure it would hurt to screw up my face like that."

"Kimberly, we really should talk about this. Let's get you to a hospital. We should probably file a police report too."

"Benny, I can't do it. I'm an heiress to a huge fortune in a Georgian town where everyone minds everyone else's business. If I file a report or go to the hospital, I'll be remembered for this for the rest of my life. Besides, with the exception of a few bruises and scrapes, I really feel fine."

"I tend to believe you're probably physically okay, but what about mentally and emotionally? Sweetheart, you can't pretend this never happened."

"I have a feeling I won't be able to pretend for long. I think I'm pregnant." She began to cry in huge gasping sobs.

Benny pulled her close to him, and she laid her head on his shoulder. He could feel her tears on his neck, and his buried feelings of love for his baby sister came to the surface for the second time today.

"I know, sis. I had strange dreams last night that I can't exactly remember, but I woke up feeling that you were pregnant."

She pulled away from his shoulder so that she could look into his eyes. "Soon we'll have a baby boy around. Can you deal with that?" she asked tentatively.

"The truth?" He smiled. "For a man who has taken a vow of celibacy, the idea of having a paternal role in the life of a little boy is like a dream come true."

They held each other for a long while, brother and sister trying their best to cope with their independent, surreal revelations of an uncertain future.

In the strange worlds of geopolitics and world finance, the known participants are more often than not the reflection of a more powerful hidden authority. Politicians and wealthy philanthropists are the face presented to the public, but the men who control the broader strategies work from the shadows. They prefer to accomplish their goals outside the purview of society. Expediency demands as much; significant investments in news agencies accomplish it. There are often rumors about the identities of these engineers of society, with the Rockefellers and Rothschilds at the top of most lists. More powerful than either family, however, is one man who commands the likes of the Rothschilds with a phone call. He is the master illuminati behind the reserve banks of the world's nations. Rarely seen in public, the mere mention of his name by associates is sufficient to ensure the fulfillment of his wishes.

This man is Lucien Begliali. His history is uncertain. There is no press kit with his biography. Rumor has it that he considers himself the first citizen of the world. To that end, he has convinced numerous governments throughout the world to grant him citizenship. His vast fortune, climbing to the hundreds of billions of dollars, is "old money," but how old nobody seems to know. The Begliali family, in nondescript fashion, pops in and out of history, as told anecdotally but never chronicled.

The current Begliali potentate, Lucien, called Luciano throughout Europe, was known to be a complex fellow. He was outstandingly handsome: a swarthy Italian complexion, high cheekbones, fine nose, gray eyes, and a head of dark black hair that he normally combed straight back. His lithe and well-muscled physique moved gracefully under the silk suits he wore habitually. Understated elegance was his hallmark. Men and women who met him were drawn immediately to his charm and charisma.

Begliali exited his limousine in the crippling heat of Washington, DC. He smiled broadly at the chance to again show his authority to the captains of industry, breaking their narcissistic fantasies that they were in control. Today the group to be cowed was the Federal Reserve's Board of Governors. Sweat poured from each of them as they sat around the table of a conference room with no air-conditioning to debate about whether to go along with the International Monetary Fund's proposal to establish special drawing rights, or SDRs.

In concept, the SDR would provide an international medium of exchange based on the value of gold. By definition, the SDR would be equal to 0.888671 grams of fine gold, the exact value of one US dollar. While certain board members could see the utility to world finance, there were two roadblocks. One was that the SDR could lead the way for developing a worldwide reserve currency other than the US dollar. The second was that the SDR was pegged to gold, and it looked to the continuation of the Bretton Woods system, which members of the Fed considered antiquated.

Lucien enjoyed the surprised expressions that filled the room when security opened the door to the sacrosanct meeting without so much as a knock. He looked around the room at the wilted board. Every armpit had perspiration stains; every tie was askew. In contrast, Lucien looked perfectly comfortable.

"Gentlemen," he addressed them as he walked to the head of the table. The security guard hastily removed fans that obstructed his view, making it even more uncomfortable for the board members. "I assume introductions are not necessary. I am here to help you decide to accept the SDR. I know of your reservations. First, let me state that the gold standard is passé. We all know it. Soon the entire world will be able to move away from Bretton Woods, and when this occurs, the value of the SDR will simply be pegged to a basket of world currencies.

"In effect, we are taking the first steps on the road to an eventual world currency. Imagine the economic boom that will occur when restrictions to the movement of goods fade away into history. Tell me, gentlemen, what country is more able to capitalize on such an economic upsurge?" He paused to let his words sink in. He said nothing that was new to them, but hearing it from his lips sounded reassuring.

"My dollar holdings are vast, as I am sure you are aware," he continued. "Betting against the dollar would be akin to betting against myself. I am convinced the opening of world markets will more than compensate for the loss of the dollar's status as the world's single reserve currency. I'm betting a personal fortune on it, and I would like to urge this austere group to join me in building a free world economy, by taking this simple first step. Be visionaries, gentlemen!"

He stared at them benevolently, watching as his opinion became their own. Behind the smile, his gray eyes danced with the delight of being able to so easily manipulate the self-proclaimed master manipulators. *This will never cease to be amusing.*

In short order, a vote was cast. The United States would support the formation of the SDR. Begliali bid the group farewell and quickly exited the room.

"Like everyone else, I had heard of the man, but I never expected to meet him!" exclaimed the youngest member of the group. "I've never met someone so charismatic. I've never been so impressed with anyone. My God, he doesn't even sweat!" He could barely contain his glee, like a child who has just sat on Santa's lap.

"He scares me to death," said the chairman. "I've met him before, and he is always the same."

"He's so decisive and subtly forceful. I'm drawn to that kind of power, even if it is a bit scary. Besides, if I were that polished, I wouldn't want to change either."

"That's not what I meant," the chairman said absently, as if looking deep into the past. "I first met him shortly after World War II. He hasn't aged a bit. He is literally the same."

"I guess good genes and a lot of money can keep a guy young."

"Yeah," the chairman said uneasily. "I guess you're right."

FIVE

It was the morning of Sarah's wedding. To Fran's surprise, Sarah didn't appear to be a bit nervous. More importantly, she didn't mention her angelic vision of the prior evening. In contrast, Fran was exhausted from the prior night's vigil and a nervous wreck about the impending nuptials. She had helped with the meal preparation, helped Sarah choose her dress, and even picked out the negligee that Sarah would wear on the honeymoon. It was now her job as maid of honor and Sarah's best friend to ensure that everything went off without a hitch. First on the agenda was to pick up Sarah's mother at the motel.

Sandy Matheson, Sarah's mother, had been widowed when Sarah was very small. She had made ends meet by working as a beautician. Like Sarah, she was not prone to the fanciful. Her life had been one of constant struggle to do right by her little girl. There were times when she would have liked the company of the opposite sex, but Sarah was the priority. Four years of tuition payments were behind her now. Her baby was marrying a good man. It was a wonderful day for Sarah, and a day of accomplishment for Sandy. Now she could kick back and enjoy her life a bit, and she had every intention to make up for lost time.

Sandy had dieted heavily to fit into the new hot-pink, short dress she had bought for the wedding. It was modern and trendy and the height of fashion.

"Mrs. Matheson, you look so slim!" Fran exclaimed when Sandy opened the motel room door.

"Awe thanks, Frannie," Sandy cooed as she spun around for Fran to get the full effect of her outfit. "I've been dieting for months to fit into this number! It's ridiculously expensive, but it's not every day that your only child gets married."

Fran smiled. She wasn't so sure Sandy hadn't gone for the wrong look. "I can't wait for Sarah to see you," she gushed.

Mother and daughter screamed and hugged when Fran brought Sandy to the dorm room. Fran was carrying the bag of curlers, combs, and brushes Sandy would use to sculpt Sarah's hair.

"You look beautiful!" Sarah squealed at her mother.

"I've been dieting for months. And I finally had the guts to do the red hair I've always wanted. It's not too much, is it?"

"I think it looks great," Sarah said. "You and I have always had to be practical. So today we get to live it up. You look glamorous! Wait here."

Sarah quickly donned the satin minidress she had chosen for this day. It gleamed white and had a tight, fitted bodice with a relatively low neckline.

"Aaaagh," Sandy squealed, "it's wonderful! You're going to look like you came out of a magazine! Now come over here and sit down while I give you the perfect hairdo for that dress. Frannie, be a doll and bring me my bag."

Sandy began teasing and spraying Sarah's hair like a madwoman. When she was done, Sarah had a beautiful six-inch poof on the top of her head; her long bangs were parted in the middle and hung down the side of her face, curling gracefully toward each cheekbone. The hair was great. Fran had to admit Sarah looked good in the Priscilla Presley hairdo. As Fran moved in to complete the look with the makeup of the day, Sandy began to give Sarah advice.

"Honey," Sandy began, "while we have a few moments, maybe we should talk a little bit about tonight." Sarah rolled her eyes and smirked at Fran.

"Men and women have different intimacy needs, darling. For a woman, flowers and candy and a hug and a kiss can be just about as good as it gets. Men, on the other hand, need sex to feel close to us." Sandy began to pace the room.

"Mom, I know about the birds and the bees," Sarah said, rolling her eyes at Fran.

"It's not them I'm worried about. I just don't want you to be disappointed. Granted, I only knew your father, but from what I hear in the

40

beauty shop, men are all pretty much alike. When they're interested in sex, they're interested in sex. Do you know what I mean?"

"It's a new age, Mom. It's okay to be interested in sex. I think it must be a wonderful feeling to lay with the man you love." Sarah began to wring her hands.

"It's not like in the movies, baby doll. I just want you to know that. It's more like a couple huffs and puffs, a grunt, and then he falls asleep." Sandy looked out the window, her back to the girls. Fran avoided looking at Sarah, knowing they would both burst into laughter if their eyes met. Sandy continued, "I just want you to know if it happens for you that way, it's not you. Women want to make love. Men want to have sex."

"Mom—" Sarah began.

Sandy cut her off, continuing as if it were a script she had memorized. "I just don't want you to set your expectations too high. The important thing is that Mack is a good man, and he loves you."

"Mom," Sarah said and smiled, "it's the 1960s. The world has changed."

"But the species hasn't, sweetheart."

Back at the hotel in Ozona, Mack Jolean was shining his black wing tips for the big day. He was thinking about his relationship with Sarah. They fit together nicely as a ministerial team. He was sure Sarah was God's choice as his partner. And he sure could use the help. For the past year he had been trying to bring some life to the little church in Riverside. The small parish was slow to respect the young man with dark curly hair and brown beady eyes. He had spent the year trying to ingratiate himself to the community. He held potluck dinners, attended Little League games, and never missed a local high school football game—this was Texas after all. He felt as if his face had frozen in a benevolent smile, his arm permanently poised in a friendly wave. The townspeople treated him politely, but they were standoffish. The reason was simple. No one trusted a young man's lusts. Everybody was waiting for the inevitable scandal that would come from a single preacher living all alone. People were less interested in getting to know him than in cataloging every conversation. Had he lingered by the cheerleaders when talking to Mrs. Pritchard at last week's football game? How many games of basketball with the young boys in the parish were appropriate? Did he smile just a bit too much? Was he too nice?

Mack knew this would all change once he arrived back in town with his new bride. He loved Sarah; that was for sure. But more importantly, he needed her to complete his ministry. She would be the key to his real effectiveness as a pastor. It all rested on Sarah.

There was a knock on his door. "Son, it's me," called his father from the hallway. Jason Jolean was a hellfire-and-brimstone preacher if there ever was one. He was a great tool in the hands of the Holy Spirit, bringing conviction of sin and the resultant confession of faith. Like so many people, however, Jason continually played to his strength. Consequently he was not very good at helping his recently saved parishioners on their road to sanctification. Week after week he spoke to them about their sins, and week after week they repented and asked Jesus into their hearts again.

Mack opened the door. "Come in, Dad."

"I thought maybe we could talk a bit," Jason said nervously.

"Sure, Dad," Mack grinned awkwardly, "is this our birds and the bees talk?"

"No, son. I'm sure you know about the hydraulics. I wanted to talk to you about the politics of a godly home."

"Okay," Mack sighed tenuously, not knowing where this conversation was headed.

"I've counseled a lot of broken marriages, and I always see a pattern. Things break down when the couple leaves the biblical picture of a working marriage. You have to be serious about assuming your position as head of the household."

"Dad." Mack chuckled. "These days people view marriage as a partnership. Sarah will be my life partner."

"No, she won't be if you keep that attitude," Jason said emphatically. "The Bible places her as subordinate to you. You have to maintain control if you want to keep her and have a happy marriage."

Mack frowned at his father's take on things. "She'll submit to me not because I demand it, but because we know it is the best way for our marriage to work."

"It may work that way in a Disney movie, son, but in real life someone has to assert authority, and that someone has to be you. Do you want to make your wife feel happy and secure in her new life with you?"

"Well, sure I do," Mack said, looking up from buffing his shoes.

"Then don't overburden her with finances and the like. Give her an allowance. Let her control the food budget so that she feels like she's contributing, but don't drive her nuts with the things you have to be man enough to take care of yourself," Jason said with staunch conviction.

"I don't know, Dad," Mack said in a bit of a pleading tone. He knew this discussion could go on all day. Nobody was likely to change Jason's views or his endless expression of them.

"You don't have to know right now. Just keep an open mind to all I'm saying. If you let her make the choices, she'll be burning her bra and saying Jesus told her to do it. Be loving, but give her boundaries."

There was silence between the two for a few awkward moments. Then Jason started again, "There's one more thing. Remember that you are the king of your castle and that the marriage bed is your throne."

Mack had feared the sex talk that was traditionally given just prior to marriage in his father's buttoned-up family. "Oh, Dad, do we have to go there?" he pleaded. Even though he and Sarah were both virgins, he really didn't want his dad's wedding night pep talk.

"You need to understand some things about women. They're not sexually driven like men. If you want to be merciful to your young bride, you'll be about your business as quickly and painlessly as you can." Jason stared intently at his son, as if to punctuate the seriousness and correctness of his convictions.

Mack couldn't meet his father's gaze. He looked away and said, "Dad, there are lots of studies out there that talk about women's libidos and—"

Mack was saved by a knock at the door. Opening it, he saw his mother and younger brother. What a pair. Silvia Jolean was tall and plain. Never had the slightest makeup, not even a touch of lipstick, come near to her face. To her, anything more revealing than a ruffled collar neckline or a midcalf dress length was unladylike at best and sinfully un-Christian at worst. Her salt-and-pepper hair was always pulled back into a tight bun, drawing attention from the length of her face to her prominent cheekbones and beady eyes. Her perfume was Ivory soap and, on special occasions, a little rose water. Her body was long and thin with no discernible bosom. The overall look was stern and intimidating, but underneath she was softhearted and loving, especially when it came to the three men in her life. She had been known to ferociously defend her husband against the slightest insult and had intervened in more than one of her boys' childhood scuffles.

Beside her was Mack's brother, Billy, the black sheep of the family. Much to his parents' chagrin, Billy had fully embraced the free-loving, freewheeling 1960s. His strawberry-blond hair flitted across the collar of his Nehru jacket. For all of his attempts to be "with it," however, he came off as a pretender. The graceless age did not define him as it had others of his generation. He hadn't found a home in the pop culture, merely a convenient avenue of rebellion against his parents. Nicely put, Billy was a jerk. Jason barely tolerated him and would have disowned him if he thought he could easily cross Silvia. Mack had a kinder view of his little brother. He thought Billy was going through a phase, one that was a bit fun to watch.

"McKenzie David Hayworth Jolean," Sylvia scolded as she strode into the room, "look at you! Finish buffing those shoes and put on your tie. Land's sakes, you're going to be late for your own wedding!"

"You just think about our talk, son," Jason said.

"He knows where babies come from, Pops," Billy said sarcastically.

"Don't call me 'Pops'! I'm not a bowl of cereal. I'm your father," Jason replied through clenched teeth.

"This is no time for bickering," Silvia said sternly. "I won't have it." Pulling out her Polaroid Instamatic camera, she demanded of them, "Now stand next to each other so I can get a picture. We are going to be the picture of a loving family today, even if I have to take one of you to the wedding in a coffin!" With Nehru and clerical collars crowned by smiles, the men dutifully posed for the photo.

Fran took stock of the little chapel with its fifty guests. About half were friends of the bride and groom, and the other half were members of Mack's new parish. They were there not only to support the new pastor, but also to show their status in the Riverside community. Mack had not invited anyone in the parish, opting instead to have a welcoming party for his new bride once they returned from the honeymoon. Certain of the ladies wouldn't hear of it. They informed him they would attend, leaving Fran scrambling to make more food for the reception to follow.

Sandy was almost too late for the "Wedding March." As she entered the chapel, Fran rushed her to her seat. Sandy seemed oblivious, but Fran felt the cold stares of Mack's mother and the women from Riverside when they got the full effect of Sandy's hot-pink dress and red hair. Fran prayed they would be a bit kinder when Sarah entered the sanctuary.

Fran made it back to the vestibule just as the "Wedding March" began. Followed by Sarah, Fran strode down the aisle. She winced at the looks on the faces of Mack's family and congregation. She prayed Sarah would be so consumed by the moment that she would be oblivious to the unmasked looks of disdain. To her dismay, she saw that Mack's eyes were wide as saucers. He seemed confused by Sarah's appearance. Next, her gaze fell to the lewd grin on Billy's smug face, and her feelings moved from concern for her best friend to outright annoyance at the intolerance in the room.

The ceremony went as planned, and the atmosphere of the chapel lightened considerably. There were no mistakes or awkward moments other than those caused by Billy's demeanor toward Fran. Whenever the two of them needed to stand next to each other, he put his hand on the small of her back, each time a bit lower. Several times she twisted away from him. Finally, as they were walking out of the chapel during the recessional, she elbowed him in the side, smiled for the guests, and said through clenched teeth, "Stop it with the hand!"

Despite disapproving of her attire, the ladies from Riverside were pleased with Sarah's graciousness in the receiving line. The shock of the day had worn off, and everyone proceeded more or less happily to the student union building for the reception. Fran and Sarah had worked tirelessly to brighten the area with streamers. Paper tablecloths and homemade favors added to the room's festive transformation. Fran looked approvingly at their handiwork.

The buffet line had ample ham, potato salad, Jell-O salad, rolls, and cold cuts. At the end of the buffet table was the punch bowl, filled with a concoction made of ginger ale, fruit punch, and vanilla ice cream. Fran stayed busy, administering the affair; there would be time to eat later. As time passed, she became aware of a significant change in the tone of the room; it had turned rowdy—too rowdy. Following her growing suspicions, she drew a glass from the nearly empty punch bowl. It was not the punch she had prepared. It had been spiked! And who was a more likely culprit than groping Billy! She angrily prepared a new bowl of punch, but the damage was done. There was nothing left to do but witness the carnage.

Thirsty Silvia had been the first to feel the punch. Striding up to Sandy, she said, "Where did you buy that dress? Jezebel's Jip Joint?"

"Oh *please*," an equally thirsty Sandy droned as she pointed at Silvia's dress. "Don't they sell this type of fashion at Nuns R Us?"

"I won't be needing this!" Silvia hissed as she huffed to the trash can, where she chucked her Polaroid.

The confrontation had struck the punch-laden ladies from Riverside as exceedingly funny. They laughed with wild abandon.

In an obvious move to best Silvia, Sandy marched to Jason. Taking both of his hands in hers, she looked at him demurely and complimented him on performing a wonderful ceremony. He smiled and thanked her, and then she reached up and kissed him on each cheek. As she walked away, she announced, "There, Silvia. Try wiping *my* lipstick off your husband's cheek!"

Shaking her head, Fran poured herself her first glass of punch as Billy came up behind her and started to rub her shoulders. As his hands touched her, he whispered into her ear, "What do you think about free love?"

Startled, Fran dropped the glass into the punch bowl. She turned around swiftly and pushed him away. "Tell me, Billy. have you ever experienced this free love you keep talking about?"

"What's your point?" he said with the lewd grin frozen on his face.

"My point is this. You're still a virgin, right? Has this act gotten you anywhere with women?"

"More than I'd care to talk about," he said smugly, barely covering the hurt.

"Yeah, right," she said scornfully as he slinked away.

The bride and groom left the reception early to begin their

honeymoon. Fran sighed with relief that the evening was finally coming to a close as Billy sauntered up to Sandy.

"Have you ever seen the movie *The Graduate*?" he asked with a leering smile.

"I'll tell you what," Sandy said disdainfully, "if you ever graduate from anything, we'll talk about it."

"Cheers," Fran said as she winked at the deflated Billy and toasted him with her nonalcoholic punch.

As the bathroom door opened into the darkened room, Mack caught a good look at his bride. Her hair was perfect. The red lipstick was flawless. Her eye makeup looked great. And the pièce de résistance: the white, transparent teddy she wore hinted tantalizingly at the naked body underneath. Just like this morning, she looked hot. A part of him wanted to jump up and ravish her, sinking deeply into her beauty. But in the back of his mind he could hear his father's voice warning him. He had to be the head of this household. If he let Sarah establish sexual control over him, how could God bless this marriage?

Gently, he sat up on the bed, moving carefully to avoid revealing how willingly his body accepted Sarah's attire. "Sarah, we have to talk about this."

"No, we don't, sweetheart. I'm not worried you will hurt me or anything," she said as her hands fell to his bare chest.

"It's not that." Mack smiled, pulling her hands away. "We have to get the protocol right if we want God to bless this marriage."

"I don't understand." Her voice quivered.

"Well, look at the way you're dressed. It's seductive," he said.

"It's our *honeymoon!*" she exclaimed. "I've worked hard to look seductive for you!" She could feel the sting of hot tears.

"Now, don't start the waterworks, Sarah," he said impatiently. "This is important. It's about the structure of our marriage. I love you, and to me you're beautiful without the puffy hair and all the makeup. I want to sleep with the girl I married, not some stranger from the cover of a magazine." His tender words brought a stop to the tears, but not before they had gouged mascara-stained gorges through her makeup. Mack wanted to hold her until the sobbing stopped, but if he did, he knew he wouldn't let her go. He had to finish what he started.

"Biblically, I have to be the head of this household. I have to be the one that initiates intimacy between us, okay? I don't want you parading around dressed like Jezebel or Delilah. Trust me on this, will you, Sarah?"

Sarah shook her head but couldn't manage a sound.

"That's a good girl," he said with a smile. "Now why don't you go wash off that war paint and come lie next to me."

After a few minutes, she opened the bathroom door demurely and found her way to bed in the darkness. She slid quietly next to her husband. The feel of her touch was electric for Mack. He had saved himself for years, waiting for this joyous celebration of his masculinity.

He remembered his father's advice. After the humiliation he had put Sarah through, he needed to spare her any more harm this night. Tenderly, he said to her, "Just lie still, darling. This will be over before you know it."

———

Mack was right. A couple of grunts and a growl later, Sarah was left wondering what all the hoopla was about. Sex hadn't shown her anything. Mack seemed to be content though, if snoring was any indication.

As she lay awake, staring at the ceiling, she realized her mother had been right. This night was everything she feared it could be but nothing she hoped it would be. Still, Mack was a good man, and she knew the angel had been right. In an undefined way, she knew she was pregnant. And she knew she was carrying a boy, just like the angel said.

She fought the annoying snores of her husband with the warm memory of the handsome angel and the soft comfort that she was on the path God wanted her to follow.

———

Miles away, another soul contemplated God's plan beside the dying embers of a fire along the shore of Lake Springfield. It was Chris's last day here. His parents' house was empty, all of its contents sold in an auction. The house itself was sold, just awaiting the buyer's bank to approve payment. Chris donated all of the funds to charity. Beside him was a box of memorabilia—those things that reminded him of his parents and the life they had shared with him.

Chris knew in his heart that he was following the will of God, but at the moment there was nothing but heaviness in his heart as he said good-bye to his life in Springfield. *I probably could have handled things better with Sophia and Coach. Given them a heads-up so that they had time to get used to the idea.* But then again, it wasn't his way. He had learned the hard way to be circumspect. *Loose lips sink ships or, at a minimum, cause car crashes.*

The sun was beginning to break through on the horizon. He had spent the night. Now it was time to get to the bus station. He stood to look at the horizon, bent to find a flat stone, and skipped it across the lake. One last stone. He broke down completely as he said good-bye to his parents, grabbed his box of treasures, and left behind everything he had ever known.

SIX

The undesignated desert air force facility had been cleared for the day. Only those who worked with the aliens were allowed on base. The alien representative, who for some reason preferred the title Lady, was already on base and would be accompanied by Lucien Begliali, whose fantastic fortune had been used to fund various aspects of the alien–Earth joint science tasks. Nobody understood the exact nature of Begliali's relationship with the aliens, but they knew he had the funds to change the world and that he desired to be a high-ranking official in the new order. As far as access to the aliens was concerned, Begliali was the gatekeeper to whom governments around the world paid homage.

The general knew he was one of the few people on Earth entrusted with this top-secret information. He should feel honored as a member of the twelve-man organization in charge of alien contact, code-named Majestic, but he couldn't escape the feeling that he was being used. This was a long way from his career's beginnings at West Point. He was a man of action. He understood the strategies of war, but now he was in charge of a group determined to keep an uneasy peace.

It all started with the crash of an alien craft in the New Mexican desert. Surviving occupants led to a fountain of information about their space brothers. Soon official contacts were made and diplomatic relationships established. They claimed to be a dying race that needed to find a way to survive. Their ultimate goal was to develop a hybrid species to contain the brilliance of their advanced intelligence with the sturdiness of the human form. To accomplish this goal, they needed to experiment on our citizens. In exchange, the government got advanced technologies and, eventually, the inclusion of the hybrids in the upper echelon of world society. Part human and part alien, these beings would usher Earth into its inclusion in a federation of advanced civilizations.

He understood the intent of the negotiations. The world would gradually be changed to the great benefit of all humankind. And yet he had this sense of doom, a pining for a simpler time when man was in charge of his own destiny. While structured as a negotiated agreement, the pact felt too much to the general like an armistice. The aliens had technology we could not hope to defend against. They established the terms of the agreement, and we complied.

Today's meeting was bound to be something special. Typically, the twelve met in secrecy and discussed briefing memos about the ongoing relationship with the aliens. Now the alien representative had requested a meeting with the group. This was most unusual.

The twelve hushed as the Lady and Begliali entered the room. The Lady moved gracelessly in jerky motions to the head of the conference table. The general involuntarily wrinkled his nose at her slightly acidic, sulfurous odor. He didn't think he would ever get used to it.

"Gentlemen, I am here today to provide an update on our progress and how I envision the future," she began in her high-pitched, inflectionless voice.

"My first point is that our joint projects are progressing, although not at the speed we had originally hoped. Your scientists are only now beginning to understand that consciousness can affect matter at a subatomic level. This understanding must be broadened if Earth is ever to take its place among the fraternity of societies in this galaxy.

"With the help of Mr. Begliali's contacts, we are promulgating an Aquarian Gospel to develop society's understanding of its place in the universe. We have also begun to communicate these doctrines directly to the humans we have culled for our ongoing hybridization projects. Together, over time, we will be able to generate a groundswell of appropriate beliefs.

"To that end, I must invoke the standard wording of paragraphs 24 and 25 of our agreement. As you are aware, the wording in these paragraphs gives us the sole right to determine when our existence will be made known to your people. The societies of Earth must be carefully groomed to accept our existence if we are to prevent widespread panic. Therefore, General, I insist that your government cease its Project Blue Book studies. To encourage the notion that your government is investigating our existence defeats our purpose."

"But, Lady," the general protested, "we weren't about to release anything that would tip our hand as to our involvement in the agreement."

"You miss my point, General," she cut him off. She did not like to be challenged. Her voice had taken on a hissing sound that signaled her annoyance.

She explained her concerns, but the general was not listening. What he heard was not the Lady's rationale but her tone of authority over him ... over Earth. He hated the feeling of subjugation. As he prepared to mount his defense of Project Blue Book, the Lady waved her hand across his forehead.

"Please be at peace, General," she said in a soothing, soft voice. The general felt instantly at peace and willing to comply. "Very good," she cooed at him.

She jerkily left the room. Following her, Begliali turned to smile at the assembly.

Later that day, the general proofread the statement prepared for immediate release to the public. He shook his head, trying to settle the sickening feeling in his stomach as he read the cover page of the release.

NEWS RELEASE
OFFICE OF ASSISTANT SECRETARY OF DEFENSE
(PUBLIC AFFAIRS)
WASHINGTON, DC 20301

IMMEDIATE RELEASE December 17, 1969 No. 1077-69
OXford 7-5131 (Info.)
OXford 7-3189 (Copies)

AIR FORCE TO TERMINATE
PROJECT "BLUE BOOK"

1979

SEVEN

Kimberly sang loudly, "I will survive" with the Gloria Gaynor tape as she sped down the highway. She thought about where the last ten years had brought her. Life had been full of surprises, all of them pleasant. She had forgotten the horrible feelings of abandonment at the death of her parents. She hadn't had recurring nightmares for years. And she loved her life.

Her days were filled with devotion to her son, Michael. When she became pregnant, she thought he would be the charge of paid nannies. But when he was born and she looked into those crystal-blue eyes, she knew she had never felt such love in her life. A nanny never touched her beautiful baby boy. He belonged to Mama. For the first three years of his life, she never left him. She had no desire to. He was her joy, her reason for living.

When the dreaded day for preschool came, her boy easily accepted the challenge. He thrived in the presence of other children. Kimberly knew he would. For some reason he had none of the proclivities of a spoiled only child. Although Kimberly shamelessly granted his every desire, from the time he was an infant, he had this bearing about him, a kind of spiritual maturity that made him a "little man." He was amazingly selfless as a toddler and had proven to be exceedingly generous with his contemporaries at preschool. Kimberly found herself constantly fascinated with this wonderful little being that had come to life inside of her.

While preschool was not hard for Michael, it was at first unbearable for Kimberly. She couldn't believe how her arms literally ached to hold him for the four hours he was away each day. To keep her mind off it, she buried herself in the details of her father's vast business holdings. It wasn't long before she, and shocked management teams at the various operating companies, realized she really was a chip off the old block. The more she got involved in the businesses, the more she could see small improvements and slight changes in emphasis that resulted in large changes to the bottom line. In the long run, the businesses came to value and seek the input of their majority shareholder. Wall Street loved a winner, and the initial public offerings of several of her companies brought her net worth to more than five hundred million dollars. Pretty good earnings for a young, stay-at-home, single mom.

She pulled into the parking lot of her bank and sat there until Gloria had finished her song. Then she entered the bank, where she was hands down the largest account holder. She had stopped to calm the fears of Doug Dean, the bank president, about her plans to invest in yet another failing business owned by the Vatican.

Kim thought Dean's secretary must have seen her pull in. It looked as if she had hauled him out of the men's room to greet her. The left side of his wide-collared paisley shirt was not tucked into his powder-blue pants, and he had a folded *Wall Street Journal* in one hand. He led Kimberly to his office, where he quickly pulled on his suit jacket as she sat in the chair in front of his desk. Kimberly was longing to tell him of the much-celebrated death of the leisure suit but decided instead to hold her tongue.

"What can we do for you today, Ms. Martin?"

"Just one thing. I need you to finalize this transaction by sending ten million dollars to this account." She handed him a paper with the account number of the French fragrance company.

"Might I inquire as to the nature of the transfer?" he asked.

Kimberly hated the question. She felt she should have the right to do whatever she pleased with her money. However, since the passage of the Foreign Corrupt Practices Act in 1977, these questions were now the norm.

"Actually, I'm taking a small percentage ownership in the company. Not a controlling interest, mind you. Just enough to give them the equity infusion they need to get over a rough patch."

"I see," Dean said, pretending he did. "How did you come about this investment opportunity, if you don't mind my asking? I mean foreign investment has all kinds of attendant risks, not the least of which is the possibility of foreign currency devaluation."

Kimberly smiled and explained. "Oh, come on, Doug. The French franc isn't going anywhere, and ten million dollars is not a large percentage of my holdings. You've done your job. I am fully aware of the attendant risks. As to how I found out about this opportunity ... well, I have friends in the Vatican Bank that made me aware of it. So you can see it is a reliable recommendation."

The fact was that it was a horrible investment. Kimberly doubted she would see any kind of financial return. But Benny was the only family she and Michael had, and like it or not, the politics of the Vatican power structure could be brought to heel with the proper investments. It appeared the Vatican was the major shareholder in this company, which would be bankrupt by the end of the year without a capital infusion. Kimberly agreed to help the ailing Vatican investment, and although she was subtle in making her wishes known, the hierarchy knew the ten million dollars was to be accredited to Benny and considered in his advancement to the administrative offices of the Church.

After assuring Dean, Kim said a hasty good-bye and sped down the road to get Michael at school. She was disappointed that privilege could be bought in the religious world. She was also disappointed that, even though she had developed a close relationship with Jesus over the years, she was pretty sure her brother hadn't. But if Kim was nothing else, she was pragmatic. Benny had suffered much at her father's hand, and this was the least she could do for him. And most importantly, he was the only uncle of Michael Cross Martin, her beautiful, gifted child.

Michael had off-the-charts intellect and had grown early into the speech and mannerisms of a man in the body of a handsome, kind little boy. Although he was young, his wisdom and compassion had led him to the place where he was most often Kim's confidant of choice when she was perplexed about a pending business deal. He had a marvelous way of seeing through to the meat of a problem.

She pulled into the school parking lot just as the kids were released from class. Kimberly had taken Michael to look at a host of private schools, but he was adamant about attending public school. Relying on the wisdom so uncharacteristic of his age, she reluctantly acquiesced.

"Hi, Mom." Her little angel waved as he approached the car. She never failed to be drawn in by his handsome features. His brown hair easily garnered silky auburn highlights in the sun and fell in beautiful loose curls that framed his high cheekbones and large crystal-blue eyes. His full lips spread easily into an engaging smile that right now contained a mixture of old baby teeth, new large teeth, and intermittent gaps.

She rolled down the window and said, "Hi back, handsome!"

"Mom, Gabe's going to spend the night with us, okay?"

Gabriel Marron was Michael's best friend. Both only children, they referred to each other as brothers ... and they could have been. The same height as Michael, Gabe had beautiful poker-straight hair that fell around his face. Coarser in texture than Michael's hair, it was just a bit darker but prone to blondish highlights. His cheekbones were high, and his lips were full, like Michael's, but his eyes were more deeply set and a stunning shade of emerald green.

"Hi, Miss Kim," Gabe said as he entered the car.

"Hi, Gabe. Does your mother know you are staying with me tonight?"

"She told me to stay with you," he said in a matter-of-fact display he used to hide his underlying concern. "The police were at our house again this morning."

Kimberly knew what that meant. Michele Marron had been arrested again. Her life was filled with drugs and men. There were rumors from the other mothers that she sold sex to get money for the drugs. Whatever the situation, she showed a lack of regard for her only child. Michael had adopted Gabe in the first grade. They were the best of friends, and Michael made it his duty to ensure Gabe had what he needed in life. He invited Gabe to go shopping for school clothes with him. He and Gabe made Christmas lists together. He threw birthday parties for Gabe at Kimberly's house. At first, Kimberly gave in to Michael because she adored him and found his generosity admirable. As time went on, however, she too began to see Gabe as part of the family. He too was a lovely little man, and she thought both she and Michael were blessed to have him in their lives.

"You're always welcome, honey," Kimberly said to him.

"Hey, Mom," Michael said as they were fastening their seat belts, "you should have seen the home run Gabe hit during recess! The ball went the whole way across the street and into Mrs. Ketchum's yard!"

"Congratulations, Gabe," Kimberly joined in. Gabe had phenomenal sports abilities. On a good day, Michael's abilities were mediocre, so he looked up to Gabe in the area of sports.

"It really wasn't that much, Miss Kim. I just whacked it as hard as I could. Sometimes the bat connects with the ball just right. Tell her about your science project, Michael."

"Oh yeah, Mom, I got an A."

"That's not all, Michael," Gabe encouraged. "Mrs. Babcock said it was the best she had ever seen."

"I'm very proud, sweetheart," Kimberly cooed. She had no doubt his project was wonderful. It had been about archaeology. Michael was fascinated with the ancient world, and he had an almost frightening penchant for languages. All of this seemed to amaze Gabe, and the boys developed an exclusive mutual admiration society.

"Mom, what is Caroline making for dinner tonight?" Michael asked.

"I had asked her to do something with beef. Why do you ask?"

"I was kind of hoping for pizza."

"Michael, I think Caroline has been nursing a chateaubriand for the better part of the afternoon." In the rearview mirror she could see Gabe smiling.

"Does that sound good to you, Gabe?"

"Whatever Miss Caroline cooks sounds good to me, Miss Kim!" Michael elbowed him sharply. "But I could always go for pizza."

"I'll tell you what, boys. It's Friday, and there's no school tomorrow. Let's eat the chateaubriand for dinner and plan on staying up late to watch *The Dukes of Hazzard* and *Dallas*. We can order a pizza to be at the house right in the middle of *Dukes*, okay?"

"Sounds great to me, Miss Kim!"

"Handle it. Handle it!" Michael said, imitating Boss Hogg from *The Dukes of Hazzard*.

"Handle this!" she shot back and put the Blues Brothers cassette in the dash. They left the parking lot singing "Soul Man."

It had been a long night for Michele Marron. Her pimp had scored a twosome for her—a husband and wife. Twice the money in half the time. Michele didn't mind the trick. It was only sex, and the money was good. Afterward, she walked the street to pick up a few more bucks. She was good at her chosen profession. On a Friday night she could stroll down the street and entice any of a number of regulars to part with their money to spend some time with her.

The last john of the evening was a friend of one of her regulars. He was a large, brutish man with long greasy hair. She could smell that he hadn't bathed in a while. That would make for an unpleasant time. She complained to the man and told him up front he would have to cough up an additional twenty dollars. He agreed, and they went into the alley.

When he started to get rough with her, Michele tried to regain control of the situation. But this man's idea of a good time clearly involved smacking her around. He slammed her hard across the face, and she reeled. Tasting blood, she scampered on all fours to get away. He kicked her into submission and then stood over her, demanding that she provide oral sex with her bloodied mouth. She assumed the role of compliance until she was in a position to make him hurt. She bit down hard. He screamed in agony as she spit a piece of him from her mouth and ran into the street. She could hear his screaming as she ran to the corner. He stumbled out of the alley after her, clutching at his damaged member.

He was barely walking, and the sight of him made her laugh. She looked at him and laughed all the harder, making sure he could hear her contempt. "Explain that to your wife, you dirty son of a—" A truck breezed down the street, cutting off the rest of her taunt.

She walked a few more blocks, where she met Jimmy. With stunning regularity he was at the corner with the heroin she craved. She couldn't wait to relax, to put this awful night behind her and just float in bliss. She had been an addict for a while, needing more and more to get high. The need for more drugs created a need for more money and the riskier back-alley sex jobs. But once she got that lovely substance into her brain, she would be all right.

She had been in love once, years ago. He was older than her and very handsome. When she became pregnant, he told her he was married and had no intention of leaving his wife. This was less than a year before abortion became legal. Tough luck, huh? Although she loved him in her own way, Gabe was nonetheless a living symbol of her bad luck. Life sucked, and she had his beautiful face to remind her on a daily basis. She listed the father's name on Gabe's birth certificate in some childish hope that someday he would come back to her and that they could be a family. That dream shattered when he presented her with an agreement whereby he abdicated all parental rights.

She made it to her run-down apartment just as it began to rain. She lit the kerosene heater to take the chill off the place. She took a quaalude to calm her nerves and drew a bath.

As the tub filled, she looked at her face in the mirror. It was bound to be swollen and bruised tomorrow. She thought about her abuser and was happy she had sent him home a little less of a man. The warm water in the tub felt fine around her aching body. This is when she loved life the most, when she was by herself, warm, and clean without Gabe's haunting eyes. She saw her real self in his gorgeous green eyes, and she hated what she saw.

After her bath, she headed to the living room and plopped on the old couch, holding in her hand the hard little brownish lump that would make everything better. She heated the lump until it formed into a liquid, which she then transferred to a syringe. She found a vein easily enough and began her mainline journey.

She pushed the plunger and awaited the rush, when she realized something was wrong. Had she taken too much? The rush hit like a sledgehammer. Her eyes rolled upward, and she began to see events of her life. She hated what she saw and wished she could be made clean. The dream shifted to a dark hill, and the wind howled around her. Looking up, she saw a man, beaten beyond recognition and hanging on a cross. His agony was palpable, and she recoiled as blood dripped down from his hands and feet.

"Oh, Jesus, I'm sorry," she muttered, and her life flashed before her again. "I'm so sorry for everything! Please save me," she barely moaned as her breathing became shallower. She seemed to have fleeting moments of lucidity when she could tell she had swallowed her tongue and needed to get help, but then the drug would wash over her again.

Suddenly she saw a bright light. A man of indescribable beauty and warmth took her hand. When she looked into his eyes, she could tell she had been forgiven for everything. She had been washed clean. He took her hand and smiled. Looking deeply into her eyes, he said, "Come home with me, little one. You are free."

"But my baby. I have a son, and I have so much to make up to him," she resisted. Her body lurched as involuntary physical responses tried in vain to wake her, to find consciousness.

"I will make sure he is taken care of." Jesus smiled. "Now it's time for Me to present you to My Father." Michele Marron took her last shallow breath, leaving the pain of this world behind forever.

Michael and Gabe lay carelessly around the family room, watching Saturday morning cartoons. "Boys!" Kimberly called into the family room. "Breakfast is ready!"

"Mom," Michael said severely as he came to the kitchen doorway, "the *Fantastic Four* is on. It will be over in ten minutes."

"Who am I to argue with the *Fantastic Four*?" Kim replied, matching his serious tone of voice. She sat down at the kitchen table with a cup of coffee. Mentally she took stock of the sprawling family mansion she had inherited. In the front of the house was a large reception area that was dominated by an intricate inlaid wood floor and a grandiose staircase that led to the second, third, and fourth floors under a rotunda at the roof. To the right of the reception area was a large parlor, which her parents had outfitted with imported antique Belle Époque furniture. On the other side of the reception hall was a large dining room, with a table that comfortably seated thirty people. Behind the formal dining room was an industrial kitchen, the domain of Caroline. Behind the parlor was a suite of offices from which Kimberly ran her business. These rooms were used throughout the week, but on weekends she luxuriated in the 750-square-foot retreat tucked into the back of the house. It was simply a small eat-in kitchen and a comfortable family room with overstuffed furniture and a fireplace. On weekends the main house was relieved of all but a single staff to answer the door and phones. Kimberly loved to celebrate the weekend in close proximity to her son, and these two rooms with sweeping floor-to-ceiling windows facing the backyard were perfect. She loved to cook in the little kitchen and to cuddle with Michael on the couch or to watch out the window while he played.

"Boys!" Kim called into the family room when she heard the closing music to the *Fantastic Four*. She knew she had to get their attention before the next cartoon started.

"I'm Johnny. Flame on!" Gabe yelled as he ran into the kitchen.

"I'm Reed!" Michael yelled as he tried to stretch his arm to reach the table.

"And I'm Sue, the Invisible Woman," Kimberly said drolly as she put down her coffee cup. "I'm set for pancakes, French toast, eggs, and bacon. What's your pleasure, boys?"

"It all sounds great to me, Miss Kim." Gabe smiled.

Michael clearly kicked him under the table to get his attention. "Remember," he whispered, "Caroline didn't cook it!" Then at full voice he said, "Do you have cereal, Mom?"

"Michael, I just told you the menu. What would you like?"

"Anything you haven't burned will be fine with me," he teased, sending Gabe into a fit of laughter.

At that moment, the intercom chimed, and Joseph asked Kimberly to come to her office.

"Watch TV for a bit more, boys, but be ready to eat when I get back. You're not very powerful superheroes if you can't stand up to my cooking!"

As Kimberly entered her office, she saw Joseph and a policeman waiting for her. She could see a pained look on Joseph's face.

"Miss Kimberly, this is Officer Denison. He needs to speak to you."

"What can I do for you, Officer?" Kimberly asked.

"Ma'am, are you in the custody of a Gabriel Marron?"

"Yes. He's my son's friend. He spent the night here."

"Miss Martin, the boy's mother died of an overdose last night. Her neighbor found her this morning."

"Oh no!" Kim shrieked and then immediately put her hand to her mouth in fear the boys had heard her. How would she tell poor Gabe?

"What will happen to Gabe?" she asked weakly, feeling the strength in her legs waning.

"He'll become a ward of the state, ma'am." The officer went on to explain that Michele's family had disowned her and that Gabe's father had relinquished parental rights.

She knew in an instant what she wanted to do. "Joseph, call my attorney. Tell him I need him now and to be prepared to make the fastest adoption in history." Joseph smiled with pride and immediately left the room to make the call.

"There's nobody to contest your adoption, Miss Martin," the officer said. "If you are serious about this, I can arrange to have social services provide a home evaluation on Monday."

"Please do that, Officer," she said, smiling though her tears. "This boy needs to have a home."

The officer thanked her and left as Joseph reentered the room.

"Mr. Markus will be here shortly, Miss Kimberly."

"Thank you, Joseph."

"Miss Kimberly, if you'll permit me, may I say I have never been more proud of you," Joseph said with moist eyes.

"Thank you, Joseph," she said as the tears began to flow. "Now I have to go back there and tell that beautiful little boy he's lost his mom."

EIGHT

J ust a bit north of the equator, the town of Ndejje, Uganda, was awakening to the morning sun, which looked like a bright orange ball on the horizon. Pastor Tom Ellis daily chose this time to spend with the Lord. The freshness of the morning air and the calls of the birds were a perfect backdrop. Soon Frannie and Gloria would awaken, and the day would begin in earnest.

Tom had come a long way from the little Bible college in Texas, but the surrounding low hills reminded him on occasion of the area outside of Austin where he was born. Both places had the big-sky feeling of an open expanse. But Ndejje was different from the affluent Texas capital. The people here were simple men and women who knew how to survive on the most meager earnings.

In days past, Ndejje had been nearly in the center of the kingdom of Buganda. The kingdom was ruled in a tribal manner by the Kabaka, members of the aristocratic ruling class. Power was distributed to Bataka, or clan heads, and further down to Saza chiefs in each county. Below them was a serf class known as the Bakopi, a word that means "the people who don't matter."

The Bakopi were the object of Tom's missionary zeal. It gave him marvelous satisfaction to see the awareness of salvation dawn on the faces of the Bakopi. Their mind-set took a quantum leap from being "one who doesn't matter" to one for whom the very Son of God gave His life. That was the touchdown experience for Tom, and he reveled in it. But there were so many first downs to get to that place of celebration! The Bakopi had endured generations of feeling worthless, of being subject to the cruelties of a heavy-handed hierarchy. For them to believe they had been given salvation meant a total change of mind-set. And in the days of Idi Amin Dada, it was hard to convince them they were anything but meaningless. By some estimates, Amin had led to the deaths of some three hundred thousand of his countrymen. And now he had started a war with Tanzania. Tom had been preaching that the people needed to resist the pull of the Bakopi mind-set and begin to play a part in shaping their political destinies.

Tom's outspoken pleas for resistance frightened his new friend, Father Chris Altenbrook. Chris also worked with the Bakopi out of Kampala, Uganda's capital. As Uganda became more and more politically unstable, his role had changed considerably. Through a series of "field promotions" that came from the departures of older priests fleeing the wrath of Idi Amin, Chris became responsible for the tiny church in Ndejje and the remnant of the Vatican embassy to Uganda as well.

From the road, Chris saw Tom sitting on his porch in the early-morning sun with his Bible. "Jamba!" he called, the local greeting.

"Jamba, yourself, Yankee!" Tom called back.

"I thought you guys might like some mandazi," Chris said, referring to the bag of local Ugandan doughnuts in his hand.

"Well, come up here with your doughnuts, Father."

"I was also hoping you would have some real coffee to go along with them, Pastor." Chris smiled as he shook Tom's hand.

"Actually, I heard Fran getting up. She should be putting on the coffee about now."

Fran stepped out of the house, bent down to rest her arms on Tom's shoulders, and said, "Did I hear my name? Hi, Chris."

"Hey, Fran, I was just telling Tom that I have mandazi to share. Do you think you could scrounge up a real cup of coffee?" Chris asked. He was referring to the odd reality that although Ugandans grew coffee, they invariably brewed a watered-down version of the drink that seemed pretty horrible to the American palate. The drink of choice in Uganda was chai tea.

"I've got a pot on. What brings you to town this early?" Fran asked. Chris worked in Kampala most of the week. His passion was ministering to the youth. He tried to battle the Bakopi passivity and the tension of an imploding regime with sports. He just wanted to give the kids a sense of normalcy, even though that meant he had to broaden his use of the term "football" to include soccer. On weekends, he came to the country to hear confessions and say Mass at Saint Andrews. He loved the simplicity in the lives of the people of Ndejje.

"Well, I was thinking it is kind of unfair that I have a soccer team in Kampala but nothing for the Ndejje youth. So, starting this week, I'll come out here on Thursday nights and stay over at Saint Andrews. Fridays will be youth day at Saint Andrews. So when the kids get out of school, we'll kick the ball around and have some locker-room talk about Jesus' love."

"Does that mean you'll be serving up some competition for my church's team?"

"Well, we can't let the Protestants have all the soccer teams, now can we?" Chris smiled.

"Now wait a minute, Chris," Tom continued the banter. "You were nearly in the NFL. I'm not sure it will be an even comparison with my coaching abilities."

"True that." Chris grinned. "But remember I'll be coaching little Catholic boys—bad knees from all the kneeling!"

"I'm going to check on the coffee, boys, before I need a shovel to get past this conversation," Fran said, lightly slapping Tom's shoulder.

As Fran entered the house, Tom said, "Seriously, I don't know how you do the chastity thing. And I'm not just talking about sex. I can't imagine I could get through the day without Fran."

"I heard that!" Fran yelled from inside.

"It takes a lot of soccer, Tom," Chris chirped, "and an occasional cold shower."

They heard nine-year-old Gloria come into the kitchen. Looking out to the porch, she yelled "Father Chris!"

"Hey," he called to her. "I brought some mandazi for you, my little mandazi." Chris found Gloria to be a beautiful little girl. Her full head of blonde hair streaked from the sunlight framed a perfect complexion and a beautiful smile. Her eyes were the lightest brown, often looking golden in the sunlight. To Chris she looked like a Barbie doll.

Gloria came out to the porch and tried to look in the bag of mandazi.

"Uh. Uh. Uh. Not until you give your old uncle Chris a hug." Chris looked over her to Tom and said, "This is what I miss most as a result of my vows."

"Yep, fatherhood is a great thing," Tom said. "Hey, darlin', how about a hug for your dear old dad?" Gloria gave him a hug and sat down beside him.

Fran came out of the house with plates and coffee, and they enjoyed the morning breeze. After breakfast, Fran and Gloria went into the house.

"I was hoping to have a chance to talk to you alone," Chris said quietly.

"What's on your mind, buddy?" Tom asked, sitting straighter in his chair.

"The war, partly. Things are looking bad for Amin. I think the fighting may find its way to Kampala."

"From your lips to God's ears," Tom responded.

Chris looked over the little town of Ndejje, nestled in the valley below. "Listen, Tom, I'm no fan of Idi Amin, but I hate to think of this becoming a war zone."

"Something's got to give though, Chris. Amin's cruelty to his own citizens is legendary. I've been trying to get the locals to drop their Bakopi helplessness. Amin is weakened by the war. If these guys would rally, they could take control and oust him before Tanzania has to march over the countryside." Tom's voice rose as his passion for the Bakopi moved him.

Chris turned to face him, drawing a huge sigh at the inevitable slaughter that would ensue. "It's not in their nature, Tom. Independence has been bred out of them for centuries. Culturally they have no sense of self, let alone a sense of responsibility for their destiny. I don't think they'll be able to take on that kind of responsibility right now."

"First of all, Chris, I think that kind of sentiment can get you into trouble. To me it sounds an awful lot like arguments made in America before the civil rights movement."

"I don't mean it that way, Tom, and you know it," Chris said tersely, waving his arms in exasperation.

"Yes, I do," Tom softened. "But at the same time, I don't want to sell these people short. I think the will for self-determination is born into the human species, and I don't think it can be bred out of people. I see it as being dormant in the Bakopi, and I honestly think I can stir it up."

Chris was getting nowhere fast. He let Tom continue about awakening new feelings in the Bakopi, but his mind wandered to the beginning of the past week. He was in the confessional when he was told by one of Amin's men that the government had taken note of Tom and his sermons. They were not pleased. People in Uganda had a way of disappearing when the government looked unfavorably on them. Chris was sure that Tom and his family were in danger, but he was bound by the sanctity of the confessional from telling Tom what he knew. His intention was to stay close to his friend and hope to defuse the situation. Tom wouldn't make it easy.

"Tom, just hear me out. What if your messages reach the ear of the government? The war isn't going well. Dada is more trigger-happy than ever." Chris began pacing the small porch with hands clasped behind his back, the heat of the day rising along with the heat of the discussion. Perspiration dotted his brow.

"You give me too much credit, Chris. I think Amin has too much on his mind to worry about a nobody preacher out in Ndejje."

"You can't know that though," Chris said. "Times could be tough for us for the next little bit. The Vatican is thinking of closing its embassy if there is a march on Kampala."

"I'll miss you if you leave, buddy."

"It won't be long, just until a new government is formed. I want to offer you and your family transport out of here if that time comes."

Tom rose from his chair to ensure that he was eye to eye with Chris. "Thanks, Chris, but I can't cut and run. This little church is my Alamo, man. You can take the boy out of Texas, but you can't take Texas out of the boy."

"It would only be a few weeks until we can get a political read on the place," Chris pleaded, maintaining the intense eye contact. "Think of it as an all-expense-paid trip to Rome. You could make it a real treat for Gloria and Fran ... and keep them out of harm's way to boot."

"There is a certain logic to it, I have to admit," Tom relented with a sigh. "I have to think about Fran and Gloria too."

"Tom, your preaching is making you into a lightning rod. It's not safe for your family."

"Do you really think that I've ruffled some feathers?"

"Yes, I do," Chris responded. Maybe his message was getting through to his hardheaded Texan friend.

Chris tried to lighten the mood, placing his hand on Tom's shoulder. "Besides, there are too many Catholics in the Vatican for it to be any fun. I'll need you around for comedic value." Chris grinned.

"Is that a fact?" Tom smiled.

"Yes, it is. Against all logic, I have come to enjoy your company, and I was thinking we should work together more."

"What are you thinking?"

"Well, your soccer team is pathetic, and mine's not likely to be much better. But if we joined forces we would have a deeper bench."

"And we could promote some ecumenical solidarity," Tom added.

"Really?" Chris asked, arching an eyebrow. "I was thinking we could kick the butts of the Anglican team."

Both men laughed. Today it was the soccer teams. Tomorrow he would talk to Tom about having the parishes come together to pray for peace in the region. Chris reasoned that by staying close to his friend, perhaps he could bring some calmness to his vitriol.

Through his laughter, Tom turned to the screen door and said with a smirk, "Come on out, Frannie. I know you've been listening. What do you think?"

"About what?

"Everything."

"First, I want to thank Chris for trying to talk some sense to you. He thinks pretty well for a Yankee." Both men laughed.

"Also, a couple weeks in Rome would be a dream. But unless he's got some of the Swiss Guard coming to help, you boys'll never beat the Anglican team. More coffee?"

After his morning visit, Chris went back to Saint Andrews to continue his studies. Sitting on the little bed in the sacristy, he opened his Bible as he remembered a conversation with Tom only a week before.

"Tell me something," Tom asked. "Where do you guys stand on eschatology?"

"I'm not exactly sure what you're asking, Tom."

"I never hear you talk about end times."

"We Catholics believe Christ will return to Earth at the end of the age, but it doesn't really come up all that often."

"What about Israel becoming a nation again after nearly two thousand years?" Tom asked.

"I definitely think God's hand was in it, if that's what you mean."

"No. What about its significance relative to the return of Christ?" Tom pushed.

Chris was at a loss for words. He hadn't really studied the topic as Tom obviously had. He looked up at Tom with a sheepish grin. "Teach me what you know," he said.

Tom moved closer, opened his Bible to Ezekiel, and showed him how the prophet saw dried bones coming together with muscles growing and resulting in an army. Then he showed him the prophecies about Israel rebuilding its temple in Jerusalem.

Tom also went to a familiar passage in 1 Thessalonians 4, in which Paul says, "According to the Lord's own word, we tell you that we who are still alive, who are left till the coming of the Lord, will certainly not precede those who have fallen asleep. For the Lord himself will come down from heaven, with a loud command, with the voice of the archangel and with the trumpet call of God, and the dead in Christ will rise first. After that, we who are still alive and are left will be caught up together with them in the clouds to meet the Lord in the air. And so we will be with the Lord forever."

It was there in black and white, the concept of the rapture. Tom explained the belief that the emergence of the state of Israel is the major sign indicating that the time of the rapture is near.

Since that conversation, Chris had spent a lot of time with the prophets. The Holy Spirit motivated his search, and he began to see God's plan unfolding. How could he have missed it?

After saying good-bye to Father Chris, Gloria got to work on her school lessons. Her mother homeschooled her. She tested very well when compared with kids who were educated in the States, but she missed the social aspects of going to school back home. Ugandans didn't have the same view of females as Americans. She got to interact with kids when they came to church and when she went to the market with her mother, so it wasn't all bad. Still, she would dream about meeting a man like Father Chris, her picture of the boy she would like to marry— handsome, strong, and exuding an air of tranquility. How would she ever meet a boy like him in Ndejje?

"Mom, can I go out and play?"

"Sure, sweetie," Fran said. "Before you go out, honey, let me tell you a little secret."

"What?" Gloria asked enthusiastically.

"There's a chance—there are no final plans yet—but there is a chance we will be going to Rome with Father Chris for a few weeks."

"Oh my goodness!" Gloria exploded. "Please, please, please, let's go to Rome!" she pleaded before skipping out of the house to consider the possibilities. She couldn't wait to daydream about it.

As she walked through the fields, she heard the birds singing. She always found Africa to be exquisitely beautiful. But today it was just divine. The blue sky reminded her of Chris's eyes. How wonderful it would be to see Rome and spend weeks with him! *Weeks!* Just the thought of it made her legs weak.

A faint shiny speck in the sky caught her eye. Occasionally she would see a plane heading to Entebbe Airport. She loved to watch them and imagine what wonderful places they had come from. Sentiments in the letters from friends in the United States sounded envious that she was living in such an exotic location, but they didn't realize how lonely life could be for a young American girl in Ndejje.

The speck grew larger, and Gloria excitedly thought the plane would not make it to Entebbe. As she was thinking this, the plane grew dramatically in size and became a rounded luminous object that hovered about one hundred feet away from her. The craft had moved so quickly she didn't have time to run away. In fact, she really didn't have time to register fear before a strong light shone from the craft to an area beside her. Stepping out of the beam was a handsome man. Everything about him shone a bright white, and everything was a bit fuzzy around him. To Gloria, it was like he was appearing to her in a dream, but she had a sense of dread that made it feel like a nightmare.

He smiled at her, put his hand on her shoulder, and said, "Don't be afraid." Instantly a feeling of peaceful drowsiness enveloped her. She smiled back at him with sleepy eyes. As she stared at him, she realized he looked a lot like Father Chris.

"Are you an angel?" she asked dreamily.

"Some people have called us angels," the being responded, "but it's a little more complicated than that."

"If you're an angel," Gloria asked, "then why are you here?"

"I came to be your friend. Would you like to be my friend?"

"Oh, yes," the lonely girl responded.

"I was hoping you would say that. I'm a lot like you. I'm far away from home and would love to have a friend to talk to. Would you like to come with me for a while?"

For a moment she was torn. She knew she should ask her mother, but then again, he was an angel. Surely her mother would trust him. She nodded, and a beam of light surrounded them. In a flash the craft was gone. So was Gloria.

NINE

B enny rolled his eyes and stuck out his tongue as he spoke into the phone at the parsonage of his new parish assignment. At the other end, Kim was excitedly telling him of her plans to adopt Gabe. "Just promise me you'll think this through before you do anything rash," Benny said into the phone.

"Okay. Bye. I love you too."

He was livid as he hung up the phone. He couldn't imagine Kimberly would seriously consider adopting Michael's little snot-nosed friend. By the time she was done, there would be no money left. What bad timing! Rome was taking notice of him after Kimberly's last investment. There was little else to do but to put more of her money to work before she did some other stupid thing.

The church he now pastored in South Carolina was not much to see, but it had factored heavily in America's participation in ceremonies during the 1960s. Rumors were that the pastor of this parish and a few parishioners had participated in a Black Mass at the same time that a similar ceremony was performed in Saint Paul's chapel in the Vatican. Benny was amused by the rumors, but he knew the truth. Luciferian societies were not devil worshippers. Far from it, they were a throwback to more basic religions that used to dominate the world. Calling the Black Mass satanic was a misnomer. It was Luciferian. The linkage of Lucifer to Satan was cleverly crafted disinformation propagated by the Jews and the early Church. If the modern Church is going to survive as the preeminent religious power in the next century, it must find the power associated with Lucifer. This business of waiting like sheep for the Holy Spirit to fall was a good pastime for the laypeople, but the clergy had to be a little bit more proactive if it wanted to stay relevant in the postmodern world.

Because of its significance to the behind-the-scenes power players in Rome, this parish had been a coup for Benny. He well understood its metaphysical power and its connection to certain members of the Church hierarchy, particularly his mentor, Cardinal Cesare Bilbo. He would have to give Cesare a call. But first he had scheduled confessions for the parish. God, he hated the life of a pastor; he had to get into Church administration before this job drove him insane.

As he was leaving the rectory, the phone rang. He knew he would be late for confessions if he answered it. *Oh, what the hell! Let them wait. A little preconfession penance won't hurt them!* He quickly answered the phone and instantly recognized the voice and accent at the other end of the line.

"*Ciao,* Cesare! I was just about to call you," he gushed.

"But it is I who should call you, Benito, to thank you personally for your sister's investment."

"I was hoping it would not go unnoticed, Eminence."

"Hardly, my friend. In fact, you may be of further service to the Holy See. Just today I became aware of a need at the Vatican Bank. If your sister would be so kind as to invest twenty million dollars in a long-term deposit with the bank, we would be most grateful."

"Unfortunately, Cesare, my sister is like her father. She believes in getting a return on her investment," Benny said pointedly.

"Of course there would be small interest to be earned on her deposit," the cardinal offered.

"I am afraid she is the type of person who would not be satisfied with nominal interest."

Cesare laughed. "Well done, Benito. You are starting to understand how to use Romanita. Never allow your lips to know the true purposes of your heart." Romanita was the unofficial language of the Vatican. It was a type of communication understood by every ambassador and secretary of state. Conversations hinted only at the tip of the iceberg, while the true intent lay always beneath the surface.

Cesare continued, "It has come to my attention that a position has opened within the Vatican's Department of State. It would report to the secretary of state, a most pious man." The plain English of the statement was not lost on Benny. If he could get twenty million dollars out of Kimberly, he could take a position in the Department of State. The job would report to the secretary of state, who Cesare considered a dullard, too locked in his Christianity to be enlightened.

"A pious man is hard to come by these days. The Holy Father is most blessed," Benny replied. "My sister greatly admires the Holy Father. I am sure she would be delighted to come to the aid of the Vatican Bank."

"We are often blessed by the generosity of the faithful," Cesare responded. "Your sister is among many who have sustained the Church throughout its history. She is to be commended."

"I will convey your sentiments to her, Eminence."

"Please do, Father. Peace to you."

"Peace to you as well, Eminence."

Following what felt like an endless stream of confessions, Benny said Mass for the parish. "The Mass is ended. Go in peace to love and serve the Lord." The organist played the recessional while Benny exited the church. Now he had to stand outside and greet the sheep. He knew what each of them would say. *Baah, baaah, baaaaah.* And yet, there was always the occasional surprise, like the time poor Mrs. Anderson went the whole way through Mass with her skirt tucked into her panty hose.

Finally, they were gone. His weekend ritual was over, and he could take some well-deserved time to relax. First and foremost, he was going to have a steak and some wine, as was his custom. While the steak was cooking, he would change out of his drab priestly attire into something ... paisley. That would do nicely. Then he would meditate. The power of his meditation was greatly enhanced here. It was as if the parish was opened to an incredible source of power. One day he would have to thank his predecessor for the dedication ceremony that had been shared with the Vatican.

As he ate, he contemplated how nice his life could be at the Vatican. No more pastoral duties! That alone was worth hitting Kim up for twenty million dollars. But there was also the opportunity to participate in restructuring the Church so that it could drop its stuffiness and use its organizational structure to embrace all religious practices. If the Mother Church could just open her arms to all men and women of goodwill, she could be at the center of a New World Order. It would only take a few doctrinal compromises. If done correctly, they wouldn't have to be viewed as compromises at all. She could simply accept that there are many paths to lord of the universe.

After a bottle of wine, Benny was feeling very relaxed. He calmed his breathing and slowly let himself sink to his meditation level. He had become quite adept at leaving his body. Some called it astral travel. Others in the government referred to it as remote viewing. Whatever it was called, it never ceased to be a rush when Benny felt it happening.

He cleared his mind. Breathe in. Out. In. Out. In. Out. There it was, a pinpoint of light on the horizon of his closed eyes. He willed himself to go toward it, and *whoosh*, he was inside the light. He felt so free of his body! How glorious to be one with the universe. The Lady grabbed his hand, exuding love. Benny held her hand and basked in that love.

Finally, she spoke. "Where do you want to go today, Benny?"

"I need to influence my sister to be kindly disposed toward my upcoming request."

"Let's go to her then."

Benny's mind was instantly pulled to Kimberly's office. She was completing adoption applications she had received from her lawyer.

"Focus on her," the Lady encouraged Benny. "Tell her mind to imagine the great love you have for her."

Kimberly put down the pen and sat back in her chair. She thought out loud, speaking to the empty room, "Daddy treated Benny like an outsider. I won't have that for Gabe. He has to be accepted as a full member of this family." She paused and uttered a quick prayer. "Oh, Lord, please help me do right by Gabe," she said aloud.

"A prayer for Gabe!" Benny exclaimed. "Let's go to my nephew. Maybe I'll have better luck with him."

Michael and Gabe were in the back of the house, quietly watching television. It was a lazy winter afternoon that had a dreamlike quality to it. Gabe had been quiet since learning of his mother's death. Michael stayed close to him but didn't say much either. Benny saw them as if he was in the room with them. He had to influence Michael to see the threat that Gabe presented to the family fortune!

Michael headed to the kitchen for a glass of water. He stopped short, put his hands to his ears, and squinted his eyes in a look of concentration. He softly but intensely commanded, "Back off!"

Benny found himself crashing back into his body. How did Michael do that? Going forward, he was going to have to be more careful around him. Benny doubted he could be as easily manipulated as his mother.

He picked up the phone and dialed Kimberly's office number.

Now that she had decided to adopt Gabe, Kimberly wanted the process to be done and over with. She already felt he was her child, and she needed to make it official. In that moment, she felt as if someone was staring at her. This wasn't the first time. Although she found it really creepy, she knew from experience the feeling would pass quickly. Usually such a feeling was followed by a phone call from Benny. They used to joke about their ESP, because when he would call, she would invariably say she had just been thinking of him.

When the phone rang, Kimberly started laughing. "Hi, Benny, what took you so long?"

"Don't tell me"—he chuckled—"you were just thinking about me."

"Okay, I won't tell you. Honestly, Benny, we have some sort of connection. It's like the kind of thing you hear about twins. Maybe it's ESP. What made you call me in my office instead of my home phone on a Sunday afternoon?"

"Just a feeling, I guess."

"See what I mean, big brother?"

"Yeah. By the way, why are you in your office on a Sunday afternoon?"

"Just filling out some papers for the adoption."

"About that, Kim. I was thinking maybe I should drive down there this week so that we can talk about it."

"We can talk all you want, Benny, but I'm adopting Gabe."

"All the more reason for me to get to know my new nephew then," Benny said cheerily.

"In that case, I think a visit would be wonderful. And while you're here, you could help me with the funeral. It seems Gabe's mom had alienated her entire family. Gabe is all she had."

"Was she Catholic?"

"I'm afraid she wasn't much into religion. I honestly don't know if Gabe has ever been in a church before today." While talking, she continued to browse through the pile of papers her lawyer had left.

"Maybe I could say a few words at a memorial Mass," Benny offered with a sigh.

"Benny, I can't tell you how much I appreciate—" Kim dropped the phone. She couldn't continue the conversation. In the stack of paperwork, she had come to Gabe's birth certificate, which listed Gabe's father as Rory Blanchett. She broke into convulsive tears at the realization Michael had found his own brother.

"Kimberly, are you okay?" Benny's voice rang from the phone on her desk.

Snatching the phone, she choked, "Y–y–yes," holding a copy of Gabe's birth certificate in her other hand. "I'll call you back in a few minutes," she managed to say before the tears came cascading down her face. She hung up the phone and cried out to God with joy. Clearly He had ordained this adoption. Gabe could never be made to feel like an outsider. He truly was Michael's brother, and soon he would truly be her son.

Benny waited anxiously by the phone. When all was said and done, his relationship with Kimberly was the only one in his life that even bordered on normalcy. Her tears drove his memory back to the little girl who cried with him and for him as he endured the trials of living with Stan Martin. When the phone rang, he jumped to answer it.

Before he could say hello, Kim sang into the phone, "Benny! Gabe and Michael have the same father. Michael has found his real brother! It's a sign I'm doing the right thing, Benny."

Wonderful! Benny thought. *The bastard son, Michael, had a real-life bastard brother to share all that money with!* Into the phone he said, "Kimberly, this man raped you! How will you explain that to these boys?"

"There has to be a way I can let them know without hurting them," she said dismissively. "Michael has never shown much interest in who his father is. Maybe Gabe will be the same."

"Promise me you won't do anything more with this adoption before I get there. Let's assess the situation and decide together the best way to proceed," Benny cautioned, nearly cussing under his breath.

"I can't promise you that, Benny. I'm going to have to go with my gut instinct on this. What can I say? I'm Stan Martin's daughter. I rely on gut instinct a lot."

Benny cringed at the reference to her pig of a father. "Fine," he said curtly. "At least I'll be there to pick up the pieces."

"Trust me, Benny, it will be okay. Can you come tomorrow?"

"Sure, sis, I'll drive down tomorrow."

He hung up the phone. "Damn!" he said to nobody in particular. This kid was a complication he didn't need in his life right now. He wished he was in Rome, working with a great man like Cesare Bilbo instead of changing this waif's diaper.

Mario Girote, president of the Bank of Italy and no relation to the Italian actor of the same name, bore a grim expression as Luciano Begliali entered the room, followed by his pet rat, Cesare Bilbo. Years before, Pope Pius XI founded the Vatican Bank shortly after he and Benito Mussolini had entered into the Lateran Treaty, giving the Vatican its current city-state status within the heart of Italy. At the behest of a reclusive papal confidante, known today as Luciano Begliali, Pius placed the Vatican Bank in the hands of Michele Sindona, a Sicilian with Mafia connections. And thus began the great siphoning of the Vatican's riches to Luciano's goals of one-world government. Alms of the poor throughout the world were recycled into the very tools Luciano and company used to further subjugate the masses. In short, Begliali had transformed the Vatican's wealth into his personal tool to bring about world domination.

Girote had been considering his own mortality lately, and he wasn't happy about the prospects of his afterlife. Not nine months before, he and Begliali held a similar meeting. The new pope, Gianpaolo I, had begun an intense investigation into the Vatican Bank just days after being named pope. He was surprisingly astute and, almost as if he were led by divine providence, was able to see through the layers of false transactions to the heart of Luciano's plan. Luciano had met with Girote, who then arranged a most heinous plot, the results of which were in the press release he held in his hand.

THE DEATH OF POPE JOHN PAUL I
L'Osservatore Romano

His Holiness Pope John Paul I is dead. His death took place in the Apostolic Palace about eleven o'clock on the evening of 28 September, little more than a month after his election. He had been elected on the evening of 26 August. The news of the pope's unexpected death caused widespread sorrow and shock ...

Girote could only guess what this smiling, ageless *bestia* would require of him today. Dropping the press release, he stood and smiled broadly at his nefarious mentor. "*Signore* Begliali, what a pleasure it is to see you again." His expression darkened a bit when he greeted that stone-faced old skunk of a cardinal. Girote knew from experience that nothing good came on the tails of this ferret-faced weasel.

"*Ciao*, Mario," Begliali said. Then he smiled broadly at Girote, a smile that brought immediate peace of mind. "Mario, we have seen much, you and I," he continued. "Please call me Luciano. Consider me a friend."

Immediately Girote felt privileged to be in Begliali's presence. The title of friend felt like a much-treasured gift. His head swam. He didn't know how Luciano did it, but he always made Girote feel like a lovesick schoolgirl in his presence.

Taking a seat, Begliali lowered his voice to a conspiratorial tone. "My friend, again we have need of some special services. Cardinal Villot has me worried. He is not of strong enough conviction to the New World Order. His conscience troubles him."

"But, *Signore*—I mean, Luciano—he was instrumental to our plan. Was it not he who ordered the immediate embalming of Gianpaolo? Did he not immediately dispose of the Papa's tainted blood pressure medicine? Confession would only point to him. He would gain nothing trying to expose us."

"He thinks he would gain the peace of mind that eludes him. No, my friend, I am afraid the dear cardinal is already late for an appointment in hell. There is no peace of mind for him, in this world or the next."

Girote grimaced at his friend's analysis. Certainly the same fate awaited him. The consternation was visible on his face as he turned first to Begliali and then to Bilbo. The latter said nothing but stared back at him, still as a stone. *This skunk has raised his tail and is ready to relieve himself on me,* Girote thought.

"You seem troubled, my friend," Luciano cooed as he took Girote's hand. "Are you well? You seem to be very stressed." Girote looked toward the cardinal of stone as he felt himself wilting under Begliali's gaze. He knew he would quickly have to create a misdirection.

"It is just business, Luciano. Sometimes the world of finance can be grueling. Interest rates are not to my liking, and the weakness of the lira is distressing." Inside, Girote's mind raced. If Luciano witnessed his pangs of conscience, he too would be sent prematurely to his appointment in hell. Not that long ago, he would have considered such an expression to be merely a figure of speech. But now he was pretty sure hell was a real place, and its proprietor was waiting for him.

"So I am to assume you are not distressed about the business that we share?" Begliali asked cautiously as he glanced at the press release on the conference table.

"I am not distressed by the business we share, Luciano. Working with you has been the highlight of my career. Of my life, in fact."

Begliali's silence sent the message that he did not fully believe his friend, sending a chill to the depths of Girote's soul.

Girote continued, "My dear friend, my service to you is my passion. Any accumulated stress in my life quickly dissipates in the performance of my duties. My commitment to you and to the New World Order is my strength."

"That's what I love about our friendship, Mario. We understand one another so well. *Ciao.*"

Luciano swept out of the room, his pet skunk in tow, leaving Girote in a cold sweat.

"He is fearful, Luciano," the cardinal said as they left the building.

"I have always found fear to be a great motivator, Eminence," Luciano said with a broad smile as he slowed his gait to match the cardinal's.

"Not this type of fear. I have seen it before. This man fears his eternal damnation."

"I thought your presence at the meeting would add a sort of Vatican approval to the acts we asked him to arrange."

The cardinal stopped walking and turned to Luciano to make his point. "His mind is too small. He actually believes the stories the Church peddles. Sometimes we are too good in our work. This type of fear will drive him to lift the burden of his conscience. He really is experiencing that which we described about Villot."

Luciano shrugged. "But we merely conjured that out of thin air to justify removing Villot. His time of service has come to an end. It is that simple."

"And I submit to you that following Villot's dispatch, the services of *Signore* Girote will also be at an end."

"Perhaps you are right, old friend. Too bad. I rather liked Girote." The pair resumed their walk.

"We all have our expiration dates, my friend," the cardinal intoned.

"As you say, Eminence." Begliali smiled, making a mental note that *Il Cardinale* would soon meet his. Not that his death would be anything special. In the long run, Luciano and his cohorts had decided that the maximum sustainable population of Earth was one billion inhabitants. Many more awaited Bilbo's fate.

NEWS RELEASE

Jean-Marie Cardinal Villot dies in the Vatican from pneumonia. Pope John Paul II will conduct his funeral Mass in the Vatican. Cardinal Villot came to world prominence last year when he verified the deaths of Pope Paul VI and then within six weeks the death of his successor, Pope John Paul I ...

TEN

The heat from the lights of the little television station beat at Mack. He could feel the perspiration beginning to bead on his forehead. He had only about a minute of the program left to film, but it was an important part, the offering. He silently willed himself to stay cool as he intoned, "If you have enjoyed this program, if it has deepened your faith, will you please dig deep in your pocket and send us whatever you can. Studio time is expensive, and we won't be able to reach more people for Christ without partners like you." Riverside Church had grown since he and Sarah had taken it over. Now they were able to tape a show each Thursday at an independent television station near Houston. The reach was only to East Texas, but it was a start. Mack's vision had grown over the years as well. He was now committed to reaching the world for Christ. He knew well Zechariah 4:10, which said, "Do not despise these small beginnings, for the Lord rejoices to see the work begin ..." One day, if he remained faithful, the Lord would open more doors to him and his ministry.

"Now let's see what Sarah has for us this week," he continued.

Sarah sang "What a Friend We Have in Jesus" while she chorded along on the piano. It wasn't an incredible rendition, but it was passable. More importantly, it fit so well with Mack's sermon. It was just the vehicle to cement the message in the minds of their viewers.

"Thank you, Sarah," Mack said at the end of the song. "And if any of you would like to have a cassette of today's service, just send ten dollars to the address shown below. That way you can share this message with friends or listen to it in your car. Folks, the important thing

84

is that Jesus loved you enough to die for you. You don't have a better friend in this world.

"From Sarah and me, I pray you have a happy, healthy, and blessed week. We'll see you next Sunday on this channel, or if you like, feel free to join us at Riverside Church. Our new, expanded sanctuary is almost ready to hold thousands of guests, so come on down and see us in person."

"And cut," called the camera man/director. "That's a wrap, folks. Guys," he called to the stage crew, "let's be set up for the Captain Cottontail show in fifteen minutes!"

"That was really nice, Sarah," Mack complimented his wife. He had always known she would be a valuable part of the ministry, but he had underestimated how wonderful it would be to have a soul mate, someone who shared his passion for the Gospel and worked tirelessly to get the message out there. Their life together was almost perfect. Almost.

"Guys, come on! It's late!" spouted nine-year-old Isaac Jolean. He had been given that name because, like the Isaac of the Bible, he was a child of promise. School friends had long since shortened it to Zack. Zack's demanding tone annoyed Mack, but he knew from experience that his correction of the boy would move Sarah into overprotective mother mode.

"Oh you!" she admonished. Mack thought it was about the harshest reprimand he had heard Sarah give to her miracle child.

"It's late, and I want to watch *Three's Company*." He pouted.

"I don't think it's a good program for you anyway, son," Mack said carefully. He longed to provide Zack with a dose of the proverbial rod, but Sarah had read Dr. Spock. "I wouldn't mind using the rod on Dr. Spock as well," Mack had said to her on numerous occasions.

True to form, Zack made a scowling face that incited his mother to action. "Mack," she chided, "he is way too young to catch the double entendres. To him it's just a lot of sight gags. If he is seeing it with the innocence of a child, then I think it's wrong of you to judge him as an adult."

Zack smiled innocently at his doting mother and turned the smile to one of victory as he faced his father.

Mack stared at him coldly. He had Zack's number and wanted him to know it. Still, he loved the boy. It would be very easy for him to follow Sarah's lead. Zack was attractive with curly dark hair and luminous blue eyes. Some might say his features were a little hawkish, but Mack saw them as chiseled and refined. As usual, he softened as he looked at the child, who would be their only one. The doctors told Sarah it would be impossible for her to carry another baby. In fact, they said Zack shouldn't have happened at all.

"Well, bright eyes"—Mack winked at his only son—"do we have time to stop for ice cream first? Your old dad could use a snack."

"Sure," Zack said, taking his father's hand. He looked up at Mack and smiled a huge loving grin. Mack melted. Sarah rewarded her man's softened expression by taking his other hand in hers. She leaned into his upper arm as the three of them headed into the dark January night.

The next day, Mack pondered their upcoming move into the new sanctuary, which was built like a theater and could seat two thousand people, more than all the residents of the small town of Riverside. That didn't matter though, because Mack expected up to a thousand attendees from his television audience. The trick would be to get the Riverside Church members to accept the television audience as their brothers and sisters.

So far, things had gone well. Mack and Sarah had made the church members a part of the television ministry. They were excited about the money that had come from the partners and were enthusiastic about the new building. Hopefully it would continue to go smoothly. Mack looked at the beautiful stained glass windows at the back of the sanctuary. There were no graven images, just blocks of color, but they cast the most fantastic colored beams of light throughout the large auditorium. The softness of the light brought a calming, dreamlike quality to the room.

"Hi, Dad," Zack called as he entered the room.

Mack grinned as his handsome son entered the auditorium.

"What's up, buddy?"

"Can we talk about something?" There was seriousness in his tone that took Mack off guard.

"Sure, we can talk. What's on your mind?"

"I have some things running through my mind, and I can't get rid of them, so I thought I would talk to you about them."

"Okay. Shoot." All kinds of images flooded through Mack's mind.

Had he heard something in school that was leading Mack to the birds and the bees talk? Mack hated to think his son's innocence would come to an end at the tender age of nine.

"I think you need a big map of the United States behind the pulpit in this room," Zack responded. Mack smiled and nearly laughed with relief.

"Why do you say that, son?"

"It just seems to me if you want a national ministry, you should have that symbol at the front of the congregation. Sort of a constant reminder that this ministry is going somewhere." Zack waved his arms at the space behind the pulpit where he thought the map should be placed.

"Wow!" Mack said in amazement. "I like it, son. What else has been on your mind?"

"Buy a video camera, Dad. Let me tape the services here and use that as your broadcast. Your television partners will contribute more if you give them a real-life church setting."

"That's genius!" Mack exclaimed. "Where did you come up with this?"

"I don't know," Zack said. "I think maybe I'm some kind of marketing guru and it's just starting to come out of me." Zack smiled at the vocalization of his superiority.

Mack ruffled his hair. "You may be right, buddy."

"Also, Dad, if we filmed the services here, then we could use the church choir. I don't want to put Mom down, but her chording on the piano and singing a hymn is really old-school. Not cool at all."

"Point well taken," Mack chided gently, "but I want to go on record as saying I think your mother's singing has been quite moving."

"Yeah, but I bet the church choir could come up with a knock-'em-dead piece every week!"

"I don't know if we want to get too slick, son. There is a point where it loses the sense of spontaneity and simplicity I want these services to have."

"Fair enough," Zack said, as if negotiating a deal, "but if you give your audience a good show, you'll be able to get deeper into their pockets."

"Zack, it's not about that!" Mack said with exasperation. "It's about helping people find Jesus and then helping them in their walk with Him."

"I guess you won't like my idea about getting rid of the invitation to say the sinner's prayer. I mean, you say it every week, Dad," Zack said as he crossed his arms.

"First of all, Zack, this is a ministry, not a sitcom. Secondly, I'd like to point out that people tune in week after week to see Jack get out of a situation created by mistaken impressions on *Three's Company*. It's the same thing week after week and yet people tune in."

"That's true," Zack said. "I guess I can *live* with the sinner's prayer."

Mack laughed out loud. "I'm happy you can live with it, buddy!"

"I just want you to build this into the biggest and best ministry that it can be."

"God will build this ministry, honey. But don't think I'm not impressed with your suggestions. I think you will be quite the helper to me going forward. I'll tell you what ..."

"What?" Zack asked.

"Let's be partners and maybe someday you'll want to take over this ministry when I get too old." Mack wrapped his arm around his son's shoulder.

"That would be swell." Zack smiled. "We'll make millions!"

Mack rolled his eyes as the boy left the sanctuary.

Sarah admired the twenty-by-thirty-foot map of the United States that had just been mounted in the sanctuary. Zack had chosen sepia tones. Once the map had been pasted on the wall, it was framed with dark cherry wood. The pulpit was changed from oak to cherry as well. The overall impression was classy. It was definitely upscale without being pretentious. She was so proud of her son. The changes he made were wonderful. His wisdom far exceeded his age. As the Bible says about Mary, she pondered these things in her heart. Sarah's conviction that Zack's conception was miraculous continually colored her view of him.

Sarah left the sanctuary and headed to the new office space. She had a small office next to Mack's much larger one. The offices were lovely. She had chosen the green paint and the multicolored shag rug, with blended strands of green, burnt orange, and brown. To that she added burnt-orange polyester drapes at the windows. The color scheme was very popular, and her selections blended the colors well.

On her desk was the morning mail. It was Saturday. The first service in the new sanctuary would be tomorrow. She doubted she would have time to go through the pile of mail on her desk. As she sifted through it, she saw thin airmail paper and postage from Africa. A letter from Frannie! She loved to hear from her old college friend.

As she was reading the letter, Mack came into her office. Seeing the smile on her face and the thin paper in front of her, he grinned.

"What does Frannie have to say?" he asked.

"She and Tom seem much less lonely now that they have befriended this Father Chris."

"You'd have to be pretty lonely to befriend a priest!" Mack chuckled.

"I think it's that he's American, you know? He's just a little touch of home," Sarah offered.

"I guess I'd want to talk to an American too if I lived outside the United States. Though I'd want to talk to someone from Texas." He smiled.

"My guess is you would be happy to be with anyone who knew who the Dallas Cowboys were," she teased.

"I guess you're right. Let's just hope Tom doesn't want to start listening to everyone's sins."

"Mack Jolean!" Sarah yelled. "They're our friends! I'm sure this Father Chris is a nice guy if they like him!"

"Pull the claws back in, woman," Mack said with a smirk. "He's probably a nice enough guy, but I've been reading that a lot of these younger priests are joining that Charismatic Renewal ... full-blown Pentecostals ... speaking in tongues and everything!"

"Oh, Mack," she chided with one hand on her hip. "Everyone knows those things were just for the first-generation church. Nobody really believes in that stuff these days."

"Well our denomination thinks it is outright demonic, Sarah, and I don't have a good feeling about this young priest that has befriended Tom and Fran."

"I think you should have more faith in Fran and Tom's good judgment," she said as she folded the letter and placed it in its envelope to signal that she was done with this conversation. "Speaking of good judgment, what do you think of Zack's innovations?"

"He's a pretty impressive kid," Mack said, "even if I do say so myself."

"I'm so happy to hear you say that, Mack. Sometimes I'm afraid you are too harsh with him."

"Sarah, sometimes you forget that I love him too. We're not enemies but partners in raising our son."

Sarah bristled at the remark. Of course she knew Mack was right, but she hated the idea of sharing Zack. After all, he had been *her* miracle. The angel appeared to *her*.

Sunday was warm for a January day. The sun was bright, and the stained glass windows gave the sanctuary a magical air. Zack thought the setting was beautiful, and to his parents' delight, the church was filled. He wandered throughout the sanctuary, filming his dad's sermon, which was titled "Do Not Despise the Day of Small Beginnings." His dad used it as a vehicle to show how Riverside had grown from humble beginnings to arrive at the lavish sanctuary filled with two thousand worshippers.

Finally, Mack used the phrase "small beginnings" to brag a bit about the changes made by Zack. He proudly announced the TV show would be a broadcast of Sunday services from now on. And he explained that Zack was filming the opening ceremony. Sarah took the camera from Zack when Mack called him up to the altar. He hugged Zack, which Zack thought was more for the congregation than for him. Then he did something that completely surprised Zack. He gave the boy a gold chain on which hung a golden cross. At the crossbars of the cross, a dove was carved. Zack looked at the cross and then at his father, and he began to cry—right there in front of the entire congregation! He could have died from embarrassment. The congregation applauded him as he quickly wiped his eyes with an embarrassed look and took the camera back from his mother.

There was an element of sophistication in Zack's videography. He had panned over the congregation, ensuring that he would get audience reactions to his father's words. He showed the television audience the new facility as the choir sang. Zack was very proud later that day when his parents saw the edited version. They watched the video several times, each time stating more emphatically that Zack should take a larger role in the Riverside ministry.

After an early dinner, Zack went outside to play in the yard as the sun began to set. The world of a nine-year-old boy is filled with dragons to slay and enemies to vanquish. He had a stick that had become his sword as he thrust and parried through the yard, heading toward the dragon's lair, which was actually a path through some trees leading to a farmer's field.

In the setting sun, the sky turned a fiery red. On the horizon, Zack saw the first evening star twinkle to life. But the star moved very quickly. Zack dropped his stick and intently followed the object's movement. He knew he should be frightened, but some other emotion was churning inside of him, a strong longing that came from the deepest part of his being.

As the star continued its arc, it grew in size and definition until Zack saw a disk-shaped craft. It came to a sudden stop and hovered over his head. His heart was burning with desire—desire to be noticed, desire to communicate in a deep way that he never had before. Certain knowledge swelled within him. He was born for this. The craft emitted a cone of light that ended in a lit circle in front of him. "Come to us," a voice rang out in his head. "We have been waiting to see you." Zack stepped into the cone of light and disappeared.

He found himself in a large metallic room, containing only a small table that seemed to have grown out of the floor. At either side was a cube that could be used as a seat. The wall on the far end of the room opened to admit a tall man with blond hair swept back into a large braid. His face shone like alabaster, and his blue eyes glowed.

"Don't be afraid," the man said with a smile. The man's voice had the timbre of a trickling brook and evoked great peace in Zack.

"I'm not afraid," Zack replied, and the sound of his voice reverberated throughout the metal room.

"Just think your answer, Zack. I will hear you," the man said, or rather, thought.

"Okay." Zack smiled in return. "How do you know my name?"

"We know a lot about you."

"Who are you? Are you an angel?"

"You could say that. My name is Baala. I'm from a race of people on a planet very far away from here. In our previous interactions with the people of Earth, they have referred to us as angels, so I guess it's okay if you want to call me that. In reality though we are from the Pleiadian system of stars. But just like the angels of your belief system, we serve the will of the Universal Intelligence. Some refer to it as 'God.'"

"Neat!" Zack thought. "Real aliens! And you're angels too! Cool!"

"You have much to learn, Zack. You were chosen before your birth to join us in serving God. In your lifetime, humanity will undergo a rapid shift in consciousness that will enable your race to join many other self-aware civilizations throughout this galaxy."

"Like the Federation in *Star Trek*?"

"Show me," Baala thought with a questioning look. Zack began to picture the starship *Enterprise* in his mind. He pictured it hovering in space and then felt Baala entering his mind. Suddenly all of Zack's *Star Trek* memories flashed in his mind as Baala read through them."

"*Star Trek* is a fine place for us to start. In your lifetime, your world will become united in one government just like Earth in *Star Trek*. Knowledge will expand, and your scientists will begin to understand the true nature of matter and energy."

"Show me," Zack mimicked Baala, who took a seat on one of the cubes. He motioned for Zack to take the other. Zack sat on the cube, but his head barely reached the tabletop. Instantly, the cube grew, raising him to the proper level to face Baala across the table. Baala reached across the table, taking Zack's hand, and Zack felt his mind rush out of his body.

In this experience, it was as if Zack were part of the universe itself. He felt as if he knew all things. He felt amazingly powerful, as if he could think something, anything, into existence. He was in total oneness with the creator.

"This feeling will not last for you, Zack," Baala's voice called from the distant reaches of Zack's mind. "You cannot remain a part of the universal consciousness at this time. Let me direct your thoughts to the knowledge that will need to grow in you."

Zack had no interest in listening to Baala or in ever returning to

Earth. He wanted to stay forever linked to the very mind of God, but he could also sense that God wanted him to heed Baala's instruction. Reluctantly, he let Baala lead, and the following knowledge became embedded in him, a part of him: "Point one. The science of *Star Trek* is wrong. Soon your scientists will discover that subatomic particles respond to the consciousness of an observer. In the years after that discovery, they will learn that consciousness is a full part of space-time. In fact, they will learn how to use consciousness to manipulate matter and energy. This knowledge is not new to Earth. There was once on Earth a great ancient civilization that had not separated spirit from science, as yours has. These ancients were part of our galactic union prior to a mass destruction that nearly killed all life on Earth.

"Point two. Once science and spirit are again united on this planet, miracles will be commonplace. Remember Jesus said his followers would do greater works than he. He was a great teacher who was trying to bring your people back to the knowledge of your greater ancestors, but he was killed."

"For our sins?" Zack thought.

"Point three. Jesus did not come to be worshipped. He came to proclaim the kingdom of God, which is actually the reunification of spirit and science. He tried to show the world how to transcend physical reality, but he did not come to die for sins. In the greater universe, there are no sinners, no saints. We are all connected to the great consciousness of the universe and connected to each other."

The knowledge imparted to Zack burned like fire in his head. Baala removed his hand, and the lesson stopped. He left the table.

"Come," Baala thought to Zack. Zack followed him through a door that magically opened in the smooth wall.

In the other room were four beds. Zack noticed a pretty girl, about his age, lying on one of them. She looked very afraid, and his heart went out to her.

"She will be fine," Baala thought to him as he directed Zack to the bed next to her.

Looking at both of them, Baala thought, "What you have seen here is too much for you to absorb at this time. You will see a bright light, and you will forget everything. It will come back to you at the appropriate time."

Zack couldn't bear to see the fear on the face of the girl next to him. "Wait," he said aloud. He reached out to her and asked for her hand. She cried at the kindness and extended her hand to his. He held her hand, pressing into it the cross his father had given him.

"Now," he said aloud to Baala, who smiled as a bright light surrounded Zack and the girl.

ELEVEN

I t was nearing dinnertime, and Frannie hadn't seen Gloria in a long while. She went to the back door and called, "Gloria! Come on. We'll be ready for supper soon."

There was no reply. It was very unusual for Gloria to be gone from the house this long. Even when she left the house, she always stayed within earshot. Fran had gotten so comfortable with their life in Ndejje that she rarely felt at risk here, but now a sense of panic was rising, constricting her throat as she tried to call out again.

She left the house and began to run through the yard. *How have I become so comfortable here?* she asked herself as the suddenly all-too-apparent dangers presented themselves. It was a rare thing, but occasionally wild animals had been known to make it to the out-skirts of town. Didn't a large cat attack a young boy just a year ago? Then there was the constant presence of Amin's men. Might they take advantage of a young girl in such an isolated place? Could the Tanzanians have sent spies this far into Uganda? What might they do with such a young American girl? Gloria's complexion and beautiful blonde hair instantly set her apart in Africa. Would she be viewed as an exotic enticement to the local population?

By now Fran was running through the fields behind the house. "Oh, God," she prayed. "Oh, Jesus, protect my baby!" Part of her knew that she needed to calm down, that there would be a reasonable ex-planation, that she would find Gloria and they would soon be laughing about how Mom panicked. But part of her, her mother's intuition, told her that her baby was in danger. She was running wildly now, her vi-sion obscured by the tears that flooded her eyes.

"Lord Jesus, please help me find my baby!" she called out. As she came over a small rise, she saw Gloria lying lifeless on the ground.

"Gloria!" She let out a bloodcurdling scream that Tom heard from inside the house. He sprang through the back door and ran to his wife, his natural athletic abilities enhanced by a burst of adrenaline. He reached Fran in seconds at the side of their unconscious daughter.

Fran immediately cuddled Gloria to her chest. Gloria squirmed and gasped for breath. As if awakening from a deep sleep, she asked groggily, "Mom, what's wrong? Why are you crying?"

Fran was now crying too hard to reply. They were tears of relief that Gloria was all right, tears of a child of God who has just had her most fervent prayers answered. Tom answered for her, "You were laying on the ground out here, honey. We thought you were unconscious."

"I guess I just dozed off, Daddy. I was having a wonderful dream about an angel. But it felt like more than a dream … and he looked a lot like Father Chris!"

Tom's anxiety let loose in a stream of laughter. Fran, still clutching at her little girl, joined in.

"Father Chris will be happy to hear you think so highly of him." Tom chuckled.

"Daddy! You can't tell him I said that!" Gloria shrieked.

"Of course he won't," Fran interjected. She knew how devastating it could be to a young girl to have a crush brought into the harshness of daylight. "Let's go. Supper's ready." She stumbled a bit as she tried to stand, looked at Tom, and said, "I'm still a little weak-kneed. When I thought of all that could have happened …"

Gloria ran ahead of her parents toward the house.

"I hear what you're saying," Tom commiserated. "Maybe it would be a good thing for all of us to take Chris up on his offer."

"Does that mean we can go to Rome?" Gloria called to her parents.

"Yes, my little dreamer," Tom shot back.

Fran noticed something in Gloria's hand reflecting in the bright sunlight. "What have you got there?" she called to her daughter.

Gloria held out a golden cross. "I … uh … found it," she stammered.

Fran shrugged off the feeling that her daughter wasn't being truthful. Where else could it have come from?

The two men were drenched with sweat. They had brought their church soccer teams together for a scrimmage of sorts. In the interest of fostering new relationships, Tom had served as player-coach to the Catholic boys, and Chris had done the same with the Baptist boys. In the end, the boys had great fun playing against their own coaches, and the teams hit it off well. Tom was more than a little impressed with Chris's athletic abilities. His tranquil demeanor and caring attitude were misleading. In sports, Chris was a fierce competitor who was gifted with incredible speed and agility.

"Not too shabby out there, Father," Tom said, breathing hard.

"You weren't looking too bad yourself," Chris replied. The two had said good evening to the boys and were headed off to Tom's house. Ndejje's tiny Catholic church was built to accommodate short visits from priests. There were only a sanctuary and small sacristy that included a cot, a sink, and a toilet but no shower. "I really appreciate you letting me shower at your place."

"I'll bill the Vatican. They can't very well have their young ambassador smelling like you do," Tom teased as they began the ten-minute walk to Tom's house on a hillside just outside of Ndejje.

Chris laughed hard at the thought. The embassy had all but shut down once everyone else had fled the country in anticipation of the Tanzanian Army's push toward Kampala. "I'm thinking I'll have to ship out in about a week. Are you and the girls up for some R & R in Rome?"

"You know I don't believe in bugging out, but you did an end run around me by making it a vacation for Frannie and Gloria. So I guess you win."

"Ah, be still my heart!" Chris mocked, making the gesture of a rapidly beating heart on his chest. "The sound of defeat coming from the lips of a Texan! We must be in the last days!"

Tom chuckled. "Sounds like you've been thinking about our eschatology conversation."

"More than thinking. I've done a lot of looking into it. In a nutshell, I think you're probably right."

"Now *my* heart's all atwitter," Tom drawled as he placed his arm around his friend's shoulder, "a concession from Rome."

"Don't get too proud. I certainly don't represent Rome's view of it. I believe the Church is a wonderful and holy institution. That's why I'm a priest. It has served itself and humanity well by moving slowly and cautiously, but I'm afraid that slowness may catch it up into a heap of trouble if end-time events move quickly. On the other hand, my time in the Charismatic Renewal has shown me there is a certain amount of beauty in the Church's slowness to action. The Spirit was literally able to revitalize the spiritual lives of millions of Catholics before the hierarchy had the chance to form an opinion. And I think that's neat."

"That whole charismatic movement is such a paradox to me," Tom said. "I'm a conservative Baptist. In most ways I would consider the Catholics to be to the right of us—an organization hamstrung by its tradition and hierarchy. Then the Charismatic Renewal happens and there are a ton of Catholics who look more like the Assembly of God, which I would consider pretty far to the left of my beliefs."

Chris smiled. "I don't see it as so much of a paradox. To me, the formal worship of the Mass is brought to its fullness by the sweeping power of the Spirit."

"I'm aware of a lot of prejudices from my side of the aisle," Tom commented. "My background would tell me you are not even saved, but my knowledge of you tells me you are in a relationship with Jesus as your Lord and Savior."

Referring to descriptions in the book of Revelation, Chris said, "No denomination has the sole claim to being the praised Philadelphian church. There may come a time when I will have more in common with people like you than I do with my own hierarchy ... and the same could be said about you."

"I think you are right, my Roman brother." Tom smiled. "There are some movements within the Protestant Church that are beginning to make me a bit nervous too. Maybe I've just been out of touch over here in Africa, but when I go back home, it seems there is no quiet time. Mark my words, in a few years, Christians in the States will be riding teacups at Jesus World and thinking they're performing worship."

Chris rolled his eyes at his friend's obvious exaggeration. He laughed. "I can see it now, swinging a sledgehammer to hit the button and see how high you can drive the heart up the cross! A water coaster that rocks the heck out of riders and then suddenly becomes still when it passes a statue of Jesus."

"Yeah," Tom quipped, "you can get grape juice and manna burgers at the concession stands."

"And stick your face into life-size cardboard cutouts of the Last Supper." Chris chuckled.

"Oh Lord, Chris, what is our world coming to?" Tom asked, suddenly serious.

"The end of days, my friend," Chris responded. The stark realization left them in silence that lasted for the remainder of the walk.

"Chris, I just assume you're staying for dinner," Fran said as he came into the kitchen, his hair still wet from his shower.

"I thought you'd never ask." Chris chuckled. "I've been smelling that chicken roasting in your oven."

"Do you mind if I ask you a question?"

"The woman who's feeding me chicken can ask me anything she wants." Chris smiled.

"I'm having a hard time figuring you out, religiously. It's like you defy all of the stereotypes I have been raised to believe."

"I have noticed that attitudes between Catholics and Protestants still have a sixteenth-century feel to them," Chris said, taking a dining chair and turning it around. He sat backward on the chair, resting his head on his arms, which he had folded over the back of the chair.

"Societal prejudices aside, I sometimes find you to be a contradiction in terms," she said.

"Such as ..."

"Such as the Mass is very ritualistic. The idea of confessions is very ritualistic. For me it seems as if there is no room for a personal relationship with the Lord—"

"Oh, but there is, Frannie," Chris interjected, shuffling in his chair.

"No. Hear me out. Then I meet you, and I see you have what I would call an enviable relationship with the Lord. There is an indefinable peacefulness about you I wish I could incorporate into my life."

"But it's nothing I've done," Chris countered. "It comes from the Holy Spirit."

"And I guess that is part of what I don't understand ... all of the Pentecostal stuff is way at the opposite end of the spectrum. Yet you sit in my kitchen, embodying both in such a marvelous way. How did that happen?"

"If it makes you feel any better, the charismatic Catholics are a bit of an enigma to a lot of other Catholics as well, including me. Let me tell you a bit of my story. When I was in high school, both of my parents were killed in a car accident—"

"Oh, Chris, I'm so sorry." Fran stopped her work at the stove and pulled up a chair.

"It was a long time ago." He shrugged as if a shrug could suppress the shadows of pain that crossed his face. He proceeded to tell her the story of his parents' death and his calling to the priesthood, looking down at his hands as he spoke.

"The house was so lonely, and I was so sad. One night I just broke. I couldn't stand it anymore. I fell to the floor crying, asking Jesus to help me. And He did. Suddenly I was warm all over. I could feel His embrace, feel Him telling me that my parents were fine with Him and that He would be with me forever. I was so moved, so grateful, I just started thanking Him and praising Him. At one point, I heard myself speaking another language. It freaked me out a little, but then I read the Acts of the Apostles."

"Wow! You know, our viewpoint is that the spiritual gifts in the book of Acts were merely for the time of the church's foundation and aren't applicable today," Fran said, implying she now doubted what she had been taught.

Chris looked up, a wry smile punctuating the sadness in his eyes. "But when it happens to you, Frannie, you can't deny it," he said.

"So you ended up a Pentecostal priest ... what I would call a contradiction in terms."

Tom had been standing in the doorway behind Chris, listening to the conversation. "So you ended up a Pentecostal priest who's chatting up my girl," he teased.

Chris turned to him and smiled.

"Tom," Fran chided, "we're having a nice conversation here. Don't ruin it."

"I have no intention of the kind, Frannie," Tom said. "I'm thinking maybe you and I should revisit the Acts of the Apostles with a more open mind."

"I agree, Tom, but we could run afoul of our benefactors back home."

"I say we cross that bridge when we come to it. If Chris can be a priest who speaks in tongues, then I should be able to be a Baptist minister who does."

Surveying the dinner table, Fran said, "It's worth considering. But for now, could you go get Gloria? We're just about ready to sit down to eat."

"Sure, but before I do, Chris, I need to fill you in on a little story. Yesterday, we found her lying unconscious in the field behind the house."

"Scared me to death," Fran added.

"Was she hurt?" Chris asked.

"No. It was more like she was asleep."

"She said she saw an angel," Fran said.

"Rome investigates a lot of supposed apparitions each year," Chris said. "Invariably they end up concluding they were products of an overactive imagination or stress."

"My thoughts exactly," Tom added. "Only the stress here may involve unrequited love."

"Sounds like our little girl is growing up," Chris chuckled.

"The reason I'm telling you this is that she said the angel looked like you."

"Oh no!" Chris exclaimed, bringing his hand to his forehead.

"It will pass, Chris," Fran said, "but we're telling you because we want you to be careful not to innocently say anything that would lead her to believe the feelings are reciprocated."

"I'll be overtly paternal," Chris said emphatically, "That's why they call me 'Father.'"

"Thanks for understanding," Fran said as she finished placing the chicken, potatoes, and vegetables on the table.

"Hi, Father Chris!" Gloria came into the room.

"Well, hello, Gloria." Chris rose to hug her. "How are you today, my little one?"

"Oh, Father Chris, don't call me little one. I'm not a child, you know."

"You'll always be a sweet-faced little girl to me," Chris said and gave her a kiss on the forehead, "like the daughter I never had."

"Would you like to say grace, oh paternal one?" Tom asked.

"I would be delighted, my son," Chris said as they bowed their heads. He gently waved his arms over the food in the shape of a cross. "Father, I ask you to bless this food for which we give You thanks. Let it nourish us as your Holy Spirit nourishes our souls. I ask your special blessing on this family as they earnestly seek Your heart. And I ask all of this in the name of Jesus, our Savior and our Lord ..."

"Amen," said only three voices after Benny had pronounced, "This Mass is ended. Go in peace." The service was held at the local Catholic church, an old building with a colonial Georgian feel. White chair rail and wainscoting decorated the bottom of the walls. A very pale blue paint donned the top of each wall, providing a soft canvas for the jeweled tones of the stained glass windows. It had been a mournfully quiet service. Even though Kim had announced the memorial service in the local newspaper, nobody came to say good-bye to Michele.

Even Gabe seemed to be detached. Last night's conversation with him rang through Kim's mind.

"Miss Kim?" he asked.

"What, sweetheart?"

"I was wondering if it would be all right if I called you Mom."

Tears flooded Kim's eyes. "It would be more than all right." She hugged him. "It would be wonderful. I didn't want to push it because your mother's death is so recent."

"I loved her," he said, snuggling closer, "but she wouldn't let me call her Mom. She used to say she was too young to be a mom, so she just told me to call her Michele."

"Oh." Kim sighed softly.

"Michele was okay, but I always wanted to have someone to call Mom." Kim squeezed him as if she would never let go, and Gabe clung even tighter to her. It was that simple. He had bonded to her as his mother. She said a silent prayer of thanks.

At the service, Gabe was controlled and somber, but not grief-stricken. As the Mass came to a close, Michael and Kim both had their arms around him. He remained quiet and resolute as a little soldier carrying out his duties. While Benny cleaned up the sacristy, mother and sons headed to the car to wait for him.

Gabe broke the silence. "I had a dream last night," he said softly. "I saw Michele, and she was in Heaven with Jesus. She told me I was in good hands with my new family. Then she hugged me and told me I would see her in Heaven someday."

"Wow," Michael said, "were you scared?"

"No. Really peaceful. She looked beautiful, and she was really happy. And I realized I didn't have to be afraid for her anymore."

"That's neat," Michael said. "It's like our new family has your mom's blessing."

"Yeah." Gabe shook his head. "I don't have to feel guilty or anything for becoming a part of your family. Michele understands."

"Cool!" Michael opined.

"Yeah," Gabe agreed and smiled a soft, sad-eyed smile.

Listening, Kim was again struck by how easy this transition was. Clearly it was a miracle that Gabe had found his way to them. She thanked God again for the entire, unlikely stream of events that had led them to this place.

Kim and the boys waited a long time in the car for Benny to change out of his priestly robes and join them. She watched in the rearview mirror as the boys fought the inevitable postfuneral exhaustion as they sat silently listening to a James Taylor tape. Kim knew they all needed a nap when they got home.

"How is everyone?" Benny asked reassuringly as he entered the passenger side of Kim's car.

"Holding up wonderfully, all things considered." Kim offered a weak smile.

"Father Cross," Gabe said from the backseat in a tone far too old for his age. "I want to thank you for the service. Michele would have been really touched."

"You can call him Uncle Benny now," Michael said.

"You are quite welcome, young man," Benny said offhandedly, ignoring Michael's invitation for him to extend to Gabe the right to call him uncle.

The coldness in Benny's tone brought a cringe from Gabe and did not go unnoticed by Kim. She knew Benny could be a tough customer and silently prayed he would eventually come to love Gabe. They drove in silence for a while as Kim busied herself with traffic, occasionally checking on the boys in the rearview mirror. Gabe had fallen asleep from the emotional exhaustion of the past couple days. Michael was just about there.

Michael willed himself not to move and to breathe slowly, rhythmically, in the hopes that sleep would come. But sleep would not overtake his rising sense of dread that Benny would never accept Gabe. Over the years, Michael had heard all of the references to Benny's bad treatment at the hands of Grandpa Stan. He also had witnessed Uncle Benny use this sad fact to manipulate his mother. He remembered Uncle Benny looking around their home and saying to him, "Someday this will all be yours, Michael." There was a strong edge of anger in his voice when he said it. *Now someday it will all be Gabe's and mine. Uncle Benny isn't going to take this well.*

Finally, Benny broke the silence. "Kim, there is something I need to talk to you about."

"Benny, you sound so grave. What is it?" Kim asked, checking the rearview mirror to be certain that the boys were asleep.

"It's two things, actually. The first is a bit of a problem at the Vatican Bank. They have an investment in this company that needs an injection of capital."

Here we go again, Michael thought.

"Again? How much this time?"

"Twenty million."

"Twenty million!" Kim stressed in hushed tones so as not to awaken the boys.

"I know. It's your father's wealth, and I have no claim to it," Benny said.

The Uncle Benny pity party.

Kim threw her head back in an expression of exasperation. "It's not that, Benny. You know that I'm here for you. Besides, Daddy's fortune has nearly doubled since his death. I call it mine now … and I want to share with you. But instead of charities, the Vatican keeps hitting me up on these banking deals."

"It's an investment, Kim. You'll get your money back with a good return."

"I'll have to see the documents. Have them sent to me. I'll look over them and discuss them with my lawyer."

"They're in my suitcase at your house … and I took the liberty of inviting Chase to dinner tonight."

Kim took her eyes off the road to stare at her brother with a furrowed brow. "You invited my lawyer to dinner? Tonight? The same day as the memorial service?"

"The Vatican will need to know in short order, Kim."

They drove on in silence for another five minutes. Michael could tell his mother was annoyed with Benny. He also knew she would cave in to his demands.

"You said there were two things," Kim finally said. "What else did you need to talk to me about?"

"There may be a position opening up in the offices of the Vatican's secretary of state. Cardinal Bilbo wants to nominate me for the position."

"Oh, Benny," Kim said, "please don't tell me this Cardinal Dildo held out the position in the same conversation that he asked for twenty million dollars." Michael fought the urge to chuckle.

"Absolutely not!" Benny protested, "It's Bilbo, with a B, and I seriously doubt he even knows about the request from the Vatican Bank." Benny patted Kim's shoulder, as if to calm her. "Everything isn't a plot, Kim. Thinking that way is a nasty habit you got from your father."

"Apologies," Kim said tersely, batting away his hand. "But you have to admit it's an incredible coincidence, Benny, that you would be offered the position at the same time you are hit up for twenty million dollars."

Benny turned his large frame in the seat to look at Kim, drawing a squeaking whine of stress from the leather. "First of all, Kim, they are totally separate matters. And if you're asking me if it is an unlikely coincidence, then I say God works in mysterious ways."

"Well, that's the comment to stop the argument." She sighed in resignation. "Tell me about this position."

"I would be reassigned to Rome."

Oh, please go to Rome, Uncle Benny!

"Oh, Benny! It seems so far away! You and I are the only family that each of us has."

"You have the boys now, and I have the Church. Kim, I'm not lonely anymore, and whether you have noticed it or not, neither are you."

She smiled at the realization. "You're right," she conceded. "You know, we ended up okay, considering the dysfunctional family we came from."

Benny nodded in agreement and sighed contentedly. The seat leather groaned in pain as he righted himself.

"Speaking of family, Benny. This day has been too exhausting for the boys and me. I need you to uninvite Chase for dinner tonight. Tell him you will send a messenger with the contract. Trust me, he doesn't want to drive an hour out to my house for dinner tonight. With a new baby, he'll be just as happy to review the contract at home. And we have a family to build ourselves."

"How is it going with your little experiment in charity?" Benny asked haughtily. Michael twitched at the coldness of the comment.

"Come on, Benny," Kim said as she stole an annoyed glance at him. "Michael and I truly love Gabe, and for your information, it is going splendidly. It is as if we always belonged together."

"Well, I'm here if you need me. There are a lot of horror stories about adopted children going bad. You know nothing of his genetic makeup."

"Not entirely true," Kim said sternly, holding up her hand to silence him. "And I don't want to discuss this in front of the boys." Michael paid closer attention.

"They've both been asleep for a while now," Benny said dismissively. "Are you going to tell them?"

Tell us what?

"Someday. When they're old enough to understand that I, and probably Michele too, were just young and confused."

"Their father's paternal instincts would kick in quite quickly if he realized his sons stood to inherit a vast fortune."

Our *father?* In his heart, Michael knew it to be true. Gabe really was his brother.

"I doubt he would ever be able to figure it out, Benny."

"Kim, you have opened yourself up to the possibility of joint custody or blackmail. It puts your entire fortune at risk.

Could that be true? Michael wondered.

"It's too bad there isn't a way to safeguard your assets," Benny continued.

"How do you mean?"

"Well, I've been thinking about it. If you put my name on your accounts and made me a shareholder of your corporations, then my holdings wouldn't be subject to any threats. As a family we would have enough to ensure that we could all live comfortably."

There it is, just another one of Uncle Benny's schemes.

"Benny, this guy is no threat. Trust me, he can't even comprehend the type of wealth we're talking about," Kim said decisively.

"A slick lawyer could." Benny floated the idea with a deliberate pause.

Or Uncle Benny could set the guy up with a slick lawyer to get at the money. Michael considered the possibilities. His uncle was the one who couldn't be trusted when it came to the family fortune.

Benny continued, "Why don't you consider putting one hundred million dollars or so into an account we share? That way it will be there for the boys no matter what."

"No, Benny, from a financial point of view, it makes no sense. We would have to pay taxes of about fifty million dollars. The only one to benefit is Uncle Sam."

"If the assets were held by the Vatican, I could get the documentation to make it look as if it were a donation," Benny offered.

"Benny, if I have recourse to the funds, it won't satisfy the IRS regulations on donations."

"You would have access to it through me, of course, even if on paper it looked as if you had donated the entire amount."

"I really have to think about it, Benny."

We both have to think about it, Mom. If we don't give him the money, Uncle Benny will find our dad.

"I just want to protect you from the worst imaginable consequences of your actions," Benny said reassuringly.

Michael was aghast. Surely his mother could see through this guy! But he knew Benny was her Achilles' heel. She wanted so much to believe in him as a brother and a priest. Michael realized he would have to be the one to stand up to Benny. His mother couldn't do it, but someone had to protect her ... and Gabe.

"Benny, I just don't think it is necessary," Kim said resolutely, looking past Benny for right-lane traffic as she prepared to exit the expressway.

"I'll tell you what. I'll send those papers to Chase as well. Let him take a look at them and see what he thinks."

"Fine," Kim said with resignation and dismay that Benny had already drawn up the documents, "but that doesn't mean I have agreed to it."

There was silence in the car for the rest of the trip. Michael's mind ran wildly through scenarios where he and Gabe would become pawns in a custody battle initiated by Benny.

"I hope you don't mind," Benny said as they pulled onto the mansion's mile-long driveway. "I asked Caroline to make duck à l'orange tonight."

———————————————

Following dinner, Benny went to his room, where he put back a glass of brandy in one gulp. Its warmth helped him to get past the excitement of the day. If he walked away with $120 million, it would be well worth saying Mass for the little bastard's trollop of a mother. He could one day be among the most powerful men in the Vatican if he could get hold of the money before little Wynken and Blinken could grow up and spend it.

Indulging in the warmth of the brandy, he settled to the floor in as close to a lotus position as his girth would allow. Closing his eyes, he counted backward from ten, letting himself fall further from consciousness at each count. He made it to the count of two when his consciousness changed. With a blinding flash of light, he saw himself sitting before the Lady.

"Oh, Queen"—he adored her—"to what do I owe the honor of your presence."

"You are not at peace in your spirit. What is troubling you?"

"This child has come into my family. I feel his presence will not bode well for me. He steals the hearts and affections of my sister and nephew. Without their affection, I won't be able to control them."

"Come with me," she said with a smile as they disappeared in a flash of light.

Outside, the boys were pretending to be the Mama Mia brothers. Somewhere between mafiosi and private detectives, the Mama Mia brothers took after criminals in an effective manner without the constraints of Miranda laws and constitutional protections. They had chased the imaginary, nefarious Johnny Black Sneaker into a clump of trees on the estate. The setting sun cast strong shadows among the trees, leaving Johnny Black Sneaker plenty of places to hide, especially since he didn't have the fashion sense to wear white high-tops.

"Over there!" Michael Mama Mia yelled to his partner.

"Got it, brother!" Gabriel Mama Mia fired back as he ran to the edge of the clearing beyond the trees. He stopped so quickly that Michael ran into him and both toppled on the ground. They would normally have laughed at their awkward situation, but both were entranced with a bright light that shone on them from about twenty feet above.

Gabe tried to get up, but his muscles wouldn't work. Michael wanted to scream, but he was too afraid. The light overtook them, and they were dissolved into its brilliance.

As the light faded, Michael found himself bound as if by glue to a metal table in a small, circular metal room. From the corner of his eye, he could see Gabe on the table next to him. What looked like a big insect was staring down at him with large, wet-looking eyes. As it looked at him, it communicated the thought that Michael shouldn't be afraid, and the fear left him. Another of the creatures extracted a long syringe from his abdomen. He hadn't even felt it.

Gabe stirred and began to scream in fright. Bug Eyes went over to him and stared at him to make him calm. Unlike Michael, however, Gabe never really became calm. He merely became manageable, softening to a whimper as they withdrew a needle from him as well.

Bug Eyes exited the room through a hatch close to Michael's head. As the door opened, Michael thought he heard his uncle Benny saying in an agitated manner, "So it's true then. They have the same father!"

Michael could not hear a response but got the impression a powerful being, maybe the Bug Commander, was confirming that he and Gabe were true brothers.

"This isn't how you told me things would happen!" Benny said in the irate tone of voice usually ascribed to a disappointed teenager.

Bug Eyes entered the room again with a burnished steel rod. It walked first to Gabe and then to Michael, telling each it was time for them to sleep. Then he touched their foreheads with the rod, anesthetizing them instantaneously.

Benny and the Lady entered the room as other creatures began to inject the boys at various parts of their bodies with large syringes of fluid.

Benny's human nature took over as he felt concern for the two boys. Whether he liked it or not, he loved his nephew, and the other one looked so small and defenseless on the table.

Sensing his uneasiness, the Lady placed a comforting hand on his shoulder. "They are fine. We are merely ensuring our plans will unfold properly. We have enhanced certain genetic features in each child. As they mature, they will be different as night and day. It will be very unlikely this new child will hold any sway over your nephew. He will grow to have great athletic prowess and strong social skills that he will be prone to use solely in the pursuit of pleasure. With Michael, we have enhanced his intellect even further. He will grow in his mastery of languages and in his love of antiquities. He is likely to prefer a solitary life, perhaps even choosing the priesthood."

"So," Benny conjectured, "Gabe will be out in the world living it up while Michael becomes a priest. Kimberly will naturally favor her own son over a philandering pretender to the throne, and Michael will get the inheritance."

"Which you will control," added the Lady, "since you will be the personal representative of the Church's authority in his life."

"Brilliant! Dear Lady!" Benny cackled with delight.

"My will must be done, Benjamin, on Earth as it is in the heavens."

"Yes, my lady," Benny exclaimed as he fell to his knees before her.

Kim settled comfortably in her favorite overstuffed chair in the family room. She loved it here, away from the formality of the front part of the mansion. There was no denying the beauty of the polished inlaid wooden floors, the oversized, ornately carved mahogany furnishings, the ceiling murals, and the Venetian glass chandeliers and sconces. But her memories of formal dinners hosted by her parents were of cold affairs where she felt too consumed with protocol and etiquette to enjoy the moment. A grin came to her face as she remembered Benny's reaction to Gabe throughout dinner. He rarely had eaten with three utensils, let alone the ridiculously ornate table setting Benny had instructed Caroline to use.

Kim wanted Gabe to feel at home, and to her mind the formal dining room was not the place to start, but she gave in to Benny's wishes. Before the meal, she explained to Gabe that he should use whatever tool he thought best, that there was plenty of time to learn about them as he grew up. She thought Benny's eyes would roll out of his head when Gabe used the teaspoon to slurp soup. He actually gasped when the child took the steak knife from his plate and used it to butter bread. To make matters worse for Benny, Michael had been keenly watching his new brother, careful to repeat any faux pas committed by Gabe. Michael, of course, wanted to make sure Gabe didn't feel out of place. She thought it was a beautiful sentiment. And Benny's horrified exasperation made it all very funny to her.

She was reflecting that these simple moments were bringing her such joy. The addition of Gabe somehow completed her family. She knew both she and Michael would be better for this new addition. Only a miracle of God could bring about such peace at becoming the mother of an orphaned nine-year-old, but here she was feeling more content than she had felt in her life.

Of course, there was always Benny to suck the joy out of the room. She had to give serious consideration to his requests, but she knew from the outset she couldn't turn that kind of money over to him and the Vatican Bank. She knew he would tug at her heartstrings about being the poor, underprivileged half brother, but she had to think of her boys. She had grown up, and maybe it was time for Benny to grow up too. She vowed not to be afflicted with pangs of conscience when he pulled out his Cinderella routine. *Or Cinderfella.* She chuckled to herself, remembering the old Jerry Lewis movie.

She moved to the window. It was time to call the boys inside. It would be dark in a few minutes. A flash of light on the horizon caught her attention. It grew instantaneously, as if it had flown quickly from the horizon to a grouping of trees in the yard.

Old memories of terror filled Kimberly. Her memories were vague, but the terror of *their* visits was not. Over the years she had found peace, but now the terror was back in spades as she realized she was not the target of their attention.

"No!" she screamed as she pounded the glass. "Not my boys! You cannot have my babies!"

She ran to the door, yelling for Benny to help her.

"Benny! Benny!" No answer.

She ran into the field, screaming at the top of her lungs. She had to get to her boys. Words failed her and only anguished gibberish poured out.

At the edge of the estate, Joseph lived in a refurbished caretaker's home. He heard Kim's screaming and ran into the twilight to find her.

Her wailing continued as she found the boys unconscious in the clump of trees. Joseph found her as she was trying to lift them both to carry them to the house.

"Miss Kimberly!" he shouted at her to get her attention. "What has happened?"

She responded to the kind old man's voice with a whimper. "I don't know, Joseph. I found them here unconscious."

"Let me take a look at them, Miss Kimberly." He moved to the boys with the commanding grace honed in his years as a major-domo.

"Master Michael!" he said sharply to the boy. "Can you hear me?" Michael stirred, and Joseph drew a sigh of relief. He moved to Gabe and repeated the process. "It is as if they are in a deep sleep, Miss Kimberly."

"Boys." Kim contained her terror and spoke to them in a soft voice. "It's time to wake up now." She jostled them, and they came grudgingly awake. Straining, Joseph picked up Michael, and Kim grabbed Gabe. They carried them to the house as silent tears filled Kim's eyes.

"I believe they are fine, Miss Kimberly, but I will call Dr. Horton as soon as we reach the house. It won't hurt for him to check them out."

"Thanks, Joseph," Kim said softly.

The back patio lights came on as Caroline met them at the door. "What happened, ma'am?" she asked softly.

"I don't know," Kimberly responded. She could not bring herself to say out loud that she thought malevolent aliens had abducted her boys. Even the thought seemed insane. Voicing it would make it seem even more ludicrous.

Awakening from his trance, Benny saw that Caroline had not yet refilled his brandy glass.

"Caroline!" he yelled. "This world is going to hell in a handbasket!" he proclaimed as he swept down the stairs defiantly. He strode past the bar, looking briefly at the brandy. He decided not to pour a refill for himself. It was Caroline's job, and he was going to make sure she did it!

He found them huddled in the family room at the back of the house. As he entered the detestable room, he saw the boys wrapped in blankets as Caroline poured some of her peppermint tea for them.

"What does a guy have to do to get a refill around here?" he demanded, oblivious to the mood in the room. "Really, Kim, Caroline can't fulfill her duties and be a nanny at the same time."

"*Where have you been?*" she screamed at him. "I was calling and calling for you to help me. Were you passed out drunk?" She snatched the glass from his hand. Stomping into the formal area of the house, she returned with the bottle of brandy. Moving swiftly to the small kitchen off the family room, she poured the elixir down the drain. "The bar is closed, Benny!"

Benny stammered in exasperation. Kim never had spoken to him this way before. "What … what happened?" he asked in a sheepish tone.

"We found the boys fast asleep at the clump of trees by the field, Father." Joseph motioned to the place at the edge of yard. "We thought they were unconscious … that something terrible had happened to them. But Dr. Horton has checked them out and assures us they are fine."

"To my mind, they're still a bit sluggish," Caroline added.

"Benny, I'm sorry," Kim apologized as she returned to the room. "I don't think I have ever been so scared in my life." Tears began to flow silently down her cheek as she lost the words she would have said.

"But we're okay, Mom," Gabe said softly, earnestly.

"Yeah, Mom," Michael added, "just a little tired."

Kim moved to the couch to be close to her boys.

"Actually, Kim, I was hoping we could spend some time discussing my proposals. Since the drama here seems to have passed and the boys are fine, maybe we could go to your office to talk. On the way, of course," he added with a smile, "I'll probably open up a new bottle of brandy."

"Tonight's not a good time," Kim said softly to him, "but feel free to open the brandy. Again, I apologize for dumping the other one."

"But I have to leave tomorrow," he protested.

"I'm not discussing business with you tonight, Benny," she said sternly. He heard her father in her voice and recoiled slightly.

"Well, all right then," he said curtly. "I will bid you all a good night."

No one responded as he stomped out of the room.

"Mom, can I talk to you alone?" Michael asked her quietly.

"Sure, honey," she said warmly as he led the way to her office.

"What's up?" she asked as they settled into the overstuffed couch there.

"It's Uncle Benny. I don't think he will ever be fair to Gabe. I don't want Uncle Benny to hurt him." Kim's eyes grew wide at the blunt statement. Michael would always be her little boy, but by the time he was five, she found his thought processes were like those of an adult.

He even offered her business insights that were often more profound than those of the executives she paid handsomely. He was an avid reader and had mastered the speech of a well-mannered grown man—when he was dealing with adults. He was also fluent in the vernacular of nine-year-olds when dealing with his peers.

"Explain," she said cautiously.

"Uncle Benny feels that Grandpa Stan cheated him by leaving things to you. I love Uncle Benny, but I have always known he resents me. He calls me a 'child of privilege' and then tells me how rough he had it."

"So you think he is jealous of you?" Kim asked, pulling him close.

"Definitely. But it's more than that. I can almost see him thinking he would get more if I wasn't around."

"Michael," she comforted, "I know your Uncle Benny loves you."

"I know that too, Mom. And that's what stops him from trying to hurt me. But he doesn't love Gabe. And I don't think he ever will."

"So what do you want to do about it?" Kim asked. "Maybe we could all talk about it or go to counseling."

"I wasn't asleep in the car," Michael said. Kim inhaled sharply. "Give him what he wants, Mom."

"What do you mean?" She stared at him.

"Give him the money and let him go to Rome. Mom, if he's busy in Rome, he won't feel like he has to find this guy you two were talking about!" Michael said, waving his arms to make the point. The thought hit Kim like a ton of bricks. Could Benny find Rory and finance a custody bid? How much would she pay to make Rory back off? More importantly, how much of the payment would Benny keep? *Would* Benny do it?

She looked at the little man beside her and threw herself against the back of the sofa. How could she have been so unwise as to tell Benny the boys had the same father! How could she have let him talk about it in the car! "Michael"—her voice broke—"I'm so sorry for what you overheard."

He patted her shoulder kindly but spoke with the incisive nature of his grandfather. "Mostly, I heard Uncle Benny threaten us. The rest is old history." She hugged him tightly and for the first time was able to forgive herself for the events that occurred so long ago at the Tic Toc Tavern. But was Michael right about Benny?

Michael pulled away from her hug so that he could face her eye to eye. "You're too easy a touch for Uncle Benny, Mom. He's your kryptonite. Let me tell him about the money. He needs to know that Gabe and I are here to stay." She and her son worked out the details of the arrangement.

"Entrez vous," Benny called to the slight knock on the door to his bedroom suite. Lying in bed, he put down the book he was reading. Michael entered quickly, opening the door just a crack and then scurrying through as children do. But the expression on his face was not that of a child. In fact, Benny saw a disconcerting resemblance to Kim's father in the boy's demeanor.

"Uncle Benny, can we talk?" Despite appearances, it was still the high-pitched voice of darling Michael, probably the only child Benny would ever love.

"Sure, Michael. Hop up on the bed with your old uncle Benny. What's troubling you?"

Declining the offer to hop on the bed, Michael instead stood beside the nightstand to look Benny directly in the eyes. "I don't think you are ever going to love my brother as your nephew."

Benny frowned. He didn't want to hurt the boy's feelings, but it would be useless to argue the point. He would never think of Gabe as his nephew. "You may be right about that, Michael. But that shouldn't make you feel bad. That should make you feel like you are special … and you are special. You're my little boy."

"Uncle Benny, of all people, you know what it's like to grow up as the outsider in a family. I don't want that for my brother," Michael lectured. Benny was amazed at the logic coming from the child. Truly, he had an adult mind and a very capable way of making his point known. When the Lady said she would enhance the boy's intellect, he had no idea he would have to go head-to-head with the child.

"I grew up okay," Benny said flatly.

"No, Uncle Benny. You grew up with scars that still hurt you. I won't have that for Gabe."

"You won't *have* that?" Benny felt his ire at Michael's tone of voice.

Intellectually enhanced or not, it was time for Michael to know who was in charge here. He opened his mouth to set the record straight, but Michael cut him off.

"I talked to Mom about it. We agreed you could have the money you asked for."

"Michael," Benny said sternly, "this has gone way beyond cute. Are you attempting to buy me off? You're a child!"

"No, Uncle Benny, I'm the heir—or more to the point, Gabe and I are the heirs now." Benny winced at the remark. He fairly hated Michael at this moment. "I'm giving you everything you want, but you won't be close enough to hurt Gabe. He's been through a lot, Uncle Benny, and he has a lot more to go through before he feels secure here."

So there it was. Just like his grandfather before him, Michael was effectively banishing him from the wealth and privilege of the family. Benny was angered, but a small voice in the back of his head reminded him that these were not paltry sums that Michael offered. He could parlay that kind of money into a cardinal's ring. Surely this was all part of the Lady's plan.

The ugliness of Stan's steely demeanor ran deep in Michael's blood. How could he not have seen it earlier? How could he have been so taken in by the love of this child as to not realize that genetics would rear its ugly head, turning Michael into the Stanford Freaking Martin redux.

"Michael, I have to tell you that you have hurt my feelings deeply. Do you really think I only care about the money?"

"No, Uncle Benny. I know you love Mom and me in your own way. And it's probably not so much the money you care about—it's the feeling of being special. That's why you keep hitting Mom up for more and more money.

"Now you won't have to. Let's talk about the one hundred million dollars. We'll lend it to you for deposit with the Vatican Bank. It will be a twenty-year loan, but only at a small interest rate, something like 1 percent. Whatever you get from the Vatican Bank beyond 1 percent is yours to keep."

"I don't recall asking your mother for a *loan*." Benny raised his voice.

"I was awake in the car, Uncle Benny. You said she could always get to the money through you. This deal just makes sure the one hundred million dollars is there for Gabe and me by the time we turn thirty."

Benny was furious at having a child dictate terms to him. "We'll see what your mother has to say about this!"

Michael produced a note, which Benny read to his horror.

Benny,
Michael is already nearly ten years old. In only eight short years, he will be responsible for helping me manage a large portfolio of companies and other financial interests. It is time for him to learn. I wish Daddy had taught me more about his businesses before he died. I had such a short time to learn so much. I don't want Michael ever to be caught that unaware. Therefore, I am giving him my full blessing in working up a deal with you. I'll go along with whatever agreement you two reach. Benny, thanks for helping Michael in this way.
Love,
Kim

Benny stared at the note as tears of anger and resentment filled his eyes. "This is unacceptable, Michael," he growled. "There is no need to set a specific term to the note. Also, if it's a loan, then your mother won't get the tax deduction."

"We'll survive without the tax deduction," Michael said decisively. "Besides, the alternative is probably worse."

"What's the alternative?" Benny demanded.

"For you to become a ward of the Church," Michael said slowly and deliberately.

Benny snarled at the very thought of living the life of a parish priest for the rest of his days: confessions, daily Mass, potluck dinners with Jell-O desserts! He hated that Michael understood him so well. *One day, little man, you will regret this conversation!*

"Do we have a deal?" Michael asked.

"Some deal. You are effectively banishing me." Benny pouted.

"I'm not banishing you, Uncle Benny. I'm finding a way to make your dreams come true while allowing Gabe the time he needs to become part of our family. As Mom would say, it sounds like a win-win."

"But you are forgetting the horror of this conversation, Michael. You have become a clone of your grandfather. He was horrible toward me. And now I'm afraid you will follow in his footsteps."

"There's a huge difference between Grandpa Stan and me, Uncle Benny. I love you." With that, Michael kissed his uncle's forehead and walked out of the room.

Benny had to admit that he loved the boy, even though he hated that Michael had taken the upper hand. Then a smile dawned on his face. *One hundred million dollars!* What power he could buy with that kind of money! The smile turned into a chuckle and the chuckle into a laugh as he pondered who really had the upper hand here.

TWELVE

I t was particularly hot in Uganda's capital when the Ellis family went to town. They had a full day planned. Sarah and Gloria would shop for some colorful clothes to wear in Rome. They had talked about it and thought that some of the African patterns of the region would be lovely and make just a bit of a fashion statement. Tom and Father Chris were going to pray with the family of one of the boys on Chris's soccer team. The child's family, like many others before it, was packing up to leave Kampala. Just a few days before, the Tanzanians had defeated Libyan forces sent in to help Amin. In the Battle of Lukuya, the Tanzanian 201st and 208th Brigades counterattacked the Libyan forces from the south and northwest, respectively, clearing the way for a march on Entebbe. Most knew that when and if Entebbe fell, Kampala would be next.

The ministers' plan was to spend the day in Kampala and then get to Entebbe for an evening flight to Cairo, with a connecting flight to Rome. By the time the Tanzanians made it to town, they would be out of the country. No one knew for sure if Dada planned to make a last stand or if he would flee. There were rumors that he had already left the city en route to asylum in Libya. If that was the case, then Kampala would fall quickly, with minimal bloodshed for the Ugandan citizens. Chris hoped this was how God would end the reign of the miserable despot. Enough Ugandan blood had already been spilled at that man's behest.

The entire city felt the impending approach of the Tanzanian troops. Many welcomed their arrival, since they were assisted by several anti-Amin groups comprised of Ugandan exiles known as the Ugandan National Liberation Army, or UNLA. For them, there was a feeling of expectation and a sense that the crushing reign of Amin Dada was nearing its end. For those who had benefited from Dada's reign, it was a time to reinvent themselves as his victims, creating the impression they were forced to conspire with him against their countrymen.

To the more clearheaded, those not driven by emotion or patriotism to one side or the other, the feeling was one of dread. While the reign of Amin had been harsh, the coming power vacuum would no doubt prove to be equally unsettling. Most thinking men and women did not believe that Tanzania, or the UNLA, had either sufficient wealth or sufficient patience to guide Ugandans toward a return to peaceful coexistence. Those with the ability to see just a bit over the horizon foresaw a looming civil war to follow the invasion. One with such foresight was Chris.

"You seem almost sad to see Amin go," Tom commented.

"Not at all," Chris responded, "but he has raped this country and left it bereft of a political will. These people are worse now than when they were a British colony. They don't know who they are, and they don't share a strong national identity. It's a golden opportunity for another usurper."

"What in particular are you thinking, Chris? Do you think the country will go communist?"

"No. I think ties with the Soviet Union and the Palestinians will seem too much like Amin's agenda for most Ugandans to endorse. But I do fear carpetbaggers coming into this country, promising the world but delivering only more heartache." Chris shook his head at the thought of it.

"For me it all gets back to this same serf mentality most of them have." Tom picked up the conversation. "Let's face it. These people didn't stand up for themselves. They will be liberated only as a consequence of Dada's attack on Tanzania. They still haven't seen the value of stepping up. It's like they don't value their lives or the lives of their loved ones enough to fight back." Tom's face flushed with his perpetual aggravation at the Bakopi helplessness.

"I'm afraid a group psyche isn't easily changed," Chris added. "These people were dominated by tribal lords, then occupied by the British. After only a few scant years of self-determination, they were subjugated to Amin, and now they will be occupied by Tanzania. For them, there is no endgame. They simply don't see what there is to fight for."

"But it's just so dang hopeless!" Tom spit in frustration.

The sky was a brilliant blue with large billowing white clouds as Fran and Gloria walked from the Vatican embassy house to the Nakasero market. Gloria was talking excitedly about going to Rome. And Fran was excited too, but for a different reason. All this week she had a sense of impending doom. She hoped they hadn't waited too long to get out of the country. Just a few more hours and they would be safely aboard a plane to Cairo and then on to Rome. And when it was safe to return, that tyrant, Dada, would be gone and forgotten.

Although she chatted with Gloria as if she was giving the girl her undivided attention, Fran was paying more attention to the dull fear rising within her. They were nearing the market, and she could hear none of the usual lively chatter of people shopping and bartering. Chris had said a lot of people were staying indoors or leaving town altogether, but he was sure the market would be open.

As they rounded the corner, they saw the marketplace, an outdoor line of stalls that usually housed anything an African shopper could want. Compared with Ndejje, shopping at Nakasero was like being on Fifth Avenue in New York City. Not today, however. The stalls had been overturned and their treasures looted, most likely by Dada's men taking plunder on their way out of town.

Fran stretched out her arm to prevent Gloria from going any farther. It was the first time Gloria had come out of her schoolgirl dreaming to take stock of their surroundings.

"Mom, this isn't right," she said in a hushed voice.

"No, it's not. Whoever did this, I hope they have taken what they want and have gone on their way," Frannie said softly with measured calmness. "We're going to turn around and walk like we're just two ladies out for a stroll. Come on."

They walked purposefully down the street toward the safety of the Vatican embassy. But they could hear heavy footsteps behind them. If

Fran had to guess, she would say army boots made them. If it was true that Amin's forces had taken to looting and plundering, she and Gloria could be in a world of trouble.

She grabbed Gloria's hand and picked up the pace. Her pursuers matched their new speed. Tears sprang to Fran's eyes as she began to contemplate that the most horrible things could soon happen to her little girl. She put her arm protectively around Gloria's shoulders and whisked her more briskly down the street. As she did, she stole a glance at the men behind her. There were two of them, and when she turned they offered her menacing, leering smiles.

At that moment, she heard bells ringing from an Anglican church up the block. She tightened her hold on Gloria and told her to run, inspiring their pursuers to break into an all-out run as well. Fear and panic distorted Fran's face, and Gloria broke into a wail.

From his church steps, the Anglican vicar saw the situation unfold. In his cassock, he moved swiftly down the stairs and walked purposefully toward them.

"Mrs. Appleby," he said, looking intensely at Fran, "you must hurry! We will be late if we wait much longer for you and your daughter!"

The soldiers stopped running when they saw the vicar's attention had fallen to Fran and Gloria. The vicar turned his gaze to the soldiers. "You too must hurry if you are going to be on time for my service."

The soldiers smiled politely and explained that they were on duty.

"Well, God bless you, then." The vicar smiled. "You randy bastards," he added once they had gone past.

"Ladies," he said sternly to Fran and Gloria, "a most terrible thing has almost befallen you. But the Lord has come to your rescue."

"Praise God," Fran said, smiling and crying at the same time. "I'm Fran Ellis. My husband is the Baptist preacher up in Ndejje. This is my daughter, Gloria."

"Oh, my dear, you would have been safer in Ndejje. Why in the world have you come here?"

"Our family has become friends with Father Chris at the Vatican embassy house. We're going to Rome with him tonight."

"I know of Father Chris. He's a nice young lad," he said with a twinkle in his eye. "Where are you meeting him?"

"At the embassy."

"Well, we can't have the Catholics being seen in such a favorable light by the Baptists, now can we?" He winked. "Why don't you and Gloria come in for a little bit of ritual the way it's supposed to be performed, and when I'm through, I'll drive you to the embassy."

Fran instantly liked the crotchety old vicar. He had a way about him that let him say the worst things but used just the right intonation, smirk, and twinkling of the eye to make him endearing.

"Why is the city so quiet today?" Gloria asked.

"No one knows for sure, little lady, but the assumption in the street is that Dada is pulling out. His soldiers have been looting and pillaging, taking whatever they can find for their lives in Libya."

"So Libya will grant him asylum then?" Fran asked.

"Of course. Qaddafi will welcome him with open arms. They're thick as thieves and dirty as rats, those two. Now hurry on into the church. The sooner I finish this service, the sooner I can see you two safely to the embassy. I'm Vicar John Ellsworth, by the way. You can just call me Vicar if you like."

They went into the church, relaxed in a pew, and thanked the Lord for their deliverance. But the anxiety didn't go away. Fran couldn't wait to get her family away from the Ugandan society that was unraveling before her eyes.

The guys walked on in the contented silence that often happens between good friends. But the silence soon gave way to uneasiness in both of them. The city streets were emptying fast, and they had never experienced this kind of hush in Kampala.

"I've got to tell you, Tom, this silence has me more than a little bit concerned," Chris said, rubbing his arms against a sudden chill.

"Do you figure most people have cleared out of the city?" Tom asked, suddenly uneasy with the solitude now that Chris had brought it to his attention.

"No," Chris said. "I've seen more than a few people ducking back into their houses when they hear us coming down the street."

"What do you think it is then? Surely the Tanzanians haven't gotten here so quickly."

"No. I'm guessing it means Dada is evacuating the city," Chris said as he slapped Tom's arm and pointed to the house on his right where the curtains were swaying from the inhabitant who had just been watching them.

"You'd think people would be running in the streets, dancing, and jumping up and down!" Tom exclaimed.

"I think there is a general fear he won't leave his capital in a state of good repair for his enemies. If he follows a scorched Earth policy, it could be really bad for the people of the city. What do you say we turn around and try to find that wife and daughter of yours?"

"Sure. If you think it's best," Tom answered. "I'm for anything that will make Fran and Gloria shop faster."

"I think Entebbe will be a lot safer," Chris said. "We'd be better off waiting in the airport. Turn left here. This street should lead us to the market." Chris sighed with relief. Soon they would all be safely on a plane to Rome together.

"You know, I was going to save this for the plane, but since we have the time, I thought I'd spring it on you now," Chris said with a smile.

"Oh, man, Chris," Tom replied in anticipation, "you've been so good to us already. What could you possibly have for me?"

"Nothing. I was just going to tell you about a story I read a while back. It seems some historians believe Davy Crockett tried to escape Santa Anna by dressing up as a woman, and—"

"I didn't hear that," Tom quipped, his Texas showing.

"I said," Chris yelled, "Davy Crockett dressed like a woman. Some people say he liked it!"

At that Chris smiled broadly and started to run down the street at a leisurely pace, knowing Tom would surely mow him down for denigrating Saint Davy of Crockett. He picked up the pace when he heard Tom coming after him. Tom was built like a bull, but he was definitely not light on his feet, whereas Chris had always loved running. The breeze blew his longish hair off his face. His breathing settled into a nice rhythm, and he was off to another place. Running always made him high as he heard the lovely syncopation of his beating heart against the thud of his feet hitting the pavement.

"Heyyyy!" he heard a bloodcurdling roar from Tom. He looked back to see Tom was nearly on top of him. But to his consternation,

Tom passed him by. It dawned on Chris that Tom was reacting to something ahead of them.

He looked and there it was. How could he not have seen it before? An army jeep with a flamethrower was parked near the entrance of an alley. Its soldiers were clearly ravaging a young girl. Two were holding her arms while one was on top of her. Tom was far ahead of him, but as Chris got closer, he could see the terror in the girl's eyes. Then it seemed as if everything moved in slow motion.

In one mad leap, Tom knocked the soldier off the girl and managed to topple the two holding her.

"Run!" Chris screamed to the girl as he approached. *"Na-kimbea! Na-kimbea!"*

The girl jumped up and ran down the street. One serviceman turned to follow her but stopped short when he saw Chris's collar, an embarrassed expression on his face.

"You are from my parish!" Chris exclaimed in disgust to the soldier. Before the soldier could offer an explanation, they were riveted by the sound of a bullet. Chris looked up and saw his friend Tom on the ground, his shattered head bleeding profusely.

Chris fell to his knees next to Tom. The blood was everywhere. He took Tom's damaged head onto his lap, as if holding it together could somehow quell the bleeding.

"Chris," Tom murmured, "I can see Jesus. He's calling me home."

Chris tried to respond, but only tears would come.

"Chris. Chris?" Tom pleaded.

"Yeah, Tex, I'm here. I'm here with you, buddy," Chris said. His voice cracked.

"You have to get Frannie and Gloria out of the country. Back to the States."

"Sure, Tom, but let's get you some help first," Chris said softly, although he doubted his friend would make it.

"No help. Jesus is here for me, and I want to go. It's what we all live for. You just tell Frannie and Gloria that I love them more than anything in the whole world."

"I sure will," Chris said, wiping the tears from his face and inadvertently smearing himself with Tom's blood.

"Chris. Chris?"

"Right here, buddy." Chris swept away the blood-soaked curls that had fallen to Tom's face and looked into his eyes.

"I love you too, friend."

"And I love you, Tex," Chris said softly through tears.

"Before Jesus takes me, I'm supposed to tell you something. He says for you to go to Rome and stand up for His name in these Latter Days." Tom offered one last wry smile to his friend. "Did you hear that? It really is the Latter Days ..."

Tom died in his friend's arms. Chris began to pray over his body, vaguely aware of the argument forming among the three soldiers. The rapist wanted to kill Chris as well. He saw no need to leave a trail. At some point he wanted to come back to Uganda and didn't want to take the chance of being seen as a criminal. The soldier who was in Chris's parish was adamant Chris was a good man and shouldn't be killed. The third was convinced that killing a priest would bring very bad luck for the remainder of his days. In the long run, they met a compromise of sorts.

The rapist pulled Chris from Tom's body, throwing him into the side of a building. The other two held him there while the rapist hit him repeatedly in the face and stomach. Chris's head throbbed both from the punches themselves and from the back of his head striking the building each time he was hit. The blows to the stomach winded him, and the other two let him go. As Chris crouched to get his breath, blood pouring from his already-swelling, broken nose, the rapist said to him, "You tell nobody, Father, and you will live. If you tell, I will find you and kill you."

Chris grabbed the man's head and pulled it down to his level. He wanted to kill the young man. He wanted to beat him senseless. Instead, he gave himself over to his Lord and did what he had been taught to do, what he had always hoped he would do in such a situation. With his own blood, he made the sign of the cross on the man's forehead and said, "I forgive you. Jesus forgives you. Go in peace."

The man stared at Chris, not knowing what to make of the pronouncement. It immobilized him for a moment. But then he hit Chris across the face with the butt of his pistol, knocking him to the ground. He joined his comrades in the jeep as they used the flamethrower to incinerate Tom's body. Chris stayed down to resist enraging them further and prayed in the Spirit as the sickening smell of burning flesh encompassed him. As the jeep was pulling away, he looked up to see the rapist in tears, trying to wipe the cross of blood from his face. "Praise God," Chris said as he passed out next to the smoldering carcass.

"Chris! Chris! Get Frannie and Gloria out of the country. Back to the States. Jesus says to go to Rome and stand up for His name in these Latter Days ..."

Chris awakened to the memory of Tom's last words. He picked up his head and reeled from the pain. He squinted to see that the sun had moved in the sky and guessed he had been out for about an hour.

Crack! A gunshot reverberated nearby. He pushed himself to his feet as panic began to set in. He had to get to Fran and Gloria. He blessed the charred remains of his friend, stumbled to the street, and began to run toward the Nakasero market. Every step sent shrieks of pain through his swollen face and head.

He began to pray in the Spirit as his mind pleaded with the Lord to keep Fran and Gloria safe until he could find them. The prayer took his mind off the jarring pain in his head, and he began to breathe rhythmically, as if he were on a pleasure run. Propelling himself down the street, he fought back tears at the thought of having to tell them what had happened to their beloved husband and father. He began to chastise himself for not having had a better read on the city. They should have left the country days before. If they had, Tom would still be alive. His eyes stung with hot tears as he ran blindly toward the market.

The peacefulness of the Anglican ritual enveloped Fran and put to rest the panic that had filled her earlier. As she praised the Lord for their deliverance, a strange sensation overcame her. It was as if everything around her was bathed in a golden light, and she experienced the tangible touch of His warmth and love for her. As she drank deeply of this experience, her mouth began to praise the Lord in a language she had never heard. *So this is the Baptism in the Holy Spirit Chris was talking about,* she mused. Just as she thought this, her mind sensed a message that had been planted there by her Lord.

My daughter, you are in a time of trial. Your husband has joined Me, but you must remain on Earth to tend to your daughter. Guard her and be strong, for I am with you, even to the end of the age.

She was filled with mixed emotions. The thoughts were so real, and they hadn't come from her own mind. At once she was in awe that the Lord of Hosts would speak to her, but she was grief-stricken at the message. She searched her heart, and somehow she knew it was true. Tom was now in Heaven, and she had to protect Gloria. She couldn't hold back the tears as she drew her daughter close.

Gloria cried softly as her mother held her. She whispered, "Mom, I don't know how I know it, but I have this strong feeling Daddy died."

"I know," Fran managed to whisper. "I feel it too." For the rest of the service, Fran held her daughter, silently prayed in her new prayer language, and allowed the Lord to strengthen her for what was to come.

The service ended, and the few Ugandans who had braved the streets to find solace in the Lord filed out of the church for their worrisome walks home.

The vicar exited the sacristy in a long cassock. He was all business, as if he was on a mission from the Lord Himself.

"Come, ladies. Let's see if we can't get you to the embassy before anything else untoward happens today. It will be a great blessing to Kampala when this day finally passes."

He led them behind the church to an old Ford Fairlane Thunderbolt. It clearly had been red at one time, but years in the sun and endless patching of rusted spots had left it a tannish-pink color.

"She's not much to look at, ladies," the vicar intoned, "but she's fast and sturdy as a truck. She'll get us where we need to go."

They silently entered the car, heartsick with the sense that their fears would soon be confirmed.

———

Chris ran blindly toward the market to find Fran and Gloria. He had no idea how long he had been running. His mind had undergone a strange disconnect from his body. He knew his head hurt terribly, but the pain had been masked by his panic-stricken need to run. As he ran he prayed continually. *Help me find them, Lord. Help me find them safe and sound.*

The sound of his feet hitting the pavement and his unending prayer broke the uncomfortable silence of a city in hiding. By the time he reached the market square, he had long since stopped looking for traffic, running through empty intersections unconcerned by the possibility of either human or automotive intervention. He heard the squeal of tires too late for him to stop for the oncoming car. It screeched to a stop inches from him, and he fell exhausted onto the hood.

"Father in Heaven!" the vicar screamed as he saw the bloodied priest on the hood of his car. He threw the vehicle into park and jumped out of the car just as Chris was finding his way off the hood.

Chris heard Fran shriek his name from the passenger seat. He thanked God for leading him to them as Fran fell out of the car in loud tears, followed by Gloria.

"Fran, Gloria!" Chris gasped. "Thank God you're all right." His bruised face carried a serious demeanor, and his hair, matted with blood, fell forward as he looked down at them.

"They killed Tom," he said with breathless grief. "It happened so fast. One minute we were goofing around, and the next Tom stopped a rape in progress and was shot in the head." Chris was crying with the women now. "He saw Jesus, Fran. Jesus came to get your daddy, Gloria. He's in Heaven now. Before he died, he told me to get you two to America and to tell you he loves you more than anything in the world."

He fell silent as they pressed against his bloodstained cassock. The three of them clung to each other and cried for a few moments.

"Where, where is his body?" Fran asked, choking back sobs.

"The soldiers torched it with a flamethrower, Fran. We have nothing to take home with us." She reeled from the shock of it, but when she opened her mouth, only her prayer language came forth. Chris saw what was happening to her. He placed one hand on her shoulder, prayed with her, and allowed the Lord to renew their strength.

Fran straightened up, wiped her eyes, and said, "Tom is right. We have to get out of here. Chris, Vicar John helped us out of trouble and was driving us back to the embassy."

Chris extended his hand. "I don't believe I know you," he said to the vicar.

"But I have heard of you, young priest. All good things. Hop in the car. No need for us to attract the attention of Amin's men."

Chris winced as he lowered himself into the front passenger seat. Fran got in the back, where she cradled her crying daughter.

"You're too banged up to drive to Entebbe, Padre," the vicar said in a voice that was just a bit too loud for Chris's sore head.

"I'll do whatever it takes to get them out of the country," Chris said with fierce determination.

"Well, relax. I'll drive you to Entebbe."

Chris looked at the old vicar and began to decline the offer.

"Don't judge a book by its cover, Padre. I'm one tough old cleric. I wouldn't offer anything I couldn't deliver."

"I'm afraid I don't have much choice but to take you up on your kind offer," Chris said, attempting a smile that moved him to instant pain.

"Wise decision," said the vicar. "I think you're more banged up than you realize." He flipped down the passenger sun visor to reveal a mirror on the back. Chris got a good look at himself. His left cheek had swollen to a red bump that was the size of a softball. It was probably broken. His nose was swollen to twice its size, and the once-handsome blue eyes were hidden in swelling bruises. He touched his blood-caked hair as he looked at the monstrous image staring back at him.

"Chris," Fran said from the backseat, "you need a doctor."

"Impossible," said the vicar. "It will have to wait until you touch ground in Rome. This country is falling down around us."

"He's right," confirmed Chris, slamming the visor back into place. "We have to get to the airport now."

"Where are your passports and tickets?" the vicar asked.

"At the embassy, with our luggage."

"Right-oh," said the vicar as he pushed the Fairlane to the limit and sped down the deserted streets to the embassy. Once there, the three moved with deliberate calm in getting their luggage and travel documents. Fran insisted on bringing Tom's suitcase. It was all of him that she would be able to bring out of the country. Fear and survival instinct had taken over them. They were all making the right decisions and in record time. The vicar loaded the suitcases as Chris came out of the embassy with some aspirin and a glass of water.

"I wouldn't do that if I were you, son," the vicar said to him.

"My head is killing me. I thought this might take the edge off," Chris replied. Even saying the words brought him pain.

"If you're bleeding up there," the vicar said, pointing to his head, "you don't want to be thinning out your blood."

"I see," Chris said. "Do you really think there is a chance of a brain bleed?"

"I'm not a doctor, but you don't look too good to me. Why take any more chances?"

"Fine," Chris said more tersely than he intended.

"I'll tell you what," said the vicar. "Come over here."

When Chris was within reach, the vicar gingerly placed his hand on the back of Chris's head. Bowing his own head, he said, "Lord of Hosts, You are perfect in wisdom. Only You know why You allowed the events of today to transpire, and we praise You for Your wisdom and for keeping these children in the center of Your will. You know the plan you have for this young servant. Please give him relief from his pain so that he can properly guide these girls to safety and take up the role You have prepared for him in Rome."

Immediately, the pain diminished, and if Chris was not mistaken, it seemed like the old vicar had a golden glow about him.

"All right, then, Padre," the vicar said, "get in the car. Your charges are waiting for us!"

Chris got in the car a bit perplexed. He hadn't told them of Tom's message from the Lord about going to Rome. How could the vicar have tapped into that knowledge? *The ways of the Lord truly are remarkable,* he thought. Without even realizing it, this rusty old vicar had prophesied his future.

Chris was certainly happy for the break in the pain, especially as the vicar sped the twenty miles to Entebbe. The old fellow may have prayed like an angel, but he drove like a demon. At first it wasn't so bad because the streets were relatively deserted. However, he chose to avoid the main roads around Lake Victoria, for fear they would run into Amin's retreating army. Mud puddles populated the narrow dirt paths through which he pushed the old Ford. No sane person would drive this quickly under such horrid conditions. All the while, the vicar kept looking out his side window at something on the horizon.

"What are you looking at?" Chris yelled over the roaring and banging of the car.

"See that little bit of smoke over my shoulder there?" the vicar asked.

"Yeah."

"That's the front. The Tanzanians are closer to Entebbe than I thought. I need to get you on the next plane to Cairo ... and fast. You can wait it out there for your connection to Rome."

Coming around a bend, he threw on the brakes, sending the occupants of the car flying. There in the path ahead of them was an oxcart. Once his passengers found their seats again, he beeped and waved at its driver and then proceeded to carve out a path in the grasslands around the cart.

"Is everyone okay?" Chris called out to the backseat. Both Fran and Gloria nodded, but words failed them. The rest of the ride was without incident until they got to the airport.

"Pull out your Vatican papers, Padre. Have them ready. There are lots of rats deserting this ship ... present company excluded. I'm talking about Dada's cronies." The airport was in a state of confusion, as many of the higher-classed people, previously favored by the Amin regime, decided to leave ahead of the advancing army.

Chris found his papers as the vicar drove around a line of cars to the airport gates. It was as if the passengers of the other cars hadn't seen the Fairlane pass them by. The vicar lowered his window and shoved the Vatican papers toward the guard.

"This is Vatican business, son. And it's a medical emergency. Look at my buddy here." Chris waved weakly to the guard.

"Here's what I want you to do," said the vicar. "Show me the fastest way to drive up to the next plane to Cairo. Then I want you to call ahead and tell them you have a State Department emergency and three will be on that flight under Vatican diplomatic papers." The request was ludicrous. Chris almost burst out laughing when he heard it. Yet, to his amazement, the guard repeated the orders, as if they had come from Amin himself.

"Sir, you will follow me," he said to the vicar. The guard then got another soldier to replace him at the gate and escorted the vicar's car to the tarmac, where a plane to Cairo was about to board.

The guard went aboard the plane to explain to the pilot he had a diplomatic emergency.

"This ought to be good," Chris said to Fran. "It's one thing to pull the wool over the eyes of a guard, but it's another to get the pilot to buy into this ..." He hadn't finished speaking when a stewardess hurried down the stairs to greet them. Within seconds their suitcases were out of the car, headed into the plane.

"Can you walk, sir?" the stewardess asked Chris.

"Yes," Chris said, looking over at the vicar in amazement, "but thank you for offering assistance."

"Vicar, I don't know how to thank you," Chris said.

"You just do what the Lord has called you to do. That's all I want," said the crusty old saint in a fatherly tone.

"Thank you, Vicar," Fran said. "You've saved our lives twice today."

The vicar responded by pulling Fran and Gloria close and saying, "Lord of Hosts, look with favor on these your servants who have suffered great loss this day. Protect and guide them in the days to come, and may they prosper and grow strong in your Word as they return to the United States."

All three said, "Amen."

"Now get on the plane, the lot of you," the vicar said. "Can't you see I'm illegally parked?"

As they headed up the stairs, first Chris and then the others turned to wave good-bye to their new friend. He was gone. Surely they would have heard the old Fairlane roaring away.

"Chris?" Fran asked in amazement. "Do you believe angels come to the aid of God's children even in this day and age?"

"I'm beginning to," Chris said in amazement.

The three were given first-class seats and first-class attention on the flight to Cairo. The pilot called ahead to clear their way on an earlier flight to Rome. As they got to the first-class section of the Alitalia flight, their stewardess greeted them warmly with hot food and extra pillows for Chris's head. At last they all felt a sense of relief, and their battered nerves gave way to troubled sleep.

THIRTEEN

The sun had risen and the Alitalia flight would soon begin its decent into Fiumicino Airport. The light pierced through his aching head as the stewardess reached past him to open the window shade.

"It's time to wake up, Father," she called sweetly to the priest. "We'll be having a breakfast service before we land." He reached up to rub his throbbing temple, wishing this past day hadn't happened. Benny still found it hard to believe he had to fly all the way to the United States to get the signed contracts for the $100 million loan. The least Kimberly could have done would have been to fly to Rome with her attorney. But, no, selfish to the last, she demanded he go to Georgia because she didn't want to leave the boys. Already those boys were a royal pain in his side.

"I'll take some coffee," he said weakly to the stewardess as he moaned and placed his seat in an upright position. From Rome to Atlanta and back in the course of thirty-six hours was just not civilized—he didn't care how much wine the stewardess could pour. Speaking of which, the wine must have been some inferior blend Alitalia had bought on the cheap. It shouldn't have left him with such a hangover.

"I guess all's well that ends well," he reassured himself. The reward would be well worth the effort. Since his move to Rome six weeks before, Benny had been shown the ropes by Cardinal Bilbo. In fact, Bilbo treated him like a protégé.

"It is important that you seek out the future church leaders," Bilbo had explained. "We are not many, but we are mighty. We have secured most positions of power in the Curia, and our hope is that one day we will have a pope from among our ranks."

"And how am I to understand who these leaders are, Eminence?" Benny had asked intently.

"I will introduce you to most of them. There is a lodge in the hills outside Rome where we meet to plan the future. We are not content with a Church stuck in the Middle Ages."

"I share your sentiments, Eminence, but how do we wean the faithful from their Christ-centered narrow-mindedness? They think they need a savior."

"They think they need something otherworldly," he corrected. "And that is how we bring them into the future, my friend. We have to begin to extol the wonder of mankind, its unique status on Earth, and its communion with other beings in the universe. Trust me, it will not be easy."

"It wasn't easy when Galileo tried to tell them the Earth wasn't the center of the solar system either," Benny mentioned, "and it has taken the better part of four centuries for the Church to admit he was right. I don't want to sound impatient, Eminence, but I don't want to wait four centuries for a more universal spiritual understanding."

Bilbo smiled broadly. "Neither do I, my friend. Neither do I. But we play a different role in this century. We will not resist the change; rather, we will be the ones to lead it. Gone are the days when we cling to our ancient ritual in defiance of scientific facts that confront us."

"One could only hope, Eminence."

"Father, there have been many interesting scientific insights lately in the realm of quantum physics. Scientists have now actually proven our thoughts influence the state of a photon. Can you imagine it? We can control creation at its most fundamental levels. Here, I brought you some papers on the matter. It is all that our members talk of."

Benny looked distractedly at the thick stack of scientific papers handed to him. *If I wanted homework, I would have taken a class.*

"The key insight here, Father, is that the most recent scientific findings validate a host of spiritual teachings that were common among mankind in the pre-Christian era. The mystery religions of the past will bring us into a glorious future. Our task is merely to direct the minds of our sheep to the power of their own inner light."

The stewardesses had cleared the breakfast service and were now announcing the final descent into Fiumicino. Benny stared out the window at the Italian countryside. He had lived in Rome for only six weeks, but it felt like he was coming home. He felt as if he had been born to live in the Eternal City, and he offered a contented sigh as the wheels touched the ground.

As the plane taxied to its gate, he gazed down at the scientific literature from Cardinal Bilbo. He had planned to read it on the plane, but the wine and the movie had taken his interest. He chucked it under the seat. *Oh, well, I guess I must have lost it.*

With a smile, he exited the Jetway, where the cardinal's driver greeted him and took his carry-on luggage. "*Grazie,* Giaccomo," he said to the burly Italian, who looked to be about one-quarter driver and three-quarters Mafia hit man. Giaccomo grunted, "*Niente,*" and walked to the luggage carousel at a pace Benny found difficult to match.

Benny was out of breath and fanning himself by the time he caught up with Giaccomo at the luggage carousel. As Giaccomo shouldered his way into the crowd, Benny's attention was taken by the scene transpiring before him. Men in dark suits, who looked for all the world to be secret servicemen, were wheeling a gurney through the airport. On the gurney was a man who looked like he had gone ten rounds with Ali. Beside the gurney were a woman and young girl, who Benny assumed to be the wife and child of the man.

As he watched, one of the secret servicemen came to him and, looking at Benny's collar, asked in Italian, "*Signore, parle Inglese?*"

"*Sí,*" Benny answered. The serviceman showed his ID. He worked for the Vatican. In Italian, he asked Benny to calm the family, explain they were from the Vatican and had been ordered to get this man to the hospital for urgent care.

"Excuse me, Mrs. ..."

"Ellis," Frannie said.

"Don't be afraid to go with these men. They have been instructed to take your husband immediately to the hospital. What happened to him?"

"He's not my husband," Fran replied, her voice quivering, as if even saying the word "husband" brought a painful rush of emotion to the surface.

At the conversation, Chris stirred. "Father," he called out weakly.

Benny bent down to him and saw that the man was in a cassock.

"How may I be of assistance, Father?" Benny asked, cringing at the swollen face.

"You must take care of this woman and her daughter. Her husband asked me to get them to the United States before he died."

"Of course, Father. Now be still and go to the hospital."

Benny told the servicemen they were to place the woman and child on a plane to the United States—a destination of their choosing. They acknowledged their orders had been as much.

"It has all been arranged," Benny said, staring down at Chris. While one eye was swollen shut, the other shone crystal blue and shed a tear as he grabbed Benny's hand to thank him.

"Bless you, son," Benny said emotionally. Something about this young priest had gotten to him. There was gentleness in him and a silent strength that moved Benny. The servicemen quickly resumed their march to the waiting ambulance as Benny looked on.

"*Don* Benito," Giaccomo grunted behind him, "*ecco i baggagli. Il Cardinale aspetta.*"

"*Sí,*" Benny said distractedly as he followed Giaccomo to the car. "*Il Cardinale aspetta.*"

Giaccomo opened the back door of the limousine to reveal Cardinal Bilbo enjoying a glass of wine.

"Eminence," Benny said as he bowed slightly, waiting to be invited into the car.

"*Don Benito, venga.*" Benny crawled into the limo, a huge grin on his face.

"Can I assume from your smile that your mission was successful?"

"Ah, Eminence, let's just say you have one hundred million reasons to like me today." Benny fairly burst with self-pride.

"*Sí, Don Benito,*" the cardinal said with a wry smile, "*ma domani?*"

Benny bristled. The question "But tomorrow?" was loaded with implications. Surely this surly old dago didn't think he would be able to come up with millions of dollars every day!

"Now, now," the cardinal chided, "don't get agitated with an old man having a bit of fun with you. We are well pleased with the wealth you have managed to bring to our aid. So much, in fact, I have a glorious surprise for you."

Suddenly Benny looked like a child going to the ice cream store. "Oh, Cardinal, do tell me!" he said with a nervous giggle.

"I am taking you to meet one of the most powerful men in the world, if not *the* most powerful."

"How wonderful." Benny smiled, not having the slightest idea of whom the cardinal was speaking.

There was an awkward silence that Bilbo broke with a fit of laughter. "Don't you want to know who it is?" he asked with a grin.

"Yes, Eminence," Benny said. "To be honest, I haven't the slightest idea who you mean."

"That is because he works almost exclusively behind the scenes. But trust me, his hand is in every major development on the planet, and he is the mastermind behind the coming New World Order. His name is Luciano Begliali."

The car whisked them from the Eternal City. As it rounded a bend in the road, Benny finally got a glimpse of the estate rising out of the vineyards that surrounded it. The mansion would more suitably be called a palace, as it had many of the classical design elements of a fairy-tale castle, complete with turrets and a huge iron gate that opened automatically to allow the car into an enclosed garden.

"It's just so beautiful!" Benny said in earnest. "I feel like I'm in a fairy tale."

"It was once a castle in the Middle Ages, but don't let its appearance fool you. Luciano has outfitted it with every modern convenience."

The car worked its way around the exquisitely manicured garden to the living quarters on the other side. Beside an open, immense oak door, a man in a morning coat stood by ceremoniously.

"*Cardinale,*" he said in a crisp formal manner. "*Benvenuto.*"

"*Grazie, Anunziatto.*"

"Welcome," Anunziatto said to Benny.

"Oh, yes," Bilbo said, "Anunziatto, this is Father Cross."

"Of course. *Signore* Begliali is expecting you."

They were led through a foyer that had been paneled in rare, light-green marble found only in Italy. The foyer was a large space, and in its center stood a huge round table made of inlaid woods, designed to look like slices of a pie radiating from the center. Prisms of light that shone through second-story lead glass windows illuminated the entire foyer.

As they passed the table, Bilbo whispered to Benny, "It is supposedly a replica of King Arthur's round table."

"I didn't know he was a real historical figure," Benny commented.

"Scholars debate it, but Luciano tells me Arthur did exist. Luciano is filled with ancient knowledge and wisdom."

Good God, Benny thought, *Bilbo must be going on ninety. What could this Luciano be like if Bilbo described him as having ancient knowledge and wisdom!*

They followed Anunziatto to a library room with no windows. Each wall was filled with floor-to-ceiling mahogany bookcases containing thousands of leather-bound books. Sconces at the intersection of each set of bookcases bore frosted peach-colored glass that bathed the room in a golden light. Sitting behind an ornate, kidney-shaped mahogany desk was a tall executive chair dressed in gold suede. It was turned with its back toward the door, its occupant working at a credenza behind the monstrous desk.

As Anunziatto announced their presence, he turned in the chair to greet them. Benny nearly gasped. He had never in his life imagined that such a handsome man could exist. His black hair was worn straight back off his face. Prominent cheekbones accentuated large gray eyes with lashes that any woman would kill to have. Perfect lips parted to reveal perfect teeth that glistened next to his swarthy complexion. Anunziatto closed the doors behind him as he left the room.

"Ah, *Cardinale*, what a pleasure," Luciano said as he offered his hand to Bilbo. "And this must be our very own Father Cross." He smiled. As he took Benny's hand, Benny felt a surge of energy pour through him.

"And how is your most generous sister, may I ask?" Luciano questioned, still holding Benny's hand and leading him to a gold brocade-tufted couch.

"She's doing very well, *Signore*." Benny's voice cracked. Luciano was looking at him with those piercing eyes, and Benny heard a voice in his head. *Relax, my pet. Let yourself go. Be free to love me. I am the lover of your soul.*

Benny pulled his hand away. "Well, she is very busy with two young sons. They consume all of her time, it seems." He was trying to calm himself. He felt like he was going crazy. Why would he have such a reaction to this man?

"Ah, that's beautiful," Luciano said as he patted Benny's knee. As his hand touched Benny, he heard it again. *You are not imagining it, dear Benito. You were born to love me with unbridled devotion.*

He knows he's doing this to me, Benny thought, panic-stricken. But beneath the fear, rising from the core of his being, Benny could feel a longing for this man. He wanted nothing more than to please him, to gain his favor. It was the closest thing Benny had ever felt to religious fervor.

"We must make sure she and her sons come to Italy one day. Two young boys would love to play in a real castle, no?"

"Absolutely," Benny agreed. At that point Anunziatto entered the room with a carafe of red wine and hot, freshly baked rolls.

"Ah, bene, Anunziatto," Begliali said.

"You gentlemen must try this wine. We make it here ourselves."

Addressing Bilbo's grimace, Begliali said, "I know, *Cardinale*, it is not yet noon, but time is all mixed up for our distinguished guest, and frankly I have found that one glass of wine with a bit of fresh bread makes for me the perfect midmorning snack."

Anunziatto poured three glasses of wine and plated the hot rolls, each with a dollop of fresh whipped butter.

"Please, gentlemen, you must try this. I honestly believe I have hired the best baker in all of Italy."

No one ever had to ask Benny twice to eat. He cut open the steamy roll. Its hard crust gave way to a delicate white center that melted the butter on contact. As he placed it in his mouth, he thought Luciano must be right. This was the most wonderful piece of bread he had ever eaten. He smiled blissfully.

"Huh? What did I tell you?" Luciano said, patting him on the shoulder. As they touched, Benny heard the voice in his head again. *This is my body, Benito. Eat it so that we may become as one.*

A chill went up Benny's spine, and he gasped, choking on a small piece of the bread. Luciano grabbed Benny's wine glass and thrust it at him. Bilbo looked on in horror and disgust at the uncouth American.

"Drink this, Father. It will help."

Benny took the cup as he heard in his mind, *And my blood, dear one.*

"*Signore* Begliali?" Benny asked breathlessly. "Can you show me to a bathroom?"

"Ugh!" Bilbo said aloud.

Begliali smiled and pushed a button. Immediately Anunziatto entered the room.

"Anunziatto, would you be so kind as to show Father Cross to the facilities?"

"Yes, sir," Anunziatto said, turning sharply on his heels. "Follow me, sir," he said to Benny, who dutifully followed him out of the room.

As Benny left the room, Cardinal Bilbo rushed to distinguish himself from the crass American. "*Signore*, I feel I must apologize for this American priest. He is not yet accustomed to the civility of the Vatican, but we will work with him."

"Nonsense!" Begliali smiled. "I quite like him."

Something about the way Begliali said it felt threatening to Bilbo.

"That's very kind of you, *Signore*, but—"

"No. You misunderstand me, *Cardinale*. I am not being kind. I have looked for one such as him for a long time. This man does not have enough of a conscience to know that he has no conscience. He will serve me wonderfully."

"But, *Signore*," the old cardinal said, wringing his hands, "he is young and has no experience." Bilbo had visions of a future having to work with this oaf in Luciano's employ.

"He is fresh, Bilbo," Luciano said. Using only his surname was a sign of disrespect. "I tire of the old Vatican flatulence. Like Pope John, I want fresh air."

"Of course, *Signore*, as you wish. I want only to please you," the cardinal said with a sickening smile. Inside he was enraged to think he had given so much of himself to Luciano over the years, only to be called flatulence. The indignity was too great for a prince of the Church to have to bear.

"If that is true, my friend, perhaps you could grant me one small favor."

"Absolutely, *Signore*."

"Be so kind as to show yourself to your car. I wish a moment alone with this American."

Bilbo's naturally ashen face turned a lighter shade of pale as he stood abruptly.

"I will take my leave then, *Signore.*" He felt a strong need to apologize or find some other way to regain Begliali's favor, but no words came.

As Bilbo entered the foyer, he paused for a second to get his balance. The meeting had shaken him. He placed his right hand on the round table for a second and took a deep breath. The pause was long enough to allow him to hear Luciano warmly greet Benny.

"*Scuzi, Cardinale,*" Anunziatto said briskly, motioning to Bilbo's hand resting on the table.

"Oh." Bilbo tried to emulate the smile of a kindly old man. "*Pardone.*"

Anunziatto ignored the response and went straight to the table with a white cloth to shine the place where Bilbo's hand had been.

Behind him, he heard the entirety of Luciano's conversation.

"Ah, *Don Benito*, I trust you are well."

"Yes," Benny said warily.

"Good." Luciano beamed. "You must come to see me again very soon. Let's make my castle your home away from home."

Bilbo grunted as if physically hurt by the comment, but he had no time to think about it. For, as he was opening the door to leave, he heard Luciano speaking more softly.

"Tell me, *Don Benito*, what is your opinion of the dear cardinal? I fear he can no longer handle my workload at his advanced age. Perhaps I have placed too much of a burden on him. And, of course, there is always the question of his ongoing loyalty. Do you think he is no longer the right man to do my bidding in the Vatican?"

"*Signore,* I can honestly tell you that today Cardinal Bilbo is the most loyal and efficient person you could have working for you."

Bilbo breathed a sigh of relief. *Good old Benny!*

Benny looked Luciano squarely in the eye and said loud enough for the cardinal to hear, "*Ma domani?*"

Chris awoke in the hospital. He had slept badly the night before. Over and over again he relived Tom's death in his dreams—over and over seeing the abysmal pain in Fran's and Gloria's faces.

His head felt huge. They had him on a lot of drugs that made him a bit fuzzy. To the best of his understanding and his rusty Italian, the doctor said he had a broken cheekbone, a broken nose, and a nasty concussion, not to mention a few broken ribs. Either the drugs or the concussion left him a touch nauseous, as well as sensitive to light and sound. In the hallway, he heard loud singing, sort of a false operatic "That's Amore."

"When the moon hits your eye. Oh, hi, doll. *Ah, que bella facia!*" Then there was a loud kissing sound.

The noise was directly outside the door to his room, which, much to Chris's surprise, swung open with a thud to reveal a small monk. Judging by the black robe and three knots in the rope around his waist, Chris guessed the old fellow was a Franciscan. He was all of five feet five inches tall with a little wisp of gray hair standing on end in the center of his head. His eyes glowed with happiness, and there was a grin on his face.

"Ah, look at you. The hero awakes!"

"What?" Chris asked.

"Listen, the Vatican's a small place. Everybody hears everything. And the word is that you're some kind of hero who went ten rounds with Idi a-Meany!"

Chris began to laugh and then winced with a bit of pain.

"I'm Vinnie Gugliamici from Hoboken, New Jersey. Glad ta meet ya, champ," Vinnie said as he held out his hand to Chris.

Chris shook his hand and said, "I'm—"

"Yeah, yeah, I know. Christian Altenbrook. It's a German name, but what the hell, we're all friends now."

"I'm American," Chris said with a smirk.

"I know. That's why I'm here. You wanna know what my job is? I'm the Vatican mucker. Whenever they want something done that doesn't involve pomp, circumstance, and a fancy dinner, they call me. That's what I do. I shovel Vatican doo-doo. And today, you're the doo-doo I'm shoveling. They sent me over here to make sure you're comfortable, maybe help you with the language a little bit, you know, make you feel loved and special."

"Thanks, Father," Chris began.

"You just call me Vinnie. I'm your friend, and trust me, they don't come easy in the Vatican!" Vinnie leaned over the bed to get a closer look at Chris's injuries.

"Thanks, Vinnie, but I'm afraid I won't be very good company," Chris said, waving him away.

"Don't worry about it! I'm a Franciscan ... vow of poverty ... we're beggars, and you know what they say about beggars—they can't be choosers."

Chris recognized defeat. Whether he liked it or not, he would have a companion for the day. The more he thought about it though, he realized it just might be the best medicine. "So tell me," he said, "what else do you do besides muck?"

"Glad you asked. I bring Jesus into the hearts of the poor. I have a simple routine I follow every day. I get up early and make, say, twenty-five, maybe thirty, sandwiches. Then I wander around Rome. The poor people know me. They know I don't want to criticize or look down on them. I just want to help. So I feed them, and then we start to talk, and I explain to them they're more loved than they could ever imagine. That the Creator of this universe sent His only Son to pay for their sins and restore them to the Father.

"Then they'll look at me and say, 'But how do you really know this?' And I say to them, 'Do you think I'd get up at five in the morning to make sandwiches and then tramp all over Rome if I didn't know Jesus loved you more than life itself? I got gout, you know.'"

Chris chuckled. He found himself really enjoying this man. "Does it work?" he asked.

Chris expected a loud, boisterous response. Instead, Vinnie's voice grew quiet and serious. "It does, my friend. The Gospel was made for the streets. It's meant to echo in the hearts of men and women, not bounce off the walls of cathedrals." He accentuated his speech with rhythmic tapping on Chris's arm, a little close to the IV needle in Chris's estimation. "If it were up to me, all church services would be on the streets and all of the collection money would be used to meet the needs of the poor. Then we would really see a world won for Christ. A few less Augustines and many more Francises would suit me just fine."

Chris gently stopped Vinnie's tapping hand. "I know what you mean. The people in Africa have so little in terms of worldly possessions. But when they come into a relationship with Jesus, it's like they won the lottery. I loved pastoring there because they bring such a passion for the Lord."

"Well, welcome to the Vatican!" Vinnie dripped with sarcasm, his voice again loud. "I'll tell you, some of these guys wouldn't know Jesus if He walked up and bit them on the leg. These guys think I'm some kind of Jesus freak, ya know. They say I'm too American in my beliefs."

Chris grimaced as yet another laugh turned to pain. "I think being American helps us to accept others more readily. But for me, the big turning point was Baptism in the Spirit."

"Ah jeez, a Charismatic!" Vinnie threw up his hands and then caught himself. "No offense."

"No offense taken." Chris smiled softly this time to avoid further pain.

"But enough shop talk, Mr. Ali. I came to make you feel better. And I brought ..." A mischievous grin filled his face as he reached into his bag. "Ta-da! Checkers!"

Benny couldn't sleep. He was absolutely giddy with excitement. The events of the day swirled endlessly through his mind: first the young priest in the airport and then meeting Luciano. *Signore* Begliali had awakened something deep inside of him. He felt like an entirely different person.

The man's eyes haunted him with their beauty, their ability to reach to the very bottom of his soul. People always spoke about a calling to the priesthood. Benny thought he had experienced it at one time, but it was nothing like this. His true calling was one of service to Luciano Begliali. He would do anything for the man.

And the best part of the day came when Luciano sent the unctuous Bilbo to the car! Although obviously angered at what had happened, Bilbo fairly threw himself at Benny's feet during the ride home. There had clearly been a transfer of power, and Bilbo immediately took the second role, offering any and all services he could provide to Benny. There was talk of an elevated position in the Department of State. It would be an office that coordinated the affairs of state with the role of Vatican, Inc., a heavy financial player on world markets. The job would, of course, carry the title of Monsignor—no more "*Don* Benito" for Benny Cross. And he would be working very closely with Bishop Marcinkus of the Vatican Bank. Benny would learn from the best of them how to sidestep the formidable courtiers that surround Saint Peter's throne.

Begliali had brought clarity to another aspect of his life: his sexuality. Begliali stirred up in him a distinct lust for men—two men, to be exact. He would love to give himself fully to Luciano, but he would never risk showing interest in him. If he put Luciano off or made him angry, then he could be banished—never to see Luciano again, never to hear his voice, never to have the opportunity to serve him. He could never take that risk. But there was another. He had felt such compassion for the young priest in the airport. Even beaten and swollen, the man was obviously handsome. And the gorgeous eyes!

Benny said a silent thank-you to Begliali for bringing these feelings to the surface. Now he had to find a way to be close to the young priest. With Luciano backing him, even the likes of Cardinal Bilbo could be relied upon to do Benny's bidding. There would be a way. Tomorrow he would find it.

FOURTEEN

Fran steadied her nerves as she drove to Riverside from Tom's parents' home. She had stayed with them for the first few weeks following the return from Africa. They were wonderful to her, and Gloria wouldn't leave Sam Ellis's side. Fran understood. Tom had been so much like his father. Gloria needed Sam right now, and he and Evelyn needed Gloria. She was all that was left of their son.

So here she was, driving alone to see Sarah and Mack. There was something so definitive in taking a trip alone. For so many years she had traveled with Tom and Gloria. Tom had done all the driving. "The only driving I want you to do, Frannie, is to drive me crazy," he would tease her. She moved to check her reflection in the rearview mirror. Her hair, in desperate need of a cut, hung limply around her face, ending just over her shoulders. Dark circles of worry and grief were like two black holes drawing all attention from the rest of her lovely face. She wondered if she would ever find her way back to the person she was just a few short weeks before.

"Oh, God. How am I going to get by without him?" She bit her lip to keep from breaking down completely and wiped the tears from her eyes. She never thought she could feel so utterly alone. A huge part of her died that day with Tom, and for all the world she wanted to just lie down and die too. But there was her darling little girl, *their* darling little girl, to look after. She had to be strong for Gloria's sake. Visiting Mack and Sarah would be a great first step. They would provide her with a loving place, halfway between family and the world. A place to become more than half of Fran and Tom. A place to become Fran again.

Pulling up to the parsonage, she bit her lip. She didn't want to break down, but she knew she would. She sat in the car for a second to gather her nerve. The door of the house opened, and Sarah poured out onto the sidewalk in a navy pantsuit and pearls, holding her arms open to hug her best friend. She was already crying, smudging the mascara and makeup she had begun to wear constantly since Fran had last lived in the United States. Fran got out of the car and ran to her in tears. The two friends held one another on the front lawn, each crying too hard to speak, yet communicating volumes.

Mack came out of the house, wiping tears from his red eyes. "Fran, I'm just so sorry. Tom was a great man of God." Unable to speak, Fran nodded her head in agreement and opened her arm for Mack to join them in the hug. He gently got between the two women and led them into the house.

Time found the three of them seated at the kitchen table, drained from the preceding torrent of emotion. Sarah brought out a homemade pie, peach praline, one of Fran's favorites. Mack put on a pot of coffee. Then they listened in stunned silence as Fran told them about their last day in Africa.

"Thank God for Chris," she said. "Without him I don't know how Gloria and I would have gotten back to the States."

Mack moved uncomfortably in his chair. Fran knew he wasn't exactly ecumenical in nature, especially when it came to Catholics. "The One to thank is the Lord," he said magnanimously.

"Of course," Fran agreed. "And I have thanked Him constantly for putting Chris in our path. I'm sad it was God's will for Tom to die so young, but the Lord let him die in the arms of a good friend, a real man of God. Then that man of God got Gloria and me home safely. And then there was the Anglican priest. Chris and I think he may have really been an angel."

"Well, the Lord works in mysterious ways," Mack said as he rolled his eyes and stood to get another cup of coffee.

Sarah grasped one of Fran's hands and said, "The important thing is that you and Gloria are safe. And you're here among friends who love you very much. We want to help you get on your feet, Fran."

"Thanks," Fran said softly. "The hardest thing for me right now is trying to imagine what to do with my life. I don't know where to go, what to do ... it is all so different from the life I loved only weeks ago."

"I know," Sarah said, nodding her head. "If I suddenly lost Mack, my world would collapse. We're college-educated women, but we were educated to play support roles to husband preachers. We lose everything when they're gone."

"One thing I know for sure," Fran said as she nervously fiddled with her fork, "I have to look out for Gloria. And that means I have to become a whole person myself. I've been looking into it, and I would only need a few more credits to get a teaching certificate. If I could get on at a parochial school, they might let me teach while taking classes."

"I hope you can," Sarah said cautiously. "The economy is such a mess with all of this stagflation. There may actually be a glut of teachers who are already certified. Finding a good Baptist school to hire you may be tough right now."

"Well, I learned a lot in Africa. Maybe life experience will count for something. If it puts food on the table, I would be perfectly happy to teach at a Catholic school. Maybe Chris would have some contacts."

Fran caught the momentary shocked expression on Sarah's face. Mack swooped to the table, filling all their coffee cups.

"Now, Frannie," Mack assured her, "I know it seems like these are desperate times, but you need to be careful not to jump to desperate actions. You're still in shock from a horrible experience."

Fran smiled sadly and rubbed her face. "Don't worry, guys. I'm just thinking out loud. I'm sure the Lord will show me His path for my life in due time."

"Of course He will!" Sarah said encouragingly. "He has a plan, and He is faithful to take care of you and Gloria."

"He sure does," Mack joined in. "Who would have thought just a few short years ago He would have given Sarah and me an expanding television ministry? Everything has been a miracle, Fran. Every dollar has been a gift straight from the Lord."

Fran welcomed the change in subject. It might be good to hear how the Lord was working in the lives of her friends. If she was smart, she would relax, let them care for her, and keep her thoughts to herself. It was painfully evident to her, if not to her hosts, that the years in Africa had changed her more significantly than she could ever have imagined. She tried to remember a time when she too dismissed the working of the Lord in other denominations. Who would have ever thought she would sit in Mack's kitchen, longing for a conversation with her most open-minded friend, a Catholic priest?

"Tell me about it." Fran smiled. "I really would like to hear."

"Well," Mack began, "from our letters you know most of the story. God has been so good. We now broadcast all over Texas. I'm looking for a syndication deal that will take us to homes outside of Texas as well. Who knows, maybe one day we'll go national."

"Is it scary to be on TV like that?" Fran asked naively.

"Not for Mack," Sarah took up the conversation. "It's like he was born to do it."

"I don't want to interrupt my wife," Mack said, "especially when she's paying me a compliment, but I have to admit I was plenty scared at first. After time though you get used to the camera. You learn how to treat it as if it were another person in the room.

"But if you want to see someone who was born to it," Mack continued, "wait until Zack comes home from school. I'll tell you, kids these days are so media savvy. It's hard for me to admit, but I take programming advise from a nine-year-old. He is just so insightful for his age!"

"He is a very special child, Fran," Sarah said to her in a deliberate, knowing way. Fran thought back to the crazy story Sarah had told her in college—that an angel predicted Zack's birth. Fran smiled to herself, thinking, *I believe an angel helped get us out of Uganda. Yet I still pooh-pooh Sarah's story. I'm as bad as all the rest!*

"I'm sure he is," Fran said. "I can't wait to meet him."

"His school bus should be here in just a few moments." Mack smiled.

They chatted for a few more minutes, mostly about mistakes Mack had made on camera in the early years. He and Sarah explained to Fran about the small studio they used previously in Houston. The screen door in the living room banged shut, followed immediately by "Mo-om. I'm ho-o-me."

Sarah jumped up and ran to the living room to greet her son. With her arm around his shoulder, she led him to the kitchen.

"Zack, this is Mrs. Ellis."

"The one from Africa?"

"That's the one, son," Mack said, rolling his eyes at Fran.

"It's a pleasure to meet you, ma'am," Zack said politely.

For her part, Fran was unexpectedly taken aback by the child. He certainly was cute with that black curly hair and those steel-blue eyes. Yet there was a harshness about his features that was hard to define. It was as if a cynical, negative energy inhabited him. Fran had never felt such an immediate negative reaction toward someone.

Collecting herself, she smiled a motherly smile and said, "Well, hello there, Zack. I've heard so many wonderful things about you."

He smiled at her in what was obviously a feigned "aw-shucks" manner. Fran looked up to see Sarah enraptured with her son. She glanced at Mack, who obviously loved his son but was not as easily taken in as his wife.

"Zack. Where are your manners, son? Shake hands with Mrs. Ellis," Mack said.

When Fran took his hand, she felt a cold chill envelop her. As she was trying to convince herself it was all in her mind, she saw a smirk light the corners of his mouth and she knew it was a reaction he intended to elicit. Quickly pulling back her hand, she said, "What grade are you in, Zack?"

"Fourth."

"That's a nice age. I have a daughter in the third grade."

"Did she come with you?"

"No. I couldn't pull her away from her grandparents. They're making up for all of the time with her that they missed while we were in Africa."

"Did you ride elephants in Africa?"

"No," Fran said and chuckled, "but I saw some."

"Cool!" Zack pronounced and then turned to his mother and said, "I just have a little bit of homework tonight. Would it be okay if I play outside first and then do my homework later?" Not even waiting for a reply, Zack darted out of the kitchen toward his bedroom to change from his school clothes.

"Sure, sweetheart," Sarah called after him, "but be back in this kitchen with your hands washed, ready for dinner at five thirty. Okay?"

"Okay," Zack called back.

Sarah turned back to Fran. "Well, that's our boy! Honestly, I don't know what I would do without him. He is just the light of my life."

Fran smiled an honest smile. "I'm happy for you, Sarah."

"I honestly think he is the most wonderful child on Earth. That boy was a gift from Heaven," Sarah drooled.

Eventually Mack retired to his study to work on Sunday's sermon. Fran helped Sarah in the kitchen. They made stuffed pork chops and brown rice for dinner, while Sarah filled Fran in on what had been taking place in the lives of their college friends and Mack's ne'er-do-well brother.

At 5:30 p.m. sharp, a freshly washed Zack came into the dining room, followed by his father.

"You must be very special, Mrs. Ellis," Zack said as they took their seats. "Mom doesn't pull out the Royal Doulton china for everyone."

"I noticed when I was helping her set the table," Fran said with a smile. "Really, Sarah, the pattern is beautiful."

"This is the one I liked the most. The lines around the edges are twenty-four-karat gold. I almost didn't take them because they were so costly."

"But the offering plate has been overflowing," Mack said. "And like Zack said, 'the Bible says not to muzzle the ox.' So this time, the ox got a little bit too."

Fran smiled, but her mind went back to the people of Ndejje. The missions had changed her priorities.

"Well, they certainly are beautiful." She smiled.

"Let's say grace, Mack," Sarah chided. "No sense in the food getting cold."

"Zack, why don't you do the honors?" Mack asked.

They all bowed their heads as Zack said softly, "For the food and friendship that we are about to enjoy, we are truly thankful. Amen."

"Amen," said the three adults. Fran was puzzled by a grace that didn't mention the Lord.

As if he could read her mind, Zack countered with information that Baala had buried deep in his subconscious, sounding more like an old sage than a young boy. "I have this theory about ministry in general. We automatically alienate Jews, Muslims, Hindus, and atheists the moment we bring Jesus' name into the equation. There's no reason to say His name over and over like maybe He's hard of hearing or something."

Fran wasn't about to argue the point with a child. She turned to Sarah and Mack.

"It's not like we disavow Jesus or His sacrifice, Fran," Mack said. "But throwing His name around like it's some kind of magical formula is not only off-putting, it's the very nature of taking the Lord's name in vain."

Fran just smiled. She didn't want to make her hosts feel uncomfortable, but she couldn't disagree more. She said, "It's just so nice to see you guys again ..."

They reminisced the rest of the dinner, retelling old stories of their time together in college. As dinner wound down, the conversation turned serious.

"Have you thought about having a service for Tom, Frannie?" Mack asked gingerly.

Even the mention of Tom's funeral brought feelings of despair and helplessness to Fran. She hadn't had a service yet because she couldn't handle the finality of it. She often daydreamed she had one last chance to hold him, run her fingers through his soft, golden curls, hear him say her name, and above all else tell him how very much she loved him—just one more time! She drew a sharp breath and answered, "It is so hard to think about. Not having a body to bury seems to make a lot of the service irrelevant. Tom loved Jesus. He's in Heaven."

"But think of Tom's parents," Sarah said, taking hold of Fran's hand. "And Gloria as well as yourself. The finality of a service may provide the closure you all need so the healing process can begin."

"Fran," Mack said, "I would be happy to hold the service for you here at Riverside." Fran was silent for a moment as she considered the offer. She had to do *something*. Maybe Mack could really help.

"Thanks, Mack." Fran smiled sadly, and tears welled in her eyes. "I would really appreciate that."

"It's settled, then." Sarah smiled. "Let Mack take care of everything."

Zack was already in bed when his father came in to say good night.

"Hey, buddy, you look all ready to hit the hay."

"Yeah, poor Mrs. Ellis made me sad today."

Mack smiled at his son's perceptiveness. "Her whole world has been shaken, son."

"That's why it's good for you to do the service, right? I mean, you could just take it over so she doesn't have to worry about a thing, right?"

"I would like to. I loved Mr. Ellis. It would be like one last act of friendship until I see him again in Heaven."

"That's a really nice thought, Dad. Don't you think it would be good for the whole congregation to see how you handle the service?" Zack asked with feigned innocence.

"No, my little marketing genius. I'm not going to televise this, if that's what you're thinking." Mack grinned and patted him on the head.

Zack smiled. "That's what I'm thinking, Dad. And for a few reasons. It may be a defining moment in your ministry. Let your viewers see you wracked with pain but pushing through it because you believe there is something better on the other side." Zack concentrated on the image, much as he had done when communicating with Baala. He imagined Mack's tears and his pleas to the audience to look beyond the veil of sadness to the joy on the other side. He could see his father soften to the idea.

"What's your other reason, son?" Mack asked, as if awakened from a trance.

"Dad, it's a message people need to hear. By reaching out to Mrs. Ellis, it will be like you're reaching out to all of them. You wouldn't be helping just one family, but countless others as well."

Zack concentrated on sending a new image to his father. He imagined the congregation, young and old, sitting in front of their televisions, crying with him. They were finding the release for pent-up sadness that was crippling them. Freeing them would be a miracle. What better testament to Tom than to have a service that wins souls.

Zack grinned in the silence as he watched the faraway look in his father's eyes. He was a farmer who had just planted a seed. He found his father not to be a whole lot smarter than a pile of dirt. Seeds grew quickly in such a mind.

"You may have a point, Zack. Broadcasting the service might help so many people who are hurting out there. You've convinced me," Mack said as he planted a kiss on his son's head.

"Good, Dad. You know, some good marketing may be what the church needs these days."

"Maybe it is, son. Maybe it is."

"One more thing, Dad," Zack said sleepily. "Wear your navy-blue suit with a gold tie."

Shortly after Mack left the room, Zack was taken in a flash of light. To him, it was as if he had a dream. The beings told him Mrs. Ellis had to leave.

There was no way Mack would be able to sleep. Already the words for his sermon at Tom's service were pouring through his head. But first things first. He rolled the mimeograph sheet into the typewriter and began to write a letter to his local and television congregations. He explained that he had a heavy heart, having just heard of the loss of his good friend in Kampala. He explained that the Lord had brought him to the aid of his friend's widow and that he would be performing the service to welcome Tom home to the loving arms of the Father. He signed it with a flourish, put the form in the mimeograph machine, and turned the handle repeatedly, printing copy after copy.

With the letter written, he was free to imagine the service in detail, and for hours he cranked and imagined. Imagined and cranked. By the time he went to bed, the letters were all bundled to be delivered to the mailing agency. By noon the next day, they would be in the mail.

"Good morning, sunshine." Sarah smiled at Fran when she made it into the kitchen. Sarah had the burnt-orange electric griddle heated and set about making French toast and eggs as Fran got some coffee. "You must have slept well!"

"I haven't slept that well since we got back to the States. I think Tom's service had been weighing pretty heavily on my mind. You'll never know how much I appreciate what Mack is doing."

"He would do it for you anyway, Fran, but you have to know he loved Tom too. He was up most of the night preparing."

"When he gets up, maybe I should have a talk with him. There are a few personal touches I want to add." Sarah placed a plate of French toast, bacon, and eggs in front of Fran.

"There's plenty of time for that," Sarah beamed. "But in the meantime, I have a surprise."

"Better than this?" Fran said, hungrily digging into her breakfast. "It's been years since I've had French toast!"

"Even better," Sarah said as she brushed a lock of hair from Fran's face. "I've booked us a spa day in Houston. We'll be getting our hair done and facials and manicures."

Fran gasped, choking a bit. She coughed and then said, "Sarah, it must be so expensive. I don't know if I could—"

"What? Pamper yourself for a change? Of course you can. You've been living in the jungle for nearly ten years. You can allow yourself a little treat."

Fran's brow wrinkled with concern she could never afford it. "It would be nice. And I could certainly use a haircut. But, Sarah, I don't have a job. There are only a couple thousand dollars of life insurance coming. I can't afford it."

"It's on me." Sarah hugged her best friend. "Like I told you, God has been good. And what's the point of Him blessing me if I can't share it with someone I love?"

"In that case, I can't wait!" Fran smiled as she returned her friend's hug.

"Besides, you were the one who took me to the makeup counter when I was getting ready for my wedding."

Fran started laughing. "Oh my, those 1960s fashions! Do you believe we actually thought white eye shadow was attractive?"

Sarah joined in the laughter, but Fran thought the memory brought just a twinge of pain to her eyes. "I just tell myself we were young then. We didn't know any better."

The girls had a great day. Fran hadn't laughed so hard in a long time. Driving home, they felt glamorous in their new *Charlie's Angels* hairdos. Fran got highlights and just enough of a body wave to make her hair look thick and full around her face, à la Farah Fawcett. Sarah's darker hair was parted in the middle and cut into layers. A soft perm yielded a Jaclyn Smith look.

"Do you think one day we'll look at these styles and feel as weird about them as we do the 1960s look?" Fran asked as she craned her neck to get a better view of the cut in her compact mirror.

"Probably," Sarah said with nonchalance. "But that's the beauty of fashion. It lets your look change with the years. When I think about how strict we were about fashion in Bible school, it makes me laugh a bit."

"Seriously." Fran laughed. "When nuns' habits started looking fashionable to me, I realized we were really behind the times."

"In some ways, nuns had more freedom." Sarah sighed. "Did I ever tell you Mack hated the way I looked on our wedding day?"

"Sarah! You were beautiful!" Fran cried out in disbelief.

"He didn't know how to react to it with the Riverside saints and his parents in the room."

"Sarah, I'm so sorry to hear that. Every woman should feel beautiful on her wedding day."

"It's not a problem. Mack and I worked through it, and he's learned to see the ministerial benefit of being culturally relevant."

"So he's not going to hate your new look?"

"No! In fact, he'll love it. He's convinced that fashion, hair, and nails are the way to reach the hearts of women for Christ. He wants me to be a standard-bearer in terms of what is acceptable fashion in the congregation."

When they got home, Mack surprised them by having dinner ready. Baked potatoes were just about done in the oven, and steaks were just waiting to be put on the hot grill. The table on the patio was set and ready to go.

"My word! Look at you two! You look glamorous!" he exclaimed.

"Ah, thanks, honey." Sarah smiled. "And what do you think of serving dinner to Ms. Fawcett?"

Fran bit her bottom lip and shook her head vacantly in an impersonation of Fawcett's *Charlie's Angels* character.

"Fran, you look marvelous," Mack said. "I would say a bit of pampering was just what the doctor ordered."

"It was a wonderful gift. I am so thankful to you and Sarah."

"It's our pleasure, Fran." He smiled warmly. "Now why don't you two take a seat while my assistant takes your drink orders."

On cue, Zack appeared with a grin, a pen, and a pad in hand. For the moment he was just a boy having fun. For that moment, Fran saw the lighter side of him and found him to be cute.

"For your drinking pleasure, madams, we have water, seltzer, grape juice, and the house special, chocolate milk."

"Oh my, *garçon*, it all sounds so wonderful." Sarah grinned with pride. "But I'm afraid I'll have to go with seltzer. I have my girlish figure to consider."

"And I'll take plain water." Fran smiled.

"Wonderful choices," he said with a bow, "and may I say you both look beautiful tonight?" Zack's look gave Fran a sudden chill, as if he saw her in a distinctly postpubescent way. His smile seemed leering for just a second. Then he looked away. Fran followed his eyes to his father's. Was she imagining it, or did Mack have the same look for an instant? She had to be imagining it. She had known Mack for years and had never seen him demonstrate an untoward manner. *Too much time in the wilds of Africa, Fran!*

"I always liked a fresh, young, handsome waiter. How about you, Fran?" Sarah asked.

"Absolutely adore them, dahling," Fran responded in her best Gabor, looking away from father and son.

Fran thought the steaks were delicious, as only Texas steaks can be. The potatoes were fully loaded with butter, sour cream, fresh bacon bits, and chives. Corn on the cob and an iceberg lettuce salad rounded out the table.

At the end of dinner, Zack turned into the waiter again to bring out a Boston cream pie, one of Fran's favorite desserts.

"Tell me you didn't make this, Mack!" Fran exclaimed.

"I'd love to pretend I did, Fran, but I'm not that talented. We do, however, have a great bakeshop just down the road."

"A beautiful end to a beautiful day." Fran sighed as she took her first bite. "Heavenly!" she said from a full mouth.

"Aside from surprising us with a wonderful dinner, what did you two handsome men do today?" Sarah asked.

"School for me. Nothing much exciting happened. But I always like Fridays, so it was cool."

"And I have been working on Tom's service. It's scheduled for a week from Sunday. It will be beautiful. I've sent letters to all of our partners who will be tuning in."

The Boston cream pie was suddenly dry in Fran's mouth, and she began to choke on her words. "Oh, Mack, I appreciate the effort, but I'm not sure I want Tom's service televised."

"We televise our services, Fran," Mack said with a slight edge. "That's the only way to keep my broader congregation involved. Riverside is a church. Some of its members come in person and some via the airwaves, but we are one parish family."

"I was thinking of something much smaller," Fran said with determination, "something intimate with family and close friends."

"Fran, I've performed a lot of services like that in my career, and let me tell you, they are really sad events. If you have a life celebration at Riverside, it will be the much-needed first steps of healing for you and Gloria, not to mention Tom's parents." Fran bristled at his condescending, parental tone of voice.

"But, Mack, I really wish you had discussed it with me before you notified everyone," Fran said with a hint of exasperation. "A week from now might be tight. I don't know if Chris can get here from Rome."

"That priest?" Mack asked in a terse voice that immediately drew the table's full attention.

Fran stared angrily at Mack even as she spoke in a kind tone. She wasn't about to cater to Mack's prejudices. "He's a good friend, Mack. He was with Tom when he died, and he got Gloria and me to safety. I know there is an inborn distrust when it comes to Catholic priests, but when you meet him, it will all fade away. Trust me."

"Well, the timing is pretty much set, Fran." Mack calmed himself. "If he can't make it, then he can't make it. It's probably God's providence."

"No, it's not!" Fran exploded. She could feel the anger blushing her cheeks. "It's blatant prejudice!"

Mack reacted as if slapped. Accusing the pastor was a serious matter.

"I don't like the way this is escalating," Sarah said sternly. "Certainly there is room for discussion here."

Mack took the cue, releasing the tension in his back and neck. "Of course there is."

"So let me get this straight," Fran said sarcastically. "The two of you agree there is room for me to have an opinion on who should do *my husband's* eulogy?"

"Eulogy!" Mack exploded, clearly annoyed at the very idea of a priest … in a cassock … preaching from his pulpit.

Zack, who had been silent, said decisively, "But the letters have gone out, Mrs. Ellis. Riverside is going to have a really beautiful celebration of Mr. Ellis's life. Maybe Father Chris could talk at a more intimate service at a later date." The kid made sense, but it was there again, the steely, unworldly nature that had taken Fran aback before.

"Out of the mouth of babes!" Mack resounded with relief.

Sarah just looked on as if it was another treasure for her heart, just like the Virgin Mary.

Fran was quiet and uncomfortable. This had ruined a beautiful day. She felt like a prisoner. These were her closest friends in the United States. If she spoke her mind, then she would endanger the friendship. Maybe it would be better to have a small service where Chris could eulogize Tom privately, away from the bright lights of Riverside. She had to lighten the atmosphere. Looking across the table at Zack, she smiled and said, *"Garçon. Café s'il vous plait."*

"Are you ready for bed, son?" Mack asked as he entered Zack's room. Zack had been concentrating on his father, trying to conjure mental images of Mack's favorite movie, *The Postman Always Rings Twice.* He was sitting on his bed, wearing a distressed look that he had practiced in the mirror in response to the subconscious command given by the visiting angel: Mrs. Ellis had to leave.

"I changed into my pajamas, but I don't think my mind will let me go to sleep tonight."

"What's bothering you?" Mack asked with concern.

"I'm sure it's nothing. It's just that sometimes I get these feelings." Zack wrung his hands in an impression of his mother.

"Such as?" Mack asked.

"I just know when things happen sometimes," Zack said softly, drawing his dad in.

"Like what?"

"I knew Mr. Ellis was dead before Mrs. Ellis called to tell us. I just knew it!"

Mack raked his hand through his hair and looked intently at his son. "You didn't say anything at the time, though."

"I tried to ignore it. It's a weird feeling to just know something." Zack could see his father's acceptance of what he said. He paused for a second as he tried to telepathically stir images of the movie in Mack's mind.

Forcing tears to his eyes, he continued, "Dad, I've tried to ignore it, but it's there. Sometimes I just know stuff … like Mr. Ellis's service. Last night I wasn't talking to you about ideas. I was telling you stuff I already saw."

"It seemed very real to me when you were talking about it too," Mack said with a faraway look as he put his arm around his son and drew him close.

"So you know what I'm talking about?" Zack asked as he snuggled against his father.

"I think I might, son. You know, the prophet Joel promised that in the Latter Days there would rise up a generation where visions and dreams would be the norm."

"So you don't think I'm weird?" Zack asked with a quiver in his voice.

Mack hugged him tighter. "Not at all! I think you are very blessed."

"I didn't tell you everything. It happened at dinner tonight too," Zack said carefully to instill a foreboding feeling in Mack.

"Tell me about it," Mack said cautiously.

"It was like watching an old black-and-white movie through a mist. I could make out some things but not others. Then there was this voice in my head asking questions. 'Where is Mr. Ellis's body? Why is Mrs. Ellis so protective of that priest?'" Zack played on his father's dark fears of Catholicism and the Charismatic Renewal, as well as his jealous rage that Fran would choose a Catholic priest over him to give Tom's eulogy.

"I've had some questions myself," Mack said cautiously.

"Dad, in the black-and-white movie there was this woman. She and her boyfriend killed her husband. Then they hid the body."

"That was just in your mind, son," Mack said resolutely, but Zack could hear the underlying doubt.

"No. It's another one of those things I just know, Dad. Think about it. Why would she try to put roadblocks in your memorial service? Why would she insist that her priest friend give the eulogy? Maybe she needs an excuse to get him back here so they can pretend they fell in love after Mr. Ellis died."

"I think we are stretching things a bit here, buddy. It could be you've just been watching too much television," Mack tried to reason.

"I hope you're right, Dad," Zack said doubtfully as he slipped his arm over Mack's shoulder. "But I have a funny feeling."

"Listen, son, I'm very happy you shared all of this with me." Mack closed the conversation. "And I don't want to trivialize it, but it is only suspicion."

"Dad, you have to go through with this memorial service no matter what Mrs. Ellis says. When it comes down to it, you and Mom might be the only friends poor Mr. Ellis had. Promise me you'll do the service, Dad."

"I promise you I'll do the service, son. Now do you think you can go to sleep?"

"Sure, Dad. I think I can sleep now. Thanks for listening." Zack kissed his father's cheek.

"Anytime, son. That's what I'm here for."

Like putty in my hands! He drifted off to sleep with a smile on his face.

Mack was tortured by dreams the entire night. Dreams of murder. Dreams of illicit love affairs. Dreams of betrayal. The words of his son buried themselves deep into his subconscious. He got out of bed early, knowing that more attempts at sleep would yield more nightmares. He went downstairs, made a pot of coffee, and thought about what to do. He couldn't let these questions burn in him. He would confront Fran as soon as he heard her stir.

Fran began her day as usual, with a morning devotional before even leaving the bed, a little time spent reading the Bible, and some time thanking the Lord for another day. This morning as she was praying, she slipped quietly into her prayer language, praying in the Holy Spirit.

Her bedroom door burst open to reveal a red-faced Mack. Fran knew immediately he had heard her. She also knew that in Mack's world, tongues could only be demonic."

"What are you doing!" he shrieked.

"Praying," Fran said with deliberate calm, trying to defuse the situation.

"You know tongues are demonic, Fran!"

"No, I don't *know* that, Mack. In fact, I believe they are a gift from God. You know, Mack, the Lord has been showering the church with fresh outpourings of the Holy Spirit. Even the Catholics recognize—"

"I don't care about the Catholics! I don't want to hear any more about the Catholics or your priest lover!" Mack screamed, waving his hands wildly.

Now Fran shrieked, "How dare you, Mack! You know that's not true!"

"All I know is you have gotten very close to this priest, your husband dies mysteriously, and you're showing evidence of demon contact!"

Fran was too stunned to answer. She heard Sarah cry as she ran down the hallway, "Mack, what is all of this screaming?"

"Did you know she prays in tongues?" he demanded.

Sarah stopped short. "No," she said gravely. "Fran, is this true?"

Fran saw from Sarah's horrified reaction that she would be of little help. She wiped from her face tears of anger and exasperation. "It happened when Tom died and we were escaping from Africa. I was so sad and so scared. The Lord met my need. One second I was praying in English and the next in a language He had given me. But that's not the problem. Your husband just accused me of having an affair with a Catholic priest!" Fran's voice broke.

"Mack! How could you?" Sarah asked in shock and dismay.

"Think of it, Sarah. Think of how much she mentioned this Father Chris in her letters. He was the only one around when Tom died. She doesn't want to have a service unless he says the eulogy. And now she's speaking in demonic tongues!"

"Oh, Mack. Are you sure it was tongues? Maybe she was just praying softly and you heard it wrong."

"It was tongues, Sarah," Fran said in a defeated tone. "And they're not demonic. As to the rest, it's just ludicrous. I loved Tom, and I always will. Whether you want to believe it or not, Tom and Chris had a great friendship. Chris got Gloria and me out of Africa *because* of his love for Tom." Now hot tears came. Fran's heart couldn't take the injustice of the accusations.

Sarah started toward her friend, wishing to comfort her. Mack restrained her by grabbing her arm. She turned to him, scowling. "You better be sure of what you're saying, Mack Jolean. These are horrible accusations."

"I wrestled with it all night, Sarah. When I heard the demonic tongues coming from her bedroom, I knew it was time to act." Mack's eyes pleaded for his wife's understanding.

"I … I don't know what to think, Mack. She's our friend," Sarah pleaded.

Fran was out of bed, her suitcase nearly packed. She felt Mack's eyes staring at her in her nightgown. *Who's the pervert here?*

"Sarah, she has to leave our house. Now!" Mack insisted.

"Don't worry about that, pal," Fran said tersely. "If you can stop ogling me long enough for me to get dressed, I'll be gone."

That comment was enough to move Sarah firmly to her husband's side. The couple left Fran's room, waiting in the living room to show her out.

Fran dressed quickly and descended the stairs quietly. Hearing them in the living room, she silently left through the back door. Pulling out of the driveway, she looked up to see Zack's smiling face as he watched from his bedroom window.

———————————

Against her better judgment, Fran tuned the television to Mack's show on Sunday morning. She was simultaneously aghast and bemused by what she saw.

"Friends"—Mack's voice cracked—"it is so hard for me to speak to you here today. It is a terrible thing to lose such a close friend at such a tender age. Tom was an inspiration to me. A trusted colleague. A devoted, passionate man of God. He was also a devoted husband and a loving father."

At the mention of the words "husband and father," the camera panned to the front row. Shot from behind, the picture showed a woman with Fran's new hairstyle, dressed in black, seated next to Sarah. Beside her was a little girl Gloria's age. Both had their heads in their hands, shoulders heaving. Sarah turned to them so that the camera caught her profile as she tearfully comforted Tom's grieving family.

Mack continued his "eulogy" with a call to the parish to help Tom's poor family assimilate back into American life. He told the harrowing story of how they had left everything they owned in order to escape the wrath of Idi Amin.

After the crowd wound down, Mack went to his office. The new office was huge with dark mahogany wainscoting and a deep-red carpet. In the middle was a large mahogany desk with a wood inlaid top. He sat behind it in an oversized leather chair and counted the largest collection ever taken from the Riverside congregation. Sarah came to his office after confirming with the call agency that telephone contributions had also risen dramatically.

"Mack, I hope we've done the right thing," Sarah said, wringing her hands.

"Of course we have, Sarah. We gave Tom the service he should have had. It is sad that Fran didn't participate, but we clearly did the right thing."

"But the money, Mack. We took in so much money ..."

"That just proves we're in God's will, Sarah. For me, the money is a tangible expression of the hearts the Lord was able to touch today. Think of it, Sarah. These people were moved by the power of God."

"But they were also moved to help Fran and Gloria. Are we going to send some of this to them?" Sarah asked resolutely.

"I'd like to, but we can't right now, not until Fran repents. What we *can* do is plow it back into the ministry. Let Tom's legacy be more souls saved in his name."

"Still, Mack, it seems that some of this should go to Gloria," Sarah argued.

"I'll tell you what. I'll put one thousand dollars in a separate bank account for Gloria. When she is old enough to be out on her own, we'll send it to her. With interest, it could grow quite a bit."

"That sounds fair. And it will probably be very touching to have a gift associated with her father later on in life," Sarah rationalized. "I can't imagine trying to give it to Fran after she accused you of ogling her like that."

"That's my girl," Mack said sweetly, and for the briefest second his mind flashed on the image of Fran in that nightgown. Thank God he had the foresight to send her packing before she could work her demonic wiles on him. He almost felt sorry for that poor priest she had gotten involved with.

FIFTEEN

After three weeks in the hospital, Chris was living in a small apartment building owned by the Church. The building was old, and its steam heat had not yet been turned down to reflect 1979's early spring weather. For the most part, Chris kept the windows open, enjoying the sweet smells of spring flowers and the occasional scent of fresh bread cooling at the bakery down the street. Most other residents were clerics as well, and the apartments were small and utilitarian. Each contained a little bedroom just large enough to fit a twin bed, desk, and chair. The living room, which was even smaller, opened to a kitchenette. Off the bedroom was what could probably be described as a bathroom-ette. All in all, the place had a bit of a seminary feel to it, but it was a good place to recuperate and was a luxury condo compared with the little sleeping area in the church at Ndejje.

Most days, Chris slept in, took his meds, and read until the headaches came. Then he would rest again. The doctors said the events in Kampala had caused a brain trauma. The cure was to be found in rest.

Today he was up early and out in the streets of Rome. The sights, sounds, and smells of the Eternal City early in the morning were glorious. And there was a beautiful smell of springtime in the crisp morning air. But this morning's walk was not casual. He was looking for someone. Following his instincts, he wound his way around to a small fountain and heard a conversation with the familiar voice. Hanging back so as not to interrupt, he followed along. His Italian was improving.

"Listen, Vito, here's what you're going to do. You're going to stop drinking and you're going to give up your girlfriend. Don't you want to be a good husband and father?"

"Yes, but I am already a good father."

"By sleeping around on your kids' mother? The first thing you have to do is buy a mirror. You're a bum!" Vinnie intoned.

Tears started to form in Vito's eyes at the mention of his children.

"Don't start crying on me," Vinnie commanded. "That's the bad news, but I have good news too. God sent His only Son to die on a cross to save bums like you … and like me." Chris grinned at Vinnie's blunt approach.

"I hope one day to get to Heaven thanks to Jesus, Father. But that is in the future. And the women … they're here and now. I love the women, Father."

Chris gasped as Vinnie slapped the guy lightly on the back of the head. "That's where you're wrong! He's here now too. He sent the Holy Spirit to change you into the man He knows you can be."

"I would like to believe that, Father."

"Good, because here's what you're going to do." Pulling a card out of his pocket and handing it to Vito, he continued, "Go to this group and tell them Father Vinnie sent you. You'll probably have to move in there while they dry you out. In the meantime, you'll come to see me here every morning at seven o'clock. We're going to talk this out and pray over it until you get better. You understand?"

"Yes, Father."

"And don't let me down, Vito. If I find out you didn't check in, it's gonna be worse than the *mal occhio* for you, believe me."

Chris raised an eyebrow at the mention of *"mal occhio,"* the evil eye.

Vinnie waved his hand dismissively and said in English, "An expression!"

"I'll go, Father," Vito assured.

"Good. Now bow your head." Turning to Chris, he said in English, "Hey! Why are you standing around with your hands in your pockets? Get over here and help me pray for this guy."

Chris moved closer, placing his hand on Vito's shoulder as Vinnie led the prayer. First Vinnie raised his hand and blessed Vito, saying a prayer of absolution. Then he continued, "Father, this man is desperate for help. Please send your Spirit to strongly settle on him, to be with him, and to heal him of the sin that is ruining his life." Chris could feel the presence of the Holy Spirit as Vinnie prayed. He could tell Vito felt it too. Hard tears came to him as he fell to his knees.

The three men stayed there for long seconds, waiting for the Glory to recede. Finally, Vinnie grasped Vito's hand that held the address of the alcoholic group.

"Go there right away, Vito. I'll tell your wife where you are. She'd probably believe it more coming from me anyway."

"Vinnie, that was wonderful!" Chris exclaimed as Vito left.

"Lots of great things happen in the morning. Maybe when that melon-head of yours gets better, you'll be able to get out of bed before half the day is gone!"

"I love the mornings. Normally, I would have been up, said morning prayers, and had a workout by now."

"Same here. I mean loving the mornings. I wouldn't know a workout if it bit me in the butt." After a momentary pause, he continued, "So, Chris, you didn't come here to critique an old monk's sandwich ministry."

"I got my new assignment, and I don't know what to make of it," Chris said, pulling a piece of paper from his pocket. The paper told him he would be working as assistant to Monsignor Benjamin Cross, who would be serving as a newly formed liaison between the secretary of state and the Vatican Bank.

Vinnie looked at the paper for a long time. The color drained from his face, and he wiped it with his hand.

"Listen, kid, the Vatican is a nightmare of politics. We have a lot of professional clerics who left Jesus behind years ago. I'm ashamed to admit it, but this town is in trouble. None of these guys gives a hoot about an old monk like me. They talk around me like maybe I am deaf or something. So I hear a lot of stuff."

"I can tell by your reaction that I'm falling right into the thick of it," Chris said with a frown.

"Well, at least this Cross guy is an American. Maybe you can find some common ground with him on that score."

"But you don't think he's a nice guy?" Chris asked cautiously as he sat on the edge of a fountain in the piazza.

Vinnie joined him. "In Hoboken we have a name for a guy like him.

Loosely translated, it's butthole. In a nutshell, this man is dangerous, and he's playing games with the most dangerous men in Italy, maybe the world. Take a lesson from your old pal Vinnie. You keep your head down, keep your mouth shut, and speak only when spoken to ... but you keep your eyes and your ears wide open."

"Sounds like I'll be some sort of spy."

"I can tell you more, but not here. Do you like gardening?" Vinnie changed the subject but looked intently at Chris, as if trying to convey that the apparently random comment carried greater significance.

"I can't really say that I have any experience with it," Chris said, wondering about the change of subject.

"Well, it's your lucky day. You're going to get some. Meet me tonight at six thirty at the entrance to the papal gardens. I'll talk to the Swiss Guard. They'll let you in."

"Why?"

"We're going to plant petunias!" Vinnie grinned.

"So how does planting petunias help me with this new assignment?"

"Working in the ground is good for the soul. And it's very quiet there. The Swiss Guard makes sure nobody gets in, so that means nobody is in earshot. In the meantime, you have an assignment."

"Let me guess." Chris rolled his eyes. "Find some petunias."

"No, smarty-pants. I'll bring the flowers. You need to read the book of Esther. Focus on chapter 7, verse 16. It's one of my favorite passages."

Cesare Bilbo had been through a lot in his life. He had survived as a young priest in opposition to Mussolini. He had been a bishop at the outset of Vatican II. But now he had been reduced to the genie that grants every wish of the fat, egotistical, American pig that had somehow become the "Chosen One" of Luciano Begliali.

Luciano had made it clear that Bilbo's value to the New World Order lay in running interference for *Monsignore Benito. Monsignore! Ha!* He had done nothing to earn the title, short of lying around Luciano's pool, being briefed on the details of the plan. So now there were two obnoxious Americans in positions of power in the Vatican. The other one was, of course, Paul Marcinkus, head of the Vatican Bank and con man extraordinaire. Marcinkus had so much dirt under his fingernails—from the sale of Mafia-made false securities to pump-and-dump schemes on the Italian stock market. None of that would bother Cesare if he could be sure Marcinkus was a true devotee of the plan. But as far as he could tell, the loud cleric from Chicago served only one god, his belly. Men like him were dangerous and, if not held on a short leash, could derail everything.

Ah, Luciano, what have you done to me now!

He picked up the phone and dialed Benny's apartment.

"Pronto," Benny answered.

"Buon giorno, Monsignore."

"Ah, Cesare. Good morning, my friend."

"Did you sleep well?" Bilbo feigned interest.

"Wonderfully. Have you succeeded in getting me that certain assistant?"

"His new orders have been delivered to him. As requested, we have researched him extensively. He is as clean as a whistle. It appears your Father Chris entered the priesthood to serve the Lord."

"A pity. Does he know there's a new Lord in town?" Benny asked.

"He does not, and it would be my advice not to attempt to dissuade him. He has attached heavy emotion to his belief system and would likely be immune to our entreaties."

"So then, how do I ensure that he will be loyal to me?"

"To a large extent, you can rely on his ethics. He will perform his duties with all integrity. As to the matter of ensuring his loyalty to you personally, I would suggest that could be accomplished with the promise of some well-placed funds."

"I thought he was incorruptible."

"From a personal standpoint, he is, but he has an attachment to the family he brought out of Uganda. I think you could entice him with a college scholarship for the young girl."

"Thereby ensuring that he stays with me for a while—"

"Exactly. You could pretend to be sacrificing to put away, say, five hundred dollars per month into a college fund for this girl."

"Well done, Cesare!" Benny exclaimed. On his end of the receiver, Cesare felt the bile rise in his throat.

"I knew you would be pleased, Benito. Have a nice day." Bilbo slammed the receiver into its cradle.

"Ciao." Benny hung up the phone, smiling. It was time for him to meditate. Since he had come to Rome, his interaction with the Lady had become so real, not dreamlike at all. He no longer had to meditate for a long period of time to invoke her; seeing her nearly immediately followed the regulation of his breathing.

"What's on your mind today?" she asked in her lilting voice.

"I just feel good about my new assistant. Tell me, is there a chance I could aspire to a more intimate relationship with him?"

The Lady smiled. "A loving relationship would be good for you, little one. But I think it may be very difficult to accomplish with this particular man. He shields himself with a strong, emotional attachment to the old faith."

"But I burn for him," Benny admitted.

"You are finding your true nature. Your attraction to this one helps to bring it out. There are other avenues of outlet."

In his vision, she reached out to him. As she touched him, her appearance became a blur of light. As the light dissipated, he could see she had changed her form to that of the young priest. She kissed him hard. He fell headlong into a bliss he had heretofore only imagined.

It had been a while since Chris had read the book of Esther. It was hard to read the book critically. It evoked an emotional response like a great play or movie. You could feel your stomach knotting when you realized the hard choice before Esther. You could see God's providence and yet understand the trepidation of her heart as she decided to throw caution to the wind in order to fulfill the Lord's plan for her life.

And there it was—Vinnie's favorite passage. Against all odds, Esther, a Jewish girl, had become the favored queen of the Assyrian ruler. The king's henchman had devised a way to rid the kingdom of the Jews. Esther now had to seek the king's favor, reveal that she was

Jewish, and ask him to save her people. A misstep would result in her death. A lack of action would result in the death of her people. Enter Mordecai, who had raised Esther from her youth. As she was pondering what to do, Mordecai said to her, "And who knows but that you have come to your royal position for such a time as this?"

Chris entered the gardens unencumbered. Swiss Guardsmen all stepped aside to allow him entrance to places that were generally off-limits. Obviously they knew he was coming. It was beginning to look as if Vinnie was not quite as unimportant as he portrayed himself to be.

At the entrance stood the venerable monk with some trowels and a box of petunias. Looking past him, Chris saw a beautiful garden decorated with exotic plants and manicured lawns. Flower gardens that had been gently cared for and cultivated for centuries were about to be infected with Vinnie's petunias.

"Something else, isn't it?" Vinnie asked.

"It's just such a beautiful place," Chris said, taking the box of petunias. "I knew these gardens existed, but I had no idea how beautiful they were."

"Kind of like the gardens of Versailles or other palaces, right?" Vinnie asked with a smirk.

"Yeah. Vinnie, are you sure about the petunias?" Chris asked as they walked down manicured paths toward the opposite end of the garden. To Chris, petunias seemed pretty mundane and out of place here.

"Let me tell you something, kid. Our pope is a good man, but his job is a killer. Every once in a while, he needs some time to think in a private space, away from the eyes of the world. Away from the constant stare of the Swiss Guard."

They got to the far end of the garden, where there stood a stone wall on which had grown thick vines of beautiful roses. They went around the wall to find a grotto on its other side.

"Ta-da!" Vinnie grinned. Chris saw a beauty of its own kind in the little grotto, which was only 250 feet by 200 feet. In the center was a statue of Saint Francis, who honored simplicity in life and in faith. Surrounding the statue was a bed of fire-red petunias as a ground cover. From the petunias rose white calla lilies. Thick grape vines climbed the wall separating the grotto from the rest of the papal gardens. Across the grotto from the wall was a wrought iron bench. On either side of the bench were, to Chris's surprise, small vegetable gardens. To the left of the bench were freshly planted tomato and pepper plants. To the right were squash and beans. Behind the bench were a lemon tree and a cherry tree, both in spring bloom. The area was alive with the scents of the trees and the earthy smell of the newly planted vegetable gardens. Along the sidewalk, a six-inch border had been overturned, ready for the petunias Chris carried. The peaceful grandeur of this small space seemed to dwarf the majestic beauty of the pruned gardens on the outside.

Chris was setting the petunias at equal distances along the walk when he heard a voice.

"Ah, Vincenzino, my master gardener! How are you today?"

Chris rose in astonishment as the pope himself entered the grotto.

"Not so bad," Vinnie replied. "How about yourself?" Vinnie knelt and kissed the ring of the sovereign and then rose to hug his friend.

"I'm learning as I go," the pope quipped.

"I can only imagine the headaches!" Vinnie said, looking up to Heaven, his right hand to his forehead. "Then there's the Curia. You know what they say, 'They get Curioser and Curioser every day.'"

The Slavic pope belly-laughed at the simple friar.

"Is this young Father Chris?" The pope beckoned for Chris to approach. Overcome, Chris knelt and kissed the ring of the fisherman. The pope subtly moved his left hand, indicating that Chris should stand, but Chris missed the signal. He was too overcome.

Vinnie slapped Chris's shoulder with the back of his hand. "Get up! What? Do you want him to get a backache bending over to talk to you?"

"My apologies, Holiness," Chris muttered as he rose to his feet.

"No apologies are necessary, son, but perhaps an explanation is. This is one of the most special places in the Vatican. It is a totally secluded space where I can be Karl. You are invited here in a spirit of peace and camaraderie. In this place it is my pleasure to dispense with the customs of state in favor of a free exchange of ideas with people I trust. If you are to continue to join us here, you will have to be at ease."

"I understand, Holiness," Chris said.

"And yet you wonder how it came to be that you are here with us," the pope said with a wise smile.

"I am very curious." Chris smiled an awkward grin.

"Let's relax under the shade of the trees." The two priests dutifully followed the pope to the bench.

"First we pray. Heavenly Father, these are perilous times indeed. We seek Your guidance and Your wisdom as we proceed. And I ask Your special blessing on young Father Chris. Let him hear completely what we present to him this day. Bless his calling and strengthen his will for the arduous times that are ahead."

There was a soft breeze as the pope said the prayer. Chris felt the Holy Spirit envelop him, and every sense seemed to be heightened. He smiled and sighed the deep sigh of someone who had finally come home. This is where he belonged, in the embrace of the Almighty.

Raising his head from prayer, the pope smiled. "You were right, Vinnie. The Holy Spirit confirms that Chris will indeed serve us well." Chris smiled, eagerly awaiting the words that would follow.

"Chris, these are perilous times. The world is racing to reinvent itself. The New World Order. There are some who believe this new world can come about through accommodation to a de-fanged Soviet Union. Others believe it can only come about with wholesale adoption of American greed. Most agree the rising European superstate will be the glue that binds." Chris found himself going back to his discussions with Tom about the alignment of nations during the end times.

"No one has made a place for Christ in this New World Order," the pope continued. "My role is to ensure that Christianity in general, and the Catholic Church specifically, have a place at the negotiating table while the details of this New World Order are hammered out.

"I cannot turn my back on the opportunity to help bring about an end to the oppression in Eastern Europe. To feed the masses behind the iron curtain who starve for the Word of God."

"A noble calling, Holiness. To raise the iron curtain would be a dream come true," Chris said.

The pope's expression clouded. "But all of life is about choices. There is a growing evil within the confines of the Vatican. My short-lived predecessor took seriously the remarks of his predecessor that the enemy had found his way to the very seat of the Church." Chris felt a chill run down his spine as a cloud passed over the warm spring sun. The once-soft spring breeze felt cold in the shadow of the cloud.

The pope continued, "Evil men have been gaining power here in the Vatican. My predecessor took the initial steps to clean house, but he met his untimely death."

"You believe Pope John Paul I was murdered?" Chris asked incredulously.

"What do you think?" asked Vinnie. "These guys are up to their eyeballs in Mafia ties. This is the real-life Cosa Nostra, only with a satanic bent. They're playing for keeps."

"And therein lies my frustration. As Holy Father, I would confront them. Even if I survived the exercise, it would take all of my time. By devoting myself to eradicating this evil, I would unwittingly be turning my back on the opportunity to help the millions in Eastern Europe. The tragedy is that I cannot accomplish both. I have chosen to bring the Gospel. These selfish, evil men will have to remain the problem of a future pontificate." There was a tear in the Holy Father's eye as he considered the gravity of his statement. He would literally have to sacrifice the Church for the chance to open the Soviet bloc to the good news of the Gospel.

"So you see, my young friend, in order to free many, I have become a prisoner. A prisoner of the Vatican. The greatest disaster would be if these unholy men found a way to eliminate me before I accomplish my work."

"Chris," Vinnie said in an uncharacteristically soft voice, "the new bad guy in town is Monsignor Benjamin Cross."

"My new boss?" Chris asked, wiping his forehead.

Vinnie nodded. "He's gotten really cozy with this guy Luciano Begliali. The guy's straight up Mafia, Freemason, and satanic ... an evil trifecta."

"It doesn't sound good," Chris muttered. The other two laughed at the understatement.

Vinnie continued, "This Cross guy is a lazy bum with selfish ambitions."

"And now I'm working for this lazy bum?" Chris asked, exasperated.

"You work for the Lord and the Church," the pope countered. "But I am afraid both have called you to a precarious position. I need you to monitor the relationship between Monsignor Cross and Bishop Marcinkus. Periodically you will visit me as you assist Father Vinnie here in gardening or other household tasks."

"What do you know?" Vinnie teased. "Turns out I'm the lazy bum you're working for!"

Chris was having a hard time taking it all in. He was being asked—no, told—to become a spy, to ingratiate himself with and then report on the very people who were dangerous enough to make the pope feel like a prisoner of the Vatican.

"I have so many questions," Chris stammered. "Why me? Why do you think I can do this?"

Vinnie answered, "Cross specifically requested you to be his assistant. Bilbo arranged it."

That news hit Chris like a blow to the stomach. "I've never met the man. Why would he choose me?"

"Do you remember a priest who met you in the airport when you arrived from Uganda?"

Chris searched his mind but drew only a dim recollection. That day was so turbulent, and he was reeling from his injuries. "I can't exactly remember it. Everything's a bit fuzzy. But I think I asked a priest in the airport to make sure Fran and Gloria got back to the United States."

"That's the guy."

"In some way, then, I'm grateful. Maybe he's not an entirely bad guy."

"There are some members of our surprisingly extensive intelligence agency who are yet loyal to me," the pope answered. "They have performed a very thorough background check on the monsignor. He's trouble."

"What makes him think I would be a good choice to be his assistant?" Chris asked, confused. The pontiff remained silent, looking to Vinnie to answer.

"Our best guess is that it has to do with that pretty mug of yours," Vinnie said, squeezing Chris's cheeks.

"Oh no!" Chris moaned. "My qualification is that he thinks I'm handsome? Could this get any worse?"

"Technically, yes." Vinnie laughed. "If he makes you wear your collar and nothing else around the office—" Chris stared at him in horror.

"Vincenzo," the pope chided, "don't tease the young man. Chris, our profilers believe that he may find you to be attractive."

"Holiness, I ... I don't know if I can do this job. I became a priest to preach the Gospel, not to be a secret agent. It all seems so far beyond my calling," Chris pleaded.

"I felt the same about my calling to Rome. But when I prayed about it, I heard the Lord speaking to me, as you will, 'Who knows if you haven't been called to the kingdom for such a time as this?'"

There it was, the quote from the book of Esther. That said it all. He remembered Tom's dying words.

"If this is what the Lord wants for me," he told the older clerics, "then this is what I'll do." He smiled a sad smile, knowing his life had changed forever. His mind fell to the memory of his father's papers burning in the fireplace. *Maybe this time the bad guys won't win. Maybe this time I can help stop them.*

A Swiss Guard appeared on the sidewalk, not daring to enter uninvited into the pope's personal grotto. Looking up, the pope saw the brightly festooned man and said, "Ah, my job beckons, gentlemen. It was so refreshing to discuss gardening with you. Please continue."

The men kissed the pontiff's ring as their familiarity was replaced with the walls of courtier etiquette in front of the guardsman. The pope raised his hand in a blessing over the two priests and left the grotto.

Chris sat on the bench in stunned silence for a few moments.

"I know it's a lot to take in, kid. But there's only one way to get over it. Work. Your petunias are waiting for you." He chucked a pair of gardening gloves at Chris.

Smiling, Chris put on the gloves and then noticed Vinnie had none. "Where are your gloves?"

"I'm not planting anything today. I got—"

"Gout." Chris laughed. "Yeah, I know."

Within a week, Chris was seated at his new desk. Although technically a liaison office between the secretary of state and the Vatican Bank, the location of the new offices was with the secretary of state

Upon his arrival, early in the morning, an old Italian monk who had been Benny's acting secretary escorted him to his desk.

"You will be seated here," he said in halting English. It was a simple desk with a multiple- line telephone in the corner. A typewriter rested on a side table within easy reach. Behind him were file cabinets. A drab existence compared to the sun-filled brightness of Africa. He missed the joy of helping those in need and the incredible thrill that surged through his whole body when someone really found Jesus. He was made for the field. There was nothing about this setup that appealed to him. But, like the pontiff, he too had become a prisoner of the Vatican.

"Dov' e il monsignore?" he inquired. "Where is the monsignor?"

The old monk laughed and went on to explain that Monsignor Cross rarely made it to his office before 10:00 a.m. Thereafter he would make some phone calls and go out for a long lunch around noon. He would return from lunch around 2:30 p.m. and take half an hour to decide the restaurant where he would eat dinner. Generally, he left by 6:00 p.m., depending on the distance to the restaurant.

When Chris inquired as to the filing system, the old friar opened the filing cabinets to reveal they were empty, save one. In that drawer were several bottles of wine and several different wheels of cheese. The cleric explained that Benny had a snack around four thirty each afternoon. *What a tool!*

At that point, Cardinal Bilbo entered the room. Technically, he was the monsignor's boss, but Chris would soon learn Benny's rela-tionship with Begliali all but negated the cardinal's authority.

"Tell him I wish to see him when he arrives," the cardinal said sharply to Chris. There was no introduction, and there was no time for Chris to introduce himself. Bilbo turned on his heels and left the office without even considering the slightest civility.

The old monk said in a whisper, "The affairs of state are rigorous. Often the men of these offices reserve all of their politeness for the art of statecraft."

The phone rang. The friar said, "That is his sister from America. A very nice woman."

"Monsignor Cross's office, Father Chris speaking," Chris said as he picked up the line.

"Ah, hello ..." Kim said in a shocked tone. "You threw me off guard! I was prepared to use the one or two Italian phrases in my repertoire."

Chris chuckled and said softly, "Hopefully they would have matched the couple Italian phrases I know."

"I'm guessing Benny hasn't made it in yet. As soon as I placed the call, I realized it was a bit early for him. He's never been a morning person."

"So I have heard. Actually, I've never met your brother. This is my first day on the job."

"Oh, well, good luck to you then."

"I might need it. I'm not the office type by nature."

"How did you come to find yourself in your current position then?"

Chris felt immediately at home with this woman. He explained the events that had taken him from Africa to Rome. She was what he would call a "constructive listener," a person who made listening an active part of the conversation. Before he knew it, they had spoken nearly an hour. *She certainly is a breath of fresh air to this dark office.*

Finally Benny arrived. "Ah, the young Father Chris is finally in my employ!" he said good-naturedly. Chris stood. They shook hands. Benny held Chris's hand just a bit too long and said, "Welcome, friend."

"It will be my honor to work for you, Monsignor," Chris said. He flashed a dazzling smile. Benny gasped.

"And it will be my honor to have you," Benny said with a slightly leering smile.

"Oh, I forgot these," Chris said as he freed his hand to pick up the messages from his desk. "Cardinal Bilbo requested that you see him as soon as you arrive. And your sister called."

"That's very efficient," Benny cooed. "Now if you could please take my coat and get me an espresso, I will prepare to meet with the cardinal."

Chris kept his head down in a servant position, remembering his larger assignment. "Of course, Monsignor," he said.

Benny looked closely at the handsome face as Chris came close to help him out of his coat.

"Your face is healing nicely."

"Thank you, Monsignor. I am very blessed to be alive. And I

understand that I have you to thank for ensuring that my friends made it back to the United States."

"No thanks necessary. You looked horrible that day. My heart went out to you."

"Well, please know that I appreciate what you did." Chris moved away with the coat toward the closet. *Not a horrible first meeting.*

As the months passed, things settled into a predictable rhythm for Chris. Benny's work habits were decidedly predictable. It was a small matter to meet his needs. And Chris had come to dismiss the occasional long glance or slightly prolonged physical contact. It appeared Benny was also too lazy to be a sexual predator. That is not to say he wasn't controlling. Early in their relationship he offered to place five hundred dollars per month in a trust fund for Gloria's education. He did it to ensure that Chris would stay with him, of course, having no idea that Chris stayed by papal mandate. Nonetheless, he accepted the money on Gloria's behalf.

Benny's late start each morning gave Chris time to work out and read his Bible on most mornings. Other mornings, he abandoned the workout to help Vinnie with his sandwich ministry. Once a week, after Benny left for the day, he would accompany Vinnie to the grotto. Most times the pope would be waiting to hear his report. So far there wasn't much to report. Benny had several meetings with Vatican Bank officials and frequent phone calls to Luciano, but Chris could not discern any devious plot. To his mind, Benny was a bit of a bumbler, not someone to whom you would entrust great power. Then again, Cardinal Bilbo's deference to Benny was unnerving. "A sure sign that Benny's guilty of something," Vinnie said, "'cause Bilbo hasn't been on the good team since I met him at Vatican II."

The pattern was frankly monotonous. It was comfortable while Chris healed physically and emotionally from his African experience, but as he gained strength, he longed for something more pastoral. He was, after all, an orphan. He needed the close contact a parish could provide—it was the only way he could attain what most people take for granted: a family.

The thing that broke the monotony and really brightened his days was conversing with Kimberly. Benny claimed he was too busy, so it fell to Chris to plan an upcoming visit from Kim and the boys. As he and Kim planned the trip, they spoke as friends, and with the partial anonymity of the telephone, they had begun to share much of their lives. Both had lost their parents at a young age, creating a bond others would not easily understand. And then there were the boys. Chris waited anxiously to hear their latest antics.

And so it was that Benny filled his calendar during Kim's upcoming visit and freed Chris's schedule so that he could do the dirty work of being a tour guide. For his part, Chris felt that he got the better end of the deal.

Sitting in the lobby of their hotel, Chris pressed a wrinkle out of his cassock. He was nervous as he waited for their elevator to descend. Their relationship had grown by telephone, and now he was to meet this family in person. As the elevator doors opened, Kim strolled forward with a grace that defied her years.

"Chris?" she asked. He smiled and nodded his head. Slight curls of brown hair with auburn highlights framed her face. She was wearing a yellow starched linen skirt and a comfortable white gauze blouse, both of which swayed delicately as she walked. Chris was a bit overwhelmed by her beauty; there was certainly no resemblance to Benny.

She hugged him, to his surprise. "I am so happy to meet you!"

"Same here. And these are the boys! Let me guess. You are Michael and you are Gabe."

"How did you know?" Gabe asked.

"Your mom gives good descriptions. She called you her little archangels. Her Gabriel with beautiful emerald eyes, and her Michael with light-blue eyes that shine from his face."

"You're right," Michael said, "and I think you and I have the same eyes."

"Let's see," Chris said as he got on his knees beside Michael. "What do you say, Gabe?"

"They look the same to me. What do you think, Mom?"

Kim gazed at the handsome face staring up at her. "It's amazing. You two could be related."

Gabe pulled on his mother's arm, and she bent to hear his all-too-loud whisper. "I like this guy, Mom. He's not like Benny at all."

"Come on, guys. Let's go. We've got a lot to see," Chris said.

Walking toward the Coliseum, Kim explained softly that Benny had been against her adopting Gabe and that it showed in his attitude toward the boy. She said Gabe had been anxious about this part of the trip, because he would have to be around Benny. As they strolled, Michael excitedly walked ahead of them, spouting facts about the historic structure. Gabe rolled his eyes with pride at his brother. Chris reached out to put his arm around Gabe, who surprised him by pressing in close for a hug.

On their last day in Rome, Chris had the family get up early for a special treat.

"Where are we going, Chris?" the boys pestered.

"For the best breakfast sandwiches in town." He smiled sheepishly. They followed him through the streets of early-morning Rome. Fresh air, tinted with the smell of baking bread, permeated the city. Traffic was at a minimum, and the daily hustle and bustle of the city was held to a soft hum. Kim and the boys fell into the peacefulness as they strode silently through the streets.

"So this is the family you've been bragging about," Vinnie called as they approached.

"Yep!" Chris smiled. "Father Vinnie, I'd like you to meet Kimberly Martin and her sons, Michael and Gabriel."

"A pleasure. What brings you all out so early in the morning?"

"Best sandwiches in town." Chris grinned proudly.

They were interrupted by a Ferrari as it sped into the plaza toward Chris. The driver parked the car inches from the group, jumped out of the car, and grabbed frantically at Chris. *"Scuzi. Padre! Sono Mario Girote."* The man broke into a torrent of Italian and tears.

Chris took stock of the man accosting him. The guy was nearly hysterical. He was wearing a fine silk suit, but it was rumpled, as if he hadn't changed clothes for days. A beard was beginning to form, and his dirty hair was uncombed.

"Hey, you guys," Vinnie said to Kim and the boys. "This man needs some privacy. Let me show you this fountain over here."

They moved to the other side of the small piazza as Chris tried to calm the man enough to understand what he was saying. "Oh, Lord," he prayed out loud, "help me to understand this man."

Girote heard the prayer. It seemed to register somewhere in his panic-stricken brain that the priest with the kind eyes was American.

"Father," Girote said in English, "I am a terrible sinner. I need confessions. Immediately."

Chris placed his hand on the man's shoulder. "Do you believe that Jesus died to take away your sins?"

The man started to cry. "I don't know, *Signore*. My sins are heavy, big sins."

Chris looked squarely into his bloodshot eyes and smiled. "He is a big God. He died for all sins. Yours aren't too heavy for Him."

"Then hear my confession, Father. Please come to my car," Girote begged.

Inside the car, the man began to tell Chris his story. Chris listened in fascination and then horror as Girote told about his participation in several murders. He had even participated in meetings discussing the murder of the previous pope. The man cried, explaining that his time had now come. His coconspirators wanted him dead, and he didn't want to go to hell.

Chris explained that repentance involved more than the fear of hell. He spoke about the love of God, explaining that Jesus loved Girote more than he could even imagine. Girote calmed. They prayed, and Girote accepted Jesus as the Lord of his life. Chris offered absolution and prepared to leave the car. While they had been speaking, Rome came to life around them. The once nearly empty piazza was now filled with Romans beginning their day.

"Father," Girote said, "because you have shown me salvation, I want to give you a warning. I have watched you. I know you work for very evil men. The cardinal and Begliali are the ones behind the murders we spoke of. And your boss, Monsignor Cross, intimidates even the cardinal. You must be very careful in your dealings with these men."

Chris nodded somberly, knowing only too well the dangers. His talks with Vinnie and the pope had already convinced him there was evil afoot, and his parents' deaths at the hands of such men still haunted him. What had he gotten into?

"The important thing is that you know you are forgiven, Mr. Girote. Maybe you could get out of the country for a while until all of this dies down. Maybe you could assume a new identity and live a new life for the Lord."

"Maybe," Girote said. He reached across to Chris and grasped his hand. "Or maybe I will go to be with my Savior. I will tell Him you say hello."

Chris smiled sadly and exited the car. Before shutting the door, he leaned his head in and said, "God bless you, Mr. Girote."

Girote said, "Amen," as Chris closed the door.

Chris was looking across the now-crowded piazza, trying to find Kim and the boys when he heard it. Three gunshots. *Pop. Pop. Pop.* He turned around to see Girote hanging out of his car. The driver-side door hung open from Girote's failed attempt to escape. He died before he could exit the car, his now-lifeless torso hanging out the side.

The crowd gasped at the sound of the shots, running to get away. Chris ran to Girote. Blood oozed from three large holes in his chest. Chris checked for a pulse he knew would not be there. He looked up anxiously as he heard footsteps pounding on the cobblestones. He saw Kim running toward him, and behind her just for a second he saw the unmistakable silhouette of Benny Cross in the crowd. It was all too much for him. Long-dormant residual terror from his parents' deaths seized him, and he found himself reliving Tom's death as he held Girote's head in his hands. He looked once more at Kim and then started to cry uncontrollably.

Kim reached him and bent down to comfort him. He was barely aware of her as she held his sobbing shoulders. The boys followed their mother in short order, Vinnie shouting after them.

"Chris!" Vinnie shouted. "Chris! Pull yourself together! You have to get Kim and the boys away from the car!"

Chris responded with concern for them. He stood on shaky legs. Tears clouded his vision as he led Kim and the boys away from the car.

Vinnie looked on as Kim put her shoulder under Chris's right arm so he could lean on her. The boys held him from the other side. Vinnie knew in that moment Chris had found the family he so desperately needed. Unfortunately it was the family of the snake that had ordered the hit.

"God help us all," he muttered and then joined the group.

SIXTEEN

hris braced himself against the early-morning chill of the winter day. Following a well-known path, he caught up with Vinnie in his early-morning sandwich run.

"Hey! Look what the cat dragged in."

"Hey, yourself, Vinnie." Chris smiled.

"What brings you out this morning?"

"Maybe I just wanted to help."

"Yeah. And maybe I'm Robert Redford! Chris, you haven't wanted to join me on the sandwich run since Girote's murder. And I don't blame you. I wasn't too enthusiastic about it myself for a while."

"Thanks for understanding, Vinnie." Chris stood with his hands in his pockets, not knowing where to begin.

"So, then, what's on your mind?" Vinnie asked.

"Christmas. Benny is going to the States for three weeks. He told me he would require my services there."

"Is he going to Kim's place?"

"Yeah," Chris answered.

"How do you feel about that?" Vinnie questioned, looking intently into Chris's eyes.

Chris waved his arm and sighed. "Frankly, I would love to see Kim and the boys again. But Benny's another story. Three weeks of him with no break! And he really talks down to me. I think it will embarrass me in front of the family."

"Hold on there, Chris," Vinnie interrupted. "I'm what you might call simpleminded. I need to break things down to understand them.

So humor me. We all know Benny's a butthole. If you have to go to the States with him, then I agree it's a problem."

Vinnie shrugged, put his arm around Chris's shoulder, and continued. "Then there's the family. I've seen you with them, Chris, and I've seen them with you. You click with Kim and those kids. There are a lot of priests I would counsel to stay away. But you're different. You're priest through and through. So I'll just ask you a simple question. Would you consider breaking your vows to be close to them?"

Chris gasped at the mere thought. "What? No! I'll be honest with you, Vinnie. I don't like my 'ministry' right now. I don't wear it well, and this is not what I envisioned when I became a priest. But the priesthood isn't a job to me. It's a way of life. It's a love relationship with Jesus. When I took my vows, to me they were a marriage to the Lord."

"Good man." Vinnie smiled. "Do you think Kim would like you as more than a friend?"

"Wow. You're hitting the celibacy thing hard today! She has alluded to some terrible things in her past that have scarred her. In a nutshell, she is afraid of sexual intimacy."

Vinnie chuckled. "Well, there you go. She can't, and you won't!" Vinnie cackled. "And what do you feel?"

Chris grinned at Vinnie's unique manner of expression. "I have a sense of belonging when I'm with them. I truly love that family."

Vinnie smiled. "Well, to the simpleminded, like me, it sounds like you get the opportunity to share Christmas with a family you love. So that's not such a problem, right?"

"When you put it that way, it doesn't sound so bad," Chris conceded and then paused and furrowed his brow. "But then there's Benny."

"Ha! You know what your problem is? You don't have a family, so you've built up a fantasy that family is all about people with shared dreams who love each other unconditionally." Vinnie shuffled his gout-ridden feet to ward off the cold. "Let me tell you about real life! I have cousins, aunts, and uncles I love. I can't stand them, but I love them anyway. Why do I love them anyway? One reason is they're important to people I care deeply about. Another reason is the Gospel.

"Here's the truth, kid. A lot of the time family stinks, but it's the greatest blessing there is. The Lord is giving you the chance to have

188

family relationships, but you have to pick up your cross—in this case, Benny Cross—and follow."

Christmas 1979 found Fran and Gloria in Dallas. It had been tough for Fran, but she had gotten a job teaching and rented this tiny one-bedroom apartment she and Gloria now called home. Thankfully, it was a short walk from Tom's parents' home. Fran was thankful for their support and care, and mostly for the constant attention they paid to Gloria. She truly believed that their love had brought Gloria through the roughest times this past year.

"Good night, pumpkin," Sam Ellis called to his granddaughter.

Gloria yelled, "Wait, Grandpa!" She climbed down from the step stool in front of the nearly decorated Christmas tree and ran to give her grandfather a hug. As she was in his arms, he looked over her shoulder to smile at Fran. His eyes carried the joy of a grandfather holding his only grandchild, but Fran could also see there the pain of losing his only son.

"Thanks so much for the tree, Sam," Fran said, smiling warmly. Sam reminded her so much of Tom. It was a comfort to have him around.

"I just figured you would be pretty busy, and you're just getting used to your finances. Besides, what's a retired old coot got to do that's better than spoiling his beautiful granddaughter?"

Fran looked around the apartment and chuckled. It was a step up from the standard of living in Africa, but not by a lot. The apartment had been carved out of the second story of an old and pretty dilapidated home. They had arrived in the United States with little more than the clothes on their backs, so every piece of furniture and most of their clothing had to be acquired. Used. Secondhand. Goodwill. Fran utilized every avenue to give her daughter a home. And while things may have been a little worse for the wear, the place looked nice. Fran discovered that she had real talent with machine-wash dyes. She was able to perfectly color-match curtains to sofas and table coverings to curtains so that everything came together in a very homey fashion. The bedroom was Gloria's. It was a wonderland of pink. You would never be able to find a pack of Sweet'N Low in that room, but Gloria thought it was great. She had a lot of girly-girl stuff to catch up on after the years in Africa.

"Sam," Fran reminded, "remember that I lined up a tutoring session tomorrow. So Gloria will be getting off the bus at your house."

"How could I forget? I'm already planning dinner." He hugged his granddaughter tightly and put his forehead to hers. "Tomorrow, kiddo, it's your favorite—we're going to have breakfast for dinner!"

"Great, Grandpa!" Gloria exclaimed, hugging him again.

Fran chuckled, knowing Gloria not only loved bacon, eggs, and pancakes for dinner, but the show as well. Sam let her help with the cooking. The two of them saw themselves as a well-oiled machine in the kitchen. Tom's mother, Evelyn, thought they were just about as messy as Sam and Tom had been in the kitchen when Tom was a child. She would usually raise her hands and say, "I'm out of this. If you mess it, you clean it!"

As Sam left, Fran said a quick prayer of thanks for his presence in their lives. Evelyn had been great too. But Sam reminded them so much of Tom that she and Gloria naturally gravitated to him.

"Do you think he'll like the tree?" Gloria asked, appraising it critically.

"Who?"

"Father Chris!"

"Gloria, he'll love your tree," Fran assured.

"I just want everything to be perfect. I guess because I'm scared."

"Why are you afraid, honey?"

"I'm afraid when I see him, he'll remind me so much of Daddy. What if I start to feel really sad when I see him?"

Fran sat on the couch and pulled Gloria down beside her. "I think you'll be fine, and here's why: I have never met anyone in this world more like your father than your granddad. Being around him makes you feel good, doesn't it?"

"Yeah. He knows how to talk to me and hug me just the way Daddy did." Gloria moved to the tree to hang the last few ornaments.

Fran joined her, picking up an angel ornament. "So, Granddad is like a bandage on the wound left by your father's death. Chris can't hurt you. He'll just remind us of some good times we all had together.

Nothing else. Besides, we might have to help your grandparents when he's here."

"Because he'll remind them of Daddy?" Gloria asked as Fran stretched to place the ornament near the top of the tree.

"That and the fact that he's a priest. They've never met a Catholic priest, let alone had one stay in their home."

"But Father Chris is just a normal, nice guy. The only difference is that he has the word 'Father' in front of his name," Gloria said matter-of-factly.

"I know that. And you know that. But they haven't met him yet. Your grandmother has been washing walls and windows since we found out Chris was coming."

"What about you, Mom? Will you be happy to see him?"

"Yes," Fran answered without conviction. She didn't want to go into detail, having just convinced Gloria the visit wasn't a time for sadness.

As Joseph pulled up to the mansion with his charges, Kim and the boys threw the door open. Benny was first out of the car, and Kim ran to give him a hug. He then reached out to hug Michael. Gabe didn't wait to give Benny the chance to ignore him. He went to the other side of the car, pulled open the door, and flung himself into a hug for Chris. At that point, Michael ran to get in on the act, and the two boys fairly tackled Chris as he tried to get out of the car.

Kim was asking Benny about their flight as Joseph opened the trunk to the car.

"Joseph," Kim said forcefully, "we have two young boys here that can take care of the luggage. I don't want you to hurt your back again."

"Thank you, Miss Kimberly."

"Don't worry about the luggage, Kim," Benny said casually. "Chris! Stop messing around and get the luggage, will you?"

Kim watched as the smile on Chris's face froze. There was a two-second pause, and he said, "Of course, Monsignor." He straightened himself and went to the trunk of the limo with both boys in tow.

"All right, crew, here's what we'll do," he said to the boys. "I'll take these two big ones, and you two—"

"Nobody's doing anything until I get a hug," Kim said as she walked into the group. She hugged Chris, and he hugged back. For a second she felt like she was the one who had come home.

"Chris, I want you to make yourself at home here. Right, boys?"

"Right!" they screamed and fell onto the two adults in a combination group hug and tackle. The four ended up on the driveway, laughing. Joseph smiled broadly in amusement.

"Chris!" Benny snapped. "The luggage!" Then he stomped into the house.

Chris stood abruptly, dusting himself off. "Come on, guys," he said to the boys, "let's get Uncle Benny's stuff into the house." Kim blushed in anger and thought about chasing Benny into the house to lay down some ground rules. But he'd just gotten there. It would be an ugly three weeks if she started it off with a confrontation. Instead, she decided to lend a hand to "her three boys."

Kim had been anxious about how Chris would react to the grandeur of the house. She watched his face as he took in the large foyer. The inlaid wooden floors yielded to the four-story expanse of stairways. The first-floor staircase began with a graceful curve that wound around most of the foyer. Nestled into that curve was a twenty-foot Christmas tree dressed in red bows.

"This is the formal part of the house," Kim said a little defensively. "Mostly we hang out in the back of the house. It's homier there. But when we have company—"

"It's not half of Luciano's castle," Benny said with a sigh, "but it will have to do."

Chris looked at Kim and rolled his eyes. Gabe saw him and started to laugh.

"Is someone going to tell Chris where my rooms are?" Benny intoned. "It's been a long flight, and I really need to lie down."

"You guys are on the third floor," Michael said. Chris started toward the stairs with the heavy suitcases, but Michael caught up to him. "Chris, there's an elevator. I'll show you."

"Me too!" Gabe chimed in as they ran ahead.

As Benny settled in, Kim and the boys showed Chris around the house. At least the first three floors. The second floor had bedroom suites for Kim and each of the boys. The third floor had a suite of rooms for Benny and five other nicely decorated guest rooms, each with a bath. The fourth floor had previously held more bedrooms and parlors but was now unused, as it had been since Kim's parents died. In their day, Kim explained, it was not uncommon to have twenty houseguests for long weekends. Since they were gone, however, the rooms had become sort of a storage site. Kim grinned contentedly as the boys joined the conversation.

"Right," Michael said to Chris with deadpan sincerity. "Plus, it's haunted. You can't go up there at any cost. Bad things may happen."

"He's right," Gabe chimed in with a grin. "The last priest that went up there came back as Uncle Benny. Wooooooooo!"

Both boys were laughing. Hiding her own impulse to grin, Kim grabbed both by the shoulders. "We need to always have respect for Uncle Benny, boys. I don't want to hear that again. In fact, why don't you guys run out back to check on Uncle Benny's Christmas surprise? The guys should be wrapping it up this afternoon." The boys scurried out of the house, laughing again at Gabe's joke once they mistakenly thought they were out of their mother's earshot.

As they descended the stairs, Kim touched Chris's arm lightly. "Chris, I really want you to feel at home here."

"Thanks, Kim. I'd like that. Since my parents died, I've kind of lived an institutional life. In fact, the few things I kept from their house are in the basement of my old seminary." Kim wished more than anything that she could share this house with him, and she worried that Benny's bad manners would ruin her attempt to make Chris feel at home.

"But how are you going to feel at home with Benny barking orders at you? Is that how he treats you all the time?"

"Pretty much." Chris grinned sheepishly.

"Why do you allow him to do that?" she asked.

Chris hemmed and hawed, as if running through several options. Finally he said, "There are a lot of reasons, but the biggest one is that he set up an account for that girl that I told you about."

"The little girl from Africa?"

"Actually, from Texas now," Chris explained. "I'm going to visit them this coming weekend. When her father died, there was very little insurance. Benny has been kind enough to put back five hundred dollars a month for her into a college fund."

Kim colored with the same protective nature she held for Michael and Gabe. Leave it to Benny to string this poor guy along at the clip of five hundred dollars a month for a little girl that had just lost her dad!

"Five hundred dollars a month? Five hundred dollars a month!" Kim was growing irate. "Look at this house! Do you know how much money Benny has at his disposal?"

"I'm starting to realize it now," Chris said with arched eyebrows.

"Follow me," she said as she marched down the stairs to the first floor. Past the Christmas tree to the west wing of the house, they marched through a large anteroom with a Chippendale desk. A tapestry pattern decorated the chair behind the desk, with a matching pattern on a sofa. She opened the door to her office, which was paneled in rich mahogany and decorated with a deep-red carpet and flowered upholstery on a camel-backed couch and Chippendale chairs.

"What is the mother's name?" she snapped.

"Frannie. Why?"

Kim hastily pulled out a large checkbook. "No, Chris, her full name."

"Frances Ellis. Kim, what are you doing?" Chris asked incredulously.

"I'm buying your freedom." She wrote quickly and handed him a check made out to Fran in the amount of two million dollars. They debated it for a long while, during which Kim opened up to Chris about her financial worth. She made him understand that, although it was a large amount, she could well afford to give it. Tears came to his eyes as he repeatedly thanked Kim for her generosity, not only toward him, but toward Fran, Gloria, and Tom's memory.

The greeting at the airport felt awkward somehow. Their entire relationship had been through Tom, and he was no longer here. Chris hugged both Fran and Gloria at the same time. They formed a little circle, and hot tears filled their eyes.

Chris thought Fran and Gloria both looked good, considering what they had been through this year. Fran's new hairdo suited her, and Gloria looked like the average American kid. But in both there was a deep, somber note, a reminiscent tone of tragedy's visit to their souls.

When they got to the house, Chris got his first taste of Sam and Evelyn.

"Father, welcome to our home," Evelyn said with a nearly imperceptible curtsy. "I want you to feel at home. So if there is anything you need or want, please let me know. I know a Catholic from town, and I borrowed a set of beads that I put in your room."

Chris fell into a chuckle. "Thank you, Mrs. Ellis, but you don't have to fuss over me at all."

"It's just I've never known a Catholic priest."

"Then don't think of me that way. I'm your son's friend, a friend who loved him a lot." At that, the walls came down. Evelyn took off her glasses to wipe her eyes. Then she grasped Chris's head and pulled it down to her height. She kissed him on the forehead and gave him a hug.

Sam, who had been running an errand, came in the front door to see them hugging. "Excuse me, Father, but she's taken," he said. Chris looked up in surprise. For a second he thought he had heard Tom's voice. He saw an older version of Tom smiling at him. A few wrinkles, the soft curls gray instead of blond, but the same powerful build. For a moment he was dumbstruck.

"Amazing resemblance, isn't it?" Fran asked with a knowing grin.

Chris held out his hand. "It's a pleasure to meet you, sir."

Sam took his hand and pulled him into an embrace. "The pleasure is all mine, son."

Later that day, the Ellis family took Chris to Tom's tombstone. It was small and reverent, bearing his name, dates of birth and death, and the phrase "Servant of the Living God." Fran, Sam, Evelyn, and Gloria stood. Chris knelt on the cold earth, looking up at Tom's tombstone.

"Father, into your hands we commend the spirit of our beloved husband, father, son, and friend. May you grant him peace, and may Your Perpetual Light shine on him. For us, Father, I ask for Your healing grace as we learn to live in a world without him. Give us the strength to carry on, and the sure knowledge we will join him one day in Paradise." Chris raised his hands in a blessing, making a cross with his right hand as he said, "In the name of the Father, and of the Son, and of the Holy Spirit. Amen."

"Amen," Fran and Gloria added, followed first by Sam and then Evelyn. Chris rose to his feet.

"I just wanted to take a couple minutes to tell you all I thought Tom was a wonderful man of God. He blessed my life richly. I was challenged by his theology, in awe of his godliness and dedication to the Lord, and inspired by his love and affection for Frannie and Gloria.

"And more than anything on Earth, he loved you, Frannie, and he loved you, Gloria. I know it seems a tragedy that your time with him was cut short. But the love you all shared was something special. It's what kept drawing me to visit. I could enter your home and just be bombarded by the love that was there.

"And you know, the Bible tells us love never dies. Tom's last words were to make me promise to get the two of you to safety. We managed to get you home to Texas, but without any of your possessions and without any financial security. That has weighed on my heart, not that there is much I could do about it. Then the Lord let me meet a wonderful lady of considerable wealth. When she heard your story, she wanted to help. So, from her heart and in Tom's memory, I present you with this."

He handed Fran the envelope. When she opened it, her legs went weak and tears filled her eyes. She handed the check to Sam. As he and Evelyn looked at it, their mouths dropped. Gloria was probably too young to understand the significance of the gift, but she saw the reaction of the adults as Chris came to her and hugged her. Soon the adults joined in. Chris led them in a prayer of thanksgiving for the provision God had given them and calling forth a blessing on Kimberly Martin.

As soon as Chris left, the fourth floor of Kim's mansion was a flurry of activity. The painters had finished their work, and the furniture was to be delivered that afternoon. In the meantime, the work in the backyard had been completed, and the boys were giddy with excitement. Her only concern was Benny's attitude. Would he appreciate the sentiment? Or would he crush the boys' spirits with his disapproval? She decided she couldn't take the chance of disappointing them on Christmas Eve.

Benny was in the dining room, finishing a late breakfast.

"Good morning, Benny."

"Good morning yourself, sis. What was all the racket this morning? I asked Caroline, but she told me I should talk to you."

"Actually, I'm happy you asked. The boys and I have been working on a surprise Christmas present for you. But the closer we get to Christmas, the more I think I should let you in on it, in case you don't agree with what we've done."

"A surprise? Oh, Kim, you know me. I'll have to know now. It will kill me to wait until Christmas!"

"Well, then, get your coat and follow me." She grinned.

She led him along the road that stretched behind the mansion to the site of what had been a sort of barn in the early years of the estate. It was made of stone, and although it wasn't a large building, it was two and a half stories tall, open from floor to roof. In days of old, it had served primarily as a smokehouse, where meats were cured.

As they got closer to the old building, Benny could see that a lot of work had been done to it. Large stained glass windows now outfitted the sides of the building. In the front of the structure, Kim had added a small steeple. The barn doors were replaced with large double doors of weather-beaten wood. Beside the doors was a sign that read, "Saint Benedict's."

"Oh, Kim," Benny said quietly.

She looked at him closely, trying to determine what to make of his reaction. "What do you think?"

"I don't want to seem like a party pooper, but why did you do this?" he asked with exasperation.

"We thought it would make you feel more at home," Kim said defensively. She knew where this was going.

"It's like giving a ditchdigger a shovel for Christmas, Kim! I'm sure you meant well, but *my* Christmas present should reflect *my* personality, shouldn't it? I don't want to sound ungrateful, but you and the boys missed this one by a mile!"

Kim's hands were balled into fists. Sometimes Benny made her so angry! But she knew his personality. This is exactly why she had given him a preview. Better she should hear him now than watch disappointment flood the faces of her boys on Christmas Eve.

"Don't you at least want to look inside?"

"Why would I? I work at the Vatican. Do you think a converted smokehouse is going to impress me?"

"Fine. Fine, Benny," Kim said as she turned around to return to the house. Benny marched alongside of her. "I still have time to get something else. Is there anything you really want?"

"I've been dropping hints all along about a very exclusive Cabernet I have my eyes on."

"Got it," Kim said sharply. She had already received a case of the wine, which she had planned to give Benny, along with the chapel.

"For unto us a child is born ..." Mack paused for a long ten seconds. He looked into the camera and wiped a tear from his eye. "I can't tell you how much these words mean to me, because this child is the hope of the nations. I don't need to tell you this was a tough year for Sarah and me. As you know, we lost a dear friend in the mission field. Those were dark days, friends, but all I have to hear is this phrase, 'For unto us a child is born,' and I know everything will be all right."

Mack paused the video when the phone rang. He was anxiously awaiting word from the station manager. "Hello," he answered on the first ring.

"Mack? It's Bob. Everything looks great."

"Thanks, Bob. I can't take all the credit, though. Zack coached me. He has an innate knowledge of how to pull the drama out of a moment."

"Well, I just want you to know it looks great. The timing is a little bit short, but I can fill in with a public service announcement."

"So we're good to go?"

"Good to go, buddy. This will air on Christmas Eve. Enjoy your cruise."

"Thanks, Bob. We surely will. Merry Christmas to you and your family."

"Thanks, Mack. Take care."

Mack hung up the phone as Sarah looked on. They would have had a terrible time getting to the cruise ship on time if Bob had decided the program needed some reediting.

"We're set to go!" he called.

"Praise God!" Sarah exclaimed. "Zack, come on! Let's get these suitcases to the car. We have a ship to catch."

"I'm on it, Mom," Zack called from upstairs.

"Oh, Mack, Christmas at sea! I can hardly believe it. I feel so blessed."

"We are blessed, honey. The donations have been pouring in. They rose when we had Tom's service, and they've stayed at that level. We can afford a little break, and we deserve it."

The days aboard the ship were lazy ones. Even Zack was uncharacteristically placid. Mostly he swam a bit between poolside naps to make up for his nighttime meanderings. Once his parents fell asleep, he would sneak from their cabin to go on deck. There he would scan the cloudless sky, hoping to see *them* again. Every shooting star filled him with expectation and then disappointment.

"Come on," he would say to the stars in the sky. "Come on!" he would scream in his mind. And so he spent his evenings, waiting.

———————

After the visit to the gravesite, the family quietly returned to Sam and Evelyn's house for a roast beef dinner. Gloria felt honored to sit next to Chris. She thought he was as handsome as ever, except for the sadness that had crept into his eyes.

"Chris, I'm in awe of this check, and I'm so curious about this Kimberly Martin. How do you know her?" Fran asked.

Chris explained about working for the woman's brother and that he and Kim began a friendship by phone. And how the friendship grew when she and the boys came to Rome for a visit.

"Chris, if I didn't know better, I'd say you were smitten." Fran grinned.

Oh, Mom, sometimes you are just so silly!

Chris colored. "I'm a priest, Frannie, and I always will be. Nothing will ever change that. But if I were ever to have been married, it would have been someone just like Kim. We connect so easily. I've never experienced anything like it." Gloria felt her face color. How could Chris say something like that? And why did it hurt so badly to hear him say it?

Sam patted Chris on the shoulder. "Physical closeness isn't the only thing that defines a relationship, son. Maybe the Lord has given you a wonderful friend. Evelyn is my best friend. She always will be."

"And Tom will always be my best friend," Fran added. "Maybe through Kim, the Lord has given you a family. Do you think she feels the same way?" Fran asked. Gloria batted her eyes to force back the tears.

"She hasn't said so. She would never interfere with my vows. But I know she feels it too."

"You need to have a talk with her, son," Evelyn said.

Chris sighed. "You're right, Evelyn."

Gloria sat quietly, taking it all in. She felt betrayed. First she had lost her father. Now Chris was in love with somebody else. Why did he need a family? He had her and her mother and her grandparents. How much more family did he need?

Kim was having coffee in the family kitchen at the back of the house when Joseph arrived with Chris. He looked so handsome to her as he walked into the room. There was a light that seemed to glow from within him. It made her feel content just to be around him.

"Damn it, Chris, where were you ten years ago?" she said urgently.

"We have to talk about this," he said in a serious tone.

"I know," Kim said anxiously. "And first, let me say I would never, *ever* do anything to compromise your vocation."

Chris sighed. "Good, because I'm already married to the Lord."

"And who can compete with that?" Kim asked as she poured him a coffee.

"Exactly," he affirmed as he took the coffee from her and sat at the table.

"But I want you in my life, Chris. And the boys do as well."

"And I want that too." He smiled sheepishly. "So I guess we live our lives as close friends."

"No, Chris," Kim answered with the stern decisiveness of a CEO issuing an order. "We'll be a family. It's what we both are searching for."

He walked to her and hugged her. She lay her head on his chest for a brief second, and he stroked her hair. In an instant, both realized this friendship could be much, much more, and they parted quickly when they saw Benny staring at them angrily in the kitchen doorway.

"Boo!" Michael screamed as he poked at his uncle's sides from behind. The startled Benny screamed and jumped about a foot, to the careening laughter of Gabe and Michael.

"What's going on here?" Kim demanded of the boys.

"I should be the one asking that question," Benny said in a huff.

"Well, obviously you were listening, Benny. Chris and I need to have a talk with you, but not before the boys apologize. Which one of you scared Uncle Benny?" She knew it was Michael. Gabe didn't feel the familiarity with Benny to pull such a trick.

"I did, Mom," Michael responded, "but it was only a joke!"

"But you scared him, Michael. What if he had a heart attack or something?"

At his mother's prodding, Michael stood before his uncle to say, "I'm sorry, Uncle Benny."

Benny replied, "I'll be damned if I allow you to pick up where your grandfather left off, Michael!" giving the boy a swift slap across the face. Kim was aghast. Michael yelped.

Kim ran to her startled son. Chris strode across the kitchen to put himself between Benny and the child and spoke quickly in Italian. "Monsignor, you are angry because of what you heard. Let's go to Kim's office so that we can all discuss it together."

After giving Michael a hug, Kim walked briskly to her office, where Benny and Chris sat in silence. She slammed the door behind her. "First off, Benny, you will *never* hit either of those boys again. Do you hear me?"

"Kim, I'll admit I lost my temper, but—"

"No buts, no excuses, no next times, Benny!" she shrieked.

"Kim, we're probably the ones that got him upset," Chris said softly.

"Chris, he'll use any excuse. Benny, let me tell you how things are. On a different day and in a different age, Chris and I could have been a glorious couple. But neither of us, *neither of us*—Benny, are you listening? Neither of us would do anything to hurt his vows. But he is now part of our family. The boys and I love him, and he loves us."

"Oh, please," Benny said wearily. "Chris, go get me some tonic water. I'm parched." Chris didn't move.

"Your days of treating him like a servant are over, Benny," Kim said with steely resolve.

Benny sat up straight, posturing for an argument. "Kim, he works for me. Our relationship is none of your business."

"Okay, Benny, let me explain to you some harsh realities. First of all, I gave money to Mrs. Ellis. You can take the five hundred dollars a month you've been holding over Chris's head and shove it."

Benny's face colored. "Chris!" he yelped. "That was between you and me. Why did you tell her?"

"It just slipped out, Benny. I didn't go running to Kim."

"Yeah, right. Well, we'll see how you like things when we get back home."

"Before you say anything else you'll regret, Benny, I want to talk about the loan," Kim said sternly.

"That's my money," Benny said. "You seemed to have great fun at my expense letting Michael arrange it, remember?"

Ignoring the accusation, Kim got to the point. "You were so interested in the money, Benny, that you didn't read the fine print. I retained the right to call the loan in consideration of the low interest rate that I receive. In other words, it's a right I bought and paid for."

"You wouldn't do that to your own brother, would you, Kim?" Benny's demeanor was far less aggressive at this point.

"I'm not an idiot, Benny. I had a private detective watch what was going on. The loan went to plug a hole in the finances at the Vatican Bank. Do you really think you'll be the apple of Rome's eye when you have to come up with one hundred million dollars to pay me back?"

Benny's complexion turned ashen. "Kim, you have no idea how much trouble that would cause me."

"And I never have to know, Benny. So here's the deal. Just like my boys, Chris has hands-off status. Do you understand me? No more talking down to him, no more petty demands, no more petulant hissy fits."

Benny was silent. He hated Kim's characterization of him.

"Benny, do you hear me?" Kim asked as she lowered her face to his. Their noses nearly touched.

"Yes, I hear you!" he spat.

"And you'll never strike out at Michael or Gabe in anger."

"Yeah. Right," Benny said with resignation.

"Chris, I'm counting on you to let me know immediately if Benny is abusive. Do *you* understand me?"

"Yes, Kim," Chris said with eyes downcast like the dutiful husband he would never become.

"Good. Now, Benny, whatever you want, get it yourself. And I mean you—not Caroline and not Joseph. You get it."

Benny left the room in a huff.

Chris said cautiously, "You have no idea how dangerous he is, Kim. I hope you did the right thing."

"I'm beginning to understand how bad he can be, Chris. And I'm also beginning to believe I'm the only one that can rein him in. I have to try." She paused to think about the implications of her statement. Finally, she stood to leave the room, saying, "Well, Christmas Eve day certainly has started off with a bang, hasn't it?"

After a wonderful prime rib dinner prepared by Kim and Chris, the family gathered by the Christmas tree to open some presents. Although they no longer believed in Santa Claus, the boys chose to open gifts on Christmas morning like in "the old days." The adults followed an even older tradition of opening presents on Christmas Eve. Generally these were small gifts of sentiment that could be opened quickly, as opposed to the open, ogle-and-play mode that filled the boys' Christmas Day.

Benny graciously received his case of wine from Kim and the boys. He brought them Vatican treasures, which Chris recognized from the souvenir booths in Saint Peter's square. All were polite and seemed thrilled, although Chris had overheard some of a conversation Kim had with the boys earlier in the day. She explained they are owed nothing in life and any gift is an act of love to be celebrated. Chris had gotten them small items that spoke to their characters, a new football for Gabe, a book of intermediate Latin for Michael, and for Kim a pendant necklace made from a piece of stone he had pocketed (God forgive him) while in the Coliseum.

"Mom, can you hurry?" Michael asked as Kim tried on the pendant.

"Yeah," Gabe added, "the suspense is killing us!"

"Okay, guys. Give him the present." The boys brought a small wrapped box and presented it to Chris. He opened it gingerly. It had been a long time since he had been given a gift in a family setting, and he knew that this gift was special to the boys as well. He tried to memorize the expressions on their faces as they handed him the present. They had no way of knowing that those little faces were the real gift. His expression turned to confusion as he pulled a key out of the box.

"Come on, Chris!" Gabe said. "Follow us!" He and Michael tore up the stairs. Chris looked at Kim, who motioned with her eyes, as if to say, "Let's go." They ascended the stairs to the fourth floor, and the boys led the adults to large double doors.

"Use your key, Chris!" the boys yelled in excitement.

As he opened the doors, he saw a suite of rooms, decorated to a simple man's taste. In the front room, the centerpiece was a huge fireplace. Around it were placed an overstuffed blue sofa and two leather recliners. Through another set of double doors at the back of the sitting room was a large bedroom decorated with mahogany furniture and a bed with high posters. Just off the bedroom was a full bath. Another room had been finished with floor-to-ceiling mahogany bookcases and outfitted with a large desk and filing cabinets.

Chris stood in awe, trying to take it all in.

"It's yours, Chris!" Michael screamed.

"Yeah. Now you have a home and a family!" Gabe yelled. Then in a conspiratorial tone, he whispered, "It's pretty easy to fit in around here. If I did it, you can too."

Chris looked over their heads to Kim. It was more than he could ever hope for, and for a brief second he was afraid to meet her gaze on the off chance the boys were somehow exaggerating. Kim nodded her head in agreement to everything the boys had said. "Don't just stand there, Chris, sit on something," she encouraged. He sunk into the deep cushions of the blue sofa and felt as if he was being cradled. From that vantage point, he saw clearly a collage of photos and memorabilia that decorated the wall above the fireplace. There were pictures of his parents, his school awards, and football trophies.

"I hope you don't mind," Kim said. "I rescued your stuff from Saint Mary's basement."

"No," Chris said softly, "it's great to see it. And it really does make it feel like home."

"We added the best part," Michael said, pointing to eight-by-ten photos of himself and Gabe on either side of the mantel.

"So you did! Come here, guys. Give me a hug." They fell on him for a moment and then jumped up quickly.

"What about Christmas Mass?" Michael asked, as if scripted. "It's getting awful late to make midnight Mass in town."

"Break time is over," Kim said to Chris. "We may have to call on you in an official capacity."

"I'd be happy to say Mass, but that privilege should go to Benny," Chris protested.

"It was offered to him. He said he's on vacation," Kim said tersely.

"Okay, then." Chris drew a deep breath. A comment like that was obnoxious even for Benny. "I guess we could use the dining room table, if that's all right with you."

"Nah, get your coat, Father," Kim said as she and the boys headed for the stairs.

As they made their way back to the Christmas tree, Benny was pretty far along in his first bottle of wine. "Let me guess. You have a room here now," he said with a drunken, sarcastic slur. They all ignored the comment as Kim handed each of them their coats. Benny waved her away. He wouldn't be joining them.

The stained glass windows of the chapel glowed like Christmas lights in the cool December air. As they approached, Chris grew in excitement.

Kim filled him in. "The boys and I have been working on this for a while now. It used to be a smokehouse in days of old. There was a ton of cleanup and demo work that the boys loved. They even helped with some of the painting. Needless to say, they got more paint on themselves than on the walls. At one point, Joseph and I seriously considered turning the hose on them before allowing them in the house." They both laughed, and Chris felt a homey, comfortable feeling that he hadn't known since his parents' deaths.

"It's gorgeous, Kim," Chris complimented as they paused outside the chapel to get the full effect. "What made you decide to do this?"

"Things had been a little strained between us and Benny. We figured this would make a great Christmas surprise for him. You know, make him feel a part of things around here."

"And?"

"And I was afraid he would react badly, so I showed it to him while you were in Texas. He said it's like giving a shovel to a ditchdigger."

"Ouch!" Chris said, thinking of both his own view of the priestly vows and how that reaction must have hurt Kim and the boys.

Of course the boys had run ahead and were now yelling to the older pair. "Come on, guys! Why are you so *slow*?" Chris and Kim picked up the pace and met them outside the double oak doors leading into the chapel.

"Check out the name," Michael said with glee.

"Saint Christopher's Chapel," Gabe blurted out, too anxious to wait for Chris to read it.

"Recently changed from Saint Benedict's," Kim added.

As they entered the dimly lit edifice, they felt a rush of peacefulness. Chris could tell the Lord had honored the sacrifice made by Kim and the boys to bring this about. Too bad Benny couldn't understand it.

Kim handed Chris an envelope. "You'll need to read this."

Chris's hands shook as he read a papal order dedicating the chapel as Saint Christopher's. The orders named him the pastor of the chapel and required that he say at least six Masses per year there.

Michael poked Chris with a pointed finger. "You have to come back, Chris. The pope says so."

"It looks like you're right," Chris said, a little bewildered at how they could have pulled this off.

Anticipating his question, Kim said with a grin, "We had a little help from Father Vinnie, patron saint of gout."

"I'm sure you did." Chris laughed.

Back at the house, Benny lamented his fate. The year had started off in a manageable place. He was second in line behind Michael to inherit Kim's fortune, and he had a plan to siphon off huge sums in the meantime. Now as the year drew to a close, his position had fallen behind the orphans, Gabe and Chris. Kim's little home for wayward boys was becoming a problem. And to top it off, the man of his dreams had fallen for his sister. Once again, everything went to Kimberly! At some point—he didn't know how, and he didn't know when—he would right these wrongs and settle the score.

For now, there was nothing left to do but gain solace from the only person who was always there for him. He closed his eyes and called softly to the Lady.

Fran and Gloria were spending Christmas Eve with Sam and Evelyn. They had joined the local church for some caroling and then settled in for an early evening in front of the Christmas tree. The soft glow of the tree lit the darkened room. Gloria loved the lightness of spirit and optimism that had come to her mother after Chris gave them the check. For Gloria, the visit was too fast. She never got to go to Rome with him, never got the chance to show him she wasn't just some little girl, and never got the chance to tell him she loved him.

Her thoughts were driving her crazy. She kissed her mother and grandparents good night and went to her bedroom, Daddy's room when he was growing up. If he had thought of her growing up without him, just for a moment, would he have still headed into that alley? She knew the answer was yes. He traded all of the tomorrows with his daughter for the chance to die for a Bakopi girl.

Her father, Chris—what was it that made these men of God so unfaithful to the women who loved them more than anything in life? Whatever it was, she knew that she had to protect herself from men like that in the future.

She found her purse and pulled from it a small Polaroid photo of herself with Daddy and Chris. It had become bent and worn from her looking at it. Crying desperately, she ripped it to tiny pieces, opened the window, and flung the fragments to the wind. She was too pre-occupied to see the light in the sky speeding toward her. For a brief second the light turned very bright, illuminating the swirling pieces of photograph. Then it disappeared, taking Gloria with it.

Pieces of the photograph danced in the wind under the light of the moon.

In the Caribbean, Mack and Sarah had left the cruise ship's nightly show and gone to the casino. Zack promised to go to bed but instead found an isolated place on deck to resume his nightly vigil. He dozed, and he dreamed. In his dream, casino machines below deck filled the air with their distant, relentless dinging noises. Nobody noticed the light in the sky far above the ship. Nobody noticed the little boy who levitated from the deck in the dark of night.

Zack awakened to find himself on board the spacecraft. He had been here too many times before to feel panic. In fact, there was a growing sense within him that this was where he truly belonged.

He saw a vision forming on the wall in front of him, as if the entire wall had become some sort of television screen. There was that girl again. She looked very sad as she peered out her window. Zack could actually feel her sadness. He wanted desperately to help her. Then he saw a flash of light, and the girl was gone from the window. In another flash of light, she appeared on an examining table in the room beside him. She never awakened, but he held her hand, hoping he could ease her pain.

1989

SEVENTEEN

Kim and her boys stood before the security checkpoint at the Atlanta airport. The boys were anxious to start a semester abroad in West Germany. As for Kim, now that the moment for their departure had arrived, she faced it with feelings of dread and despair. While Michael bought a magazine and Gabe went to the men's room, she took a brief moment to think about her boys. Michael had grown to a handsome man. He was leanly muscled, which he masked with the oversized clothes that were the current fashion. His dark-brown hair was shiny and carried soft curls, and his blue eyes were like crystals. Slightly shorter than Michael, Gabe had honed his thicker body to solid muscle. His hair was thick and poker straight. He wore it long and swept straight back off his face. The result was a look that was slightly fierce, as his high cheekbones accentuated his green eyes. His smile wasn't as perfect as Michael's, but it came to his face with reckless abandon, softening the otherwise intense features. In all, Gabe came off as an energetic, capable, extroverted, and lighthearted individual, but he carried it with an undertone that subtly threatened anyone who would hope to take advantage of him. In contrast, Michael's presence was more somber and reflective, and his demeanor was more graceful and refined.

She had done a good job raising them, with Chris's help. Chris had been a steadying hand to both boys over the years. And his influence was noticeable. Both boys had developed his politeness and quiet strength. Michael related to him on a mental level as they spoke of antiquities and ancient languages. Often they spoke in Latin, which

Kim found to be a bit silly. How many languages were in the world and these two chose a dead one in which to converse!

Chris related to Gabe on a more physical level, guiding him through a host of athletic activities. It seemed Gabe had no interest in anything that didn't involve movement. He was perpetually active.

"Don't forget I want you to call me every day," Kim said to Michael as he returned with a *Time* magazine. "I don't care about the time difference. Call me when you can."

"Mom, we won't be able to call every single day," Michael said, chuckling.

Gabe returned from the restroom. "Let me guess," he said, making fun of his mother, "Michael, promise me you boys will call every hour!"

"It wasn't quite that bad." Michael smiled at his best friend and brother.

"Mom, I'll take care of him," Gabe said with mock sincerity. "I'll make sure he gets to class no matter how many girls he had the night before. No. No. Forget that. I'll limit him to two girls a night, and they both have to carry a 4.0."

"I'm not laughing, Gabe," Kim chided. "I reluctantly agreed to this semester abroad. West Germany is a long way away."

"Come on, Mom. We've been through all of this," Gabe pleaded. "We'll be living on campus, and egghead here is just about fluent in German. How much trouble could we get into?"

"I'll keep us out of trouble, Mom," Michael said earnestly.

"Michael, I know you have a good head on your shoulders, but when Gabe gets going, there's no stopping him."

"You mean I don't have a good head on my shoulders?" Gabe asked in mock despair.

"It's more like you have good shoulders under your head, honey," Kim responded.

"But, Mom," Gabe countered, "think of it. With his head and my shoulders, just imagine—"

"The trouble you can get into. I know," Kim interrupted. "Maybe we should have notified NATO that the two of you were coming."

The boys hugged her one last time and moved to the security checkpoint. Michael looked back at her with a furtive glance. Gabe checked out a stewardess. Kim barely saw it through her tears.

At his desk in Rome, Chris was dealing with Benny's recovery from plastic surgery. "Chris, could you get me some ice, please?" Benny moaned from his office. The nip and tuck were fresh. He had his eyes done and a little bit of tightening of the face muscles. Since he was in the hospital anyway, he got some hair plugs as well. The plastic surgeon was world famous and had been recommended by Luciano.

"No problem, Benny," Chris said with a grimace as he looked at the bruised, swollen face before him. "Why don't you go home, Benny? You're looking pretty bad."

"I will as soon as I finish up this paper. Bilbo wants my comments today." Chris quickly scanned the paper and found it to be of little importance. Over the years he had become very adept at speed-reading through the things on Benny's desk.

As Chris wound his way to the commissary to get some ice, he thought about his work over the past ten years. Benny's avoidance of work had enabled Chris to build files of information about nefarious goings-on in the Vatican Bank. His work resulted in the firing of Bishop Marcinkus, who had used his ties with organized crime in the issuance of fraudulent securities. The best part of the entire affair was that the pope handled matters in such a way that no fingers pointed to Chris as the spy, or Benny as the leak. As successful as Chris had been with detecting financial scandals, he could uncover no evidence of Benny's part in darker, more spiritual pursuits. He had no doubt they existed, but he was never able to find evidence. He surmised Benny's participation in plots to bring about a New World Order took place only at Begliali's castle, and aside from bragging about Luciano's wealth, Benny was silent as to what he did there.

On his return, he ran into Vinnie, who was carrying a large, potted calla lily. "Where are you going with that monstrosity?" Chris asked.

"To your office. This flower was on the altar at San Giovanni for the past week. They were getting rid of it, and I thought it was a shame to throw it away."

"So you carried it the whole way from San Giovanni?"

"Not easy with my gout, I'm telling you. But I thought I could give it to your boss. You know, show some sympathy for his face stretching."

"Bull!" Chris laughed. "You can't fool me, Vinnie. You just want to see what he looks like."

"True. And I like the idea of giving him someone else's garbage. What does he look like?"

"It's horrible." Chris chuckled. "I seriously wonder if this surgeon is some kind of hack."

"Maybe he's just allowing Benny's inner beauty to come to the surface," Vinnie challenged with a shrug.

"I know there's a lot wrong with Benny, but I really hope this surgery heals better than I think it will. Benny's concerned he's aging prematurely."

"Why not?" Vinnie asked. "He's got to look at you all day! Have you aged a day in all the time I've known you? I don't think so. In fact, I think Benny's greatest punishment comes when he looks at you and then in a mirror." Chris rolled his eyes and then put a finger to his mouth to silence Vinnie.

Chris entered Benny's office with the ice and took stock of the patient. His eyes were swollen and puffy. They seemed to be pinned in the corners, giving the overall impression of a fat, sleepy cat. His hairline was bright red where the hair plugs had been installed, and there were bright-red incision marks along the edges of his face.

Vinnie followed, saying, "There's the patient! How are you feeling, kid?"

"What do you want?" Benny demanded.

"I just wanted to bring you this flower and say get well," Vinnie said, acting a bit hurt.

"Well, thank you. But I'm really not receiving at the moment." Then he said sternly, "Chris, show him out."

"Sure, Benny. Father, if you'll be kind enough to give the monsignor his privacy," Chris said with a wink.

Vinnie left the office, and Chris closed the door behind him. Chris knew he would be standing on the other side of the door to hear Benny's reaction.

"Don't you *ever* let that little flea-ridden monk in my office again! My God, Chris, I'm recovering from major surgery! Do you have any idea of the germs he's carrying?"

"Sorry about that, Benny," Chris said nonchalantly as he read the paper currently on Benny's desk. From the looks of it, Benny was being summoned to Begliali's castle.

"Just leave me alone for now, Chris. I don't want to be disturbed!"

Too late, Chris thought as he exited the room.

Vinnie stood there bemused. "What a mother!" he exclaimed in Hobokenese. The two laughed so hard they had to go into the hallway for fear Benny might hear them.

The first week in West Germany had gone well enough for the boys. They were at a school that catered to the large population of US military families in Berlin, enabling them to choose classes taught in either German or English. Gabe had no penchant for languages and opted for an easy course load in English. On the other hand, Michael had chosen to build his fluency by taking two business courses and two science courses in German. The first week was an eye-opener for him, and he struggled to keep up. To make matters tougher, Gabe was treating the semester as an adventure vacation. He had barely been sober since they arrived, and the thought had crossed Michael's mind more than once that alcohol might not be the only chemical recreation pursued by his brother.

"Michael, I need an interpreter," Gabe said as he burst into their dorm apartment, which consisted of a room that housed two bunk beds, two desks, and two closets. It was sparse but luxurious, because it was connected to a private bathroom. Following Gabe was a pretty, young girl who was visibly upset.

"What did you do now?" Michael asked with a sigh, looking up from his desk.

"Apparently she thinks I want to be friends or something."

"Why would she think that, Gabe?"

"Duh. We had sex. She looked me over. I looked her over, and before I knew it we blew off class and were in her room."

"Let me get this straight. You met her and jumped on her, but you haven't even had a conversation yet?"

"Something like that," Gabe said dismissively. "Now can you just tell her I'm not looking for a friend?"

"Er liebe Sie nicht. Er wurde nicht Ihren Freund sein," Michael said cautiously as he approached her. Upon hearing that, the woman let loose a string of German that Michael could only assume were profanities. Her gesticulations indicated something more than a young girl whose feelings were hurt.

"Langsamer, bitte," Michael said, asking her to speak more slowly. As she spoke more deliberately, Michael's face showed burgeoning awareness.

"Hey, Romeo," he chuckled, "she doesn't want to be your girlfriend. She wants you to pay her for services rendered."

"What?" Gabe exclaimed. "She wanted me!"

"Wieviel?" Michael asked. *How much?*

"Sechzig."

"There! See what I mean?" Gabe exclaimed, pointing his finger at her. "She's saying that *'sex-sig'* thing. That's how I knew she wanted me."

"That's the word for 'sixty' in German!" Michael said in exasperation. "Why am I even talking to your head? Let me see if I can access your brain." He bent toward Gabe's crotch and said, "She wants sixty dollars."

Gabe fished three twenty-dollar bills out of his pocket. Before handing them to her, he said in a whisper, "Michael, is it the cultural norm to give a tip? I don't want to look like the ugly American."

Michael erupted in laughter. "Give her another twenty dollars, Gabe. She had to chase you to your dorm room to get paid, and time is money to this one."

Gabe gave her the money, which she took with a sneer.

When she left, Michael fell to his bed laughing. He was at once exasperated and delighted by the fun Gabe brought to his life. Gabe attempted to sit beside him, and Michael pushed him away with his foot. "Don't even *think* about sitting on my bed, bro. I *know* you need a shower."

"Do you think I was her first?" Gabe asked with growing concern.

"No, Gabe," Michael said with mock condescension, hitting Gabe on the head with his pillow. "I don't think you were her first."

"No, I mean today. Do you think I was her first today, at least? I mean it's pretty early in the morning," Gabe said, his face taking on a pleading look. Michael shook his head in disbelief.

216

"Gabe! Why do you think they call them 'ladies of the evening'? Face it, buddy, you were overtime on a twelve-hour shift. I hope you wore a condom." The look on Gabe's face told Michael he hadn't.

"Funny you should mention that. I was going to ask you today how to ask for them in German. Man, I've got to get into the shower!"

"If I were you, I'd just cut it off," Michael teased.

As Gabe let the shower water get hot, he came back into the living area wearing only a towel, his six-pack abs supporting a perfectly carved chest. "Michael, do you think you could go with me to the dispensary and explain the situation for me?"

"I think I better. Syphilis can drive you mad. For you, it's a pretty short drive."

"Thanks," Gabe said earnestly, obviously concerned.

A few moments later, while Gabe was in the shower, the phone rang. *"Guten Morgen,"* Michael answered.

"Hi, honey. I couldn't sleep, so I thought I'd call to see how you guys are making out today."

"I'm fine, Mom. And from what I can tell, Gabe made out just fine this morning." He could barely contain himself.

"Michael!" Gabe yelled from the bathroom. "Do we have any bleach?"

Covering the receiver, Michael yelled, "You can't use bleach on that!"

"Is that your brother? Why does he want bleach?"

"He's worried about germs."

"Wow," Kim said with pride, "I didn't even think he had an idea of what household cleaning supplies were. What's he trying to clean?"

"Um ... a pipe in the bathroom. I'm afraid bleach will corrode it. You can tell it's been used hard."

"Let me talk to him."

"Ga-abe! Mommy wants to talk to you," Michael teased in a singsong voice. Gabe exited the bathroom wearing a towel and a grimace. "Did you tell her?" he mouthed.

"No." Michael grinned.

"Hi, Mom." Gabe turned the receiver so that Michael could hear.

"Hi, honey. Listen to your brother, sweetie. If you use bleach on that pipe, it may never work again."

Tears were forming in Gabe's eyes as he tried not to laugh into the phone. Michael was bent over with laughter.

"Ah. I won't use bleach, Mom. I was just concerned about germs. That's all. I read an article recently about how dirty drains can get."

"Especially by the end of a twelve-hour shift." Michael cackled in the background.

"I'm just happy to hear you're taking an interest in having a clean dorm room. You know, Gabe, I'm really proud of you two boys. A semester abroad means extra schoolwork, not to mention getting used to a new culture. I have faith in you guys."

"Thanks, Mom. I appreciate it. I'll make you proud. I really will." Gabe's voice was somber.

"Okay, honey. I think I'll be able to sleep now that I've spoken to my boys. You guys have a good day."

"Thanks, Mom. We will. You get some sleep."

Kim immediately dialed another number.

"*Buon giorno, questo é il ufficio del Monsignore Benito Cross.*"

"Hi, Chris."

"Oh, hi, Kim. Why aren't you asleep?"

"Call it mother's intuition. Something is going on with the boys. I can feel it."

"We've talked about this, Kim. We're going to have to give them room to grow. They'll have some hiccups, but at least they have each other to lean on."

"Just humor me on this, Chris. There may come a time when I ask you to take a trip up to Berlin and check in on them."

"I'd be happy to. I love to spend time with them. You know that."

"No, I mean in an emergency. I just have this feeling that before the semester is out, they're going to find themselves in some trouble they can't get out of."

"Of course I'll be there for them. And I'll be here for you right now. I think you are having some serious empty-nest syndrome. You lay back and cast these cares on the Lord. I'll be praying on this end that you get some sleep."

"And pray for our boys, Chris."

"I will."

"One more thing, Chris. How does Benny look after the surgery?"

"It's still early days, Kim."

"That bad, huh?"

"Right now he kind of looks like Chairman Mao. Once the swelling goes down though, I'm guessing it will heal to more of a Genghis Khan look."

"And I'm supposed to sleep with that image?" She chuckled.

"Put it all in the hands of the Lord, Kim. All three of them are out of our control."

"I guess you're right. Good night, Chris."

"Good night, Kim. Sleep tight."

Later that day, the sun seemed really bright compared to the subdued light of the campus clinic. The boys shielded their eyes. Gabe carried a small pouch filled with antibiotics, and Michael carried a look of slight bemusement.

"Thanks for the help in there, Michael."

"Don't mention it," Michael said with a sarcastic grin. "Seriously. Don't mention it."

"Just one thing. I don't know much German, but it seems to me that you and the doctor were referring to me as *Dumkopf.* That means 'idiot,' right?"

"More like stupid head." Michael grinned.

"Oh, that makes it much better! I don't feel nearly so bad," Gabe protested, staring at Michael as they walked.

"Come on, Gabe. We've barely been here a week, and I'm translating your sexual misadventures to a doctor at a VD clinic. By the way, a little kinky, don't you think?"

"Not kinky. Adventurous."

"Well, if I had any idea, I would have let you use the bleach."

"You won't have to worry about me and dirty hookers again, Michael," Gabe promised.

"Thanks, Gabe, because I was hoping to see more of Europe than cheap motels and VD clinics."

"Yep. We're going to Amsterdam."

"Amsterdam!"

"Yes, sir. Three days from now, we'll be in Amsterdam: Where the grass is green and the whores are clean!"

"Forget it." Michael stopped walking. Gabe moved in front of him to plead his case.

"Prostitution is legal there. And they have head shops that are like cafés. You walk in and order your weed from a menu. It's like Disney World for adults!"

"You don't even do drugs!"

"Not in the States," Gabe corrected. *Well, there it is. He's experimenting with drugs!*

Three days found them in Amsterdam. Michael loved the city's Van Gogh Museum, even if he had to see it with Gabe tugging at his sleeve to hurry. After dabbling in the arts, Gabe led them to the dark side of town. The boys strolled along a canal as Gabe checked street signs against an address he had written on a piece of paper. Soon they found themselves standing before a storefront. Its large green banner read, "The Seed Shop," and the writing on the windows said "Coffee Shop."

"The Seed Shop?" Michael asked.

"They sell more than coffee," Gabe said with a raised eyebrow.

Peering through the window, Michael said, "Dude, they sell weed in there!"

"Of course they do! How can you know so much about museums and so little about culture?" The remark stung just enough to motivate Michael to go into the shop with his brother. To his surprise, it was lovely—not the dirty, dingy, smoke-filled hashish den that he had conjured from Hollywood movie images. There were wooden bistro tables with small chairs, and the walls were painted alternately a golden yellow and a muted green. Above the counter was a large chalkboard with three columns: one listed types of weed, another hash, and another rolled products. The list was in English.

"How do you know about this place?" Michael asked, still in awe of the ambiance.

"I read about it." Gabe shrugged.

"No doubt in some men's room."

"Funny," Gabe said drolly. "Michael, check it out. It's entirely legal here. Look at the chalkboard. They're cultivating taste. This is no different from going to a wine tasting. Look at the people in here. Do they look like they're suffering from reefer madness?"

Michael chuckled as he looked around. There were men in business suits, well-dressed ladies, and a few younger people in fashionable jeans and nice shirts. The clientele looked very upscale. No one was rowdy or out of control. In fact, the place was peaceful, and the air had a pungent, sweet smell, almost like incense.

"I have to admit, it's a respectable-looking crowd." Michael grinned as he became more at ease.

"Ah, what to choose. What to choose," said Gabe as he studied the board. "It's a toss-up between Purple Haze and White Widow. I think I'm more of a Purple Haze kind of guy."

When the waiter came to the table with the Purple Haze hand-rolled creation, he lit it for Gabe and waited to see if he liked it. Gabe inhaled and held his breath. Then he sighed, allowing the smoke to billow out. He sat back for a second, looking at the cigarette, and said, "Gut. Gut."

"And for you?" the waiter asked Michael.

"Nothing." Michael smiled. "I don't want to smoke anything."

"Ach. A brownie and some coffee maybe?"

"Actually, that sounds good." Michael smiled. All the while, Gabe was busy with the Purple Haze.

"Pfennig for your thoughts, Gabe." Michael grinned.

Gabe, who was already feeling the effects of the Purple Haze, found the remark to be hilarious. He laughed, wiped his eyes, and tried to speak, only to burst out laughing again. The laugh was infectious, and Michael found himself joining in. Slowly Gabe calmed himself enough to say, "You know, Michael, you could probably get a bit of a contact high here. Don't panic if you feel a little buzzed."

"I feel fine," Michael said, taking a big bite of his brownie. This threw Gabe into another fit of laughter, and Michael joined in.

As the evening wore on, Gabe tried several more types of weed, vowing that tomorrow he would check out the hash. After the brownie, Michael was feeling pretty good himself.

"Gabe," Michael prodded.

"What?"

"I know nothing!" Michael said in a *Hogan's Heroes* accent, sending Gabe into a new fit of laughter.

They rolled into the street and began their trek into the evening. The neon lights along the perimeter of shop windows beckoned in the red-light district. Each window contained a woman waiting for the next trick of the evening. All were dressed provocatively, of course, but there was an air of respectability that concealed the more base nature of their profession.

"Like a kid in a candy store!" Gabe exclaimed. "Everything looks so good, but I only get to choose one morsel."

The marijuana brownie had lightened Michael's mood, and while he was not as enthralled as his brother, he could certainly get into the spirit of the evening. He stared intensely at each window they passed.

"Anything you like?" Gabe asked.

"There was the thin brunette back there. I liked her eyes. And she had a young, innocent look."

"Good for you, bro! Let's go get her," Gabe encouraged.

"Do you have to put it that way?" Michael asked in a tone of disgust.

Gabe looked at him incredulously. "You're not taking her to the prom, Michael. You understand that, don't you?"

"The entire red-light district is about fantasy, Gabe. Let me have my fantasy."

They backtracked until they found her sitting calmly in her window. A lovely smile lit her face as Michael knocked on the window. She opened the door to him.

"Michael!" Gabe yelped, striking his own forehead. "Take these." He handed Michael a pack of condoms.

"Where will you be?" Michael asked.

Turning to the next window, Gabe eyed the large-bosomed woman with platinum hair and a been-there-done-that attitude. "I'll be right here. She looks like she has some tricks I could learn."

"You always were very education-minded." Michael grinned at his brother as the door closed.

Michael's awkwardness was readily apparent. While the thin woman had looked innocent in the light of the window, Michael could see that her eyes carried a haggard wisdom in the light of the bedroom lamp. She took control, pushing him onto the bed and undressing him. She took off her clothes and moved slowly over him. Her hands and mouth were everywhere, her perfume intoxicating. And then she was on top of him, and his mind shattered with pleasure.

"You're mine," Michael heard her say with a hiss. He opened his eyes to find himself not in a fantasy but a nightmare. The young, innocent-looking hooker had turned more than a trick. She had transformed into a strange, alien-looking being. Michael looked in horror as the Lady rode him like a wild beast. He closed his eyes again, thinking this was some sort of trick his mind had played on him. He felt his finger being sucked and looked again to see it in the Lady's toothless slit of a mouth.

He screamed loudly. Surely people on the street could hear.

"Quiet, my pet," she purred. "Almost through."

He tried to push her off him but couldn't move. She was in control of him. It was a stifling, suffocating feeling. And she smelled of old, rotting flesh. Michael could only compare it to the smell of some street people he had encountered on a visit to New York. And still she grinded against him. He gagged and choked on his own bile.

"Get off me!" he screamed. She put the spiny fingers of her hand across his mouth. They smelled foul and left an acidic taste on his lips. Turning his head, he saw for the first time he was no longer in the bedroom. They were in a rounded room with metallic walls. He was lying on a metal table; his entire body seemed to be stuck to it. His panic was near complete as he realized he was still physically excited. He felt terribly violated and had an inner knowledge that this horrible smelly *thing* was stealing his semen ... and his body was participating!

"Relax. Enjoy, pet."

"Aaaaghhhhh!" Michael screamed in anguish and ecstasy, squeezing his eyes shut against the horrible vision on top of him.

As he opened his eyes again, he was back on the bed. The girl was gone. He quickly grabbed his clothes, dressing as he left the bedroom. He managed to get his pants and shoes on before succumbing to his primal need to get out of the building. He fell onto the street as he was buttoning his shirt.

A small group of people had gathered. They were looking into the sky. Some spoke English, and Michael could hear they were talking about a bright light that had hovered above them and then disappeared. He couldn't care less. He needed to get out of there. He ran to the next storefront and pounded on the door. It was locked. Seeing nothing more in the sky, the crowd turned to the commotion next door.

"Are you all right?" a man called with a British accent.

The sound of his voice and the golden glow of the streetlights reinforced Michael's sense of being in the real world. Embarrassed, he said he was fine. Then he found a park bench to wait for his brother.

It had to have been a combination of guilt and the effects of the brownie, Michael assured himself. Of course he knew there was pot in the brownie. Sometimes it was better to just go along with Gabe. He also thought he would need the extra push if he was going to lose his virginity. But the pot had induced a horrible vision. Surely that's what happened. He began to wonder how weird he must have seemed to the poor girl he was with. *Maybe I should talk to her. I haven't paid or anything.*

Making his way back to the storefront, Michael was shocked to find it empty—not only empty, but the building had been closed for a long while. There were no neon lights. The window was smudged with months of dirt. He could see dust and cobwebs inside. He went to the door to knock and saw a sign on it. His German was good enough that he was able to make his way through the Dutch sign. The business had been shut down months ago by order of the health authority.

I just came out of that door not twenty minutes ago!

"You're mine, pet." He heard that hissing voice in his head. He felt the panic rising and knew he wanted to be far away from this place. He found his way back to the bench and began to cry with confusion and fear. After the tears had dried, Michael sat with his feet on the bench, knees drawn up in a near-fetal position, and head down on his knees.

He looked up as Gabe gently sat beside him and leaned into him until their shoulders touched. "Are you okay, buddy?"

"I'm not sure," Michael said, barely audible.

"Nothing's easy the first time, dude."

"It's not that, Gabe. I had this really strange vision. It was like I was in a real-life horror movie."

Gabe's heart sank. "Oh, man. Michael, listen to me. That's my fault. The brownie you ate was laced. I didn't tell you because—"

"I knew it was laced, Gabe. I just thought of it as a cup of courage for this evening."

"Must have been more than weed. Maybe you got hold of some kind of hallucinogenic."

"Whatever it was, it was scary," Michael said, wiping his eyes.

"What about the rest of it? Did you ... you know ..."

"Yeah."

"Well, how'd you like it?"

"In my vision, that innocent-looking girl turned into some weird alien creature."

Struggling not to laugh, Gabe asked, "So did you mind-meld or something?"

"I know it sounds stupid." Michael chuckled sadly. "But it felt so real." Jumping off the bench, he said, "In fact, look at this." He led his brother to the now-vacant storefront.

Gabe looked at it in disbelief. "Michael, this is weird. I don't like weird stuff. Let's get out of here!"

There was no need to ask Michael twice. He took off in a run. Gabe caught up to him easily, and the two ran into the night.

EIGHTEEN

The air was hot, but the humidity was low. The dorm wasn't air-conditioned, but Gloria was fortunate to have landed a corner room. Two windows meant a breeze. It was enough to keep the room from being stifling. She had developed into an extremely attractive young woman. She had Tom's bright eyes and his soft, curly, blonde hair, which she wore long. Her figure was perfect, too perfect for her mother's liking, with large breasts and a small waist that accentuated anything she wore.

The first bit of time here had been wonderful for Gloria. She liked her new roommate a lot. And she was thriving in the "anything goes" culture of the University of Texas. It was so liberating, so unlike the Bible school she had previously attended. Today, for instance, she was wearing a pair of short shorts and a midriff-baring top, something sure to bring frowns, if not a threatened probation, at Bible college. Here it garnered admiring glances both from women who envied her figure and from men who wanted to possess it. She found the attention to be exhilarating. She imagined writing a letter to her poor mother. *Dear Mom, who knew exhibitionism could be such fun!*

She spread a blanket on the lawn in front of the dorm and stretched out for some sun as she studied. It was hot, but this mama was getting even hotter. It was time to attract a little more serious attention from the opposite sex. She started into her behavioral psychology text. Thank God she had found a major she could sink her teeth into. She loved learning what made people tick.

She had become engrossed in the material when she heard three young men walking down the sidewalk. "Check it out," one whispered to the others. Gloria could feel them undressing her with their eyes. It felt as good as the rays of the sun beating down on her.

She pulled down her sunglasses in what she hoped would be a provocative stare. The one in the middle returned her gaze with the most penetrating steel-blue eyes. She hadn't seen anyone with such an arresting gaze since her crush on Father Chris years before. As their eyes met, his angular face broke into a broad smile. She knew the smile was for her, but he quickly turned it to the guy next to him. He said something under his breath, and the three of them laughed as they continued down the street.

There was something about that guy. Of course, she was horny and had lots of catching up to do in that department. The time at Bible school and the summer with her mother had taken a toll on her sex life. Could it be she was just so hungry for the touch of a man, or was there something about him in particular that she found fascinating? *Wonder what Dr. Freud would say about that.* She returned to her psychology text but couldn't escape that warm feeling that comes over you when you fall for someone. She would read awhile and then wonder who he was. What was his major? Where was he from? Did he like blondes?

"Hey, chick," her roommate, Berta, said to her as she walked toward the dorm. Gloria liked Berta. She was fun and had a lot of style. She was attractive enough to be popular and know the guys on campus, but not so attractive that she outshone Gloria. Berta's auburn hair and light-brown eyes filled out a fleshy face. She could stand to lose a few pounds, but her engaging personality and her love of a beer made her a favorite among the frat brothers of the Theta house.

"Hey, yourself." Gloria smiled. "What's shaking?"

"My bum!" The two laughed.

"Any takers?" Gloria asked.

"Maybe tonight. We're going to the Theta welcome-back party."

"Nice." Gloria smiled. "I've never been to a frat party. Is it like *Animal House*?" Despite Gloria's pretense to worldliness, there was innocence about her that she could not completely bury.

Berta laughed. "No, Gloria, imagine it: loud music, kegs of beer, some drugs if you want them, and guys, tons of guys. If you ask my opinion, the Thetas are the best-looking on campus. And they invite tons of people. You literally can't walk a step without rubbing against a handsome man."

"Sounds like it's just what the doctor ordered," Gloria said, pointing to the author of her textbook.

Later that evening, as Gloria and Berta walked up to the Theta house, they could hear the din of loud music and screamed conversations. They got behind another group of kids and took their turns pushing into the house. Gloria had never been to New York, but she had seen pictures of packed subway cars. This seemed to be a realistic comparison.

Berta grabbed her arm and tugged at her, pulling her through the crowd toward the bar. As they moved, Gloria was buffeted by the full-body contact with the crowd. Occasionally, they would pass a handsome man and the contact would slow. They wouldn't just brush by but stop for a short second and smile. Gloria could feel herself becoming aroused by the sheer proximity of testosterone and muscle.

The bar was little more than a corner of the first floor that contained kegs of beer. Theta brothers dutifully filled large plastic cups with the brew. Gloria wasn't much of a drinker. In the past, she had taken a sip now and again, mostly to prove to herself that she wasn't some throwback to the temperance league. It seemed daring then, but she was in a different world now. *When in Rome ...* She took a big gulp of the beer. It was surprisingly refreshing in the heat of the packed fraternity house. The foam tickled at her lips, and the taste of hops and malt delighted her tongue.

Pushing through the crowd, she and Berta made their way to some of Berta's friends. Introductions were made, and the girls made up for time they had missed with each other over the summer. At first Gloria tried to listen to the conversations, but it was too hard to hear over the din of the crowd. She drank her beer and felt entranced by the hum of the room. The alcohol gave her a slight buzz, and she swayed listlessly to the music.

She felt a tap on her arm and turned to find a handsome young man with long blond hair. He held out another beer to her and smiled. She took the beer and said thanks. He said something, but she couldn't hear him. Then he leaned very close so that his mouth was near her ear. The smell of his cologne, the muscled tone of his body, and the heat of his breath in her ear said far more than his words ever could. "I thought to myself, 'What's that pretty girl doing without a guy to talk to?'"

Gloria smiled again. He was handsome. Certainly he appealed to her physically, and the old morality had died long ago, hadn't it? She leaned into him to say, "You're not so bad yourself. Why is there no girl on your arm?"

"Transfer student." He smiled.

"Me too." She grinned, pointing to herself.

"Would you like to dance? This is a great party for old friends to reacquaint, but we newbies are going to have to stick together if we're going to have fun."

"I'd love to," she said and smiled.

"Great. Let's just drink these beers down a bit first." He gulped his beer, and she followed his lead. He then led her to the dance floor, which was just as crowded as the rest of the party. He pulled her close. His warmth blended with the warmth of the beer, and she nestled her head on his shoulder as they danced and talked. She learned that his name was Jake, and he was a biology major who had transferred from a college in upstate New York. He hated winter and moved to Texas. As the evening wore on, they made several more trips to the bar together. Soon they settled to a soft sway to Roxette's "Listen to Your Heart."

I could get used to this. For the moment she felt warm, safe, and cared for. She looked up to smile at him, when she caught something out of the corner of her eye, causing her to turn her head. The guy with the arresting eyes from this afternoon was headed toward the bar. Even in the dim light of the dance floor, she could feel those penetrating eyes. There was a sense of purpose in his gait. He looked past her, hadn't noticed her at all, but there was something about him that drew her. After seeing him, Jake's once-warm embrace began to feel like a stranglehold, and his cologne assaulted her. She found it all very confusing.

"I have to go to the ladies' room," she said to Jake, breaking the spell for him.

"Oh, sure. Do you want me to come wait for you?"

"No, thanks. I'll be back. I just need a couple minutes."

Jeff Healey's "Angel Eyes" played in the background. Gloria changed the lyric just a bit as she sang along. "What can I do? What can I say … to turn your angel eyes my way?"

She scanned the crowd for him. He wasn't at the bar. There were hundreds of people here, and all but a handful were strangers to her. She began to despair that she wouldn't find him, when she caught a glimpse of him leaving the party … alone. She felt like a fish swimming upstream as she pushed through the crowd toward the door. Her heart pounded with the lunacy of what she was doing. Even if she managed to catch up to him, what would she say? It was crazy, but she was no longer in control.

Finally, she pushed through the doorway and burst into the night. She took a deep breath. The night air was so refreshing after coming from the crowded frat house. As her eyes adjusted to the sudden darkness, she scanned the area. She walked toward campus, thinking he had to be going in that direction. Soon she was by herself on the little road. The air was clear, and the stars were brilliant. Even if she didn't find him tonight, it had been a good evening. As she mused about dancing so close to Jake, she smiled, thinking of Audrey Hepburn in *My Fair Lady*. With nobody around, she felt free to spread her arms and sing, "I only know when he began to dance with me, I could have danced, danced, danced all night."

In her imagination, she was the star of her own play. She could feel the warmth of the spotlight as she danced, danced, danced through the final chorus. In a flash, the light was gone. So was Gloria. Overhead, the spacecraft darted into the distance.

Hurricane Hugo pounded into the coast and sent shock waves far enough inland to inundate Kim's estate. The wind howled, and the rain was torrential. Kim's mood was just as somber. The house seemed so lonely with the boys gone. When they were in college in the States, there were constant visits, even if just to drop off laundry. What she wouldn't do to have the pleasure of a laundry visit right now.

Joseph had retired from service to live out his life in the cottage at the corner of the property. The caregiver now needed care himself. Nurses stopped by each day. Often Kim cooked for him and carried it to his house. There she would eat with the old gentleman and whatever visiting nurse was there that day. Caroline was semiretired, enjoying life with her family and coming to the estate to help Kim when there was a large dinner to serve.

Today Kim's mood was more than lonely. Deep inside she was upset. She couldn't put words to it, but she felt anxious about her boys. Maybe it was empty-nest syndrome. Maybe it was a mother's intuition. Either way she was too anxious to stay seated. She wandered around, looking for projects to keep her occupied as the large manor house creaked and moaned in the strong wind. The television news said the storm was likely to pound away all night long. If she thought for a moment that driving wouldn't be treacherous, she would have forced herself to go somewhere—anywhere to push this feeling away.

After calling to check on Joseph, she hunkered down for a long evening. She sat in the den at the back of the house, alone with her memories of her two little boys. Soon she dozed off in front of the television.

Kim heard a soft hiss that slowly awakened her. She looked around to realize she wasn't in her home any longer. She was in the rounded metallic room from her past. The room that haunted all of her dreams. The dreams that prevented her from ever being able to trust physical intimacy with any man. The dreams that had made her a vigilant and overprotective mother. The dreams that disappeared into a vapor whenever she prayed to Jesus.

A screen on the far wall began to show images, visions of her past. She saw herself entering the bar on that night long ago, desperate to soil her womb before the Lady could. She watched in horror as she paraded herself in front of the Blanchett brothers. The screen caught every nuance of that evening. Kim was awash with emotion. She wanted to hug the poor, scared young girl, driven to this point by desperation. She wanted to kill the owners of this room. Their experiments had done this to her, to that poor young girl. And yet the boys had been the joy of her life. If not for that evening, she wouldn't have her two beautiful boys.

Kim cried softly as she saw the acts of the brothers. Her guilt and shame overwhelmed her as she thought of Chris. If not for this night, maybe she would have met him before he became a priest. After that night, she was far too soiled for someone as lovely as him.

The scenes droned on and on. Kim would not allow herself any more of this. She started to scream at her unseen captors. She pounded her fist on the screen in front of her. Then the screen froze on a picture of Kim with her boys. It was taken just before they went to Germany. A chill went down her back as she looked at their smiling faces. The chill became a soft breath, and she turned to see the Lady staring at her with those passionless eyes.

"What have you done to us?" she asked in disgust.

"They're mine now," the Lady said with a decided air of smugness.

The insect queen was asserting her dominance. Kim couldn't take it anymore. She had hated this thing from the time she was a young girl. In a quick motion, she grabbed its scrawny neck. It hadn't expected any action from her. She loved seeing the look of surprise in those horrible eyes. The ugly slit of a mouth opened in a silent "Oh" as Kim brutally wrung the neck in front of her.

She awoke to the ringing phone. She answered it tentatively as she looked at the framed picture of her and the boys.

"Kim, are you all right?" Chris asked. "I felt the Spirit leading me to call you. How are you doing in that storm?"

"Chris? Oh, Chris, I had the worst dream about the boys." She began to cry, and Chris spoke to her in soft, soothing tones from his bed in Rome.

It felt so good to be with him. They made love in a weightless space, free as angels. His desire matched her own as they moved like one person to that moment of ultimate pleasure.

Gloria awoke with a start. The early-morning sun had just begun to shine. She sat up and took stock of her surroundings. Bushes around her. Birds singing. She was sitting on a patch of grass alongside the road leading from the frat house. The morning dew was still on the ground. She absently wiped her hand across her face. *What happened?*

She remembered leaving the party, following that guy. She remembered dancing down the road to the song from *My Fair Lady*. Then things got fuzzy, like in a dream. There was this bright light. When it faded she was floating in a brightly lit circular room. Across from her was the guy she had been following. He was naked. Her eyes followed the form of his muscular, thin body. His eyes shone as he looked at her and smiled. Looking down, she realized she was naked as well. The only thing she wore was the cross.

Seeing him want her made her want him all the more. They swam to each other through the ether and had the best sex she could ever imagine. At one point in their passion, her necklace broke, and the cross drifted off into the night.

What a dream! More to the point, how did she come to awaken in the weeds hours after leaving the party? She picked herself up and began the walk back to her dorm. Could she possibly have been *that* drunk? She tried to count the beers she had over the course of the evening.

By the time she reached the dorm, she had come to the inescapable conclusion that Jake had slipped her something. She had heard stories of the date rape drug. Thankfully, the cute boy had diverted her. For a brief second, she wondered if God had spared her from being raped by the new transfer student. *That's just the remnant of two years at a Bible college, Gloria. God has a lot to do running the universe. He isn't safeguarding your panties.* She laughed at the thought. Whatever happened, she was fortunate to get away with only a drug-induced dream and a sore body from sleeping on the ground.

Lesson learned. No more drinking with abandon just because some cute guy is bringing the beers. No more spending all of her time at a party with some guy she had just met.

The door to her dorm room opened as she fumbled for her key. A guy she had never seen brushed past her as he exited the room. Inside, Berta was putting on a housecoat.

"Hey there, stranger! I was worried about you."

Looking around the messy dorm room and smelling the last vestiges of pot, Gloria said, "I can tell."

"No, seriously," Berta responded. "I looked all over the party for you. I was upset that I couldn't find you, so this guy walked me home. He had some pot. We agreed to smoke it while we waited for you. Then one thing led to another, and we sort of passed the time horizontally, but I was concerned the whole time."

Gloria chuckled at the story. "Well, I appreciate it. But I'm fine."

"Well, I'm not," Berta said as an annoyed tone found its way into her voice. "We have to get something straight. We should have each other's backs. If we go to a party together, the first to leave should tell the other."

"You're right," Gloria said. "I really had you worried, huh?"

"I haven't known you all that long, but I like you enough to know I don't want anything to happen to you."

"Thanks. I won't do it again."

"So now that we have that out of the way, what happened? I saw you with that guy Jake. He's so cute!"

"I'll give you that."

"Unless he was hiding something in his pants, that guy's got it going on. So tell me, was he as great in bed as he looks?"

"I wouldn't know," Gloria said. "I didn't sleep with him."

"I understand, you're fresh from Bible school and don't want to kiss and tell," Berta offered as she worked with a brush to establish some sense of order to her hair. "But we're roommates. Hell, I'll tell you everything Dave did last night. By the way, I wouldn't recommend him. Terrible lover. Got the job done, but barely."

"Berta, I didn't sleep with Jake. There was this other guy I wanted to talk to. I saw him leaving the party and followed him," Gloria said with a sigh. She sat on her bed, comforted to be in her own space.

"Must have been a total hunk if you threw Jake over. Tell me all about it."

"That's about it. I never caught up with him. I was walking to the dorm one minute, and the next minute I was laying in the grass beside the road—in the morning!" Gloria lay back on her bed, realizing how ridiculous it all sounded when spoken aloud.

Concern began to furrow Berta's brow. "You don't remember anything?"

"No. I'm beginning to think Jake slipped me a date rape drug or something. Thankfully, that other guy caught my eye, and I followed him."

"Are you sure you don't remember anything?" Berta asked with concern as she moved to Gloria's bed.

"I had this wild dream about sex with the guy I followed out of the party, but that's about it."

"How do you feel now?" Berta asked deliberately.

"Fine. I feel good, in fact."

She took Gloria's hand and looked sternly into her eyes. "I think we need to call the police."

"What? Why would I do that?"

"Gloria, your blouse is inside out. Someone undressed you and then dressed you again in a hurry."

The new parsonage looked like a manor estate as Sarah drove the Mercedes around the circular driveway to the double-door entrance. She stopped the car and bustled to the trunk, where she muscled out a wheelchair. After setting it up, she added the padded seat and positioned it by the passenger door of the car. Inside, Sandy Matheson sat. She was finally out of the rehab facility following her stroke.

"All right, Mama, let's see if we can get you into the chair."

"Oh! There it is again, the royal 'we'! 'We' didn't have a stroke, and 'we' aren't going to *get* me anywhere!" She pulled herself up by the open door of the car and managed the few steps to position herself into the chair. Sandy hated the way she sounded. Originally, the stroke had left her paralyzed on the left side. Now she was able to walk short distances with a cane, but the left hand hung dead at her side. One moment she had been fine, and the next moment she was imprisoned in her own body. But mobility wasn't the only thing the stroke had taken from her. It robbed her of her privacy and her dignity. Now she was forced to give up her home to live with Sarah and Mack.

"Mama, that was great! I'm proud of you," Sarah cooed. Sandy couldn't stand the condescension. Two months ago she was still running her own beauty parlor. Now she was being applauded with singsong praise because she sat her fat butt in a chair. Didn't they know she wasn't some kid in potty training? She didn't want such lighthearted praise.

"Proud enough to get me off of the lawn?" she barked.

Mack opened the door and placed a foldable ramp up the few steps into the house. "Welcome, Meemaw." He grinned as he used Zack's name for her. "Our house is your house."

"My house is a little pretentious, don't you think?" She was thrown backward a bit as Sarah abruptly began to push the chair up the ramp.

"God has been good," Mack said with a grin.

"The sheep have been sheared," Sandy said with the flatness of tone that can accompany a stroke.

Mack bent down and planted a kiss on her cheek as the chair made its way into the foyer.

"You know I love you kids," Sandy said, softening with the kiss. "Since the stroke though, my mood has been bad, and my mouth even worse. I have no filter."

"We haven't even noticed, Mama. We're just happy you survived the stroke," Sarah said in a too-animated tone.

"Bullshit!"

"I forgot to tell you that Mama sometimes cusses now." Sarah blushed, looking up at Mack.

Mack let out a hearty laugh. He got down on one knee and took Sandy's hand in his. "You've worked hard all your life, Sandy. You've always been there for us, and now it's our time to be there for you. I truly want you to be at home here. I want you to rest and rebuild your life."

"Thanks, Mack," Sandy said as tears formed in her eyes. She pulled her hand from his and brushed his cheek. "Thanks for understanding. This isn't a dead end. It's just a speed bump."

"You say it, sister." Mack grinned.

"This is a new beginning for me."

"You bet!" Mack smiled, slapping his knee. Sarah's eyes lit up as she saw the change Mack was bringing.

Waving her good hand, Sandy complained, "Don't just stand there grinning like Mickey and Minnie. Get me a Rolaid. I've got gas."

Gloria sat with her head in her hands as Berta brought coffee to the table. She hadn't wanted to call the police, so Berta suggested they discuss the matter further over breakfast in the cafeteria.

"I can't call the police, Berta! I don't have a serious complaint. They'll say I got drunk and slept it off. We're the only ones that saw the blouse. And besides, I feel great. Don't you think I would feel violated in some way?"

"Yeah, I do. The way you wolfed down your breakfast makes me believe you aren't traumatized. But what could have happened?"

Gloria was about to respond, when she noticed the cute guy coming into the cafeteria. He was alone. His eyes shone, and she would have sworn he looked in her direction. She raised her hand, as if to wave, and then stopped herself.

"Who's that?" Berta asked, her face looking like she had just unexpectedly tasted a lemon. "He looks like something pretending to be human!"

"That's the guy I followed out of the party," Gloria said defensively.

Berta took a long, hard look. "Him? If you threw Jake over for him, you *must* have been drugged."

"I know his looks are unconventional, but it's like his eyes see through me. And in my dream, his body was all lithe and muscled."

"Must have been some dream!" Berta shook her head in disbelief.

"I've never felt anything like it. In the dream there was so much passion. It was like we truly were becoming one person, you know?"

"Can't say as I do. I'm not much of a romantic. When mama wants her something-something, she gets it. That's about as emotional as it gets for me."

"The dream was like a Hollywood love story. Even when the chain broke and I lost the cross, I didn't mind ..." She felt around her neck with horror, noticing for the first time the cross was really gone. "Oh, Berta, I lost the cross!" Panic struck her. She had worn that cross every day since she had gotten it in Africa. It was her link to her past and to an event that would otherwise have seemed only to be a fairy tale. *I have to find the cross. I have to find that cross!*

Gloria's near panic was heightened when she heard the tension in Berta's voice. "Gloria, either Jake drugged you and had his way with you, or some other guy did. But either way someone dressed you badly and made off with your necklace. Now we have something to report to the police."

"Okay. But before I embarrass myself by telling the police department my most vivid sex dream ever, will you go with me to look for the cross along the road? Maybe it's there. I don't care about anything else right now, Berta. I have to find that cross." Now that she was aware of its absence, Gloria could think of nothing else.

"Fine. Just give me a minute to go to the ladies' room first," Berta said as she left the table. Gloria stacked their trays to take them to the dishwashing area. In the corner of her eye, she saw a hand place her cross onto the table. Looking up she saw the guy she had followed. She knew those beautiful eyes, and she understood the knowing smile.

"Hi. I'm Zack."

NINETEEN

A re you sure that everything is fine?" Fran asked. She had this unshakable feeling her little girl was in trouble. It wasn't rational. It was just a feeling, but mothers know when their babies are in danger.

"Mom, I'm fine! In fact, I've been having a great time. I really like Berta a lot. And classes just started, so it's not like I'm behind in work or anything. The weather's been great. I don't know what you're feeling. Maybe your mother's intuition is wearing out."

"Not a chance." Fran chuckled. "When you have kids one day, you'll know the feeling." Zeroing in on her concerns, Fran said, "Last night I couldn't sleep at all, and when I called your room, there was no answer."

"Berta and I went to a frat party last night," Gloria admitted. Fran could hear tension in her voice.

"And?"

"It was fine, Mom. I didn't feel much like I fit in. I'm the new kid on the block. It was an entire evening of feeling like a fifth wheel."

"That will all work itself out, honey. Sounds like a bit of a lonely evening."

"In the end, I left the party and went for a long walk."

"I wish you wouldn't be out late at night by yourself, Gloria." Fran was starting to calm a bit. Her daughter had been wandering in the night alone. Perhaps that was the cause of her unease. It was more than mother's intuition that had driven her, though. She was sure the Holy Spirit had alerted her.

"What about guys?" Fran was fully aware of how Gloria filled out a pair of jeans. She couldn't imagine the guys allowed Gloria to be a flower on the wall for too long.

"I danced a bit with a guy named Jake. He's a transfer student too."

"And?"

"And we danced, Mom. He's very handsome, but something didn't click. And then ..." Gloria stopped short. Fran could tell that there was something she didn't want to say.

"And then what, sweetie?" Fran coaxed.

"And then the music and the drinking. It was all too much for me. I had to get out of there."

Fran breathed a sigh of relief. Maybe there was hope for this child after all. "You're going through a bit of culture shock, honey. You've been pretty sheltered, and the world is a tough place. Are you praying and staying in the Bible?"

"Not so much, Mom. That's more your world than it is mine."

"God is eternal, sweetie. He always has time for you. You just need to make a little time for Him."

"Oh, shoot! Mom, I've got to go. I'm supposed to meet Berta and I'm late."

Fran sensed that she was getting the bum's rush. "Okay, honey. I love you. You know, if you ever need to talk—"

"I love you too, Mom. Bye."

In *Ospitale Santo Spirito*, Cardinal Cesare Bilbo was recovering nicely from pneumonia. He was resting peacefully when he heard yet another nurse come into the room and fiddle with his IV tube. He kept his eyes closed against an apparent conspiracy among the nurses to prevent him from sleeping. His eyes snapped open as he startled to a sharp pinch on his arm. Standing before him was Benny Cross.

"Benito," Cesare said weakly.

"I came to say good-bye," Benny said with mocking sadness.

"You're a bit early, my friend. I'm recovering," Bilbo managed to say just before his body was rocked with a spasm.

"Succinylcholine—an amazing drug, dear friend," Benny said as he held up the syringe. "A few spasms and it will all be over. The important thing is that my new beautiful face will be the last thing you see in this life."

Wild panic filled Cesare's eyes as the drug began to take effect. In seconds he began to lose control of his body. His mind screamed out for help, but he couldn't make his mouth move. The neurotoxin was shutting him down, muscle by muscle. It was impossible to swallow, and saliva pooled in the back of his throat. Soon he felt himself suffocating. His mind panicked as it fought for oxygen, but the chest muscles would not respond. All the while, Benny had planted his face in front of him. He couldn't even close his eyes. Benny would indeed be the last thing he would ever see. From the depths of his mind he cursed Benjamin Cross.

The panic subsided as his brain acceded to the fact that he was dying. He began to feel a lightness that gave way to total freedom as his spirit left his body. Looking down at his dead body, he had never felt more alive. From the corner of the room, he saw a blinding dot of light. It grew exponentially until the room was filled with pure brilliance. He saw her in her blue garb, walking out of the light. The Virgin had come to take him to Heaven. The last laugh was on Cross!

She opened her arms to him. He ran to her, and she held him close. She felt so frail in his arms. He pulled back to see her face.

"Surprise!" said the Lady as he gasped at the sight of her mutated face. She wore a crooked smile of victory on that toothless slit of a mouth. The light vanished, along with Cesare and the Lady.

It didn't feel good to suspect that her daughter was lying to her. Fran was a jumble of emotions as she walked through the supermarket. First, she was angry that Gloria would lie to her. Then she would tell herself she wasn't really sure Gloria had lied. Then she would feel sad, thinking she was losing the girl. All in all, it produced heartache in her. She was sure her little girl was in trouble, and it hurt her to think Gloria didn't trust her enough to reach out. She distractedly placed a melon in her cart.

"You won't be able to eat that," a man said with a smile.

Fran shook her head, as if to clear the distraction. "I'm sorry?"

she asked, noticing his eyes. She hadn't seen that depth of kindness in someone's eyes since the death of her father-in-law.

"That melon isn't close to being ripe. They picked it too early. I think this one will rot before it ripens."

For the first time, Fran really looked at the man. He was well dressed. His full face broke into huge dimples when he smiled, and there was a sense of peacefulness about him. "Thanks," she said, putting the melon back. She returned his smile. It would be impossible not to.

"You have to thump it, like this." He gave the melon a surprisingly hard thump with his index finger. "Do you hear that sound? Now *that's* a fresh melon." He handed it to her.

"I heard it." Fran chuckled. As she took it, she noticed his cologne—sandalwood, very manly. "Thanks again."

"You seemed pretty distracted back there. Is there something on your mind?" he asked. "I would be happy to pray for you."

"Are you a Christian?" Fran asked, sensing in her spirit this was a divine appointment, when you meet someone God has put in your path.

The man laughed loudly. "I kind of hoped it showed! I'm David Treadhill, the pastor at the Alliance Church in town."

"Hi. Fran Ellis," she said, extending her hand. "Nice to meet you."

"Nice to meet you too, Fran Ellis," he said as he grasped her extended hand. "Are you a Christian?"

"I kind of hoped it showed too! Yes, I am. My husband and I used to be missionaries before he was killed in Africa." A woman behind them groaned in protest as she tried to get past Fran's cart. They moved out of the produce section to the end of an aisle where there was more space.

"My word," David continued the conversation, "that must have been horrible."

Fran nodded her head, the pain of Tom's murder hitting her afresh for a moment. After a few seconds she spoke. "I'm sorry for the tears. It was ten years ago. I guess I've been so focused on raising our daughter that I still have some untapped emotion there." As she spoke, she was aware of how immediately she had felt she could trust this man with details of her life. It was very much out of character for her to be so open with strangers, and yet this man didn't feel like a stranger.

"Where's your daughter now?"

"University of Texas."

"You have empty-nest syndrome. I've gone through it myself."

"Are your children raised?" she asked.

"My wife and I couldn't have children. She died two years ago of cancer. I've spent many a night walking through an empty house, wishing I could see her just one more time." He sighed. Fran nodded. She knew the feeling. To this day she would sometimes awaken thinking Tom was lying next to her, only to feel a recurrence of the pain of his loss.

He continued, "But the Lord is faithful, and He's bringing me through it."

Fran liked his direct style. There was no guile in this man. He placed his hand gently on her shoulder, bowed his head, and said, "Father, we just ask that the peace of Your presence surround Fran and that the healing indwelling of the Holy Spirit free her from painful memories and fears for the future. We ask all of this in Jesus' name. Amen."

Fran said, "Amen," and her mood lifted.

"That was really nice." She smiled at David. "I really appreciate it."

He touched her hand softly. "We are called to bear each other's burdens. If I can be of help in the future, just drop by the church. I'm there most of the time."

"Thanks again," Fran said. She smiled at him with her mouth and with her eyes. She felt a connection to him. Between teaching and making a home for Gloria, she hadn't been much involved in church. She was committed to daily prayer and Bible reading, but she had placed church activities on the back burner … and not only because of work and child rearing. The truth was she and Tom had shared a vision of ministry. When he died, he had taken the dream with him. Maybe it was time to get involved again. She watched David walk away. He was just a little overweight and jolly as Santa Claus as he hummed to himself. Almost as if he knew she had been watching, he turned around.

Yelling down the aisle, David said, "Potluck dinner at the church Thursday night at six thirty. You're more than welcome to come."

"Thanks. I think I will."

"If you're not doing anything, come to the church hall around four o'clock to help me cook. I like to minimize the 'luck' part of potluck!"

Fran chuckled at the attention. "I get out of school at three forty-five. I may be a few minutes late."

"I'll be waiting." David smiled, but for a brief second Fran could see the remnant of sad loneliness in the wake of his wife's death.

It was a beautiful fall day in Rome. The air was crisp but not cool as the heat of August slowly gave way to the balmy days of fall. Chris was ecstatic with the change in weather. Running in the heat and humidity of August had wearied him, yet he ran anyway. It was his only real stress reliever. True enough, he had found a workable relationship with Benny, but it was definitely not what he had signed up for when he joined the priesthood. He patently didn't like Benny, but his love for Kim and the boys always kept him in check. All in all, it was for him a lonely existence. Much like the pope, he considered himself to be a prisoner of the Vatican. Thankfully, Vinnie and the pope had the foresight to mandate that a number of Masses per year be said at the chapel on Kim's estate. At least he got the chance to break the "island fever" that came to Vatican residents.

The sun was moving lower in the sky as he made his way to the papal gardens. Vinnie had told him there was some special "gardening" that needed their attention this evening. He could only imagine it had to do with Benny. In the wake of Cardinal Bilbo's death, Benny had been acting aggressively, almost as if he had been promoted to Bilbo's position. *God forbid!* The likes of Benjamin Cross wearing the scarlet of a cardinal was enough to take Chris's breath away.

When he arrived at their meeting place, Vinnie was already there, cane in hand. The gout and age had worn him down to the point that he needed the cane if he was walking more than a short distance. They hadn't diminished his spirit, though. In fact, he had grown through the adversity. He still walked daily in Rome to meet the needs of the poor. He still had his rapid-fire wit. And, more importantly, his faith had grown exponentially.

"What! Did you take the long way around?" he demanded.

"What?" Chris smiled, knowing he was in for a teasing.

"I've been here ten minutes already!" Vinnie exclaimed, patting the space beside him in invitation for Chris to join him on the bench. "Ah, what's it matter, anyway?" Vinnie sighed. "I'm still happy to see you." After a brief pause, he tapped Chris on the chest with the top of his cane. "This is the place where you say, 'I'm happy to see you too, Vinnie.'"

"I'm happy to see you too, Vinnie," Chris said and grinned.

"John Barrymore, you're not!"

"I'm just wondering what we're going to hear tonight, Vinnie. I'm sure it's about Benny."

"Probably is." Vinnie turned serious. "Some people say he offed Bilbo."

Chris shrugged. "I don't know if Benny is capable of actually committing murder. I could see him ordering a hit but not actually getting his hands dirty."

"Whether he did or didn't, God help Bilbo now."

"I'm so tired of this, Vinnie. I didn't become a priest to be the servant of some fay, Mafia wannabe."

"You joined the priesthood to serve the Lord and the Church. His Holiness has been able to maneuver around the Curia more effectively from the information you provide."

"I'd rather be pastoring a church."

"I'm sure that's what Saint Paul said when he came to Rome," Vinnie quipped.

A voice joined from the entrance to the grotto. "That's what a younger Karl said when he came to Rome." The pope took a seat next to Chris. "These are difficult times, Chris. We are all called to be where we would rather not be. Vinnie is right. You've helped me more than you will ever know with the information you have brought to me."

"Thank you, Holiness. I apologize. I didn't mean to sound as if I was complaining."

The pope patted Chris's shoulder. "No need to apologize. I understand completely. But we no longer belong to ourselves, Chris. We belong to our Redeemer, and He has placed us at the crossroads of history. That is why I have asked to see you. We have great news, friends. We are on the cusp of the dissolution of the Soviet Union."

He paused for a few moments to let the gravity of his statement settle in. "I, myself, have spoken with Mr. Gorbachev. He doubts the Soviet economy will survive long without an influx of capital, but Western bankers are pulling back their support. Without serious democratic reform, the Soviets will not be able to borrow all they need."

An end to Soviet communism! An end to the Cold War! Chris and Vinnie could scarcely take it all in. Literally, the world would change overnight.

"Holiness, I'm overwhelmed," Chris said incredulously.

"Even I'm speechless!" Vinnie exclaimed, to the laughter of the other two.

"The pinnacle of my papacy is about to occur, my dream from my earliest years growing up under Soviet oppression. And it couldn't have happened without you, my friends."

Tears began to well in Chris's eyes. A bit embarrassed, he waited for Vinnie to tease him but instead heard a huge sound as Vinnie blew into his handkerchief.

After an awkward pause, the pope drew a deep breath and said, "There's something else. I have received a recommendation that Monsignor Cross perform the duties vacated by Cesare Bilbo. In fact, the Curia believes he would be a wonderful cardinal."

Chris was reeling. *Benny a cardinal! Come on!* "Holy Father, I can't stress enough that I think it would be a mistake to make him a cardinal," he said in measured tones. Even in the glimmer of twilight, fire shone in his eyes.

The pope continued, "I have told them he can perform Bilbo's duties as a bishop, while I take time to decide whether he will be offered the appointment of cardinal."

"Benny the bishop! Now I've heard everything!" Vinnie exclaimed.

"We live in curious times, my friend," the pope answered, smiling at Vinnie's outburst.

"But, Holy Father, there will have to be a decision at some point. How long can you hold open the cardinal's seat?" Chris asked.

"There are no limits. The position remains open until I decide, and as you know, not all papal business is complete when a pope leaves this world."

"So he'll perpetually be a—what would you call it?—cardinal-in-waiting?" Vinnie asked with a mischievous look.

"He will be perpetually challenged to find my good grace. With prayer and the Lord's help, perhaps he could see the error of his ways and return to more faithful practices. We must never underestimate the Lord's power to redeem."

"So wait a minute," Vinnie surmised, "if I take all kinds of actions against the Church, maybe sleep with a really wealthy man and help to sell worthless securities, maybe I could become a bishop too?"

Chris chuckled.

"It is vital that I dedicate myself to helping the transformation of the Soviet bloc nations," the pope said seriously. "I have neither the time nor energy to rout the Curia of suspicious characters. We have had this discussion. Besides, I have a fail-safe." The pope smiled ambiguously.

"What's that?" Vinnie asked.

"His assistant, of course, Monsignor Chris here."

For a second, Chris was honored by the title, but only for a second. The idea of another "hitch" at Benny's side was disdainful.

"Holy Father, it's my desire to serve you, but I have been finding myself more and more frustrated in the role of Benny's assistant. I beg of you, send me to a cloister somewhere ... or to the farthest mission, but don't make me work in the Vatican at Benny's side."

"Of course I wouldn't force you, Chris. But you know the stakes. I am asking you to help me do nothing less than free those enslaved by communism. In the light of such a global endeavor, can you sacrifice your time to the role I wish to assign to you?"

"Since you put it that way, I guess I can," Chris said with reluctant resignation.

"Thank you, Chris. I appreciate all you have done for this papacy, and I know the Lord will bless you, Monsignor."

"Damn, he's good!" Vinnie said to Chris in reference to the pope. All three chuckled as the sun fell below the horizon.

It was a surprisingly warm and sunny fall day in Rome as Benny lay out along Luciano's pool. His head was covered with a towel. New plastic surgery didn't fare well in the sun, but that didn't stop him from tanning the rest of his body. His tiny European thong left nothing to the imagination.

Strolling down the pathway in a silk suit was the nearly perfectly proportioned Luciano Begliali. He could have been in his twenties. Grimacing at the sight before him, he said, "Benito, it is time for you to change. Come into the house. I have much work for you to begin."

"What kind of work?" Benny asked, pulling the towel from his face.

"Let me ask you a question. Does the word 'Mahdi' mean anything to you?"

"No. Should it?" Benny asked as he sat up.

"Yes, Benny, it should. Not to worry though, you will become an expert on the subject." Begliali turned his head away and extended a robe to Benny.

"So what is a 'Mahdi'?" Benny asked, not taking the robe.

"It is the Muslim concept of a messiah."

"How interesting," Benny said as he lay back and returned the towel to his face.

Begliali threw down the robe to snatch the towel from Benny's face. He said tersely, "Yes, it is. But I don't have the patience to watch as you attempt to figure it out. So I'll help you. In seminary, you were taught what is often referred to as an amillennial view of Bible prophecy. Basically, you were taught that Christ will not reign over a literal kingdom on Earth at His return."

Luciano's harsh tone drove Benny to quickly sit up and slip into the robe. "That's right. His reign is in our hearts … supposedly."

"Well put, Eminence. But do you know what your fundamentalist brothers believe?"

"Not a clue. Does it have to do with handling poisonous snakes?"

"No." Luciano chuckled. "They believe Christ will return to Earth to rule for a thousand years."

"Good for them. Water to wine everywhere!" Benny tied the robe's belt.

"It may sound silly to you, but that's what they believe. And do you know what the Muslims believe?"

"I'm guessing it has to do with this Mahdi character," Benny offered.

"Yes. They believe he is coming to Earth to rule the world."

"That might get in Jesus' way," Benny said pertly.

"Not only that, but the Jews are awaiting their Messiah now that they are back in their ancestral lands."

"Could get crowded. It seems to me that too many messiahs will spoil the soup," Benny said drolly.

"But what if there was one man, someone we controlled, who could satisfy enough of the criteria to deceive all three groups? Their expectations of a coming deliverer will have made them quite gullible." Begliali smiled, waiting for Benny to fully grasp the implications.

"Then we could exercise control over the Muslims and Protestants," Benny said thoughtfully.

"Add that to the number of Catholics in the world, and the Church would have unprecedented power. And, of course, with that power comes unprecedented wealth," Begliali completed the thought.

"Genius, Luciano! Simply genius!" Benny cackled.

"The key is to put the Church in a place to take advantage of these delusions. That is why you must get dressed. I have arranged for a Muslim scholar from Turkey to educate you on the myths surrounding the Mahdi. I have also shipped to your apartment books from America that lay out the returning Jesus myths believed by the Protestant fundamentalists. There are similarities. There are ways to fulfill everyone's expectations."

"But aren't these guys supposed to work miracles? How do we fake that?" Benny questioned.

"If we have the right man, we won't need to."

"So, you actually *have* a messianic figure that can do miracles?"

"No, my friend. But the Lady and her companions are close to achieving an alien–human hybrid that will fit the bill very nicely."

"I'm starting to see how it would work. I am quite close with the Lady, you know."

A look of disgust blew past Luciano's face. "I know. The point is that once we have the undying loyalty of the faithful, we can implement strict birth control measures and a controlled eugenics program to reduce the world's population to the sustainable size of one billion souls who will embody the best of what humanity has to offer."

"Good luck finding a billion people that are exemplary!" Benny cackled.

"We may have to start with a smaller number," Luciano said and smiled.

Achmed Kurtoglu had a proud Ottoman past. He was Kurtoglu, which meant "Son of Wolf." His family had been part of the ruling caliphate for centuries before Ataturk brought Turkey to the modern world. At the time, many thought that westernizing Turkey would bring the nation from the Middle Ages to a place of equality with its European neighbors. In reality, modern Turkey was neither fish nor fowl. Too long had his proud people been at the tail end of Europe, always hoping to be treated as an equal, but forever branded a barbaric culture in the hearts of the West. Too long had they forsaken Sharia and the call of Allah.

If Kurtoglu had his way, Turkey would rekindle its Muslim roots, expand into the Middle East, and reestablish the caliphate. So how did he find himself in Rome of all places? Worse still, he was teaching a papist about the Perfect One, Allah be praised. How could an infidel understand the fierce purity of the coming Mahdi? Actually, "infidel" was a misnomer. This Benny was more of an "infidelette." Son of Wolf chuckled to himself. The nickname fit. If he was to go through with this and remain in Rome to teach this simpering wimp, then he would forever be infidelette in Achmed's mind.

Kurtoglu, Son of Wolf, tossed in his bed. He found it hard to believe this infidelette had shown the strength to commit murder. Yet Luciano described him as being a fearless warrior within, someone who would one day do wonders in bringing the West to the ways of Islam. Could it be? The infidelette? Son of Wolf was indeed perplexed as he fell asleep.

"Kurtoglu, awaken!" Son of Wolf heard the command and slowly opened his eyes to find a huge, swarthy man in his room. His first instinct would have been to reach for his knife, but he felt paralyzed as he gazed at the glowing figure before him.

"Who are you?" he asked.

"An angel of Allah, may He be praised. Some may call me a jinn. In reality I am merely a messenger of the Most High."

"What do you want with me?" Son of Wolf demanded.

"I bring you greetings from Paradise. You have been chosen to play a great role in the fulfillment of Allah's desire to bring Islam to the entire world."

"And how is it to be?"

"You will train this man you call infidelette. He has a purpose in the great plan."

"But he is a Christian cleric. And yet you wish me to tell him the mystery of the Mahdi?"

"Indeed, fine warrior. You must engage the world to conquer it."

"Then it shall be. I will do as Allah wishes, praises be to Him."

"And you will be rewarded richly in Paradise, Son of Wolf."

With a flash of light, the angel disappeared. Kurtoglu was perplexed. He went to the floor, faced Mecca, and prayed.

TWENTY

t was mid-October and the East Texas town of Riverside was beginning to show muted signs of fall. Sarah busied herself around the house. She wanted everything to be perfect. Zack hadn't been home for six weeks, and this weekend would be special. He was bringing his new girlfriend. Sarah was anxious. Zack had been circumspect in describing her, but he assured his mother this was "the one." The thought of losing her perfect little boy to another woman brought a chill to her. It seemed that such little time had passed since the angel told her of his arrival. She closed her eyes and let her imagination drift back to that wonderful night. It had changed her life. And now it was time for her baby to make his own way. As much as she hated the thought of sharing him, she knew he had been born to a great purpose. Her role in his life now was supportive. Whatever it took, she would force herself to love the girl Zack had chosen.

"Mack! Mack?" she called to her husband.

"In the study, Sarah," Mack called. "What's up?"

Sarah made her way through the rambling mansion to Mack's cherry wood–paneled study. "Should we serve wine with dinner? I'm having prime rib, and a dry red wine would taste sensational with it, but I worry what kind of message that will send." Sarah was worried about more than the wine. The introduction of Zack's girlfriend into the family caused her to see everything in a new light. She had spent a week making sure everything in their home looked perfect. She also placed herself on a strict diet to put a dent in the thirty pounds she had gained since her college days. She even tried a frightfully expensive new cream to attack the crow's-feet and laugh lines that had formed so subtly over the years.

"Personally, I'm okay with an occasional glass of wine," Mack replied. "The Bible tells us all things are lawful, but we should take care not to offend new believers."

Sarah took a good, hard look at Mack. He also had gained a few pounds and wrinkles over the years, but combined with some gray hairs at his temples, they conjured the appearance of wisdom and dignity. Aging was so much easier for a man! She unconsciously wrung her hands and said, "I know, and I want the meal to be perfect for Zack."

"Then serve the wine," Mack said as he began to massage her neck. "We could always ask her if she objects, but I find it hard to believe she would. She's going to a school known for its drinking."

The massage felt so good. Sarah could feel the tension fading away. "Good point. Mack, we know Zack has an occasional glass of wine, but do you think he gets drunk at school?"

"I'm guessing he has tried it and decided it isn't for him, honey. I know in your eyes he'll always be your little boy, but I think he has gone through all the temptations of youth."

She frowned. "I guess you're right. You don't think they've slept together, do you?" She shuddered at the thought.

"Times have changed, Sarah. If I had to guess, I'd say there is a fifty-fifty chance they have. He wants to marry this girl someday. He's very much in love."

"Did you ever have a heart-to-heart with him about that?" she asked him, rotating her head as he concentrated on her stiff shoulders.

"You mean like my father had with me? Or like your mother had with you?" he asked with a smirk.

They both laughed as they remembered those awkward conversations.

Chris had just said morning Mass at the chapel and had gone for a run in the beautiful Georgia countryside. Kim stayed behind to make breakfast. Each time he came home, they fell into an easy pattern.

Although their relationship was chaste, they functioned together like a well-oiled machine. Much like a couple that had been married for years, they seemed to anticipate each other's thoughts and emotions.

Kim loved his visits. The family business had thrived, and Kim was a tireless and generous owner. She was hands-on all the way, but when Chris or the boys came to town, she had lieutenants who were told to handle everything in her absence. Her boys were her major priority in life—all three of them. As for Benny, it had been years since he visited. It was a simple matter of taste; he preferred Luciano's castle.

On a whim, she called the boys' dorm room. Although it was morning in Georgia, it was well into the afternoon in Germany. The phone rang and rang. *Pretty stupid to call and expect an answer, Kim. They're probably in class.*

"Huh, hello?" a voice slurred on the other end of the conversation.

"Gabe? Gabe, is that you?"

"Mom. Really tired."

"Gabe, are you sick? What's going on?"

No answer.

"Gabe! Gabe … what's going on?" Kim demanded. Her grip on the phone tightened as she paced the kitchen. Something was wrong—very wrong. Images from her recent nightmare rushed through her mind.

There was a rustling sound as the phone was moved.

"Hello? Mom?" Kim heard Michael say.

"Michael! What's going on? What happened to your brother?" She unconsciously twisted the phone cord tightly around her fingers.

"Not to worry, Mom. He partied hardy last night and is sleeping it off."

"He's not in college to 'party hardy,'" she snapped. "Put him on the phone." She unwound the cord and twisted it again as she felt the familiar motherly instinct to protect her son. But he was so far away!

She could hear Michael rustling him. Gabe was a bit more coherent when he came to the phone this time.

"Hi, Mom."

Kim was relieved, but only slightly, to hear him sounding clearer-headed. She launched into the well-worn lecturing tone she had come to use with her risk-taker son. For years she had lived in fear that his birth mother's weakness for drugs would prove to be an inherited disposition. And those fears had grown steadily since the boys went to Germany. Too often Gabe was "out" or "busy" when she called. She knew Michael well enough to know he had been covering for his brother the entire semester.

"Gabe, I don't care if you have a good time once in a while, but I don't expect to find you hungover on a Wednesday afternoon. Think about the choices you're making! What are you doing with your life?"

"I'm fine, Mom. Really I am. I just got a little out of control last night. I'm fine. Don't worry."

Famous last words! Parents know to worry as soon as their children tell them not to. "I'm disappointed, Gabe. You can do better than this." There was silence on the other end of the conversation and then a heaviness of breath. She would swear he was crying.

A quick sob escaped. "Don't be disappointed, Mom. I'll do better. I promise."

Her heart melted by the sob, Kim offered a softer tone. "Okay, sweetie. Listen, I love you and I'm here for you. If you're into something you can't handle, I'll help you."

"I know, Mom. I love you too."

"Okay. Go back to sleep, and let me talk to your brother for a moment."

"What's up, Mom?" Michael asked.

"You tell me!" she demanded of her more responsible son. "What the hell is going on with your brother? He never cries, but I only said two words to him and he's sobbing."

"Maybe he's not so much hungover as still a bit drunk. It was pretty much an all-nighter," Michael offered weakly.

"And not only alcohol, I'm guessing." Kim opened Pandora's box. She winced as she said it, but she had to know.

No response from Michael. She knew his silent assent well.

"Michael, is your brother a drug addict?"

"Mom, you're getting worked up over nothing," Michael said sternly. Kim knew if it was untrue, Michael would have denied the allegation vehemently instead of turning it back on her.

"I think I'm going to pull the rug out from under this little experiment in living abroad," she said, matching his tone. "You two aren't ready to be on your own."

"Mom, please believe me. Everything is fine. Let him sleep it off a bit and he'll call you tonight. I promise," Michael pleaded.

Chris returned from his run. Seeing the expression on Kim's face, he stopped and mouthed "What's wrong?" to her.

"I need to think about it, Michael. I don't like what I'm hearing. Chris is here. I'll talk it over with him."

"Can I talk to him?" Michael asked.

"Sure," she said crisply. "Chris, Michael wants to talk to you." Chris took the phone, looking at Kim intently for some sort of hint as to what was going on. "Drugs," she mouthed silently.

With a grim expression, Chris demanded, "Michael, what's going on?" Kim moved close, and Chris tilted the receiver so that she could hear Michael's side of the conversation.

"Mom caught Gabe sleeping off an all-night party. Now she thinks he's some kind of skid-row addict."

"Is he?" Chris asked with a stern tone.

"No."

"Well, why don't you tell me what he is?" Chris demanded. His look told Kim that he too sensed something was wrong.

"He's a guy who likes to party too hardy. He likes to chase skirt, and he's not the most industrious student. But he's not an addict. You have to calm Mom down, Chris."

"Let's be clear, Michael. None of that is exemplary behavior. I want you to tell me straight. Do you think Gabe is in danger?"

"No! I think Mom called at a bad time and is blowing things out of proportion."

"Are you being truthful with me?"

"Yes!" Michael blurted too emphatically. "Chris, you're like a father to me. I wouldn't lie to you. I think he's experimenting with his freedom right now, but I don't think he's some kind of freaking addict."

Chris's tone mellowed to a "don't shoot the messenger" conciliatory one. "Okay. And how are you doing? Are you reading your Bible and brushing your teeth?"

"I'm probably unbalanced toward the teeth side of the scale, but I'll get on it."

"Okay, buddy. I love you."

"I love you too, Chris. Talk to Mom." Michael hung up.

Chris hung up the phone and looked at Kim with a furrowed brow. "Gabe's in trouble," she said.

"Could be."

They ate breakfast in silence as each thought about the situation. "I think I should fly to Germany and bring Gabe home with me," Kim finally said as she finished her eggs.

"It might be a bit early to do that, Kim. Michael says we just caught Gabe at a bad moment. They're adults now. If you go marching in there only to find nothing is seriously wrong, you could hurt your relationship with them. It would be like saying you don't trust them. That you think they're liars." Chris stood to get more coffee.

"Maybe you're right. But, then again, there's this mother's intuition telling me they are in trouble. What if I hired a private detective? They wouldn't know he's there, and I'd get some peace of mind."

"You're not serious!" Chris exclaimed as he returned to the table. "Kim, you can't hire a private detective to make sure the kids aren't partying too much in college."

"Why not?" Kim asked defiantly.

Chris spoke gently. "Kim, a certain amount of partying is a rite of passage for a young man. I understand your concerns, but you are going to have to put this into the Lord's hands. At least for now."

"What do you mean, 'at least for now'?" she asked.

"I'll be here for Thanksgiving. We'll monitor Gabe carefully. If we think he needs an intervention, we'll take care of it like a family. No private detectives. No panic-stricken flights to Berlin."

From anyone else, Kim would have found the words to be condescending, but from Chris she only heard his concern. "Okay, Thanksgiving it is. On one condition."

"What's that?"

"If I get one of those really bad mother's intuition moments between now and Thanksgiving, will you be willing to check in on them for me?"

"I probably owe them a visit anyway. Does that make you happier?"

"Yes, it does. Trust me, something's going on with those two. Michael is too devoted to Gabe to tell us there's a problem."

Chris nodded his agreement. "In the meantime, let's pray ..."

Fran and David had been inseparable since they met. She loved his kindness, sense of humor, and passion for his church. And she loved the way she felt when she was with him. As they prepared yet another church dinner, she marveled at his abilities. Early each Wednesday morning, David would canvass local restaurant suppliers for products that were about to expire. After finding what would be donated or could be purchased at a steep discount, he would determine a menu and start to work, often producing fabulous restaurant-quality meals for nearly two hundred people at the unheard-of cost of about $1.50 per head.

"Where did you learn to do this?" she asked incredulously.

"I've always had a knack for cooking. It just comes easy to me."

"It's more than a knack, David. If you ever decide to stop preaching, you could open a four-star restaurant."

"And give up pastoring the best church dinners in all of the Republic of Texas? Not a chance, sister!"

Fran laughed. She laughed a lot when she was around David, and it felt good. No, it felt great. She missed so much about Tom, but mostly she missed his friendship. David brought laughter and friendship back to her life. They ate together about four times a week, and she volunteered at church events on Wednesday and Sunday evenings. In fact, she was sure the other women in the parish were wondering what was going on.

"I think we're becoming a bit of a scandal in the parish," she said with a demure smile.

"Wagging tongues like to wag, Fran. We aren't doing anything wrong. We're just enjoying each other's company. We haven't even kissed!"

"Why is that?" Fran asked suggestively. "Don't you find me attractive?"

David stopped his work at the stove to look her in the eye. "I find you incredibly attractive!" he protested. "And I enjoy your company. If it were up to me, I'd spend all my time with you."

"Me too," she said, biting her bottom lip.

"But to do that, we have to get over the awkward feeling that we are somehow cheating on our spouses," David said seriously.

A tear came to her eye. "My memories of Tom are all I have left. I don't want to lose them."

"And Jill was the love of my life," David added.

"So how do we hold on to them and let go enough to find each other?" she asked.

"We've already found each other. Now we have to figure it out."

"David, there's no man on Earth right now I would rather spend time with."

"But if Tom were here, I would be second," David finished her thought.

"Yes," Fran said, "but please don't take it badly."

"I don't," he said. "I love you, but if Jill were here ..."

Fran smiled. "Did you just say the L word?"

"I guess I did. And it didn't bother me now that we have given Tom and Jill their rightful places in our lives. I promise you to always respect Tom's memory."

"And I promise you to always respect Jill's memory."

David sighed contentedly and then said with excitement, "That was easier than I thought it would be. You know—"

"David?" Fran interrupted.

"Yeah?"

"Shut up and kiss me." They had time for one kiss before the volunteer kitchen help arrived.

After the meal had been served and dishes washed, Fran and David were again alone. As they were leaving the church, David wrapped his arm around Fran and asked, "Do you think Gloria will accept our relationship?"

"She considers herself a pretty liberated woman," Fran answered. "But she worshipped her father. I'm guessing the grown woman in her will be grateful I've found someone, but Daddy's little girl is going to be hurt."

"What have you told her so far?" he asked.

"Nothing. She has no idea of our relationship. In fact, I had no idea of where it was heading until we had this talk tonight."

"I see," he said uncomfortably. "I have to tell you, Fran, I don't believe in long engagements. If we want a life together, it needs to be aboveboard. The best thing for us and for the church would be a wedding. It will put the wagging tongues to rest and allow us to move on with our life together."

Fran had to catch her breath. "David! Are you proposing?" she asked.

"I guess I am. Frannie Ellis, will you marry me?"

"Yes," she beamed, "but maybe not as quickly as you would like. I need to be fair to Gloria. Let me introduce her to you over Thanksgiving break first … give her a chance to see how wonderful you are. Okay?"

"Okay. So let's plan a Christmas wedding."

"It's all so fast, David!" Fran yelled.

"We're not kids, Fran. We know what we want in life," David said as he pulled her close.

"I suppose I could manage it. After all, I wouldn't want a large wedding."

"We can have a small ceremony and then a reception in the church hall. We'll have so many volunteers that we'll have to turn some away. And I could supervise the meal in my sleep! All you need to do it put on a pretty dress—"

"And sell the idea to Gloria at Thanksgiving," Fran said and sighed.

Gloria was quiet on the drive to Zack's house. They had pieced it together that their parents had known each other years ago. She remembered Fran's disappointing visit with them shortly after Tom died.

"Nervous?" Zack asked. They had left the interstate and were only minutes from his home.

"I just wish our parents didn't have a history, you know?"

"First of all, it was years ago. I'm sure everyone has grown since then. Secondly, I kind of like the idea. We can each stand up to them, let them know we're going to lead our own lives," he said as he pulled the car around the circular driveway in front of the mansion.

"You grew up here?" she asked in awe.

"No. I grew up in a much smaller place. The church just built this place about a year ago."

"It's beautiful!" Gloria's eyes were wide as she took in the view.

"A well-run ministry takes care of its pastor."

"I guess it does!" Gloria exclaimed.

The front door opened, and Sarah ran to meet the car as it stopped.

She threw herself on Zack, nearly knocking him off balance as he exited the car. "I've missed you so badly," she cried as she hugged him.

Mack came out to the car and opened the door for Gloria. "Welcome to our home," he said with a broad smile.

"Thanks, Pastor. Zack has told me so much about you. I feel like I know you already."

"Call me Mack, dear. Unfortunately, Zack has been pretty secretive about you. All we know is that he's head over heels. I don't even know your real name. He calls you 'G.'"

"His nickname for me," she said and smiled. Putting out her hand, she said, "I'm Gloria. Gloria Ellis."

Gloria saw Sarah stiffen at the mention of her name. Sarah pushed herself away from Zack and plastered a pretend smile on her face. "I think I went to college with your mother, dear."

"I think you were roommates." Gloria smiled with a twinkle in her eye.

"Yes. We were. How have you been? I can't tell you how sad Mack and I were when we heard of your father's death."

"It was a tragedy. But my mother went to work as a teacher, and my dad's parents were there to help raise me. It ended up okay."

"I think we are already beyond a handshake, young lady," Mack said as he embraced her. "Welcome to our home."

"Yes," Sarah said warily, "welcome. Let's go inside. Meemaw is waiting to meet you."

As they entered the foyer, they found an unhappy Meemaw sitting in her wheelchair.

"I can't believe you stood out there all the time with the front door open. It's October, you know," Meemaw chided. "I've had that cold breeze blowing up my skirt for five minutes now. My down under is starting to feel like Antarctica!"

Gloria laughed out loud. She really liked something about this old lady. Maybe it was because she missed her own grandparents.

Zack laughed heartily. "Hi, Meemaw. I'm so happy to see you."

"Back at you, blue eyes." Sandy grinned. "You could have rushed in here to see me, you know. What were you waiting for, rigor mortis to set in?"

He hugged her and gently kissed her cheek, melting her temper tantrum. "Meemaw, I want you to meet my girlfriend, Gloria Ellis."

"Oh my word! I think I would have known you anywhere," Sandy exclaimed. "You have your mother's kind eyes, and if I'm not mistaken, your dad's hair and cheekbones."

"I think you're right." Gloria grinned as she bent to kiss the old lady's cheek.

"And your dad's smile, honey." Sandy held Gloria's face in her hands. "I loved your mom. I haven't seen her since happy pants over there danced all over your dad's memorial service."

"I was a child. I don't have any memory of that service," Gloria said, quickly righting the conversation. "But we're here today. And I finally get to meet Zack's Meemaw. I'm thrilled."

Zack, Sarah, and Mack all looked on in silent consideration of the way Gloria disarmed that potential bombshell. She turned to them and said, "Seriously. I am very happy to be here. Maybe it's time we put a past misunderstanding behind us."

"Do you like my dress, dear?" Sandy interrupted.

"Why, yes," Gloria cooed. "I think it's beautiful."

"Oh, good. Now that I've made a good first impression, would you mind if I changed into a housecoat? These control-top pantyhose are squeezing the gas—"

Sarah rushed to her mother's side and shoved something in her mouth. "Have a Rolaid, Mama." She pushed the wheelchair to the dining room, and the others followed.

As they sat down to dinner, Sarah stared at Mack, silently prodding him to ask about the wine. He said, "Gloria, we're having prime rib. I have a nice bottle of red wine that will taste great with it, but if you don't believe in drinking, we won't open it. I want you to be comfortable."

"I'm fine with the wine, Pastor Ellis."

"Mack," he corrected.

"Mack." She smiled.

"Good going, girl," Meemaw added. "A little vino would be keen-o!"

"Mama, just a little for you. You take so much medicine!" Sarah said with exasperation. She had planned every detail of this day for weeks, but there was no planning what her mother would do!

"I've read every bottle, Sarah. Not one of them says I can't have a glass of wine with dinner. Or two or three if I want to," Sandy challenged.

"But, Mama, you never drank in your life!" Sarah exclaimed.

"Well, it's high time I started," Sandy said, mimicking the haughty smile of a bad girl from a 1940s film. Sarah glared at her, hoping to silence her.

Zack calmed the building storm by saying, "Oh, come on, Mom, what could it hurt?"

"It's your party, Zack." Sarah bristled. "Do whatever you want."

"Meemaw, I will pour you a glass myself," Zack said with a smile. "That way we can all toast Gloria and welcome her to the family."

"Thanks, sweetheart. And as the matriarch, I want to welcome you to our family, Gloria. God knows I could use the company. Living here with Sarah-Scare-a and Mack the Knife is getting the better of me. I think I'm starting to slip mentally."

They all sat with frozen smiles. There was no civil way to respond to such a comment.

Zack poured Meemaw's glass first, saying, "You're doing fine, Meemaw. Don't worry. And we all love you very much, especially Mom and Dad."

Sarah mouthed a thank-you to her son as Mack picked up the conversation. "Your mind is pretty sharp, Sandy. Don't sell yourself short. Tell these guys your theories on the Kennedy assassinations."

"It's simple," Sandy responded. Sarah scowled, knowing Mack was playing her mother for a fool. "Ethel killed Jack, and Jackie killed Bobby. That Marilyn Monroe thing was the final straw, so the girls took action. I would have done the same thing if it happened to me."

Everyone but Sarah chuckled. Mack was on a roll, and Sandy was his sight gag. "Tell them what you've been reading about Bible prophecy."

"Dad, a toast first," Zack protested. "To Gloria. May she feel welcomed and loved by our family as she and I start our lives together."

"Here! Here!" Sarah said in an obviously overenthusiastic cheer. Zack's toast sounded like something you would say at a wedding. She wasn't ready to lose her son. Not yet. And with this girl, she would not only lose him to his wife, she would have to share him with Fran. What a thought!

"Cheers," Mack added.

Meemaw slammed her empty glass to the table and belched. Sarah startled, as if unexpectedly slapped.

"Mama, you're supposed to sip it," Sarah scolded.

"Now you tell me! Since when has the cat got that tongue of yours?" Sandy spit back. "Pour me another, Zack. I'll sip this one and tell you about the Second Coming. I've been reading a lot lately about the book of Daniel and the book of Revelation. I'm going to start reading about Ezekiel soon. They all predict what the world will be like before Jesus returns. I think we're living in the last generation."

"Oh, Meemaw." Zack chuckled. "Guys like this Hal Lindsey are just out to make a buck. We are far more likely to build the Kingdom of God on Earth ourselves. That's the real meaning of Christianity. It's the ultimate expression of the Golden Rule."

"You sound like your father, and if you're not careful, one day you'll be wearing a 666 on your forehead," Sandy warned. Mack burst out laughing. Zack joined in. Sarah silenced them with a scowl.

"Stop teasing her, Mack," Sarah chided. "She really believes this stuff."

"That's right. I do. You know old age isn't always a curse. The years add a different perspective. I may be slipping on some things, but I really think I'm right on this one."

"I think it is wonderful that you engage your mind like that," Gloria commented. "You don't sit all day watching *The Price is Right*. You read and think about things. I hope my mind is as sharp when I get older."

"Not that there's anything wrong with Bob Barker," Sandy said. "He could put his shoes under my bed any day!" Sarah slapped another helping of mashed potatoes on her mother's plate.

Zack continued the original conversation. "Dad, do some people seriously think we're close to Christ's return?"

"Some people think so. Gloria's daddy believed we were living in the last generation. I never really felt it. There is a lot of scholarly work that points to the idea that those prophecies were never meant to be taken literally. A lot of us believe it is our job to build the Kingdom of God on Earth."

"One dollar at a time, right, preacher?" Meemaw cackled.

"Mama, I've just about had enough," Sarah said in a low growl.

"I don't want to hear a peep from you for the rest of dinner. Do you understand me?"

"Yes," Sandy said, looking like a chastised child. She remained quiet until a caregiver took her to her room after dessert.

"Okay, now that she's gone, let me say this," Sarah scolded. "I don't ever want to see her with alcohol again. She takes too many pills, and God only knows how they'll interact. I think she's drunk."

"Will do, Mom. I didn't realize she was going to chug it," Zack said sheepishly.

"Thank you," Sarah purred. She just adored her handsome son.

"I need to turn the conversation to another important matter," Zack said rather formally. "Gloria and I want to get married. I guess you could say we're engaged."

Sarah bristled as Mack took up the conversation. "Son, you're so young, and this relationship is so new. I think it's great you're dating with an eye toward marriage, but an engagement might be premature."

"We're not naive," Zack said. "It's not like we're planning to run off and get married. We were thinking after we both have graduated in two years."

Mack's entire body deflated with a sigh of relief. "That's a different story. I think we can all work with that time frame. What do you think, Sarah?"

There was no response. Sarah's eyes were filled with tears as she looked to the day she dreaded. This meant that he was gone for good. She had always hoped he would come back home to live for a few years after college. Well, Fran Ellis had gotten her revenge, hadn't she?

"It's not my decision," Sarah said. "If this is what you want, son, then I guess I have to go along with it."

"Thanks, Mom. I know if you had your way, I'd stay your baby boy forever, but that's not the way of the world." He left his chair to give his mother a kiss on the cheek.

Gloria had sat quietly throughout the conversation.

"Penny for your thoughts," Zack said as he returned to his seat beside her.

"I'm just wondering how my mother will feel about the news. She doesn't even know we're dating."

"Really?" Sarah perked up. This presented some real opportunities.

If Fran reacted badly, maybe Gloria would reconsider the marriage. Failing that, if Sarah played herself off as the more compliant mother, she could win "favored mother" status with the new couple. She could cut Fran out.

"I was thinking we would break the news to her over Thanksgiving. I think it may take her a couple days to come around to the idea."

"Well, you're part of our family now, dear." Sarah dripped with sweetness. "If there's anything I can do for you, you let me know."

"Thank you, Mrs. Jolean." Gloria grinned at the apparent change of heart.

"Call me Sarah. Or call me Mom if you like. It will be so nice to have a daughter."

"Okay ... Mom." Gloria fumbled with a smile. "And thank you so much for your support."

"Thanks, Mom," Zack said with a sigh of relief.

"I'm happy you're being so supportive, Sarah," Mack said with a curious look that betrayed his desire to know her true motivation.

"You even sound surprised." Sarah smiled as her eyes warned him to back off. "Of course, I would be supportive of my only son! Mack, you never understood that a mother's ultimate joy is to be there for her child." Then looking at Gloria, she said, "There's a certain care that only a mother can bring—"

She was interrupted by loud music from Sandy's room. "Oh, no," she moaned. "Not that Jimmy Buffet song again!"

"I like 'Margaritaville,'" Gloria said.

"It's not 'Margaritaville.'" Mack laughed.

Just then they heard Sandy's once-lovely voice, now only loud and out of key, singing with Buffet, "Why don't we get drunk and screw?" followed by Sarah's heavy footsteps as she stomped back to Sandy's room.

———

Benny winced at the thought, but he gave it another try. Son of Wolf wanted him to memorize the ninety-nine names of Allah. Some of them he found interesting. There was a brutality about this god that Benny admired. He admired Son of Wolf as well. He was dedicated to his religion and was serious about teaching Benny. He had been a bit harsh at the start, but Benny found that a little bit of automobile anti-freeze in the man's tea did wonders for his disposition. Not enough to kill him, mind you, at least not right away. But it was enough to slow him down and make him a little less ornery. The sweet taste of the antifreeze played to Son of Wolf's sweet tooth, a combination made in heaven.

Heaven! The thought nearly made Benny laugh. Studying Islam allowed him insight into a faith structure completely different from his own. The training gave him a new vantage point, one from which he could see the overriding fundamental in all religions, namely control. The stories of Islam seemed to him to be as mythical as the stories of the Bible. Their mystery was neither in their veracity nor in their spiri-tuality, but in the way that they created levers deep in the souls of their believers. The one who understood this was the one who would be able to pull the levers. And Benny was learning that, with the right nuance, one solid push could move levers in Muslims, Jews, and Christians. Luciano was right. The Lady and her extraterrestrial friends should be able to create the signs and wonders that were attributed to Mahdi. The beautiful part of the Mahdi story is it involves Jesus as his right-hand man. Played properly, huge numbers of Christians of all denomina-tions could be persuaded this dynamic duo created a perfect synthesis of faiths. Judaism was trickier. Even though he was part Jewish, Benny realized that Hebrew obstinacy may mean many would have to die in order to bring all of Abraham's children together. There was a chance for the Jews, but they would have to be so tired of conflict that they would bend a bit for the sake of peace. Arab–Israeli tensions were crucial in creating the pressure to bring about a change in the Jewish mind-set. There was also a chance the Jesus character, friend of Mahdi, could be received as the long-awaited Jewish Messiah.

The possibilities were endless. Benny's job was to find the com-binations that would bring about the subjugation of the most peo-ple. Given time and the possibility of his ascendancy in the Catholic Church, he could greatly assist the Curia in their training of a billion souls who were apt to believe even the most outlandish claims if they appeared to have Roman backing. Then there were the name-it-and-claim-it Christians in America. They really just wanted a piece of the pie. They could be lured pretty easily into a larger amalgamation of Abraham's children. As for the mainline denominations, well, Rome already had a dialogue with many of them. They were beginning to realize that ecumenism may be the only way to preserve their dwindling institutions.

There were others, however, who followed a straight biblical path. They were harder to manipulate. They seemed to share a psychosis in which they actually felt led by the Holy Spirit. For days, Benny had pondered how they could ever come into the fold. Finally, the Lady explained to him that certain of these Christians would have to be removed if there were to be a New World Order. At first Benny thought she meant by war, but she then showed him that her people would literally take them out of this world.

Kurtoglu entered the room. "Have you learned the names, infidelette?" he demanded.

"Of course I have," Benny said and smiled. "I even had time to make you some of your favorite tea."

"You know well how to serve your master," Son of Wolf complimented. He drank the tea and nodded his approval. "Proceed with the recitation of the Holy Names."

"Of course," Benny said, looking like a willing student. He began the recitation but barely made it to number ten before Kurtoglu fell fast asleep.

Benny stopped talking and threw himself into a chair. *What to do? What to do? Dare I. Oh, why the hell not!* He quietly went to Kurtoglu and undid his pants. The man certainly didn't live up to the fantasy.

In a high-pitched voice he sang, "I know seventy-two virgins that are going to be pretty disappointed."

TWENTY-ONE

G unter Schabowski was the new party boss in East Berlin and the spokesman for the Politburo. On November 9, 1989, he had been on the job only a few days. Events had swirled into a vortex of political action that swept his boss to power only a few weeks before. As spokesman for the Politburo, he had to have the facts down cold. He reviewed them in his mind. In August 1989, Hungary opened the iron curtain to Austria. This prompted a mass exodus of East Germans who would pass through Hungary to Austria and then to West Germany. Sensing the cry of freedom in the air, East Germans staged huge rallies throughout the fall, resulting in the resignation of Erich Honecker, East Germany's head of state, on October 18, 1989.

Hoping to stem the tide of exodus through Hungary and quell the burgeoning crowds, the new East German government prepared to lighten travel restrictions for its citizens by allowing them to enter West Germany. And now it was Gunter's privilege to make this announcement on November 9. He read it in his most authoritative voice to the cheering crowd. Following the announcement, at around 7:00 p.m., he was asked exactly when the easing of travel restrictions would come into effect. Looking down at the memo he received, he found no date specified and went with his gut to answer the question. "As far as I know effective immediately, without delay." The cheering crowd turned into a tsunami of people pushing toward West Germany. Throngs of East Germans rushed to the gates in the Berlin Wall, anxious to visit their long-lost brothers in West Germany. Security guards were not prepared for the onslaught, and the crowds poured into the West for their first taste of freedom since Hitler's ascent to power.

Peering out at the chaos, Schabowski realized that he had been wrong about the date of the regulation's implementation.

Michael jumped at his desk as the slamming door broke his concentration. He looked up to see Gabe out of breath. He had clearly run home.

"Dude! Drop the books, man! History is in the making!" Gabe yelled with excitement.

"Let me guess, there's a huge cocaine shipment about to take place," Michael said, tiring of Gabe's antics.

"In fact, there is," Gabe said and smiled, "but that's not what I'm talking about. The East Germans have stormed the wall. They're pouring through the gates."

"What?" Michael asked incredulously.

"You heard me. We've got to get to the wall, man! We're part of freakin' history!"

Michael slammed shut his books and grabbed his coat. "Where do you want to go?"

"Brandenburg Gate," Gabe answered over his shoulder as he headed out the door.

As the boys ran toward the Brandenburg Gate, the entire city was alive with emotion, and Berlin residents were crying in the street as they saw their brothers come to the free side of Germany. The atmosphere was at once solemn and party-like. Older residents remembered the horrors of the past that had led to this moment. They carried with them the stain of World War II; it pricked their hearts every day that they looked at the horrible wall bisecting their city. Younger residents, who had grown up with the wall, were jubilant as they contemplated the birth of something new in their society.

The streets were filling with Trabants, small East German cars that looked more cartoonish than functional. People were shaking hands and hugging as the boys pushed through the crowd to the gate.

Pulling up short, Gabe looked through the crowd until he spotted a familiar face and waved.

"Who's that?" Michael asked.

"He's a ... connection."

Michael scowled as the young man, obviously in need of a shower, worked his way to Gabe. The recent concerts by the new group Nirvana had brought grunge to West Germany. Though, by the looks of it, Michael guessed this guy had the grunge thing down well before Kurt Cobain hit town.

As Michael looked on, Gabe held up four fingers. Four ludes would do the trick once the party mellowed. But for now it was coke, which the man had in carefully measured bags in his backpack. "Better get the stuff now," he said in a thick accent. "These easterners are crazy to try it." Before this, Gabe had been careful to use his drugs out of Michael's sight. Michael had relied on that fact to support his lies to Chris and their mother—after all, he had never *seen* Gabe take drugs. Only the frenzied atmosphere of historic significance stopped Michael from lashing out at Gabe.

Gabe finished the transaction. "Okay," he said, "but check back with me later. I think this party could be days long." To Michael's continued horror, Gabe pulled a thick wad of German marks from his pocket, selected a few bills, and handed them to his "connection."

As the man left, Michael grabbed Gabe's arm, intending to at least take care of the one situation that could be managed this night. He shouted to be heard above the crowd, "Why are you carrying that kind of money? And flashing it around in a crowd?"

"I cashed a check, and I guess I forgot to leave some of the money back at the room. Don't sweat it, bro. Even if I lose it, we can afford it."

"I know, Gabe, but I don't want to get jumped for it either. Just keep it in your pocket, okay?"

Gabe was looking at a long-haired blonde who was clearly on a buzz, swaying and laughing in the crowd. "The money, you mean?" he asked with a smirk.

"Everything!" Michael screamed above the crowd.

A few beers and some German sausages later, Michael was relaxing into the situation. It was wonderful to be a part of history. The euphoria of the crowd was contagious. Vendors and restaurants near the wall were offering specials as people milled through Berlin on their way to or from the Brandenburg Gate.

Down and out with a cold, Kim went to bed early but couldn't sleep. The big house creaked in the winter wind. It seemed very lonely without her boys. Her boys. They were the real problem—not that they weren't home, but that she was having a hard time letting go. She tossed in bed with an almost palpable fear they were in trouble. Repeatedly she told herself it was all in her head, but sleep wouldn't come.

"Father," she prayed, "please take away this anxiety I feel for my boys. If you aren't behind these feelings, then let them pass as I sleep in Your presence. I ask in Jesus' name. Amen."

She rolled to her side, confident that her prayer would be answered. She focused on the glory of God and prepared to fall asleep in His embrace. As she drifted off, she fell immediately to a dream. She saw Michael and Gabe helplessly jostled by crowds of people. Michael looked forlorn, trying to steer his brother out of the fray. Gabe looked stoned to the point of losing consciousness as Michael half-carried him along.

With a jolt, Kim sat upright in bed. "Father, are my boys in trouble?" she prayed. There was no audible answer, but the response in her heart was as loud as if He had yelled to her. She had a distinct impression she needed to turn on the television. Feeling the Spirit was urging her, she turned on the set and saw news reports of the startling events in Germany. There were the crowds, just as she had seen in her dream.

She quickly dialed the boys' apartment, but there was no answer. *Of course not. No doubt they're at the center of the action.* She slammed down the receiver and placed another call.

In Rome, Chris had gathered with Vinnie and several other priests to have silent prayer before the Blessed Sacrament. Their intent was to thank the Lord for the rupture in the wall, to pray for the continued safety of East Germans wishing to cross to the West and to ask the Lord to further dismantle the communist machine in Eastern Europe.

Prayer before the Blessed Sacrament is a ceremony without ceremony. The priests gathered in silence and knelt in reflective prayer. While corporate in their number, each was engaged in his personal relationship with the Lord.

Vinnie shifted uncomfortably, sighed, and opted to be seated for the event, mouthing the word "gout" to Chris, as if Chris wouldn't have known. An elderly friar came to the meeting dressed in a brown tunic and a hood that, even pushed back from his head, was thick enough to go around the bottom of his face like Joe Bazooka's turtleneck. He knelt next to Chris and began to pray. Sensing something familiar, Chris looked over to the man at his left. On close inspection, the man's brown hair appeared to be a toupee. Chris recognized the blue eyes of the pontiff, who in turn leaned in to whisper in Chris's ear. "Thankfully, I was an actor in my youth," he said with a proud grin. "Don't tell the Swiss Guard I sneaked out. It makes them nervous."

Vinnie reached behind Chris to pat the monk on the shoulder, as if welcoming an old friend. Then the three men of God joined their brothers in honest, contemplative prayer.

At first, Chris's mind wandered. *What if someone recognizes the pope? Will he be safe? Someone could harm him and the Swiss Guard wouldn't even know where he was!* Chris surveyed the chapel, which was lit only by candles. He strained to see every man in the room, looking for a potential threat. He knew most of these men, and the ones he didn't know certainly didn't look like a problem.

As he settled into prayer, Chris could feel the Holy Spirit tugging at him. There was a sense of disquiet, as if his name were being called. *Speak, Lord. I'm your servant. I am listening.* As Chris closed his eyes, he was assaulted by a vision, a sort of movie that played on the screen of his eyelids. Crowds swelling in the streets of Berlin. He was running through them, searching each face, trying to find Michael and Gabe ... before they died!

Chris gasped and jumped suddenly. There were slight titters of laughter throughout the chapel. Chris wouldn't be the first to drift off to sleep in silent, contemplative prayer, but those closest to him knew different.

"The Lord is calling you to action," the pope whispered into Chris's left ear.

"Holy Father, Michael and Gabe are in danger. I need to go to Germany."

"My camerlengo will arrange it for you. Tell him I sent you."

Chris genuflected toward the altar and rushed out of the chapel as Vinnie looked after him with concern and began to whisper in the pope's ear.

The papal offices were open late on such an auspicious evening. As usual, the pope's camerlengo kept things running smoothly. He was a short man with straight hair and vortex baldness that would have made him look like a stereotypical monk, but this man had intelligent eyes that twinkled in the office light and the smile of someone from Hollywood. Chris knew him only in passing, but from the smile and recognition in his eyes, Chris surmised he knew of the meetings in the papal gardens.

"Not a problem, Chris. I can get you on a flight to Germany that will get you into Berlin at 3:00 a.m."

"I guess that will do. Thank you so much," Chris said with a desperate smile.

"The Holy Father wouldn't have sent you if he didn't think the Lord had told you to go."

"One question," Chris said. "Why did you believe me when I said His Holiness sent me?"

Grinning mischievously, the camerlengo pushed a button on his phone. It sent an intercom message to the head of the Swiss Guard.

"Pronto, Signore."

"Can you please tell me where the pontiff is right now?" the camerlengo asked in English.

Responding in English, the head of security said, "He is still at the Chapel of Saint Martha, disguised as a monk." He sighed, as if to say, "Do you believe this?"

The camerlengo chuckled softly. "Make sure he gets home safely."

Chris rushed to his apartment to grab his passport and a change of clothes. As he turned the key, he heard his phone ringing. Quickly opening the door to his apartment, he ran to answer it.

"Pronto," he said, slightly out of breath.

"Chris, I've had a really bad dream about the boys."

"I'm on it, Kim. I think the Lord gave me the same dream."

"Where are you now?"

"Grabbing my passport. I have a flight to Berlin in an hour."

"Oh, thank you, Chris! I wanted to go myself, but I'm thinking it will be too late to help them by the time I get there."

"No need to thank me. I love them too."

"I know you do. Does Benny know you are going?"

"I haven't told him, and I don't have the time. You can tell him if you like."

"Will do. Call me the moment you know anything. And, Chris?"

"Yeah?"

"Be careful."

"I will. You keep praying."

"I will."

The screaming and cheering made the boys thirsty. They opted to celebrate again with several beers in a nearby pub. Around them, others were doing the same. With each beer came a growing sense of ease. A new world had come. The world was on the threshold of a new reality, and they were watching the birth of something never before seen.

Gabe's coke had run out, and as he grew mellow on ludes and beer, his eyes shrunk to mere slits. Michael looked pretty much the same, due to alcohol and fatigue. But they couldn't go back to their apartment. There was every possibility they would never again have the chance to be on the forefront of history.

"I have to drain the monster," Michael said, standing to go to the toilet.

"No, you don't. I won't let you in my pants." Gabe smiled.

"I was talking about me." Michael grinned, knowing full well he was setting Gabe up for another quip.

"Then you meant to say 'minnow. I have to drain the minnow.'"

Michael clipped his brother across the top of the head as he left the table.

When Michael returned from the men's room, Gabe was talking with his "connection." The grunge guy had an equally dirty-looking friend with him.

They looked up at him as he approached the table.

"This is my brother, Michael," Gabe said.

"Michael, this is Gunter and Franz."

"Hi, how are you doing?" Gunter, aka grunge boy one, asked in perfect English.

"I'm well," Michael said. "What an incredible evening for your country!"

Franz looked at Michael and said, *"Abend Deutschland ist sehr froh."*

Michael made a puzzled face. Something inside told him not to let them know he was fluent in German. He didn't trust them.

"My friend's English isn't so great as mine," Gunter apologized. "He says tonight all of Germany is happy."

"Ja." Michael smiled, as if saying "yes" in German was new to him.

"Michael, these guys are going to grab a bite to eat with us. I'm buying," Gabe announced, patting the wad of bills in his front pocket.

"Great," Michael lied. "I would love to see tonight through the eyes of a German friend. Welcome."

Gunter smiled at Franz. Michael stared at Gabe in disbelief. They were going to spend the evening with drug pushers! Gabe ordered large steins of beer for each of them.

Benny slapped the screaming Kurtoglu and felt the now-familiar warm sensation. Soon he would take Son of Wolf yet again.

The phone rang several times in the background.

Slap! Benny tried to keep the fantasy alive, ignoring the phone.

It rang again, and his fantasy burst. Kurtoglu became the Lady and then vanished in a pool of light.

Panting, he picked up the receiver and said curtly, *"Pronto!"*

"Benny, it's Kim. Are you all right? You sound out of breath."

Gathering himself, Benny said, "I'm fine, Kim. Just doing a little exercise, but I'm not as young as I used to be." He cringed as he said it, doubting Kim would believe such an obvious lie.

"Benny, I couldn't sleep. I dreamt about Michael and Gabe being in the crowds around the Berlin Wall. In my dream, they were in trouble."

"You need to try to get over this empty-nest thing, Kim. They're not children anymore. They can take care of themselves."

She said, "Actually, Chris feels like God is telling him the same thing. He's on his way to Germany now."

"He didn't tell me he was leaving," Benny snarled.

"I know, Benny. He had to rush to catch a plane. I told him I would call you."

"He reports to *me*, not to you. His duty is to *me*," he barked into the phone.

"He's not shirking any duty, Benny. He's checking up on Michael and Gabe. They're *your* nephews after all!"

"You're right, Kim. I overreacted." *Chris, the hero! What a pain in my butt!*

"Kim, I'm sure everything will be all right. They're just young boys. They're probably partying and enjoying the moment."

"I hope you're right," Kim said, struggling to hold back tears.

The pain in her voice touched Benny. "They're good kids, Kim. You've done a great job with them. Now it's time for you to trust yourself and the great job you've done."

"Maybe you're right. If you are, then I sent Chris on a wild goose chase. Can you forgive me?"

"Yes, of course," Benny said and chuckled, "but only if I reserve the right to say, 'I told you so.'"

"I guess that's what big brothers are for."

"That … and to tell you to get some rest for that cold. You sound terrible. Hang up and go to sleep. Everything is going to be fine. Trust me."

"Thanks, Benny."

As soon as Kim hung up, Benny placed another call.

After one ring, he heard a voice on the other end say, "Schmidt."

"It's me. Find your guys. They need to do it soon. There may be some interference."

Chris made his flight with moments to spare. He wore his full cassock, thinking that clerical garb might make it easier for him to get around once he got to Berlin. *Berlin!* It was a big city with a big wall. What were the chances he would find the boys? Practically nil outside of receiving some help from the Holy Spirit.

After the safety instructions, he closed his eyes and prayed for guidance. He lingered for an hour in the Lord's presence, thinking he might get some sleep there, but he had a feeling that irked him, the feeling that someone was watching him. He undid his seat belt to look around at the other passengers. No one looked familiar. Most were already asleep. Eventually sleep overcame him, but it was a fitful sleep in which he dreamed about Tom dying in his arms in a back alley of Kampala.

The restroom door opened just a crack. When the occupant saw Chris was asleep, he returned to his seat.

The beers did quite a bit to calm Michael's nerves. Franz and Gunter didn't seem all that bad. He would rather they had no influence in Gabe's life, but they were fine to hang out with during an event as momentous as this.

People around the pub were all singing songs the boys didn't know, prewar German songs that were known on both sides of the wall. Each song sparked new emotion as the once-and-future brothers united in song.

At one point, Franz nudged Gunter and moved his eyes toward the door. Gunter's eyes followed. Michael saw the light of recognition in Gunter's eyes as they fell upon a stern-looking man in a black overcoat at the door, carrying a knapsack. His sharp features and round-rimmed glasses made him look like the caricature of a Nazi in old films.

Gunter saw Michael's expression and said with a grim smile, "My father."

"Invite him over," Michael said, waving the man over to the table.

The man walked awkwardly toward the boys. Gunter got up quickly to meet him. They spoke briefly together. The music and noise of the crowd prevented Michael from hearing what they said. Gunter brought him over to the table. Michael and Gabe stood to greet him.

"This is my father, Herr Schmidt," Gunter said cautiously. "Father, this is Michael and Gabe."

"A pleasure to meet you, Herr Schmidt," Michael said.

Gabe was already into his ludes. He smiled broadly and said, "Likewise."

"*Bitte, Sitzen Sie sich,* Herr Schmidt," Franz said, offering his chair.

"*Nein. Nichts abend,*" Schmidt responded. Then in English, he said, "Pardon me if I do not join you. It is a night of many memories for me. I don't want to sit in a pub. Gunter, you forgot to take this when you left home," he said, handing the knapsack to Gunter.

Gunter took the pack, looking bewildered for a moment.

"*Vergessen Sie nicht Ihre Arbeit,*" he said softly to Gunter. *Don't forget your task.* Michael found it curious Herr Schmidt spoke to Gunter using formal verb forms instead of the informal "you" most parents used with their children.

To the group, Herr Schmidt added, "I took the liberty of adding a hammer and chisel. The crowds have begun to chip at the wall to get souvenirs. At the rate it is going, I wonder if anything will be left by tomorrow. You should all get your piece of history tonight."

"Neat," Gabe said with a bit of a slur. "We got to do it, guys! It's freakin' history in the making."

"Sounds good to me, "Michael added.

"Well, I will take my leave. Good night," Herr Schmidt said as he turned to leave.

———

There was no way Benny could sleep. Occasionally, he would doze only to fall into dreams of the boys. Michael was such a beautiful toddler. In his dreams, Benny was eighteen years younger, holding the boy as he fell asleep. At other times, he would dream of Gabe looking like a waif when he came into the family. Each time he awakened in a panic. Deep inside he didn't want any harm to come to the boys. They were an impediment to getting Kim's money, but he didn't wish them dead.

Jumping out of bed, he derided himself. *You're just an old softy, Benny.* He dialed Schmidt to tell him the deal was off.

No answer.

He called again.

The phone rang and rang. With each ring a wave of panic rose in Benny. What if he was too late? How could he have put himself in such a position? What was he thinking?

He slammed down the phone, thought for a second, and then dialed another number. *"Pronto"* came the response on the first ring.

"This is Bishop Cross. I must speak to *Signore* Begliali. It's an emergency."

Chris's head pounded as he ran down the streets of Kampala. He could feel the blood drying on his face. He could feel Tom's blood on his hands. His body hurt everywhere, but he had to keep moving. He had to find Fran and Gloria.

Kampala was a big city. If he was ever to find them, it would be with the help of the Holy Spirit. He began to pray as he ran.

"Guten morgen, Damen und Herren." Chris startled awake at the pilot's announcement of their descent into Berlin.

Chris recognized he had more than a dream. It was more like a flashback known to US soldiers when they returned from Vietnam, and there was another deeper meaning. He pondered it as he exited through the Jetway in Berlin. Although he had no luggage, he paused at the luggage carousel, because the feeling of being watched had come back strongly. Looking around, he saw nobody he knew, and the airport was nearly deserted in the wee hours of the morning.

He walked toward the exit intending to get a taxi. Instead, he found a man holding a card with his name on it. The camerlengo had apparently thought to arrange a car service for him.

The driver ushered him into a dark Mercedes. When Chris had buckled up, the driver placed a red flashing police light on the dashboard and sped away.

"I hope you don't mind the light, Monsignor, but it will assure us the quickest passage to the Brandenburg Gate." The driver had learned British English and eliminated all but the slightest trace of his German accent.

"Thank you. I really appreciate it."

"God always finds a way for His children to do His work," the driver pronounced.

"Yes, He does." Chris was reminded of the Anglican priest in Uganda. He certainly had been the Lord's provision. Maybe even an angel.

That was the greater message of the dreams! The Lord had cleared his path in Africa, and He would do it in Germany as well. *Thank you, Lord!*

Michael struggled to the top of the wall. Gabe made it easily.

"You amaze me, bro," he said into Gabe's ear, to be heard over the crowd. "Even stoned you did that better than me."

"I'll tell you a little secret," Gabe said with a grin, the slur noticeably gone. "I'm not all that stoned. A little chemical engineering pulled the buzz back."

"Meaning what?" Michael asked, afraid to find out.

"I did a little speed to counteract the ludes. I can always take more when things calm down for the night. But until then"—he removed his cupped hand from Michael's ear and yelled into the crowd in an impersonation of John Kennedy—*"Ich bin ein Berliner!"*

The crowd around them clapped him on the shoulders. Franz dug the hammer and chisel out of Gunter's knapsack, and the boys took turns chiseling and throwing pieces of the wall to the crowd.

Unlike his brother, Michael hadn't taken speed to move him through the evening, and was very tired. Gunter was chiseling away, and Franz bent down to talk to him. Had Michael been more energetic, he would have missed the encounter. Although he couldn't hear them well, he was pretty sure he caught some of the German conversation between the two.

Franz: "When ..."

Gunter: "Relax. Plenty of time."

Franz: "But the bishop—"

Gunter: "He'll be fine. This is history, brother!"

Michael found the bishop reference to be weird. Could they know Benny? *Not a snowball's chance in hell.* He laughed to himself. Benny wouldn't go near grunge. Still, the reference wouldn't leave his thoughts.

Michael looked approvingly at the damage he and the other three had done to the wall. There was something marvelously spiritual in the event. He could actually feel the tug of history in the making. But he was cold and tired and needed to relieve himself.

"Gabe," he yelled to his grinning, singing brother. "Let's go home, buddy."

"What? Are you kidding me?"

"History will still be here tomorrow."

"It *is* tomorrow!" Gabe screamed. "What time do you have?"

Michael checked his watch. He was shocked by what he read. "Three in the morning!"

"So let's at least hang out until sunrise. You know, kind of welcome in the new dawn."

"It sounds good," Michael said with a grin, "but how about a beer to help me get warm? And I need a bathroom. I need to get off this wall."

"Actually, I've been thinking about peeing on East Germany." Gabe smiled. The thought of East German guards shooting up at an un-zipped Gabe made Michael laugh heartily.

"Let's go. Save your member for another fight on another day," Michael said as he climbed down.

As Gabe followed, Gunter grabbed his arm. "Where are you going?"

"We thought maybe we would grab another beer, find a toilet."

"We're coming too," Gunter said.

"Whatever. Do you still have some stuff you can sell to me?"

"I saved the best for you. You're my favorite customer." Gunter smiled broadly.

"Then by all means, please join us," Gabe said and grinned.

Gunter tapped Franz, motioned to the brothers, and started down the wall. Franz followed.

———

Benny was well on the way to Germany in one of Begliali's Gulfstream jets. It could fly higher and faster than commercial flights and would land at a private airport much more convenient to the city of Berlin.

The steward brought him two slices of cucumber for his eyes. It really didn't matter anyway. His sleep was so badly interrupted that they were bound to be puffy. As he absorbed the luxury of having a private jet all to himself, for a brief moment he questioned his decision to rescue the boys. Then he relented.

"When it comes down to it, you're too soft for your own good,

Benny Cross!" He moaned to himself as he lay back and put the cucumbers on his eyes.

Chris couldn't believe it, but his driver had somehow managed to get him to the Brandenburg Gate. He knew the boys' apartment was within walking distance, but he didn't intend to go there. At their age, those two wouldn't be able to resist the party atmosphere that had developed. In the news reports he had seen earlier in the evening, the crowd was composed of people of all ages. The older men and women and the younger children had obviously left to find their beds. At this point the crowd probably had an average age of about nineteen. A raucous frat-party atmosphere now replaced any somber nature the earlier crowd had shown. Chris felt very conspicuous in his cassock as he pushed through the crowd to the wall. *Oh well, if I don't see the boys, maybe they'll see me. I definitely stand out in this crowd.*

As Chris walked along the wall, he found his presence evoked kind feelings in those he passed. Several young men slapped him on the back, saying things like "What a blessing, huh, Father?" and "Father, do you think this is the beginning of the Kingdom of God on Earth?" He would chat briefly, describe Gabe and Michael, and ask if anyone had seen them.

"There were two American brothers with a chisel breaking off pieces of the wall and throwing them to the crowd. Maybe those are the ones you are looking for, Father."

"No doubt." Chris smiled and continued on. Michael was one thing, but Gabe's need for adventure could compel him to try to jump off the wall into East Germany. Chris put the image out of his head and continued to look into the crowd.

Gunter and Franz offered to buy this round. They stood at the bar, where weary bartenders worked well past their allotted shift to serve their elixir to the new Germany.

Michael sat next to his brother after returning from the men's room. "After sunrise, we're going to crash, right, Gabe?"

Gabe pulled two tablets out of his pocket. "I'll be ready. Gunter says these guys will really mellow me out."

Michael stared intently at his brother. "You've got to put that stuff down, Gabe, before it ruins your life—ruins *our* lives."

Gabe winced and nodded. "I've been thinking a lot about it. It was fun at first, but now I'm beginning to remind myself of my birth mother."

"Let's talk to Mom about it. She can get you rehab treatment in the States."

"Fine. Just let me finish the semester here with you, okay?"

"If you promise me you'll try to bring it under control. Hold it at bay for another six weeks. Can you do that?"

Gabe looked at the pills in front of him. "I know I can try. I really will try, Michael."

"That's all I'm asking, bro. All I'm asking. If not for yourself, then do it for Mom and me. We'd be lost without you. Probably happier," he teased as he ruffled his brother's hair, "but lost all the same."

"I'd do anything for you and Mom."

"Back at you. So at Thanksgiving, let's talk to Mom and Chris. Maybe Chris knows of some programs or can find one through the Church," Michael said.

"I'd do anything for Chris too. But don't ask me about Benny. I've never been drunk or high enough to say I'd do anything for him." They both laughed.

"Good," Michael added, "because God only knows what Benny would ask you to do."

The hallway of the apartment building was dimly lit. The building had been quickly erected in the rubble of Berlin at the end of World War II. It was built to be functional and had all the charm of a Soviet-style barracks apartment. Finding apartment 4B, Benny knocked on the door. No answer. He could hear snoring inside.

Benny knocked louder.

No answer.

This time Benny knocked and called the man's name. "Herr Schmidt. Herr Schmidt!"

"*Ja. Wie ist dort?*" came the muffled reply of a man roused from a deep sleep.

"Schmidt! It's me," Benny continued in English, careful not to say his name aloud for the entire apartment complex to hear, "your friend from Rome."

Schmidt opened the door, shocked to see Benny standing there dressed in jeans and a sweatshirt.

"Bishop Cross!" he exclaimed.

"Shut up!" Benny whispered fiercely, not wanting anyone to know he was there.

"Why have you come?" Schmidt whispered in reply.

"If you would answer your damn phone, you would know I have called off the entire operation. Where are your boys?"

"I don't know. Somewhere near the wall with your nephews. I saw them earlier at a pub. I told the boys the job had to be done tonight, just like you said."

"What's the name of the pub?" Benny asked in an annoyed tone.

"Heinlickers."

"Write down the address for me."

"Yes, Eminence." Schmidt moved into the dimly lit one-room apartment to find a piece of paper. Benny readied himself.

Schmidt sat at a small table, scribbling an address. As he stood to hand it to Benny, his eyes opened wide with shock as he saw the bishop's gun with silencer pointed at his head. With two quick thuds from the gun, he fell onto the table.

Benny took the piece of paper.

"Have a good rest, Herr Schmidt. Can't leave behind any messy details. I hope you understand."

———————

Gunter and Franz returned with the beers. Franz was careful to give Michael the beer that they had spiced with drugs.

Gunter handed a beer to Gabe and slipped him two tablets at the same time.

"How much do I owe you?" Gabe whispered, reaching for his pocket.

"On the house, my friend. A toast ... to a united Germany!"

They all drank deeply. The cold beer tasted good in mouths parched by hours of cheering in the crowd.

"We shared history, my friends," Gunter said proudly. They clinked glasses and drank again. The beers went down smoothly as they shared their impressions of being on the wall.

Gabe fell into a comfortable daze, a perpetual smile on his lips. Michael began to feel strange, as if overcome by exhaustion, yet his mind was working furiously. His eyes became slits, but he willed himself to stay awake to listen to the German conversation between Gunter and Franz.

Gunter: "We should get them to the alley while they can still walk."

Franz: "Are you sure you gave them enough to get the job done?"

Gunter: "Schmidt gave us enough to kill a horse."

Franz: "Too bad. Such fine young American boys dying of overdoses."

Gunter: "Happens every day."

Franz: "What does that bishop have against them?"

Gunter: "Who knows? Just remember never to tick off the Vatican!"

Michael's head swam. *Aw, Benny! Did you really want the money that badly?* He fought to retain consciousness.

"We have to go home now," he slurred to Gunter and Franz.

"Gabe ... Gabe, wake up. It's time for us to go home."

In Michael's mind, he was screaming at Gabe. In reality, the words came as a mumbled slur. He felt himself standing with the help of Franz. He opened his eyes a bit to see Gunter helping Gabe. Gunter looked at the bartender and shrugged. "Americans."

In response, the bartender said, "We are all Germans tonight. Get them safely home."

Michael tried to scream to the bartender for help, but no words came.

The search felt pointless. There were just too many people. Chris had looked into each face he encountered. He just couldn't find Michael and Gabe. To make matters worse, he still felt as if he was being watched, as if being about town in a collar and cassock at this strange, drunken hour wouldn't naturally draw attention.

They're probably at home, sleeping it off. Might as well try their apartment. I'm not getting anywhere here.

He turned away from the wall and prayed, "Lord, please let me find them safe at home."

He started toward their apartment, the town growing darker as he moved away from the festivities at the wall. Ahead of him he saw four young guys stumbling out of a bar. *Kids!* he thought to himself, suddenly hoping all the more fervently he would find his boys safe in their beds.

Then his eyes played a trick on him. For the briefest moment, he thought he saw the Anglican priest from Uganda. In the second Chris saw him, the priest pointed to an alley beside the bar.

In a sudden flash of lucidity, Gabe became aware of the fact that this was no normal high. Something horrible was going on inside of him. Gunter had given him some bad stuff. He hadn't even asked what it was.

What an idiot! Michael would never let him live it down. He forced his eyes open to find his brother. Michael could call an ambulance. It took a few moments for him to understand what he saw. Franz was nearly carrying Michael along.

This is no accidental overdose. They mean to kill us!

"Oh, Jesus," Gabe prayed silently. "I don't even know if you're real, but I need your help. I've done a terrible thing. I've led Michael to his death. Please give me the strength to get us out of this."

Gathering his prodigious strength, Gabe pushed himself away from Gunter, swung around, and landed a fierce roundhouse punch. He felt it connect with Gunter's jaw before he felt the fury of Gunter's response. Franz dropped Michael in the alley and joined Gunter in battering him and pushing him to the ground. One of them reared back and kicked him hard in the stomach. Gabe threw up before losing consciousness.

After speaking with Benny, Kim filled a thermos with coffee, grabbed her Bible, and went to the chapel to spend time with God. Ignoring the electric lights, she lit several candles and let the serenity of the surroundings and the Holy Spirit calm her. She prayed repeatedly and faithfully though the evening for the safety of Chris and the boys.

When she felt that she was peaceful enough to go to bed, Kim extinguished the candles and prepared to leave the chapel. She hadn't made it to the door when a horrible wave of nausea came over her. It was her boys. She knew they were near death. Falling prostrate to the cold floor of the dark chapel, she again asked for the Lord's help. "Please save them, Lord. Let Chris find them and save them. Please!"

———————————————

Chris rubbed his eyes. The Anglican priest was gone, but in his heart arose an urgency to reach the alley. He ran down the street, his cassock billowing around him. When he reached the alley, he saw two men standing over the boys.

"Hey!" he screamed as he ran toward them.

A startled Franz jumped back at the sound, but the yell brought about a more primal fear response in Gunter. He leaped at Chris, arms swinging. Lowering his head against the blows, Chris threw himself at Gunter, knocking him down to the ground.

Franz dug in Gunter's knapsack to find the hammer they had been using on the wall. His hand found it just as Chris landed on top of Gunter.

"What have you done to them?" Chris demanded of Gunter. He was so intent that he didn't sense Franz coming up on him with the hammer.

One fierce blow to Chris's head knocked him off of Gunter. Pain exploded in his head. In a fury, he pushed himself up from the ground and attacked Franz, knocking the hammer away. By this time, Gunter had recovered and both were attacking the priest savagely.

"Hey," a voice called from the entrance to the street, "want a sandwich?"

"Vinnie?" Chris asked, momentarily taking his eyes off of his opponent. Seizing the moment, Gunter got him hard in the face with a left hook. For the moment, Chris was down, and the young Germans looked at the old American who was approaching.

Vinnie dropped the sandwich as the boys turned on him.

"You ever hear of Joe DiMaggio?" he asked as he quickly turned his cane around and swung for the fences. He connected squarely with Gunter's face, sending him to the ground.

Franz didn't have time to get to Vinnie before he swung again, this time connecting with Franz's neck. The boy didn't fall, but he had seen enough. As Chris was standing up, Franz pushed past Vinnie and ran into the night. Gunter followed.

"Hey! You forgot your sandwiches!" Vinnie screamed after them.

"The master race, go figure," he said to Chris with a twinkle in his eye.

Chris cradled the boys, looking for signs of life. Each was still breathing, but the breaths were shallow.

"Vinnie, get the bartender to call an ambulance," he yelled.

"Already on it," Vinnie said as he turned the corner.

"Father, in Jesus' name I ask you to save these boys," Chris prayed fervently. To each of the boys he said, "Hang in there, buddy. We've called an ambulance."

"We got a couple ambulances on the way," Vinnie called to Chris.

With a flash of incredulity, Chris asked, "Why are you here?"

"You're welcome! Nice way to thank an old friend who followed you all this way to save your tail. This little trip will be hell on my gout!"

"Thanks, Vinnie. But why did you follow me?"

"From my perspective—and the Holy Father's, I might add—you're a kid yourself. Why send a kid to save a kid? Besides, I was curious about the wall. So I figured I would shadow you. If you needed me, I'd be there. If not, then I would fly back to Rome, and you wouldn't be any the wiser."

"Which explains why you're not in your clerical clothes."

"A sweatshirt is better cover," Vinnie said and shrugged.

The ambulances arrived. Their crews went to work on the boys. From what Chris could tell, they seemed to be more concerned about Michael's condition than Gabe's. They loaded the boys into the ambulances. Vinnie went with Gabe, and Chris rode with Michael.

Once the boys had been loaded into the ambulance, Benny left the shadows and returned to Luciano's plane. Buyer's regret filled him as he rubbed his hands on the burled wood paneling in Luciano's private jet. If he had only been tougher, by now he would be so close to having one himself. His own jet. *Imagine it!* His plan would have worked too if he hadn't been so weak.

It had been a simple matter to feed Gabe drugs. Schmidt was happy to provide the connection. Benny figured the boy would have an inherited weakness to controlled substances. Michael was a tougher matter, but the two were together enough that he could easily have gotten caught in what appeared to be Gabe's drug deal gone wrong. Benny thought the circus surrounding the wall would be a great time to pull it off. The press would take a pass on the drug-related deaths of two Americans when they could cover the fall of the Berlin Wall. After the deaths of the boys, it would have been a small matter to get Kim committed to a mental health facility. As next of kin, Benny would take care of her assets ... and he had such plans for those assets!

Then the plan was ruined by the stark realization that some part of him loved those boys. Even Gabe! Benny could hardly believe he had been struck by a conscience attack at this point in his life. Clearly this was a display of weakness on his part.

"Oh, Benny, you're too sensitive for your own good," he said as he sipped red wine. Still, there had to be a way for him to control the family fortune without killing everyone. Michael was the key. *Michael.*

"You're right," the Lady's voice suddenly burst into his mind. "That's why I wouldn't let you kill him. We need him."

"I'm so sorry, my lady," Benny pleaded aloud to the empty plane cabin. He feared he had offended her. "Why didn't you stop me earlier?"

"It was important for both of us to know how far you are willing to go to bring about the new kingdom."

"Again, I am sorry if I offended you," Benny offered.

"Not at all, my pet," she purred. "You did just fine. You gave me three sacrifices, didn't you?"

Michael wasn't aware of the jostling ambulance or its blaring siren. He had no sense of the emergency technicians working feverishly to stabilize his vital signs. He was surrounded by light. He felt free and weightless.

I must be dead.

"Not dead," came a lady's voice. "Between life and death. Your time on Earth is not complete. There is much for you to do, Michael."

What is it that I'm supposed to do?

"There are great discoveries, ancient knowledge that you will learn. Michael, you will touch the world with the Light."

Chris felt as if they were surrounded by spiritual darkness. He prayed harder, commanding evil to leave the boys, praying that the Blood of Jesus would protect them.

One of the EMTs gave a little shout. Michael's vital signs had miraculously stabilized and were rapidly improving.

"The Light," Michael mumbled as he opened his eyes slightly into the glare of the EMT's examination lights.

Chris heard the words, and tears came to his eyes. The EMT turned to him and gave a thumbs-up sign. Michael would be all right!

Chris took Michael's hand, leaned into his ear, and said, "You'll be all right, son. You're going to be fine."

In the other ambulance, Gabe's condition stabilized as well. Around the world, those praying for the boys knew by the Spirit that they would live.

"Thank you, Lord," Vinnie said out loud.

"Oh, God. Thank you. *Thank you!*" Kim screamed.

"Thank you, Lord," the pontiff prayed, "for saving their lives. Please give Michael the strength to resist the evil that beckons him."

EPILOGUE: THANKSGIVING

Michael was nervous as his plane approached Atlanta. He had a lot to tell his family. Would they be supportive of the decision he had made? They probably would, but it would come to them as a bit of a surprise.

The real issue was what to make of his feeling that Benny had been involved with the attempt on their lives. The doctors said he and Gabe were given more than enough drugs to kill them. The Berlin police told Michael that Schmidt had been shot in the head and that Gunter and Franz had met a similar fate less than a block from where they had attempted to kill him and Gabe. The police said they had no leads on who the killer was.

Who was "the bishop" Gunter and Franz referred to? Could it possibly have been Benny? Michael desperately wanted to talk to someone about it, but how did you bring up something like that? To make matters worse, if Benny actually had orchestrated the plot, then he also could have sent Gunter to befriend Gabe and addict him. It was too horrible to think about, but it wouldn't leave his mind. How could he tell this to his mother? Or to Gabe?

His mother met him at the airport, running to hug him. "Thanks for coming, Michael. I know it's messing with your class schedule." It was a hard decision. Thanksgiving was an exclusively American holiday. Michael had to miss class, and he was already behind from time he had spent in the hospital.

"I'll make it up. I had to get home, you know? That last bit of excitement made me long to come home, to a place that feels safe. Besides, I missed you, and I want to take advantage of the opportunity to see Gabe. Have you heard from him?"

"He's still in a silent period, but I talk to the administrator at the facility every day. She tells me he is doing very well."

"Does he know we're coming for Thanksgiving dinner?"

"Yes. And she tells me he's excited to see us."

"Why wouldn't he be?" Michael asked.

Kim's voice cracked as she tried to verbalize fears that had remained hidden in her. "What if I did something wrong? What if he didn't feel like an equal part of our family? What if I'm the reason he turned to drugs?"

Michael pulled his mother close, comforting her as she had comforted him through the years. "Mom, I know Gabe better than anyone else. I can tell you he feels like an equal member in our family. And he loves you very, very much. You're not at fault."

"Then why did this happen to him?"

"He inherited a weakness from his birth mother and got involved with some bad fellows. That's all. Don't look any deeper, Mom. None of this is your fault."

She dried her eyes. Pulling herself together, she said, "We don't have much time to get to Chris's gate."

Gabe was lonely in rehab, but he liked the feeling of being "clean." He was hitting the gym hard these days, and that felt really good. He had not realized how much damage the drugs had done to him. He had less strength, less speed, and less agility than at any time in his life.

Right now he was bench-pressing, leaving a minute between sets—a minute after each set to think. His mind wandered to the therapy sessions. They were trying to figure out what led him to drugs. Certainly genetics was a factor, but he really couldn't find any emotional reason to have slid so far. He loved life. He loved his family. For the therapists, he played up the feeling of abandonment when his birth mother died, but the truth was that life had been pretty grim before Kim and Michael adopted him. When he found out that he and Michael shared a deadbeat father, it just confirmed the fact that he belonged with Michael and Kim.

When he looked back on it with the clarity of sobriety, he saw that

Gunter pursued him, zeroed in on him like a target. Gunter was his "connection," but he had never seen Gunter sell drugs to anyone else. When Gabe mentioned him on campus, nobody knew him. And why would Gunter and Franz try to kill him ... and Michael?

He changed the weight and pounded out another set. *Who would want us dead? Who would stand to gain from our deaths?* There was only one answer: Benny. But how could he ever say this to Michael and their mom?

Without Zack, it wouldn't be much of a Thanksgiving. Sarah's heart ached to be with her son. And her brain ached to be away from her mother. That's why she suggested that she and Mack serve Thanksgiving dinners at the shelter this year. It was quite the event. Mack's camera crews were on hand, of course, to get images of their charity.

Dressing for these things was always so hard. She had to look like the diva of the show; after all, she was. Still, she had to be careful not to overdo it, or it would look like she was flaunting. She decided on a deep-green sweater dress, a vest in Thanksgiving floral colors, and a single strand of pearls.

Mack's cameraman was not the only one at the shelter. Mack had invited a local news crew to come by and film as well. Both cameras were rolling as homeless and poor individuals stood in line for a taste of Thanksgiving. Sarah was at the head of the serving line. She greeted each person theatrically: "Come and taste the goodness of the Lord. I don't have much, but what I have I freely give."

At the other end of the line, Mack offered grace and a small prayer with each person who exited.

All was going well until a particularly downtrodden woman made her way in line to Sarah's station. "Give me them pearls."

"What? What did you say?" Sarah asked.

"You said what you have, you give me. So give me them pearls ... or do you just talk the talk. Know what I mean?" The cameras caught it all, and the woman seemed to glory in her fifteen seconds of fame.

"I'm sorry, dear," Sarah said, stalling for time. "I'm not sure I understand."

"If you believe in Jesus like you say you do, *give me them pearls!*" Sarah glanced at the cameras, both of which were now moving in for close-ups. She pulled off her rubber serving gloves and gently removed her pearl necklace. With great care, she reached over the counter and handed it to the woman. The woman's stench filled Sarah's nostrils, but she had to smile for the cameras.

"There you are, dear," Sarah said sweetly, looking into the camera. "Know that the love of God is real!" After that moment, Sarah didn't take her eyes off of that lady or her pearls. When the woman finished eating and left the building, Sarah told the staff she needed to take a break. She followed the woman to the small parking area behind the shelter.

"That was a funny thing you pulled in front of the cameras," Sarah said to the woman with the pearls.

"You gived 'em t'me," the woman said with eyes downcast. "Isn't that what yo' Jesus is all about?"

Sarah spat angrily, "Don't preach to me, missy. Give me those pearls back. They're not yours."

"I could sell 'em t'ya," the woman offered with a toothless grin as she held out the pearls in her grimy hand.

"Give them to me!" Sarah said as she snatched at them. The woman pulled her hand back, and Sarah stumbled forward, falling into the woman and knocking them both down. The shocked woman released the pearls. Sarah snatched them and stood quickly. Brushing at a smudge on her dress, Sarah looked down in distain and said, "Now look what you've done!" and gave the woman a kick in the butt.

"Cut!" yelled a member of the local news crew that had quietly followed them.

The woman cackled loudly as she stood to make a face at Sarah, who stood in tears as the newsmen entered their van.

Zack returned to bed and swept Gloria up in his arms. "I don't think your mom will like me, G. There's more about our parents' history you don't know."

"Like what?" she asked, rubbing the hair on his arms.

"Like the real reason our parents don't speak."

"It was a disagreement over my father's funeral service. I know all about it."

"That's what everyone says. Look, when your mother came to visit, my parents kept getting this strange vibe. She talked so much about that priest. What's his name?"

"Father Chris."

"Right. Father Chris. Well, anyway, she seemed to be more into adoring Father Chris than mourning your father. Finally it got to be too much, and my father asked her if she and Father Chris had an affair."

"That's ridiculous! It never happened!" Gloria pulled away from him.

"She didn't deny it. She just stormed out of the house."

"But that's crazy! Chris was a good friend. He loved my father! He was there with him when he died."

"He was the only one, right?"

"Yeah. What are you getting at?" Gloria demanded, staring at him harshly.

"You only have this priest's word on how your father died."

"You think Chris might have killed him?"

"Or just left him to die."

"That's nuts! It didn't happen like that, Zack!" she said in a tone that closed the discussion. She hastily got out of bed, banged drawers as she got her clothes, and stomped to the shower. Zack smiled. Another seed planted. The last thing he needed was a wife who wanted to be filled with the Holy Spirit, like her mother!

Fran had lived in Sam and Evelyn's house since they died. Neither she nor Gloria had been willing to sell this last vestige of Tom's life. Thanksgiving dinner smelled wonderful as she sat in the living room and peered out the front windows, awaiting the arrival of Gloria and her new boyfriend. Fran knew precious little about him due both to Gloria's circumspect nature and to the fact that Fran's news about David had dominated most of their telephone conversations. As the car pulled into the driveway, Fran ran out the door to the passenger side of Zack's car. Gloria barely made it out of the car before she was swept into her mother's loving arms.

Over Gloria's shoulder, Fran caught sight of Zack. She would know that smug, hawkish face anywhere. He flashed her a knowing smile, which she took at once to be malevolent. Involuntarily she stiffened as a chill ran down her spine. She *really* didn't want this man for her daughter, but she had to be wise. If she turned them away, he would win, and she would lose her little girl.

"Hi, Zack," she said. "It's been a long time." Then feeling that she sounded cold, she lightened her tone and cooed. "You were a little boy when we last met. You've grown up nicely. My compliments to your parents."

"Hi, Fran. I'm surprised you remembered me." Zack grinned in a manner that was boyish enough to fool Gloria, but threatening enough to let Fran know he could see she was lying.

"Well, let's not stand out here. Come in! David and I have been cooking a feast for us. I'm so happy you're here." Looking Zack in the eye, she said, "I've missed my little girl."

David came to the front door just as Fran and the kids were entering.

"David," Fran said, "this is Gloria, the best thing that ever happened to me."

"Gloria, I am so pleased to meet you. Your mother talks so much about you. I feel like I know you already."

Gloria smiled and put out her hand to shake his. Although not obvious to everyone, Fran sensed that her daughter immediately disliked David. He was very different from her father. Maybe it was a bit much for Gloria to meet him in Tom's parents' home. Fran wished she had thought to have their first meeting at a neutral place, like a restaurant.

"Mom," Gloria said, trying to cover, "I really have to go to the bathroom badly. Can you introduce Zack?"

Fran played the role Gloria handed her. "David, this is Gloria's boyfriend, Zack Jolean."

Both men smiled as they shook hands.

"As it turns out," Fran said in a lighthearted manner, "there is a bit of a surprise here. Zack's mother and I were roommates in college."

"I see." David's eyes widened knowingly. "Well, it's great that you all know each other." Then quickly changing the subject, David moved Zack into the living room, saying, "So, Zack, what's your major?"

"Marketing," Zack said and smiled. "I kind of have this knack for it. I just seem to know the buttons to push to get the behavior I want from people."

"That's marketing, all right," David said. "Every time I go to the supermarket, I'm lured by this 'new' thing or that 'new' thing. Invariably I find only the packaging has changed."

"And the price," Zack added with a smile.

"And the price," David conceded.

"I never forget the money, David." Zack grinned. David bristled, as if struck by a cold breeze. "That's what makes marketing fun. So, I hear you're a local pastor."

"Yes. The Alliance Church on Main Street. We're the 'Little Church with the Big Heart.'"

"You've probably heard of my father then, Mack Jolean. He has a weekly television program."

"I knew your name sounded familiar," David said. Fran involuntarily chuckled at the sound of sincerity in his voice. She had told him all about this family, and he had spent some time watching Mack's programs. He agreed with Fran that the productions were slick, the messages were sparse, and the sales pitches were never-ending.

"You know, my dad uses my ideas a lot. I would be happy to come to your church sometime and give you some pointers. Who knows? Maybe you could become the 'Big Church with the Big Heart.'" Zack grinned broadly. Fran's eyes widened as she saw David will himself not to move a face muscle lest his opinion of this boy shine through. He turned his eyes to Fran, who stared back, as if to say, "Do you believe this?"

They pulled up to the treatment facility. It was a sparse-looking institutional building of red brick. The windows were necessarily narrow to prevent patients from escaping. There were lovely rosebushes in the front and climbing vines along the security fence that ringed the yard. Still, the overall appearance was one of a prison to Michael. He faltered for a second as tears clouded his eyes. Chris was the first to notice, and he tugged gently at Kim's sleeve. They got on either side of him. Chris put his hand on Michael's shoulder. Kim grabbed his hand.

"It's okay, Michael," Kim said softly. "He is well cared for here. I check his progress every day."

"I know," Michael said. "It just hurts that he has to be here."

After they had checked the contents of their pockets, and Kim had forfeited her purse, the three were led to the facility's dining room. The cinder block walls were painted a bright yellow. A series of small tables was decorated with alternating yellow and orange tablecloths. A cutout pilgrim graced each table. Their hostess, who was in a doctor's white coat, led them to their table, where an anxious Gabe awaited them.

Michael felt a fleeting sense of awkwardness that happens when people have been estranged, even if for a few weeks. If that feeling came over his mom, no one would have known it. She ran to Gabe and hugged him fiercely, kissing his bearded face.

Michael and Chris followed, and all awkwardness fell to the wayside.

"You look great!" Chris exclaimed with a smile, looking deeply into Gabe's eyes, which were now bright again.

"Love the beard, dude," Michael said, tugging at Gabe's facial hair.

"No razors allowed." Gabe smiled. "You're starting to look human again, Chris."

"The bruises are fading. For a while there, I looked like your uncle Benny after his eye surgery."

Kim laughed. Michael smiled, but even the mention of Benny's name brought about the concerns that he had been behind their latest catastrophe. Gabe's halfhearted smile mirrored Michael's. They caught each other's eyes, and just as twins seem to be able to communicate telepathically, each realized what the other had been thinking.

Thanksgiving dinner was surprisingly good for institutional food served on paper plates. Chris was impressed. And the company was wonderful. The conversation and the laughter flowed freely. It was good for all of them to be together.

"Don't tell any good stories without me," Kim said. "I have to find the ladies' room."

"I think you have to go all the way out by the entrance to the building, Mom," Gabe lied.

Kim barely left the room before both boys leaned in toward Chris, speaking in staccato, conspiratorial tones.

"Chris, I've been thinking about it," Michael said.

"Same here," Gabe added.

"We think Uncle Benny paid Gunter and Franz to kill us."

"I'll go one further, Michael," Gabe said. "I don't think Gunter pushed drugs to anyone but me. I think Benny paid him to get me hooked as well."

The news shocked even Chris, who had seen a lot of Benny's evil actions. One of Benny's few redeeming qualities was that he loved Kim. If he tried to hurt the boys, he was more evil than even Chris had imagined.

"Listen, boys, your uncle Benny is not a nice man," Chris said softly, seriously.

"Hey, spare us the Disney version, Chris," Gabe said. "We know he's a twisted pervert with suppressed feelings of rage."

"Suppressed feelings of rage?" Michael aped.

"All I do is go to counseling and the gym here," Gabe offered apologetically.

Shaking his head, Michael smiled and said, "Amazing what you can pick up in the gym these days." Turning to Chris, he said, "We know Benny's a bad guy, but is he capable of something so horrible?"

"Guys, I don't know what to say."

"You're with him every day," Gabe said. "Do you think he could pull off something like this?"

"Could? Yes. Your uncle has amassed a large group of ugly friends on the wrong side of the tracks. But would he? I don't know. I've seen him be absolutely evil with people, but he always pulls in his claws where your mother is concerned. Even when it comes to me, he's not threatening because he knows your mother loves me. If he is okay with *me* for your mother's sake, why would he hurt you?"

"I can think of about 950 million reasons," Michael said.

"That much now?" Gabe asked.

"Last time I checked."

Chris whistled. He had no idea it was that much. What would Benny do for nearly a billion dollars?

"Let me think about it. You know, watch him a bit to see if I come up with anything," Chris stalled. If Benny had sunk to this, then it was a new low. His personality was degenerating into pure evil. Then casting a dead-serious look at the young men, Chris said in a lecturing parent tone of voice, "In the meantime, there are a couple things you two can do."

"Like what?" Gabe asked.

"First of all, you have to go to God and forgive Benny."

"I'll pass," Michael said.

"Not so fast, Michael," Gabe announced. "Repressed feelings can be really unhealthy. Unforgiveness only hurts the person who refuses to forgive."

"Gym?" Michael asked.

"Actually, I had nothing better to do, so I paid attention in group therapy. It's true though," Gabe quipped.

"Okay," Michael said to move the conversation forward, "what else?"

"Watch your backs," Chris said. "Even if Benny was behind this last situation, you guys fell into it. You can't hook someone on drugs if that person doesn't take them. You can't beat someone in an alley in the middle of the night if that person has the common sense to be home in bed."

"Fair points," Michael said.

"So what do you say?" Chris asked, still in a paternal voice. He grabbed their hands and said, "Let's pray. Father, we ask your forgiveness for Gunter and Franz and whoever was behind their attempt on the boys' lives. And we ask your forgiveness for our actions that led us into their trap. We offer to you our forgiveness as a gift, celebrating the love of Jesus that freed us from the pain of sin. And we thank you for bringing us through this intact, as a family. As always, we pray ..."

"In Jesus' name. Amen." David finished grace.

"Well, dig in, guys," Fran said. "Gloria, I made Grandma's stuffing for you."

"I see," Gloria said softly.

They ate quietly for a while. Then Gloria asked her mother, "When is the last time you heard from Father Chris?"

Fran's complexion flushed with sudden anger. She could sense from the question that Zack had been telling her little girl the same stupid accusations his father had leveled years before.

"We got a Christmas card from him last year, remember?" she said with purposeful nonchalance. "I'm sure we'll exchange cards again this year. Why do you ask?"

"I was just wondering. He came to mind this morning." Gloria looked at Zack, as if to show him nothing had transpired between her mother and Chris.

"He was with your husband when he died, right?" Zack asked.

Fran was not about to let this punk try to put her on the witness stand. "Yes, he was, but that was a long time ago, Zack. We all have the future to consider. Gloria, I'm going to need a maid of honor next month. Would you do me the honor?"

"Yes, Mom, but what's the rush? Why next month?"

"We're not getting any younger," David joked.

"This is between my mother and me," Gloria snapped.

"Gloria, that was uncalled for," Fran said sternly.

"Gloria, some people don't like long engagements," Zack said and smiled. Turning to Fran he said, "I'm happy to hear you prefer short engagements. Gloria wants to wait, but I say why not get married now?"

"What?" Fran fairly shrieked. "You two are babies, and you just met! Give yourselves some time."

"We met before you met David, Mother. And we're in love," Gloria challenged.

Fran was nearly nauseated at the thought, but she knew she had to rein in this conversation. "So the two of you are engaged?" she asked as calmly as she could.

"Yes, Mother, we are," Gloria said curtly, "but back to you. Where are you and David going to live?"

"That's still up in the air. We should probably move into the parsonage, but I don't want to sell this house."

"So your choices are to sell my home out from under me or to bring your lover into my father's house?"

Fran ignored the comment. "David, could you pass the gravy?"

Fran's deliberate calm set the stage. At first the conversation was stilted. She asked Zack about his classes. David told of his wife's death and explained that he never would violate her memory. Neither would he tolerate a violation of Tom's memory.

Fran's tension eased as Gloria warmed to the conversation. She seemed engaged and gregarious when David asked about some of her favorite memories of her father and grandparents.

Fran believed David may have turned the corner with Gloria, but she wondered if she could ever get comfortable with Zack. Periodically she had to fight back the sting of tears that threatened to erupt. She was thankful to get away from the table to answer the phone in the kitchen.

"Hello?"

"Ah, hello, Frannie, this is Mack. I don't want to interrupt your Thanksgiving dinner, but something has come up, and I need to speak to Zack."

"Oh. Sure, Mack, I'll get him right away," Fran said in response to the urgency in his voice. Then, considering that they may someday share grandchildren, Fran added, "By the way, happy Thanksgiving to you and Sarah."

Mack sighed. "And to you as well, Fran."

Fran rushed to the dining room. "Zack, your dad is on the phone. He wants to talk to you. It sounds kind of urgent."

"I swear he can't run that ministry without me." Zack smiled as he hurried into the kitchen. Within a minute, he rushed through the dining room, his face unusually pale. "I need to see something on TV," he blurted as he ran to the living room.

"What is it, Zack?" Gloria followed.

Fran arched her eyebrows at David and motioned they should join the kids in the living room.

The roof antenna picked up the Houston stations, but not clearly. Through the snowy reception, they watched in horror as the newscaster presented the story of a local minister's wife beating up a homeless woman.

Zack's anger at his parents was palpable. "Those idiots! They'll ruin everything! Gloria, get your coat. We have to get to Riverside."

Gloria rose to get her coat, and Fran said, "Gloria, why don't you stay here?"

"Because I *need* her!" Zack screamed at Fran as his nose came to within inches of hers.

"I'll call you, Mom," Gloria said as the two hurried out of the house.

"Oh, David," Fran cried as she sank to the couch. "What is Gloria getting herself into?"

As Chris finished his prayer with Gabe and Michael, Kim returned to the table. "Gabe, for your information, there's a ladies' room just down the hall. I wouldn't have needed to go the whole way back to the reception area."

"Sorry, Mom." Gabe smiled sheepishly, and Michael chuckled. Chris was slow to join the conversation as he pondered what had befallen the boys in Germany. Evil men with no compunction about killing could wreak havoc. He knew it only too well.

"Well, at least we know he's not lurking around women's restrooms," Michael said.

"Thank God for small favors." Kim laughed.

"Thank God for *all* favors," Chris said seriously. "We're very blessed to all be here safe and sound."

Kim touched Chris's hand briefly. In another day and a different relationship, they would have held hands. "You're right, Chris. The Lord has been so good."

"Guys, there's something I have to tell you," Michael announced. "I guess this is as good a time as any. I think I may have died in that ambulance a few weeks ago."

"Don't even say that," Kim said as tears filled her eyes and she patted her son's shoulder.

"No, Mom. I think I did. Something happened to me while I was gone."

Remembering the feeling of extreme evil that surrounded the ambulance, Chris looked deeply into Michael's eyes and expected to hear that he had become plagued by obsessive thoughts or evil desires.

"Look, there's no easy way to say it. I've decided to become a priest," Michael said.

The saga continues! Here is the first chapter from the thrilling sequel, *Pentecost*.

1999

ONE

Michael's plane would soon land in Miami. He smiled at Gabe's idea to bring the family together for a cruise and wholeheartedly endorsed the idea of doing something special to honor Chris's twenty-fifth anniversary as a priest.

Chris was hoping to celebrate the time quietly and in prayer. He relented to the cruise only on the condition that it not be on the actual date of his anniversary and that no fuss be made. Michael knew Gabe had one surprise up his sleeve but didn't think Chris would mind.

Subtlety was never Gabe's strong suit. Michael was well aware that he had also planned the cruise to be a sort of bachelor party week for Michael before his ordination in the spring. Typical Gabe—he viewed the very notion of celibacy to be a fate worse than death.

Celibacy! The concept involved a renunciation of physical pleasure in the pursuit of spiritual purity. Well, there was nothing to renounce for Michael. His horrifying experience with the Lady in Amsterdam ten years earlier left him with a fear of intimacy. He had not so much as kissed a woman since, but he often wondered about it—about the joy of belonging to one woman, about whether he would be a good lover, about whether he would be a good partner, about whether he would be a good dad, but most of all, he wondered about the priesthood.

Over the past decade, the seminary had offered solace and protection against the memories of his otherworldly encounter with the Lady and a hedge against its recurrence. If he was in the seminary or at a lonely archaeological dig, the Lady was far away—never in his thoughts or dreams. But when he deviated from those two pursuits in favor of what would be considered normal relationships by the world, he felt her there, ready to burst into his reality. The mere threat of her reappearance served as an invisible fence, blocking him from finding love and herding him toward a solitary existence.

The life of a cleric wasn't all that bad. In fact, it would be fine if somewhere along the way he had acquired a strong faith or love of God, like Chris, but it had never happened. He had spent too much time with antiquities to believe there was an inherent superiority to Judeo-Christianity, and he seriously doubted he would ever find an emotional attachment to Christ or the Church. So what made this life livable? In a nutshell, the Church fed his passions for languages and the antiquities. It had a seat at the table of every major archaeological discovery, and there were many, although the bulk of them never saw the light of day in press reports or scholarly journals. The Church had used its considerable influence to silence some of the most amazing finds because they didn't fit a biblical account of ancient history. Strangely enough, science itself had been the Church's ally in the area of suppression. Evidence of a very ancient, very advanced global civilization on Earth didn't fit the conventional scientific paradigm, so more often than not, the sciences worked with the Church to deny and refute any evidence leaked to the public. If Michael wanted access to the most marvelous discoveries in his field, the Church was the answer. It had access to the ancient knowledge he was destined to bring to the world.

The archaeological opportunities were unparalleled, but Michael hadn't yet been ordained. He was years behind the men in his seminary class. They had been ordained and moved into ministry, but Michael hadn't made that final commitment. There was always an archaeological dig that he would administer for the Church. The urgency of the project invariably interfered with his studies, and that was just fine with him. Each delay offered him more time to find a compelling reason, other than archaeological access and fear of the Lady, to become a priest. Unfortunately, he had run out of time. His orders were to finish his studies and be ordained or leave the seminary. If he didn't become a priest this spring, he never would.

He weighed his options, wondering if the week with Gabe would shed any insight. Clearly Gabe's life wasn't an example to follow, but was there something there for Michael to learn? Would it be so bad to find a woman in the coming week? Not for some kind of vacuous sexual fling, but to have the opportunity to be attracted to a woman who was also attracted to him. A little flirting? A romantic kiss? If it felt right, maybe more. At least then he could make an informed decision to take his vows. And if he was lucky, if God really was there and wanted him in ministry, maybe he would finally hear the call.

The plane landed, and Michael ran from his gate to the luggage carousel and then to the taxi stand. If he wasn't careful, he could miss the ship's boarding time. As he advanced in the taxi line, he kept thinking, *Mom will* kill *me if I miss this boat!* He looked up just in time to see Chris heading to the end of the line. "Chris? Chris?" he called. It would be a lot easier to show up late if he was with Chris.

Chris had barely aged in the last decade. He still wore his hair a bit long, even though there was now an occasional gray hair. A few crow's feet at the eyes made him look more distinguished.

"Michael!" Chris called as he walked briskly up the line to hug the younger man. "We are seriously close to missing this boat. Your mother is going to kill us!"

Michael laughed. "If I have to helicopter out to the ship, I'll get there. First because we need a family vacation, and second because I want to see Gabe leading an aerobics class. I might not be able to contain myself."

"I always thought he would do something more substantive than become the activities director on a cruise ship," Chris conceded, "but he seems to have found his niche. What about you? Are you going to be ordained in the spring?"

"That's my intention," Michael said sternly. This was shaping up to be yet another of Chris's attempts to assess Michael's commitment to becoming a priest.

"Between you and me, Michael, it's a hard life," Chris said. "Are you really in love with Jesus? I mean enough to be married to Him?"

"I wouldn't say I'm in love with Him, but I understand what the Church teaches about Him, and I'm interested in helping to correct some of the things we got wrong over the years."

"Like what?" Chris asked with a look of displeasure. A cab pulled up. They hopped in and told the driver where they were going.

Michael drew a sharp breath. How could he explain the archaeological significance of Vatican secrets that he hoped to explore? "Chris,

I have worked on several different Vatican archaeological digs in the Middle East. It's a tremendous honor. You should see some of these ancient texts. They're astounding!"

"Will you be helping with the translations?"

"Yeah." Michael beamed. "And some of these things predate what we previously thought to be recorded history!"

"So, a five-thousand-year-old shopping list is going to correct our stand on Christ?"

"Maybe not directly, but it may change our views of biblical history. Chris, I'm not talking about shopping lists, trust me."

"So you're an archaeologist, Michael, but are you a priest? That's what I'm trying to determine."

"I will be, and I'll have the opportunity to find out what was really happening thousands of years ago on this planet."

They rode in silence to the terminal. Michael knew it wasn't the answer Chris wanted to hear.

Sunday was a busy day for all those in the cruise industry. On that day, cruise ships would dock in Miami to say good-bye to thousands of browned, satiated, and spoiled passengers. Then a rapid cleaning of the entire ship would precede the introduction of thousands of new passengers—pale, sun-deprived, and in need of some special attention. The special attention was what it was all about, especially when it came to the ladies. On an average week, Gabe, now the activities director on one of the new grand ships in the Caribbean, could count on about five different ladies to share his cabin. The pattern was always the same: pursue during morning activities, make vague sexual suggestions in the afternoon, bed them in the evening, and apologize for letting things get out of hand the next morning. It was a hard life, but somebody had to do it.

Since his stint at rehab, Gabe had been careful never to touch drugs again. Nonetheless, he still favored alcohol. His job was to create a party atmosphere, and he worked on a "booze cruise." The two went hand in hand. But Gabe was a highly functioning alcoholic. You would never know that his day started and ended with alcohol. He was fit—buff, in fact—with a great tan, bright smile, long hair, and glistening green eyes. He could bring even the most unwilling participant into the cruise activities. He had been gifted with the ability to read people, to know how to quickly gain their trust. He could have used this ability to take advantage of others, but he never did, with the exception of sex. But even in that circumstance, he saw himself as generous. He was fulfilling the beach-stud fantasies of most of the women he bedded.

This Sunday was different from most. At the terminal, waiting to board, were his mother, his brother, and Chris. None of them had ever been on one of his cruises, opting instead for yacht or sailing vacations. The cruise was Gabe's idea—to give Michael something like a bachelor party. Not that Michael would chase, especially with Mom and Chris around, but Gabe wanted him to have a reckless, sun-drenched week away from dusty old libraries, musty monasteries, and sandy archaeological pits.

To top it off, this was the year of Chris's twenty-fifth anniversary as a priest. Where would they all be without Chris's influence in their lives? It took a little bit of subterfuge and sneaking around in Chris's files, but Gabe had managed to find the address of the woman who was in Uganda with him in the early years of his priesthood. He was able to coordinate things so that Fran and her husband could bring a young-adult group from their church. He arranged to have the group's assigned dinner table next to his family's, and he couldn't wait to see the surprise on Chris's face when he saw her.

It was also an opportunity to reconnect. He and Michael had been inseparable for years, but there was little place for Gabe in Michael's world once he entered the seminary. To make matters worse, Michael had been a seminarian longer than almost anyone. Gabe wished Michael wouldn't go through with the ordination, but if he did, Gabe hoped for him to pastor a little church somewhere once he was ordained. Maybe with a more normal schedule and living in a rectory, Michael would be more accessible to him. He wondered if Michael knew how much he wished they could be closer.

David's church group sat in matching T-shirts, waiting to board the ship. Ten members of his young singles group accompanied him and Fran.

"I feel like a glorified chaperone," Fran whispered to David with a grin.

"It's more like a sorority house parent," David suggested.

"That makes me feel a lot better!" She laughed.

"Aw, they're good kids, and we'll have a great time. Besides, who would have thought that Zack and Gloria would agree to come along?" They had maintained a nice relationship with the couple, but every time they tried to do anything together, Sarah would find a way to come up with an alternate plan to pull the young couple back into her orbit.

"They're not here yet," Fran said, "and Sarah's pretty resourceful. I don't know how Gloria puts up with Sarah and Mack's constant meddling."

"I don't think she's happy, Fran. But to her credit, she loves her husband and is trying to make it work."

She floated the idea. "Maybe a baby would help …"

"I don't think a baby is ever the solution to a rocky marriage. Babies add stress to a relationship. Hey, look to your right," he said surreptitiously.

To Fran's right, Danny sat staring at Tina as she read her Bible. Danny weighed all of 120 pounds and had large horn-rimmed glasses and a tendency to produce too much saliva, which pooled and stretched into little bands from his upper to lower teeth as he talked. By contrast, Tina was the church heartthrob. She had a radiant, full face and luxurious brown hair with bangs that framed her hazel eyes. Her figure was nothing short of voluptuous, and she was seriously saving herself for Mr. Right, not only in terms of keeping her virginity but dating in general. She refused to say yes to a date until she felt the Lord had placed the man in her life as a potential mate.

"It's cute, but it's sad," Fran said. "She's not going to fall for him. He's read too many novels where the knight wins the fair lady's hand."

"On a more selfish note, it kind of makes our chaperone role pretty easy, don't you think, my lovely missus?" David grinned and arched his eyebrows.

Just then they heard a chant rising from the crowd behind them. "Give me an R!"

"R!" yelled about a dozen people in wheelchairs, heading toward Fran and David, who could do nothing but look on in disbelief. The group continued to spell "Riverside." Of course, at the head of the parade were Sarah and Mack.

"Fran! What are you doing here?" Sarah asked in mock surprise.

"You know why we're here, Sarah. We've brought some of the young singles from our church."

"What a coincidence! We brought our challenged seniors," Sarah said, continuing the charade. Turning to Sandy, she said, "Mama, you remember Fran, Gloria's mother, don't you?"

Sandy shook her head with dismay at her daughter; she turned to Fran and said, "And they say *I'm* brain damaged!" Her tone softened as she said, "How are you, Fran?"

"I'm fine," Fran said with a smile. "How nice for you to get to go on a cruise."

"I'll say. Now if I can just find a way to cut loose from old iron girdle and shake my maracas!"

Kim sat at the other end of the terminal in the VIP section. She was the first one in her family to arrive. *Of course!* Michael was like the wind. He blew in and blew out. And Chris was Chris; their entire friendship was about varying availability. They had been careful to strictly respect his vows over the years, yet they were emotionally entwined. Each felt lighter and happier in the other's presence. That was enough for her.

In the background, the terminal speakers played Cher's "Believe." *Sing it, Cher!*

The years continued to be kind to Kim. She had kept her figure and added a little bit of dye to color the beginnings of gray hair. Her well-maintained face showed few signs of aging, amazing considering the day-to-day stresses of running a financial empire. She had her father's sense of when to buy and when to sell. Her cell phone rang. As she fished through her bag, she thought, *This better not be Michael or Chris calling to cancel!*

"Kim, it's John," said the president of Kim's holding company. She was training him to do more around the office. The business needed a clear succession plan, and it didn't look as if either of her boys was interested.

"John, what's up?" Kim asked curiously. She had left instructions not to bother her unless it was an emergency.

"I just wanted to say, 'Have a nice trip,' and to talk to you one more time about Enron stock."

"Don't go there, John. I'm telling you, I met with those guys. They're too full of themselves," she lectured. "I don't want to get involved. Hear me on this."

"I know you don't want to invest *your* money there," John said cautiously, "but I was hoping to get your approval to invest some of our pension funds in Enron. The pension fund isn't your money; it belongs to us employees."

"No!" Kim yelled into the phone, not so much to be difficult with John as to be heard above Cher. "I can't approve it, John. How could I, in good conscience, allow the employees to invest in a company I think will implode?"

"Okay," John said in a pacifying tone. "I just wanted to put it by you one more time."

"I appreciate your concern, John, but trust me. You'll be thanking me in a few years. Those guys are a phenomenon, but they don't have a sustainable business. I'll see you in a couple of weeks." She hung up, wishing one of her boys would go into the business.

"Ms. Martin?" an attractive redheaded woman wearing the standard cruise line navy blue suit, white blazer, and multicolored scarf asked.

"Yes?"

"I'm Clara, your VIP representative. I'll take you to your suite now."

"Thanks." Kim smiled weakly. *If those two stand me up, I'll kill them!*

The door to the lounge opened just as Kim and the rep were passing by. In poured Chris and Michael, who had clearly been in a dead run to get to the terminal on time.

"They're with me," Kim said with a dry smile to the rep. "They're cute but not very punctual."

The rep laughed as Kim hugged her guys. The rep then pushed through the crowded terminal, and the three dutifully followed as onlookers wondered who they were to merit such VIP treatment. The rep led them into an elevator at the far end of the terminal. Just as the elevator doors were closing, Kim noticed Chris was staring out at the crowd of people in the terminal.

"Fran?" Chris said softly.

The presidential suite was lavish and overdone as only a cruise line could do. Crystal chandeliers, wall sconces, and a baby grand piano appointed the sitting room with its facing crimson couches. The three bedrooms were decorated in bright Caribbean colors and gold-and-silver taffeta drapes.

Michael chuckled at the unrepentant gaudiness. "A little under-done," he chirped, "but I like it."

"It's a bit much, but we wanted three bedrooms, and this is what your brother booked," Kim said.

"The guy has definitely spent too much time in houses of ill repute," Michael added as Chris chuckled.

"Ah, the asexual musings of two vicars in sweet accord," Gabe pronounced as he entered the apartment. Michael and Chris ran to hug him, but they couldn't beat Kim.

"Hands off, fellas," she said. "Gabey can't come out and play until he gives his mommy a hug."

"Hi, Mom," Gabe said as he hugged her tightly. "So what do you think of my home away from home?"

"I haven't seen much of the ship yet. They kind of whisked us up here, but it seems beautiful."

Gabe conceded, "Look, I know it's gaudy, but that's true of cruise ships in general. This is a nice ship, though. It's one of the newest and biggest in the fleet."

"Maybe you could take us on a tour once you finish saying hello," Kim said.

"Sure," Gabe replied. He released his mom and held open his arms for a hug from Michael and Chris. "Hey, guys—"

"Michael, did you hear something?" Chris asked with studied nonchalance.

Michael chuckled softly and then joined the ruse. "Just a member of the crew looking for a tip. If we ignore him, he'll go away and pester someone else."

In a second, Michael was airborne as Gabe rushed first him and then Chris, knocking them into the facing sofas. Michael protested as he stood and hugged his brother hard.

After a while, Gabe said, "Ready for your tour, Mom?"

"Sure. Let's do it," Kim said as she took his arm.

Over his shoulder, Gabe said, "Clergy, follow us."

As they entered the hallway, Michael heard the porter taking another family to their suite.

"Here is your apartment, Reverend Jolean."

"Thanks, I appreciate your kindness," the reverend said.

"This should do nicely," the reverend's wife said to the porter. "After all, we're on vacation. I guess we can't have every convenience of home."

Behind them, an old woman in a wheelchair sat in the hallway with her caregiver, waiting to enter the room.

"It's not fair," the old lady complained to Kim. "Why should you have all the good-looking men on the ship?"

Kim smiled sweetly at her, bent toward her, and said softly, "I'm just lucky."

Michael thought it was all cute, until the old woman lightly slapped Gabe's butt and said, "This melon is just about ripe." Then he laughed hardily at the surprised look on Gabe's face. Chris rolled his eyes, covering his mouth to hide a laugh.

"I'll tell you a secret," Kim whispered. "He's my son."

"Well, it's just an old lady's opinion, but I think you should let him out to play every now and again." They all chuckled, except Gabe, who stood with a polite smile frozen on his face.

"He'll be teaching the morning aerobics classes. You should stop by," Kim said proudly and gave Gabe a mischievous wink. Michael and Chris snickered loudly, as did the woman's caregiver.

"I think I'll take you up on it." The woman grinned.

"Mama, get in here!" the reverend's wife yelled from inside the suite.

"The warden calls," the old lady said with a sigh and motioned with her hand for the caregiver to take her inside. "Nice meeting you. See you around."

"Nice meeting you too." Kim grinned.

As the door closed and they proceeded down the hallway, Gabe asked his mother in exasperation, "Why did you tell her I was teaching that class?"

"She'll balance out the young jiggly crowd, and I want Michael and Chris to remember the upside of celibacy." Kim laughed.

"Worked for me," Chris said as he high-fived Kim.

"Worked for me," Michael echoed.

Gabe shrugged and said, "I've had worse," to a chorus of laughter.

———————————

The cabin was small and had a tiny porthole for a window. Fran would have been happier with something a bit less cramped. She and David could afford it, but such accommodations would have been prohibitively expensive for the young singles group.

"Second thoughts?" David asked as they surveyed the small bathroom.

"Not really," Fran said. "When you think about it, how much time will we really spend in our cabin?"

David hugged her from behind and said softly, "Well, I was hoping for a little alone time."

There was a knock at the door. Fran opened it to reveal several of the young singles in their group.

"Come on, guys, we're about to set sail. Let's go on deck and say good-bye to Miami!"

"Knock on Gloria's door to see if she wants to join us," Fran said to Tina. To David, she said, "You'll have to unpack your stuff later." He shook his head and rolled his eyes.

Gloria met them in the hallway.

"Where's Zack?" Fran asked.

"He went to his parents' suite because he refuses to spend a week in the bowels of the ship," Gloria said with unbridled disdain. "Just a warning, Mom; he'll be a pain this whole trip. Nothing will be good enough for him while his parents are around."

"So hang out with us and have a good time," Fran offered. "Maybe he'll get tired of the wheelchair group they brought."

"It doesn't matter, Mom. Trust me, I'm happy to have some time without him—without the whole famn damily."

They walked in silence for a few seconds, when from behind them Danny spoke up, a little too loudly and a little too rehearsed. "They say a bon voyage kiss is good luck," he said as he stared at Tina.

"Not your lucky day, Danny," Tina said briskly as she pulled away from him and moved closer to Fran and Gloria. The older women laughed quietly.

Fran put her arm around Tina's shoulders and pulled her close. "Men," she said, "you can't live with them and—"

"You can't live with them," Gloria finished as the three smirked.

The group burst out of the stairwell onto the deck just as Kim and her family were coming down from an upper deck.

"Fran!" Chris cried as he ran to her. They hugged awkwardly as Fran pulled Gloria into it.

"Gloria!" Chris said, smiling. "You grew into a beautiful lady, sweetheart!"

"And you haven't aged a bit!" Gloria exclaimed.

"Kim, guys, look here!" Chris called to the group, who had pulled back to give him some space.

"Kim, this is Frannie and Gloria Ellis, the family from Africa."

"Oh well." Kim laughed. "We were going to surprise you at dinner. Gabe invited them in honor of your twenty-fifth anniversary."

Chris briefly hugged Gabe as Michael patted his back. Then he introduced Fran to Kim.

Fran hugged Kim and said, "You're the one who sent us the check. I don't know how I would have raised my daughter without your kindness."

Kim hugged her in return. "Don't even mention it. I'm happy to know things turned out well for you." Fran knew in an instant she could easily become friends with this woman. She introduced David to Chris and Kim.

Chris proudly said, "These two handsome men are Michael and Gabe. I wrote to you about them."

"I would know them anywhere from your descriptions." Fran

grinned. She hugged both guys, and Gloria followed suit. Fran couldn't help but notice the way Gloria looked into Michael's eyes, or the way Michael returned her stare. She looked at David with dismay.

Fran wasn't the only one to notice Michael and Gloria. Kim saw it as well. For years she had hoped and prayed Michael would either develop a passion for the priesthood or meet the one woman who would change his mind. If she never had met Chris, she would have dismissed out of hand the concept of love at first sight, but she knew she loved Chris the moment she saw him. Would it be that way for Michael as well? She took a second look at Gloria and drew a sharp breath when she saw her large diamond-studded wedding band.

Kim tried to get Gabe's attention, to see if he had noticed Michael's interaction with Gloria, but Gabe was staring intently at a young girl from the youth group.

"That's Tina," Fran said with a smile. "She's a great kid."

"I love Gabe," Kim said, "but he's trouble for young ladies."

"Tina will shut him down," Fran said with a confident smile.

The ship blew its whistle and moved slowly from the pier. The customary celebration began, and the deck turned into a New Year's Eve celebration. Everyone onboard waved and cheered. Couples hugged and kissed. David kissed Fran, Chris and Kim hugged, and Gabe kissed a surprised Tina. As they came out of their respective embraces, they watched aghast as Michael and Gloria shared a passionate kiss.

Fran made her way to Gloria and said, "Gloria! Look at the ocean!"

Chris followed her to move Michael out of the way.

Kim looked to David in shock. He wasn't looking at the couple but to the balconies above. She followed his gaze to a balcony where the woman in the wheelchair sat. With her were several others, but one in particular caught her attention. He was a thin man with hawkish looks and an expression of absolute rage. It sent a shiver up her spine.

David leaned into her to be heard above the crowd. "Gloria's husband," he said somberly.

"Bon voyage," Kim said. She sighed as the ship's whistle boomed.

SELECTED BIBLIOGRAPHY

Anderson, R. *The Coming Prince*. Three Rivers, UK: Diggory Press Ltd., 2008.

Berliner, D. with Marie Galbrath, and Antonio Huneeus. *UFO Briefing Document*. New York: Dell Publishing, a Division of Random House, 1995.

Colman, J. *The Conspirators' Hierarchy: The Committee of 300*, 4th Edition. Las Vegas, NV: World Intelligence Review, 1997.

Dolan, R. and Bryce Zabel. *A.D. After Disclosure: The People's Guide to Life After Contact*. Rochester, NY: Keyhole Publishing Company, 2010.

Dolan, RM. *UFOs and the National Security State, Chronology of a Cover-up 1941–73*. Charlottesville, VA: Hampton Roads Publishing Company, Inc., 2000.

_____. *UFOs and the National Security State, The Cover-up Exposed*. Rochester, NY: Keyhole Publishing Company, 2009.

Estulin, D. *The True Story of the Bilderberg Group*. Walterville, OR: TrineDay, LLC, 2007.

Flynn, D. *Temple at the Center of Time, Newton's Bible Codex Deciphered and the Year 2012*. Crane, OR: Official Disclosure, a Division of Anomalos Publishing House, 2008.

Foden, G. *The Last King of Scotland*. New York: Vintage Books, 1998.

Fowler, RE. *The Andreasson Affair: The Documented Investigation of a Woman's Abduction Aboard a UFO*. Newberg, OR: Wild Flower Press, 1979.

———. *The Andreasson Affair, Phase Two*. Newberg, OR: Wild Flower Press, 1982.

Grant, JR. *The Signature of God: Astonishing Bible Codes*. Colorado Springs, CO: Waterbrook Press, 2002.

Griffin, GE. *The Creature from Jekyll Island: A Second Look at the Federal Reserve*. Appleton, WI: American Opinion Publishing, 1994.

Hamilton III, WF. *Project Aquarius: The Story of an Aquarian Scientist*. Bloomington, IN: AuthorHouse, 2005.

Hitchcock, M. *The Complete Book of Bible Prophecy*. Wheaton, IL: Tyndale House Publishers, Inc., 1999.

Hogue, J. *The Last Pope: The Prophecies of St. Malachy for the New Millennium*. Boston: Element Books Limited, 2000.

Horn, T. *Apollyon Rising 2012: The Lost Symbol Found and the Final Mystery of the Great Seal Revealed*. Crane, MO: Defender, 2009.

———. *Nephilim Stargates: The Year 2012 and the Return of the Watchers*. Crane, MO: Anomalos Publishing, 2007.

Horn, T. and Nita Horn. *Forbidden Gates: The Dawn of Techno-Dimensional Spiritual Warfare*. Crane, MO: Defender, 2010.

Horn, T. and Cris Putnam. *Petrus Romanus*. Crane, MO: Defender, 2012.

Horton, M., ed. *The Agony of Deceit: What Some TV Preachers Are Really Teaching*. Chicago: Moody Press, 1990.

Hunt, D. and TA McMahon. *America, the Sorcerer's New Apprentice: The Rise of New Age Shamanism*. Eugene, OR: Harvest House, 1988.

Imbrogno, PJ. *Interdimensional Universe, the New Science of UFOs, Paranormal Phenomena and Otherdimensional Beings.* Woodbury, MN: Llewellyn Publications, 2008.

_____. *Ultraterrestrial Contact: A Paranormal Investigator's Explorations into the Hidden Abduction Epidemic.* Woodbury, MN: Llewellyn Publications, 2010.

Jeremiah, D., with CC Carlson. *The Handwriting on the Wall: Secrets from the Prophecies of Daniel.* Nashville, TN: W Publishing Group, 1992.

Knight, C. and Alan Butler. *Before the Pyramids: Cracking Archeology's Greatest Mystery.* London: Watkins Publishing, 2009.

Lindsey, H. *The Late Great Planet Earth.* Grand Rapids, MI. Zondervan. 1970.

_____. *There's a New World Coming, an In-depth Analysis of the Book of Revelation.* Eugene, OR: Harvest House, 1973.

Marrs, J. *Alien Agenda,* New York: HarperCollins Publishers. 2008.

_____. *The Rise of the Fourth Reich,* New York: HarperCollins Publishers, 2008.

_____. *Rule by Secrecy,* New York. HarperCollins Publishers, 2000.

Martin, M. *Windswept House,* New York: Doubleday, 1996.

Milor, JW. *Aliens and the Antichrist: Unveiling the End-Times Deception,* Lincoln, NE: iUniverse, 2006.

Missler, C., Dr. *Prophecy 20/20: Profiling the Future Through the Lens of Scripture,* Nashville, TN: Thomas Nelson, Inc., 2006.

_____. *Cosmic Codes: Hidden Messages from the Edge of Eternity,* Coeur d'Alene, ID: Koinonia House, 1999.

Picknett, L. and Clive Prince. *The Stargate Conspiracy: The Truth About Extraterrestrial Life and the Mysteries of Ancient Egypt,* New York: Berkley Books, 1999.

Redfern, N. *Final Events and the Secret Government Group on Demonic UFOs and the Afterlife*, San Antonio, TX: Anomalist Books, 2010.

_____. *The NASA Conspiracies*, Pompton Plains, NJ: New Page Books, 2011.

Rice, Andrew. *The Teeth May Smile but the Heart Does Not Forget: Murder and Memory in Uganda*, New York: Metropolitan Books, 2009.

Richardson, J. *The Islamic Antichrist: The Shocking Truth about the Real Nature of the Beast*, Los Angeles: WND Books, 2006.

_____. *Mideast Beast: The Scriptural Case for an Islamic Antichrist*, Washington, DC: WND Books, 2012.

Romanek, S. *Messages, The World's Most Documented Extraterrestrial Contact Story*, Woodberry MN: Llewellyn Publications, 2009.

Rothkopf, D. *Superclass: The Global Power Elite and the World They Are Making*, New York: Ferrar, Straus and Giroux, 2008.

Seftel, A. *Uganda, the Bloodstained Pearl of Africa and its Struggle for Peace, From the Pages of DRUM*, Lanseria, South Africa: Bailey's African Photo Archives, 1994.

Sherman, D. *Above Black: Project Preserve Destiny, A True Story*, Kearney, NE: Order Dept, LLC, 2008.

Sherman, ER. with Nathan Jacobi, PhD and Dave Swaney. *Bible Code Bombshell, Compelling Scientific Evidence that God Authored the Bible*, Green Forest, AR: New Leaf Press, 2005.

_____. *Bible Code Bombshell: Compelling Scientific Evidence that God Authored the Bible*, Green Forest, AR: New Leaf Press, 2005.

Shoebat, W., with Joel Richardson. *God's War on Terror: Islam, Prophecy, and the Bible*, USA: Top Executive Media, 2010.

Shriner, S. *Bible Codes Revealed: The Coming UFO Invasion*, New York: iUniverse, 2005.

Smith, WB. *Deceived on Purpose: The New Age Implications of the Purpose-Driven Church*, Magalia, CA: Mountain Stream Press, 2004.

Strieber, W. *Breakthrough: The Next Step*, New York: Harper PaperBacks, a Division of HarperCollins Publishers, 1996.

_____. *Communion: A True Story*, New York: Harper, 1988.

_____. *Confirmation.* New York: St. Martin's Press, 1998.

_____. *Transformation.* New York: Avon, 1998.

Vallee, J. *Messengers of Deception: UFO Contacts and Cults*, Brisbane, Australia: Daily Grail Publishing, 1979.

Ventura, J. with Dick Russell. *63 Documents the Government Doesn't Want You to Read*, New York: Skyhorse Publishing, 2011.

Yallop, D. *In God's Name: An Investigation into the Murder of Pope John Paul I*, New York: Basic Books, 2007.

Internet Sites

Apollo Moon Conversations and Pictures Show NASA Cover-Up. August 31, 2010. http://www.ufos-aliens.co.uk/cosmicphotos.html.

Air Force Advisory Panel Briefing January 12, 1967. http://www.cufos.org/1967 01 12 AF PanelBriefing.pdf.

Booth, Billy. 1959–The Papua, New Guinea UFOs. August 26, 2010. http://ufos.about.com/od/bestufocasefiles/p/papua.htm.

Coast to Coast. Full Interview with Father Malachi Martin. https://www.youtube.com/watch?v=DEDXYPgsp9M.